RETREAT TO LOVE

MELANIE GREENE

This book is a work of fiction. References to real people, events, establishments, organization, or locales are intended only to provide a sense of authenticity, and are used fictitiously. All other characters, and all incidents and dialogue, are drawn from the author's imagination and are not to be construed as real.

RETREAT TO LOVE.

First edition: March 2015

Retreat to Love/by Melanie Greene

Cover Design by The Killion Group

ISBN: 978-1-941967-06-5

What happens when the seams of your life are ripped apart?

Quilter Ashlyn May attends a retreat in the Texas hill country, not expecting to learn a wrenching family secret there, or for the arms of photographer Caleb Kendall to hold her together.

Sharing the secret would break her grandmother's heart. Keeping it runs contrary to every value Gran has taught her.

Will Ashlyn be able to patch up the past and stitch together a future with Caleb?

To all the Jennifers I love

CHAPTER 1

"Hey!" I straightened up, glaring at my brother Zach. He'd pulled one of his favorite tricks: stomping on the brakes so the lurching of the car woke me. Yawning, I took in the rolling hills and barely-paved side roads fading to obscurity in the dusk. "Where are we?"

"Just coming up to the turnoff. Thought it was time for you to stop playing Sleeping Beauty and start playing creative genius."

My nap hadn't left me feeling exactly enchanted. But they never did. Of everything I'd inherited directly from our beloved Gran, the only tedious one was our tendency to fall asleep the moment we got into a moving vehicle. She claimed hers started in 1929 when her family was on the ship from Rosslare to New York. I claimed mine started the hour of my birth, when she'd taken my squalling self from her daughter and rocked me to peaceful sleep.

Either way, it meant no one loved the idea of my driving myself from Houston to the small town of Wimberley, Texas, where I was beginning a two-month residency at FireWind, an artist's retreat Zach had badgered me into applying for. Since my trip there was all his fault, he'd driven in from Austin to chauffeur me, along with my sewing machine, bags of fabric and supplies, and hopefully none of the emotional baggage that had weighed down my attempts to let my art soar over the past year.

"What's the time?"

He tapped the dashboard clock so I could see it was nearing seven, before slowing at the almost-neon sign for FireWind. The blacktop gave way to a cattle guard—most of this area was ranch land before the vacation-home and bed-and-breakfast crowds moved in—and then to an unevenly pitted uphill drive. I checked the spidery handwriting on the instruction sheet I'd been sent. "My cabin is straight up the main road until the turn-off for the Main House. Take the right fork and I'm the second one, on the right."

"You wanna unload all this first or go straight to your big welcoming party?" The first group dinner and general meeting was due to start.

"What am I missing? The low-down on the rules and regulations, maybe some appetizers? Let's get this taken care of."

"How you gonna get inside?" Zach asked, parking outside a neo-rustic log-faced cabin, totally square except for the five by four foot porch notched in by the front door. It was about what I'd expected, but the size of the wrap-around windows surprised me and the fact I could actually hear a babbling brook somewhere off to the north of my cabin was cool, in a hokey way.

"They sent me the code for the front door. Everything here is state-of-the-art, yet rural." I unbuckled, repressing my need to stretch until I stood up outside. Zach got out the first load of bags while I climbed the three porch steps and peered at the dark keypad until I could make it out well enough to punch the four digits. The control panel beeped twice at me and the door clicked. "Freaky," I said, entering what would be my home for the next eight weeks.

I stepped into a little living area, with windows overlooking a counter with a bar sink and mini-fridge, a small sofa and coffee table, and waist-high bookshelf in the corner. I'd been in roomier waiting rooms. But the bedroom, which led off the den, was spacious enough for the antique double bed (covered with a machine-stitched green-on-green Log Cabin quilt), dresser, armoire, and side table, all functionally arranged around the two windows and two doors. The second door led to a short hallway past the equally functional bathroom, and to the studio.

The studio was perfection. As Zach brought in bag after box of fabrics, dyes, beads, threads, and my sewing machine and quilt frame, I flipped on the track lights hanging from the high ceiling and sighed. Double sinks in a large steel work counter lined the short wall, a bank of storage cabinets under the low wall divided the studio from the den, and the rest of the huge room was nothing but rough-hewn hardwood floors, vast windows, and a couple of easels and wood tables. The chair at the tilted drawing board was ergonomic. A rolling chair at the desk was smooth enough to slide me across to the supply cabinet with a single push.

"You wanna grab your suitcase when you're done playing in here?" Zach was using his grumpy voice.

"Oops, you caught me. Isn't it awesome?"

"Big room."

"Big flawless room," I did five pirouettes before I had crossed to him.

He rolled his eyes, but snickered. "I'm glad you like it. Now aren't you lucky you have such a great big brother looking out for you?"

"Sure, take the credit, I don't mind. As long as I get some work done here, you can have all the credit you want."

I'd spent most of the year since Gran had kicked me out of her house, and the converted henhouse I'd used as my studio, attempting to browbeat my creative instinct into appearing. Not shockingly, it hadn't worked. I could work on traditional quilt commissions no problem, but my fiber art was not flowing. Once I got over my petulance that Zach had strong-armed me into applying for FireWind, I began to suspect it would be just the space I needed to kick-start my floundering career as an artist. And the undulating hills and fragrant cypress air around me had begun to work their way through my root chakra. Already I was more centered than I'd been that morning, turning my accursed rental over to the sublessee.

I looked around. "I don't feel like unpacking now. Come to the meeting with me and I'll share what's left of my dinner with you."

"You sure they won't mind?"

"I have no idea. But nothing ventured, eh?"

Zach closed the trunk and we tramped down the road until we hit a lit footpath which crossed a stream and dead-ended into a set of steps for the long porch of a clapboard house. We peeked in the windows of the dining room. Around a huge table sat eight people, seven of them leaning back in their chairs or up against the table listening to a curly-haired woman in a granny skirt and woven Tibetan-wool jacket. A double-sideboard at the back of the room had a series of covered bowls, but no one was eating.

"I'll hang here for a while," Zach said, sitting in a rocking chair on the porch. "Get me when y'all start to chow."

"Okay." I opened the folding door and walked in.

They all turned to glance at me, and the woman sitting next to the only empty chair shifted over so I could have some room.

"Hey, everyone, sorry I'm late. I'm Ashlyn May."

Granny Skirt glanced at her watch. "I am Margie Roya, the facilitator. You have missed the general introductions and the tour of the Main House. I am just coming to the part about the food. Everything else you should ask someone else about later, because I have not allotted time for late-comers."

I nodded, and caught the eye of the woman next to me. She was about thirty with straight blonde hair pulled back in a loose bun. Tapping her watch, she gave me a stern look. I shrugged, rolled my eyes, and smiled at her grin.

Margie kept talking. "As I was saying, you have each been

assigned a food partner, with whom you will be responsible for preparing the communal meals for two weeks of the retreat. In deference to the three vegetarians here, each meal must offer an adequate array of non-meat options. Allergies and food aversions, according to the information supplied on your applications, are on the laminated sheet hanging on the pantry door. I will drive to San Marcos between two and three each day to pick up whatever supplies the day's cooks have requisitioned." She must have rehearsed the spiel nightly.

"Each week will have two teams of cooks. This week, Team One will make breakfast and lunch, while Team Three makes dinner. Next week, Team Two will make breakfast and lunch, while Team Four makes dinner. It is not confusing, but for clarity's sake there will be a laminated schedule posted next to the allergy list on the pantry door." All of that, and she only paused once for breath. Why was it so easy to picture her carefully carrying her neatly printed pages to the copy center for laminating, perhaps wincing if the clerk sneezed as he handled her documents?

"You may take snacks and small meals to your cabin for consumption, but gathering in the cabins to eat is discouraged, as it disturbs the sanctuary-like seclusion you should feel upon entering your working space. At no time may you eat or drink anywhere in the Main House other than the kitchen and the dining room. Are there any questions?" Clearly, the answer was supposed to be no.

"What if we hate to cook?" asked a skinny dark man in a black turtleneck.

Finally, she paused. Then, from somewhere in her repertoire of instructions, she came up with: "Often food partners divide the labor so that one is in charge of meal preparation, and the other sets and clears the table and washes the dishes. The reliance on pre-packaged foods is discouraged, although, naturally, one may choose to supplement fresh foods with selected ready-made ingredients."

I just stopped myself from snorting out a laugh, earning a quick glare from Margie and a nudge under the table from my blonde neighbor.

"And who are the food partners?" she asked, diverting Margie.

"Team One: Angelica Starlight and Theo Ribelles. Team Two: Ashlyn May and Caleb Kendall. Team Three: Lauren Phillips and Rafael Quezada. Team Four: Lizzy Murphy and Brandon Brayton. I have already purchased breakfast and lunch groceries for tomorrow, but Team Three will have to come up with a dinner menu before I go to town tomorrow afternoon."

Blonde leaned in to me. "All boy-girl. Coincidence? I don't think so. And way to go on getting the cute one." She tipped her chin at a man sitting next to Margie. He was watching her, so all I got was a one-quarter profile, but I noted the dark wavy hair and pleasantly broad shoulders. "I'm Wren, by the way."

"Nice to meet you. Which one's yours?" I whispered back. "Not the cook-hater?"

"No, the quiet one next to me. Hasn't said a word since he told us he was a painter. Can't say I see him whipping up a delicious primavera while I sit back and grate the cheese, though."

"You know they sell the cheese already grated. Or is that too convenient?"

"Excuse me, ladies," Margie interrupted our sidebar. "You are free to discuss whatever you like over dinner, but I would appreciate your full attention now while I finish my general meeting."

We nodded solemnly at her and she went on. "You all—or, all of you who were here on time—saw the stairs off of the laundry room. They lead up to my private quarters. There is an intercom in the laundry room, which you may buzz between the hours of seven a.m. and ten p.m., if you need access to the television, or to discuss anything related to the running of the colony. Outside of those hours, you may only use the intercom for emergencies. I will keep the first-aid kit in the laundry room fully stocked, and the doors for the Main House are always open. This is our eleventh session at FireWind, and by now, I think we have anticipated every need that may arise. Are there any questions?"

Margie scanned the table. The heads of eight artists shook back and forth, and she smiled. "Well, if you think of anything, you know where I am. Now, tonight's dinner is to be served buffet-style. The dishes and cutlery are in the sideboards, and of course, Team Three will be doing the washing up when you are all done. I will take my meal upstairs, as always. Welcome to Fire-Wind, and good night."

We all stood up when she moved from the table, wishing her a good night and reaching to uncover the dinner platters.

"I can't believe you missed the first half, you lucky wench," Wren said. "Yes, ma'am, no, ma'am, we won't try to watch TV when we're not allowed, ma'am."

"What does she do, time us?"

"Yes."

I laughed. "No, seriously? Oh, Goddess, what a regime."

"It seems she's a stickler for the rules. We sit in our studios working unless we're eating our communal meals or taking inspirational walks through the hills of beauty that encompass us."

I glanced outside. Zach was making faces at me through the window. "Oops. Be right back," I said, moving to open the door.

"It went from quiet to laughter within, and I figured I'd been neglected," he said.

"I wasn't going to eat without you." I protested, half-truthfully, as I led him to the food. "This is my brother, Zach. He brought me up from Houston. Zach, this is Wren, a fellow inmate in Margie Roya's penal colony."

He shook her hand. "Wren?"

She executed a quick half-shrug. "It's Lauren, actually. Got stuck as Wren when my little brother was learning to talk, you know?"

He nodded. "I was Aackie for a while there with this one." Almost sweetly, he leaned his elbow on my shoulder. "Kind of a cross between disgust and fright, I think."

Her flutter of a laugh was interrupted by a hail from someone at the table. "Zeke!"

"Ned?" Zach looked around. My food partner was standing up, grinning. "Ned!" Zach repeated, and strutted up to him. They bumped chests, exchanged a double high-five, locked hands and grunted loudly at each other.

"I thought you said Zach?" Wren looked at me.

"I did."

"Then?"

"I have no idea."

Zach and Caleb laughed, and joined us. "Caleb was at Berkeley with me. We were computer lab nerds together."

"Hi, Ned, I'm Zeke's sister, Ashlyn."

"Hey, I'm Caleb." He cleared his throat. "Um, we all called each other Zeke and Ned at Berkeley, kind of a code for the CS guys."

I didn't reply. My initial impression of him as kind of a hunk had dissolved as he and my brother revealed their dorkiest sides.

I guess my thoughts translated, because his cheeks flushed. "Okay, it's a little silly now. You can call me Caleb."

"I think that would be best."

Wren handed Zach the plate she'd picked up from the corner of the sideboard. "You eating?"

"If nobody minds. What's on the menu?" he asked, peeking over the skinny guy's shoulder to scope out the spread. "Oh, artist food," he said. "Salads, fruit, and quiche."

"Not store-bought, I hope," said Caleb. Zach raised an eyebrow at him. Caleb elaborated. "True artists only eat food made from scratch. Preferably all organic and from their private gardens."

"Zach's a computer programmer," I told them. "He wouldn't understand. All they eat is fast food and frozen pizzas."

We loaded up our plates with what was, admittedly, pretty

appealing food and sat down. Caleb joined our half of the table, taking the seat deserted by Wren's food partner. Rafael had stayed at dinner long enough to eat a slice of quiche and a scoop of Salad Nicoise, minus the olives, judging from his plate. "You suppose he'll be back to help me wash these?" Wren asked, utilizing his napkin to move his dish to the kitchen pass-thru.

"From the way he slinked off down the porch I'd say he's gone for good," said a woman on the other side of Caleb.

Zach and I asked simultaneously, "South Dublin?"

"Dalkey. How'd ya know?" she said, pushing her gold-rimmed glasses up her nose and studying me.

"Pappa was from Dalkey, Gran from Rosslare, and they trained us to tell the difference—to them it was obvious. I'm Ashlyn. This is my brother, Zach."

"Hi. Lizzy Murphy." She nodded at us, her glasses slipping back down in the process. She had the traditional Irish freckles and fair skin, but a startling, almost punkish combination of black eyes and very light spiky hair. With a blunt rough-nailed hand, she picked up her fork and gestured toward the man sitting beside her. "I was just discussing with Brandon here that the only thing I cook is rice, so he should be prepared to do a lot of cooking next week."

Brandon nodded at us, flipping back his long dusty locks to get a clear view. "I thought guests weren't allowed."

"Don't worry, I'm leaving soon. Right after we help Wren do the washing up."

"Suit yourself," he shrugged. "I just woulda brought my girl-friends along if I knew."

"More than one?" Lizzy asked.

I suppose he thought his smirk was a sly grin. "They like to travel in pairs, what can I say?"

His food partner sized him up. It didn't look like she thought his measurements were sufficient. "Just let me know if they're going to show up. You cook for a week for each one that flirts with me."

"Yeah, well, whatever." Brandon stood up and stacked his dishes with the others. "See you all later."

"Good night, partner!" Lizzy drawled after him as he shut the porch door behind him. She asked us, "You think I made him uncomfortable?"

"God, I hope so," said Caleb. "He was on the bus from Austin with us, and he thinks that he's the hottest new photog in the world. If you call running every shot through a diffuser either 'new' or 'hot', I'm in serious trouble."

"You're a photographer, too?" I asked. Having missed Margie's introductions, as well as the informative shuttle from Austin's airport, I was out of the FireWind loop.

Turned out that Brandon and Caleb were the only photographers. I, to exactly no one's surprise, was the only fiber artist. Lizzy, Wren, and the other woman there, Angelica Starlight, were all sculptors, but Wren concentrated on small-scale ceramics while Lizzy and Angelica worked on larger pieces. The skinny guy, Theo, as well as the amazing disappearing Rafael were painters. So was Margie, to judge from the small watercolors of hummingbirds in flight strewn about the dining room and hallway, but the consensus was she might be better off trying her hand at cross-stitch or stained glass or something else with which she could use a pattern. Caleb suggested quilting for her, but at least had the decency to redden at my look.

AFTER THE MEAL was cleared and the dishes dried, Zach and I walked first Wren then Caleb back to their cabins, all of which had the requisite earthy names. Wren was at RiverStone and Caleb at LakeFire, but mine stole the prize for most uncertifiably organic: ValeSong. It wasn't even in a valley, more of a dip in the road.

The guys planned to have some sort of 'Zeke and Ned' reunion, so Caleb invited us in while he fetched a notebook for Zach's email address. We'd all be banned from bringing our cell phones, and apparently I wasn't the only one who'd followed the rule. LakeFire shared darkroom facilities with Brandon in the adjoining cabin, but otherwise Caleb's layout was almost a mirror of mine. I forced myself to admit to a stab of jealousy. He'd only been there a few more hours than I, but already his studio looked not only organized but like it had been worked in. Three cameras were out of bags, a portable light table was on a desk near his bedroom, and a multi-pocketed safari vest and light gauge hung over a chair near the door.

Back at ValeSong we surveyed the carload of unpacking ahead of me. "You need any help with all this?" Zach asked.

"No, thanks. You'd best to get back home. Some of us have to work in the morning and need their rest." Zach programmed for a firm in the Silicone Hills of Austin, and not only did he pull some tidy cash, he also got to set his own hours and telecommute most days. "Hey, listen, I appreciate your coming to get me and bringing me up here and all. And, you know, sorry I was a little brusque in the car."

"A little brusque? I was ready to call the exorcist by Bastrop. But what are brothers for? I'm glad you're doing this thing. I hope it helps."

I hugged him and walked him to the door. "It should. I feel good here already, and that's always a plus. Will you give Gran a call in the morning; let her know I'm settled in okay? I'll email her later." The computer room in the Main House was already shut up tight for the night.

"Sure, and I'll drop a note to Frank and Bernadette, too." Our parents would hardly have been looking for a message from me, but they'd be overjoyed to hear from their precious Zach.

"Thanks, hon." I smiled and gave him one last squeeze. "Safe home."

"Good night, then. See ya' later." I waved as Zach got into his car, lowered my hand as he backed out onto the main road and headed towards Austin.

Unpacking my clothes and toiletries didn't take long, nor did arranging the few books and photos I'd brought. But other than storing the boxes of fabrics and threads in the studio cabinets and setting my machine on one of the wood tables, I was at a loss as to how to arrange my new working space. I would use the easel for sketches, the drafting table for layout drawings and making templates, and the floor as a canvas for my cloth. That much I knew from experience with the way I worked.

But I had no idea, despite my bravado with Zachary, what my first project at FireWind would be. I hoped in the eight weeks I would compile a number of sketched ideas and renditions, and complete three or four large pieces. I couldn't waste too much time wandering in the woods or socializing, but lacking any concrete idea of where I would begin, I couldn't envision myself doing anything else. I'd had the same problem when I moved from Gran's to my accursed rental on the outskirts of Houston's museum district, except there I lurked in galleries and cafes instead of wooded clearings and cabins.

I'd been in the rental since the previous fall and had only completed twelve pieces, ten of which were commissioned via my online storefront. I'd had to up my part-time hours at the fabric store and run a couple of quilt-making classes to make ends meet, which was distinctly not in the plan when I'd projected my costs and time ratios before moving out. I'd found myself dropping in on Gran more often than planned, and even spent a winter weekend with our parents, since Zach had come in to absorb the brunt of their Yule-season festivity. He'd pretty easily figured out from my restlessness that my work wasn't working for me. Gran knew it, too, and broached the idea of my moving back in with her, even though she was the one who'd pushed me from her comfortable nest to let me figure out how to fly on my own. And I was determined to prove her faith in me justified.

Lying on my back on the studio floor, I watched the treetops disappear in the darkness. My spine wanted to rebel against the solid floor, but I forced it straight and still, my muscles relishing the stretch. This close, the hardwoods smelled almost musty, but in a more woodsy than moldy way. It was peaceful.

The wind blew a bit, and I caught sight of a star through the waving branches, and smiled. I hadn't seen a lot of stars since moving to Houston, and added 'stake out a good gazing spot' to my mental to-do list. It didn't hold much else: finish unpacking, find out if there was hot cocoa mix I could take to my cabin, create something new and marvelously expressive of my inner self.

A few deep breaths as I concentrated on the smell of the floor and the sound of the cicadas, the feel of the groove between planks on the pads of my fingers. I'd been entirely too disjointed in recent months to tap the creative core I knew was lurking somewhere within me. Eyes closed, still, I gently willed it to surface, to let the artist in me know any old time would be a great time to decide to thrive. I meditated for a good half-hour, but never felt a change.

I hauled myself off the floor, and off to bed, hollow and alone.

CHAPTER 2

I woke up confused. It felt for a moment like my room at Gran's house, but there wasn't enough light from the north and west facing windows to make that possibility plausible. And the north window was tapping. I sat up and looked out at Wren, who scraped a long branch of deadwood against the pane. She dropped it and waved, then headed towards the front door.

I met her with the log cabin quilt around my shoulders.

"Did I wake you?" she asked, entering.

"Do you always do this?"

"No, I swear I won't make a habit of it. But I've been up for two hours and I'm bored and breakfast won't be for another forty-five minutes."

"Maybe you should have tapped on the windows of Team One to make sure they're going to serve you on time."

She sat on the love seat and tipped her chin towards the road. "I saw Angelica walking out by the lake already, so I figured we were okay. She's bound to wake up that Theo guy if he's not up already."

I went through the bedroom to the studio. "Make yourself

cozy. I'm going to shower." Yawning, I shut the bathroom door behind me.

The hot water heater, at least, was working well. It seemed the coldest room in the cabin was the bedroom, and I regretted leaving my clothes behind in the chilly armoire. Once I'd figured out the arcane neo-Victorian shower controls, I rapidly shampooed and conditioned my hair and scrubbed myself with the oatmeal body bar I'd found in a basket of toiletries on a shelf above the commode. The shower was in a garden tub with a window looking into the woods, and if Wren hadn't been sitting in my cabin I would have slept past breakfast then soaked in a bathtub of bubbles long enough to be almost late for lunch.

As it was I made quick work of my morning ablutions, threw on yesterday's jeans and a Berkeley sweatshirt I'd stolen when Zach was a freshman, and went back into the sitting room with my hair in a towel and my sneakers and socks in my hands.

"Is the heating in your cabin this screwy?" I asked, sitting beside her.

"In a word, yes. I was wondering if it was the goal of the HVAC engineers, to keep us working till all hours instead of lying abed."

"I guess it worked for you this morning."

"I'm an early bird on East Coast time, so I woke up just after five with enormous hunger pangs. I went to the Main House to get coffee, but Margie was in the kitchen so all I did was grab a cup and retreat."

"You're from Connecticut, right?"

Half-shrug. "It's where I live now."

"Oh. Where's home?"

"Everywhere. Nowhere. Military brat, you know? That's what I'm trying to do now, really."

"What is?"

"Defining home. Or creating it, maybe. My brain is full of images of homes—of houses—and I'm sorting them out, trying to categorize what makes them the same, or keeps them distant."

"Wow."

A slight snort, and Wren said, "Well, wow if it works. If it doesn't…."

"Did you get any work done this morning?"

Wren laughed. "Yeah, right. I've just been wandering around, thinking, getting oriented. I've found two shortcuts to the Main House from my cabin, and one from yours to Caleb's, plus I've been along the river bed until it headed uphill pretty steeply."

I went to drape the towel in the bathroom and comb out my hair. "We've still got half an hour until grub," she called. "I'll show you around if you want."

"Sure. Let's go."

Wren waited by the front door for me to join her. As she opened it, I glanced back at the huge east-facing windows of the studio, and saw the growing light land upon a fat, probably pregnant, whitetail doe in a clearing twenty feet from the cabin. There was a salt lick set up there, and she stood rather confidently enjoying it in the otherwise still landscape. By the time we'd gone outside and rounded the wall of ValeSong, she was gone.

The clearing was edged with cypress and pine trees, which crowded out the view of Wren's porch across the creek. Turning away from the water, she led me to a path with an almost overgrown entrance, but which widened out and was lined with pine bark once we were on it.

"This is the way to Caleb's?"

She nodded. "Lucky you. You can have private rendezvous and we'll never know to gossip about it."

"I'm not sure that's really on the cards." I shook my head. "He's nice and cute and all, but I'm not sure he's my type. Too intense. Or intent, maybe."

"I don't know. He seems promising to me. We sat together on the bus down from Austin, and he's got quite a charming crinkle to his eye when he smiles."

I shrugged. "My Gran says crow's feet on a youngun' are an

indication a person won't age well." I glanced at Wren, who was smiling inwardly. "But if you think he's so all-mighty, why not do something about it yourself?"

Her smile opened up. "I'm thinking about it. I just don't know how to approach him. But, then, if I knew how to approach men, I wouldn't be a desperate single woman at thirty-two."

"That's hardly old."

"How old are you?"

"Twenty-six in September."

"No wonder. The blush of youth is on you yet. I'm turning into an eccentric old crone, just me and my clay, all day long."

"So, maybe you and Caleb are destiny. Find out."

She'd reached her fingers around my wrist when I'd said 'destiny.' Stopping, she glanced towards LakeFire, so I did, too. We were too far away for sound to carry through his lit bedroom windows, which Wren fixed her eyes upon as she talked. "The destiny thing. You know, Ashlyn, there really has to be something to it. I mean, I haven't left the state of Connecticut for over a decade. I haven't been on a plane in a dozen years. Then all this happened with my house—I'll tell you about it later, it's a long story—and the same day I read about FireWind. It seemed like destiny, so I applied. And here I am, and here he is. Doesn't it seem predetermined somehow?"

I nodded, hesitant, but she wasn't looking at me.

"Thing is," she said, finally releasing her clutch on me. "I don't know what to do about it. I've been mulling it over all morning, but I don't know what my next move should be. Will you help?"

"What do you want me to do?"

"Well, you know him. At least, your brother does. Plus he's your food partner. I just thought, maybe you could sound him out a little. Or invite me along if you and Zach do something with him?"

Her glance rested on me for half a second before she fixed her bright eyes again on Caleb's window.

"Sure," I smiled, "whatever I can do."

She hugged me. "I knew you'd do it! I could tell from the moment you walked in last night you were great. Thanks so much."

For such a soft-focus looking woman her grasp was bone hard. I stepped away from her and took her arm. "Well, if we're going to be friends, we may as well try to make each other happy, right?"

"That's just what I thought when I woke up this morning." She looked at her watch. "They've got to have something ready to eat by now. Come on, I'm starving."

We skirted past LakeFire and walked up the drive to the Main House. Wren was humming off and on, and I caught sight of a blue jay rising from an oak near the little lake.

When Lauren'd made room for me at the general meeting, she'd had no idea Caleb and I were vaguely connected. However, something about her waking me up to lead me off towards his cabin, love plans on her mind, put me off. I sighed. Maybe I was just tired and worried about work.

And hungry. When we entered the dining room and smelled the coffee and biscuits, my stomach responded greedily enough to deserve personification. Theo and Angelica were hard at work, making omelets and a melon salad. Caleb and Lizzy were already at the table, Lizzy looking jet lagged and raccoon-eyed, Caleb reading the thin local paper. No sign of Rafael, which it seemed already was norm, nor of Brandon.

I sat two seats away from Caleb when Wren told me she'd get me a cup of coffee, and pushed back the chair next to him when she brought it to me. Her blue eyes were wide as she sat, but I figured if I had a friendship mission, no matter how genuine the friendship, I was going to complete it as quickly as possible. We only had eight weeks at FireWind, and the last thing I wanted to be doing for the bulk of it was devising ways for Wren to run into her intended.

Putting down my mug, I stood. "Talk amongst yourselves, I'll be back." Caleb folded the paper and smiled at me as I passed him to reach the hallway. I didn't see any crinkles in his eyes, but maybe it was a special thing for Wren.

Outside the dining room was a hallway running the length of the house. Doors to the kitchen and a half-bath were on the dining room side, and the far end of the hall widened into a laundry room under the stairs to Margie's lair. The other half of the house had two rooms, the lounge and the computer center. Brandon was in the latter, using the scanner and whistling in a way I guessed meant he knew I was there but wanted to pretend he was so absorbed he could ignore me. There were three other computers and two printers, and hummingbird feeders hanging outside each of the four windows.

I backed out and went to the lounge. Two walls were covered with bookcases, filled mostly with art books and biographies, interspersed here and about with thick paperback novels. A keyless locked hutch undoubtedly hid the TV and DVD player. Two accessible side doors to it revealed the colony's selection of movies, which tended towards old Oscar material but ranged from *Max Headroom* to *Howard's End*. The telephone on a side table had a sign taped to the base: *Local, Collect, and Emergency Calls Only!!!*

Taking a pencil and unopened sketchpad from the coffee table, I settled myself into a wing chair and began to draw. I traced in a largish portrait of Gran in the upper left corner, and just a light impression of me alone in the woods in the lower right, and connected the two with a few tentative diagonals. As I found the angle I liked and emphasized it, rotating the pad to give my hand more freedom and reach, I realized the lines were just the beginnings of the pattern. Flipping to the next page, I blocked out a rectangle and filled it in with a traditional Double Irish Chain quilt design. Then I redrew Gran in the upper left diamond, but this time she was the locus of a web, and my likeness at the other end was just one of the elements extending from her, and bound up by her.

When I paused to look at the overall effect, I was pleased. Generally, I'm not happy with pencil sketches, because the way the fabrics feed into and bounce off each other is so much different than the diffused scratchings of a #2 lead, but I quite simply liked this layout. I was thinking about the ways I would fill the other spaces, and how best to make the chain into the unifying element, when Caleb knocked on the door.

"Sorry to interrupt, you look so lost, but we're about to eat your share."

"No, it's okay. Only lost in creation." I closed my sketchpad and stood, indicating the pile of pads on the table. "I hope these were for general use."

He smiled, and then I saw what Wren had meant about his eyes. "They were. Margie gave us some inspirational lecture at that point of the tour, telling us how the founders felt it was important to encourage us to create whenever the urge took us, even if it was in the middle of *Judge Judy*, and crates of these pads were ordered direct from the manufacturer and placed about the house and grounds. There are even a couple in the bathroom."

I laughed and let him lead me back to the table, where Angelica passed me a pitcher of orange juice. "Fresh squeezed," she explained. "There was no ready-made. And no juicer. Theo had to strain it with the colander."

"But it was good for my soul," Theo said, with more than a touch of sarcasm. Angelica laughed an in-joke sort of laugh, but it looked like everyone else had heard it already.

No one spoke for a while. The silence was less than easy, but it was only our second meal together and few of us had become bosom pals yet. Then Caleb leaned past Wren to catch my eye. "So what were you making?"

"Oh, just sketching out an idea. I'll have to play with it a little, but I think it's going to end up taking off from a traditional pattern. A story-telling piece."

"What is it you really do? I mean, is it basically just quilting?" Lizzy asked.

Time for the big eye roll. "'Oh, I thought quilts were just for sleeping under!'" Our gazes locked. "I'm not making fun—I just hear it all the time. Traditional art form, blah, blah, not just Wedding Rings and Flying Geese, blah, blah, creativity, technology and history intertwined, etcetera."

I sipped at the pulpy juice, stifling my impatience. "I make art. Just because it's related to something anyone can manage with a bit of technical know-how doesn't make it less valuable as an art form. It's like asking Caleb or Brandon what's the difference between my iPhone's photo stream and what they do."

Wren nodded at Lizzy. "Or why what we make is more important than some Hummel figurine."

Lizzy's counter was instant. "I don't know about that. Sculpture has a long tradition as art. Collectibles are fine for what they are, but no one's going around asking why *The Thinker* is magnificent." She stopped and let out a breath, then turned more calmly to me. "Do you have any here?"

"Hummel figurines?"

"No, quilts. I mean, examples of your art. Or photos of them? I'd like to see the difference for myself."

I finished wolfing down my omelet. "Sure, come along now if you like, I've a couple with me." We stood and stacked our dishes, then headed outside.

"They do make fiber arts in Ireland, you know," I told her. "Tapestries for one thing, and some extraordinary lacework, but there's quilting, too."

"I've never spent a lot of time on traditional arts. I've been to the National Gallery and all, but between working and my art I don't have just loads of time to spend on the kind of culture not speaking directly to me."

"What's your day job?"

"I was a chef at a brassiere my ex owns. But we broke up over Christmas and it's been hell, so I gave my notice when I found out I'd been accepted here. When I go back I'm taking over for a friend of a friend going on maternity leave, at this trendy and wholesome café in Temple Bar. It should be easier. I won't have breakfast to contend with and the menu is smaller and less ambitious than Carmel's."

"Was that her name?"

"The brassiere's. She's Moira." As we turned onto the path to ValeSong, Lizzy added, "Don't you dare let it get back to Brandon I cook. I need a break from all that, and if it means eating canned soup because it's all he can manage, it's fine with me."

"Your secret is safe." I entered my door code and gestured her in. "This your first trip to the States?"

"No, my parents brought me on holiday when I was fifteen, we toured all round New England and parts of the south." She wandered rather freely around my studio, opening the cabinets and playing with the lights while I unpacked the bag with my work. "I had my very first lesbian encounter in Maine, of all places. At this kind of day camp for the surly teenagers who didn't want to go on the lobster-boat tours with their parents. She and I wandered off together when we were supposed to be picking blueberries and mauled at each other in a little wood. I think the camp director—he was barely older than we were— knew, but he never said a word to our parents. He just asked if Cindi and I wanted to join him at a beach party with some friends."

"Did you go?"

"We told our folks it was a cookout for all the campers, and then we disappeared under the pier. We were going to take a dip in the ocean, but it was fekking cold, so we got dressed again and went to a bar and she bought us coke and chips—french fries— and talked about how we would always remember each other and always be friends." Lizzy shook her head just slightly. "She's living in L.A. now, and has twin boys."

She came up behind me where I was spreading *Sprung From Spring* on the drafting table. "This is one of them?"

I nodded. "It's one of my favorites. Spring is the town I used to live in, a little bit out of Houston. I did this just after I'd moved away from my parents, so it felt, you know, like a release from a kind of moral prison."

Lizzy moved around me to touch the surface, fingering the hanging silver manacles and following the spiral of freedoms (boots made for walking, needle and thread of expression, a condom wrapper, a clock stopped at 2:18 am, a net-purse full of coins) as it expanded across the cloth. "I wouldn't have thought it was so sensual," she said, looking at me. "The fabrics invite you to touch them, don't they?"

"Mmm," I said. "I tried painting in college, but it always seemed too static to me. Oils dry so hard and relentless. Even when I paint the cloth," I indicated the brush strokes of the dust storm and tint of the sunrise, "I try to do it as lightly as I can, so it can still flow with the same motion as the quilt."

"'Tis okay, touching them, isn't it?"

"Sure. Same as with sculpture; they wear out with time but you can make them as functional as you want when they're new. When I'm commissioned for baby quilts I always pad them with terrycloth or wool instead of batting, to make them washable."

She scrunched her brow at me. "How can you switch so easily from fighting tradition to making something that ends up so functional?"

I shrugged. "A gal's gotta eat. And it depends on the piece. My baby quilts are celebrations of the new life, but they also have visual and tactile appeal, because that's so important for developing brains. Besides, I'm not exactly to the pick and choose point in my career." I moved *Sprung* aside and unfolded another, an abstract collage of blues, greens, grays and purples with a distant boat askew in the upper right corner and a glimpse of a turreted tower in the lower left. "I've known people to encase my work in glass, and to set tables on it, so I try to be flexible in how I make them. This is called *The Irish Sea.* Does it look right?"

"This a Martello tower?" she pointed.

"Yeah, it's supposed to be the one in Killiney. My Pappa always told us about it being the last he saw of Ireland. He watched it fade into a speck, then turned his head and never looked back."

"When was that, then?"

"In '37. He was eighteen and had done as much as he thought he could in Dalkey, so he went first to Liverpool, didn't like it so much as a haven for Irish Catholics, and caught the next boat to America. It docked at Galveston and he moved up to Houston because he was offered a job timbering."

"Did he bring your granny over?"

"No, they hadn't met. She was already living in Houston, had been since her parents emigrated here when she was six. It was bad timing, just before the Depression, but they fell in with some good people, a community of local Irish who looked out for each other when they could." I ran my palm over the rough kaleido-scopic waves on the tightly stitched top. "Pappa met Gran through the same crowd when he had only been in America a couple of weeks. It was on her fifteenth birthday. Fourteen months later, they got married."

"And she from Ireland. Traveled across the world to marry the girl next door."

"I made this shortly before Pappa died, when I was fifteen. It was to commemorate his arrival in America." I didn't fold away *The Irish Sea,* but I walked off to stare out the window. "Of course, I hadn't studied art at all at the time, but I'd been quilting for years. Gran had me piecing quilt tops when I was just a kid, six or seven. I'd made others of my own by then, too. Zach still has the one I did when he went to college."

I looked around to see Lizzy still handling *Sea.* "So, have I convinced you I'm an artist? I know that one's a little raw, but surely you see it's not just traditional craftwork?"

"No, I think I do believe you. I shouldn't have questioned you in the first place. No one ever challenges me for wanting to sculpt, not that I give them much room, but, then, when they find out I'm a chef it seems to fit some sort of pattern in their eyes."

"Creating marble art is an extension of creating culinary art, which in turn is an extension of the womanly art of putting a nice meal on the table?"

"That's it exactly. So even though I'm a freak in some ways, especially in that I'm gay, I'm a very womanly freak. Whereas I feel quite anti-womanly-anything at times. I mean, loving women is a man thing. Chiseling at rocks is a man thing. Being a successful chef, usually a man thing. Those are the traditions I'm battling. Men are the ones who do all the exhibitionist sort of creativity, who get their names in the papers for their big passions."

"Women are supposed to do quiet things like quilt," I said.

"Yes, or if they indulge in art it should simply be about flowers blooming in the spring or the look of love in an innocent newborn's eyes."

"Or hummingbirds in flight. Don't you worry you're being stereotypical? Isn't society advanced enough to see past that?"

Lizzy began to pace. "Maybe in America. I can't really know. And there've been wonderful women artists in Ireland for decades, eons, but I still think when most people I've met hear of an artist achieving something, they assume 'man' first and only chide themselves a little when they find instead it's 'woman.' Do you not find that?"

"Stop, look," I said, pointing. The doe was back. In the brush behind her, I saw a buck eyeing the clearing, trying to sense the difference my morning walk there with Wren had made to it. "They know I was there, I think," I told Lizzy. "She seemed much more at ease earlier. She must seriously like salt."

As we watched, I thought about our debate. I decided the issue for me was less whether I had an innate right to create art than it was whether what I did was indeed art. In addition, most fiber artists, like most quilters, were women, so I wasn't crossing any gender barriers, stepping on anyone's balls, in doing what I did. I could see how Lizzy would be more threatening to a male than I would, in almost all she was. She was hard and intelligent and the things she made were thrust at the world. I was smart, too, but quieter and what I did grew from things women had always done in America. Virtually everyone who bought my work was female. Men commissioned my quilts, but generally as gifts for their beloved women.

The buck started suddenly and dashed off, and the doe followed more heavily. Her fawn was imminent, I thought. "They seem large," Lizzy said. "Are all American deer that size?"

"So far as I know." Someone knocked at my door. "That's what scared them, I bet," I said, going to open it. Wren was there.

"You two deserted me," she accused, tossing herself onto the love seat.

"I thought it would be wise. Let Team One disappear with the washing up and Brandon go back to his computer and it would be just you and Caleb."

Lizzy scooted in next to Wren as I sat cross-legged on the coffee table. "Is there a FireWind fling happening, then?" Lizzy asked with a grin. "I love gossip, tell me everything."

I laughed. "You're hilarious. One second you're raging against the world pinning you to its expectations of women, the next you're digging for dirt in time-honored fashion. And you accused me of double standards?"

She pushed her glasses up her nose again. "I'm very complex."

"Well, I'm not sure I'll be of much help to your gossipy side, unfortunately," Wren said glumly. "We were sitting there chatting and all the sudden he pulls out his newspaper again. As if it takes more than two minutes to read a rag like that."

"What, in the middle of your conversation?" I asked.

"Well, I was running out of things to say. I told him about the houses I was going to make here, and he told me about some big series he's got going of buildings over landscape, construction and deconstruction or whatever, and then he told me a little about California, and I rambled on about Connecticut, then I stood up for a last cup of coffee and he opened out the paper. So instead of drinking the coffee I gave my cup to that Theo guy and left." She looked rather wistfully at the empty coffeepot on my bar.

"Coffee all 'round?" I asked, rising. They nodded. "Still and all, Wren, it doesn't seem too disastrous. I mean, you only met yesterday, you shouldn't be jumping into bed with him today."

"Oh, definitely not," said Lizzy. "You should wait until at least tomorrow."

Wren hunched her legs up under her and leaned forward on her hands. "It'll be decades before I have sex again, at this rate."

"Don't mope. If you get desperate there's always me. I'm right next door, you know," Lizzy said, hugging her with one arm.

Wren leaned into her. "Thanks. I may have to."

I regarded them on the sofa. "What a cute couple you make. I think she's too tall for you, Lizzy."

"A woman can never be too tall or too blonde. Or too busty. It's my credo."

"Well, in the immortal words of Meatloaf, two out of three ain't bad," Wren said, and sat up again. "But what are we going to do about Caleb?"

"Ash here knows him, why doesn't she set the two of you up?"

"That's just what she told me to do this morning. Now you're ganging up on me." I rummaged in the cabinet next to the sink until I found three mugs and a spoon. There was sugar but no creamer. "I hope you all like it sweet and black. What's the plan, then?"

"We could all go somewhere some night."

"Not this week, you're on dinner duty."

"Next week. Sunday night."

"That counts me out of the fun, I'm watching Brandon cook that night," said Lizzy. "But as long as I get the full account the next day, you have my blessing."

"So you'll call your brother and set it up?" Wren leaned forward to take a mug from me.

"Set what up? I don't even know what either of you like to do."

"Dinner or a movie? A gallery? Something. Is there even anything to do in Wimberley?"

I flashed back to the hill country guides I'd browsed. "There's some restaurants. There's a great barbeque place not far off, but it's a meat market, and loud. Hayes is a dry county, no booze, but there's a couple of places where you can get a 'membership' to a drinking club for a night and get served."

Lizzy snorted. "That's the most asinine thing I've ever heard. How the hell am I meant to get drunk every night? I can't count on Margie supplying me, now, can I?"

"Well, stupid or not, it's that or driving to Austin or San Marcos, and unless there's some event on that's stretching it a little. I mean, why would you come with us on a Zeke and Ned reunion unless it was local or it was something special?"

Wren nodded. "You're right. So see if Zach will come down here and we'll go to the club place and get drunk and throw stones in a river or something, whatever passes for excitement in small-town Texas, and then I'll seduce Caleb and we'll live happily ever after!"

Her exuberance was fetching. "Whatever you say, darlin'. I'll email him right after lunch. For now, you two get out of here. We're only here for eight weeks and I'd damn well better get a thing or two done while I'm here besides helping you find the love of your life."

"You go girl!" laughed Lizzy in her pseudo-American voice. "Come on, Wren, we're in the way of Ashlyn's work, and if she tells Margie we'll be in big trouble. I don't want to come away with demerits on my first day."

I made them promise to return the mugs they were taking, and sent them off. Closing my eyes and inhaling my own coffee, I decided the chain part of the piece could be a collage of reverse sides of the fabrics making up the other patches. The patches themselves would all center around Gran, of course. It would be the first large thing I'd make for her without her supervision. It would be my way of saying thank you to her for her love, and her encouragement, and her offering up of her home as my refuge. And my way of saying to myself....

Well, I had ideas. I didn't have anything definite, but I had ideas. As I went to rummage in my fabric stash, it occurred to me that the best thing that had happened in the past twenty-four hours, and perhaps in the past twenty-four weeks or so, was that I finally had some ideas.

CHAPTER 3

"*B*ro -

"You miss me yet? I'm working away here. (Okay, I'm taking a break, but I've been at it since breakfast. You're probably still asleep, right?)

"Hey, I know I'm clueless, but can you remember Gran's little brother's name? I got Brian, Albert, Danny, Maura, 'someone,' Mabel. And Berneen. Trust me, this is work related.

"Long story, but how would you feel about coming up here this Sun. for a Z & N thing? I could bring Wren along & the four of us could have some laughs (gee, what a brilliant idea, which just now popped into my head! Perhaps C & W will hit it off & start a relationship or something! Wouldn't that be great –> we could be the matchmakers!). Since C & I have to cook that day, it'd have to be a night thing. We could meet at my cabin if you'd be so kind as to pick us up, or we could take the shuttle to town & hook up at John Henry's (remember THAT place?) Let me know.

"Okay, here's the other part. I suppose you should email C on your own & suggest this—I thought I'd swing by to see sis, how bout dinner, etc. So as it'll be a surprise, you know.

"Catch up w/ ya later!

"Love,

"A

"PS—Bring some booze for our pal Lizzy, who's about to dehydrate from a lack of whiskey. A more complete order will follow. Gracias!"

I HIT SEND JUST as blondie walked into the computer room.

"Hey, gal, I hope you're still on for this thing. I just told Zach to set it up."

She lounged into the chair next to me. "I am. Trust me, I am. I've been fondling clay all day. My houses look more like dildos."

"Please. Stick with the need-to-know, okay?" I logged out. "How many houses are you making?"

Wren squinted as she thought. "The first series is four. My grandmother's house in Juneau, the row house on the base of Ft. Stamhood where my brother was born, the ranch house in San Antonio from when I was thirteen, and a little cabin in the hill country I hope you'll recognize. White, blue, red, yellow. After that, we'll see. If it goes well I'll move on to orange, green, purple, and black." Wren had decided to create intricate scales of typical American houses, mono-colored to symbolize the life-phase she was experiencing while she lived in each abode.

"What were you saying earlier about the house thing in Connecticut?"

"Oh," she shrugged. "It's kinda strange, I guess. I've been living in the same duplex for eight years. The landlord told me when I moved in he was wanting to remodel and sell the thing one day, so that ax has been over my head the whole time. But all this long, nothing, not a word from him about it. Or if there was word, it was 'we've just lost in the market and can't fix it up now' or 'interest rates are too high, no one's buying' or something. Then, three months ago, out of nowhere, a decorator shows up on my doorstep to take room photos and measurements. I mean, the place is like a second skin to me now!" She dabbed at her eyes, and then rolled them self-deprecatingly. "So I called him up, the land-lord, to see what was going on. Seems his wife's parents just left them some major cash, and house prices in the area has gone way up, and he gave me two months to get out. The same day—I was taking a house-hunting break to surf some art boards—I ran across the FireWind info, and something just, I don't know, made me apply. Isn't it strange? There I was, devastated about losing my home, having to move—which I hate, of course—and this new sanctuary threw itself in my lap. That's why my cabin is one of the important first pieces of my series."

"Awesome." It seemed more like well-aligned events than destiny, but I got that the move here moved her. And the emotion would drive her art. "Sounds like they'll be great, your houses."

She snorted. "If I ever manage to make them."

"You don't have anything sculpted yet? Just the sketches?"

"And the concept. It took me ages to figure out what I wanted to do with all houses we've had. Like, make them into tree orna-ments so I could give them roots, or nesting in each other like one of those Russian dolls, kind of interactive, you know?"

I nodded.

"But clay's no good for interactive, and I didn't want to go with anything more delicate, less structural. So this is where we're at. If I can just get my mind off you-know-what I'll be able to focus." She scratched her nails along her scalp. "But besides all that, I have about three minutes to find Rafael and place the order for dinner. He's not at his cabin, down any obvious trails, or around here."

"Get Margie to find him."

"She's on her way to San Marcos to pick up the groceries I haven't ordered."

"I haven't seen him all day. Suppose he's bailed?"

She double-clicked on the supermarket program. "Either way, I guess the menu's up to me. You have any favorites? If I'm solo cooking for eight it'd better be pretty damn simple. Like, hot dogs and potato chips simple."

"Do they have tofu dogs?"

"Oh, God, you're one of the veg-heads." She crossed her eyes at me. "Pizza it is, then. Let's see—frozen cheese pizza, with some added flourish. Green peppers, tomatoes, corn, ground beef for the normal ones here. Salad on the side. What else?"

"Up to you, Team Three. I'm off to soak up inspiration from the hills around me." I stood and squeezed her narrow shoulder on the way past.

BY TUESDAY DINNER, Rafael had been declared among the missing. Margie claimed he was still on the grounds, and merely nocturnal. The trail of dirty dishes Theo discovered in the rec room every morning supported her claims. Over pasta, Wren declared war.

"Look, you've all been nice about helping to clean up and stuff, but no more. No more saving leftovers for him. No more washing dishes for him. If Margie can't bother to make him follow her precious rules, I'm figuring out a way on my own."

"Guerrilla training at the base camp at dawn?" asked Lizzy.

"If it comes to it. I'm no sergeant's kid for nothing. But I think we'll start with Operation: Palmolive. Stack the sink so high he can't get his midnight snack without clearing it, and leave a nice little note pinned to the rubber gloves."

Angelica and Theo started in at the same time. He deferred to her. "And what about when he's ignored them and we need to make breakfast and there's dried primavera on the bowls?"

"Drag me out and I'll do them. But if that happens, tomorrow I'm lugging the dishes to his porch. And if that doesn't work, I'm ordering paper plates and you're all eating frozen food the rest of the week. Just so you all know."

I took my plate to the sink and returned with a cup of chamomile tea.

"...Sunday night," Caleb was saying. "I'm sure they'll be happy if you join us. Right, Ashlyn?"

"Right what?"

"I told Wren she should come with us Sunday, since she seems to need a break already."

"Come where?" I asked, as Lizzy nudged me under the table.

"Hasn't Zach told you? He emailed he's coming in to see you and suggested we all go into Wimberley for a meal. I told him it had to be Sunday night because of the cooking and everything."

"Oh. Well, fine with me, I guess. I told him to come back and see me sometime, but I didn't think Austin would be boring him already."

"I guess Wimberley has its attractions," Caleb said, crinkly brown eyes tracking from me to Wren.

ZACH'S MESSAGE mostly complained about his spring allergies kicking in, but reported he'd accomplished my mission and Sunday was good for him. When I got back to my cabin, the lights were on.

"I knew I shouldn't have told y'all my door code," I said to Wren as I joined Lizzy on the sofa. "What did you think of that, then?"

She grinned the first true face-splitting grin I'd ever seen. "I'm pleased."

"Don't let her lack of euphoria fool you," Lizzy deadpanned. "I forced her to stop asking me after the eighth time if he really said what she thought he said and did it seem to me too he was saying what he might be saying. I mean, obviously he is smitten and my hopes of taking her on the rebound are forever crushed."

"So next time poor Zach and I are going to be left all alone?"

"Let's toast to that," Wren said, handing us mugs of the cocoa she'd remembered to order for me from San Marcos.

THE NEXT MORNING I ignored the tapping at my window, figuring setting Wren up with the hottest guy at FireWind was my good deed for the week and she could get Lizzy to wash up the mess Rafael had obviously left. After sleeping late, I took my long-awaited bubble bath then lounged in my robe as I watched the deer from the studio window and pretended not to look at the sketches on the drafting board. Once it was bound to be quiet at the Main House, I dressed, gathered my notebook, and headed for the computer center.

It was empty, and I set myself up next to the plotter printer, which was a luxury on my artistic wish list. A few times, I had taken designs to a copy center to print out full-scale patterns, but for most of my quilts, I tiled the pattern pieces to a page each and used the old-fashioned cut-and-paste method. It took me most of the morning, accompanied by illicit slices of coffeecake, to create the *Gran Chain* (or whatever I would call it). When it came off the plotter I made a few adjustments and corrections on paper, then on screen, and sent a line drawing to print.

Brandon came in. "Can I see?" he asked, approaching.

"Nope."

He pulled his hair back. "Oh. 'Kay. I get it." Turning his back to me, he switched on another terminal.

"It's the way I work."

"Yeah. It's cool. Some people are insecure about things until they're done. They don't think anyone else can see the big picture but them."

"Some people don't want the flow of their ideas interrupted by the comments of others, actually," I said, and rolled the final print-outs to take back to my cabin.

~

THREADING my machine is my mantra. Before each project, I start by cleaning the feed dog, shuttle race body, and hook to remove any lint, and then I oil the moving parts of the take-up lever, needle shaft, winder, and bobbin casing. Next, I make my bobbins. I like a full one for each thread color ready to drop in the casing as soon as I need it. But it's when I tighten the stop motion knob and take the thread from the spool pin through the upper guides, down around the tension dial, and up again to snap into the check spring that I begin to focus on what's ahead for the day.

Snaking the thread through the take-up eyelet and dropping it past the thread guard, weaving it through the lower guides, I anticipate the dry taste of the frayed end. I moisten it to a sharp point before I finally thread the needle. My drops of saliva won't make it into the actual project, but in my gut I know the process of licking the thread that will appliqué, embroider, or quilt together my creation solidifies the connection between me and my artwork.

I'd spent the afternoon crouching on the floor rearranging fabric, and was ready to develop a backache based on hunching over my sewing machine. After a few shoulder rolls, I selected a spool of forty weight yellow rayon and swapped the machine's patchwork foot for the open toe applique foot. I stretched a scrap of bright green fabric over a small oval embroidery hoop. My first step was always to monogram 'Ashlyn May' with the date and title of the piece, if I knew it. I could embroider my name on the reverse side of the fabric freehand now, but had to trace the title in a dark fabric marker on the front. I'd named this piece *Chains of Love*. The yellow thread gleamed golden against the green; perfect. A nice bright mood, energetic. Before the final stage, I would appliqué the title patch to the backing in the lower right corner. Meanwhile, it would be pinned to the wall near the machine.

Just as I finished cutting the upper thread to tie it up, Lizzy knocked on the front door.

"Dinner's in about a minute. You coming? Wren sent me to ask."

I popped my spine and turned to get my shoes. "I lost track. Ignore the mess." We headed out. "Wren mad? I told her I'd help set the table and stuff."

"No, I did it. She figured you were working. Which is not to say she's fine and all; Rafael is still among the missing and Margie never went over there today."

I sighed. "Tomorrow get me early if he's not around and you are. I'll help her cook."

"I wish I could, but it would blow my cover with Brandon."

"Have I told you the latest Brandon-as-ass story?" I asked. We had already compiled quite a few, but that didn't stop me from relating what he'd said in the computer room.

Caleb was on the porch. "What are you laughing about this time?"

"An annoying photographer we know," I replied, winking at him.

"Geez, be more subtle, will you? I'll back off already."

Lizzy walked up the steps to look him in the eye. "We'll let it go this time, boy, but just remember you've been warned. None of your macho man stuff from now on, eh?"

Caleb literally did back off. "No contest, Lizzy, you are way tougher than I am. I'll keep away, I promise."

"Poor Caleb," I said, holding the door for them both.

"Poor nothing," Lizzy replied. "He's had a little too much of being the dominant paradigm, in my opinion. Time to spread the wealth."

"Wren, can I sit next to you?" he asked, taking the bowls of sour cream and guacamole from her as she held open the kitchen door with her foot. "These two are too domineering for my sensitive soul."

"From what I've heard, Wren is into domination herself," Liz said, grinning as Wren stumbled on her way to fetch the platter of spinach quesadillas.

The banter slowed down once the others came in. Most of talk revolved around Angelica's photos of her most recently completed sculpture, a life size baby. It was a pure pink marble, and the infant was clenched in the palms of a woman's hands; the tendons between her knuckles standing out, the smooth nails pressed into the baby's ribs. The baby was curled upon himself, listless and pursed-mouthed.

"It's modeled on my nephew Tommy. I wanted to express the strength my sister in labor and the fragility of his little preemie body."

Theo's eyes sparkled a little when he looked from the photos to her. "It's amazing. You've really got something here."

Wren and I glanced at each other. Her side-eye suggested she shared some of my doubts.

"That's a gorgeous piece of marble," Lizzy said, peering at the close-up of the infant's balled fists.

"I just looked for beauty, and this spoke to me. I knew it was right from when I started."

We passed back the photos and moved on to general criticisms of Margie, who had kicked Theo out of the TV room in the middle of a documentary on Picasso. Caleb volunteered to help Wren haul the night's dirty dishes to Rafael's porch, but insisted she leave a note about their rebellion tacked to the newel post of Margie's staircase. Lizzy winked at me and I had to pretend to be choking on the salsa to cover my laughter.

THE WEEK WENT on in the same vein. Theo and Angelica were never seen apart. Rafael was never seen, although the dishes did show up clean after the porch dump. I dyed three yards of percale with indigo and spruce swirls, and ordered more cut glass beads from my favorite online supplier. By Saturday morning, the fabric was ready to rinse and set, and I strung a clothesline between two trees in the deer clearing to hang it out. One of Gran's quilting legacies was a predilection towards working with sun-drenched cloth, carefully ironed.

"Hey, that's going to scare away my subject," Caleb said, coming out of the path towards the cabin.

When I turned towards him, startled, he snapped three or four quick shots of me spilling the corn kernel offering I was leaving the deer.

"Well, one doe is as good as another," he shrugged.

"Not funny."

"Point of view. Add your expression to the fact I'm taking some revenge for your ruining my morning's shoot, and it's enough to make me smile."

"She doesn't even come around this late."

"I know; I've been stalking her. But I wanted some good daylight establishing shots, then this afternoon I was going to get her coming out. Which she won't do if you've got some curtain thing flapping all over the place."

"Too bad you don't have a right to dictate the world the way you want it, isn't it?"

"A haven for artists working side-by-side, isn't it?"

I shook my head. "Pulling a Margie line isn't gonna make me take it down. It needs to dry, and this is the only good place to hang a line. Take your pictures tomorrow."

"I've got to set up downwind well before she shows, and your brother's coming just past dusk. I sure don't want to offend your and Wren's delicate sensibilities by going to dinner in the sweaty work vest I spent hours crouching in."

Goddess preserve us from Caleb smelling bad in front of Wren. He crossed the clearing towards me, presumably without considering if his work vest reeked. It didn't, but I was counting thoughts, not reality. I admitted, "I forgot about the dinner thing. And the cooking. What are we going to make?"

He pulled a spiral notebook out of a side pocket. "I made a little bit of a shopping list. Figured on eggs and pancakes or muffins in the mornings, maybe some soups like gazpacho for lunches. What do you think?"

I took it from him. His handwriting was all block capitals. His pencil was blunt. "You actually planned all this? Raspberry-cream cheese blintzes? I was thinking more like cereal and raisin toast."

"It's not hard. Some fresh fruit for smoothies, a few dairy products. There's a food processor in there, we can make anything." Oh, the confidence of a man who could cook. It knew no bounds.

Handing back the notebook, I said, "I'm game, as long I don't have the smell of bacon frying every morning to deal with."

"Wouldn't have it any other way. Unlike your little project here, which I'd really like to get rid of now."

"Look. I know it's thrown a kink in your works, and I'm sorry, Caleb. But I can't just not dry the cloth now, it has to set properly. Can't you take your shots in a couple of days?"

He kind of growled, quietly. "Sure, it's okay for you to progress at your so-important pace, but my stuff just gets shelved. No problem."

"Relax. Doe probably wouldn't have shown tonight anyway."

"Yeah, she's so inconsistent."

"You seriously want me to ruin my whole dye job for this one shot? There aren't other pictures you can take in the meantime?"

"You're drying it, right? Like, same thing you could do in the laundry room?"

"And waste all that electricity? I'm sure the founders wouldn't approve." I was flippant, but I'd calculated the overall look of the cloth based on a slow dry time, not the heat-set it would get with a tumble in the dryer.

"Thanks a hell of a lot, Ashlyn, damn considerate of you,"

Caleb's Hershey kiss eyes went narrow on me before he turned sharply and strode out towards his cabin. Except, somehow, he didn't start exactly on the path, and a black willow branch snapped at him. "Fuck!" he yelped out.

"Goddess, you okay? What happened?"

He limped back towards me, hand gripping his upper thigh. "Fucking tree attacked me."

"Are you bleeding?"

"Uh, crap, yeah, I think so."

I reached him and pulled him back into the clearing. "Come on, let me help." The eyes judged me briefly, almond-round once more, and Caleb nodded. He balanced against me as I guided him up my steps.

We limped to the love seat. "Let me look." Wincing, he lifted his palm. "Wow. Good thing you're not a couple of inches shorter, you'd never have children."

"Ha, ha, hardy ha."

"You're going to have to take those off, you know, so we can clean it."

"Are you enjoying this? I'm hurt here."

"I know, I know. Poor Caleb. Aren't you glad you don't have to crouch on this thigh for hours later today?" Poor Caleb's thigh. It looked bad. Well, not the thigh itself; the thigh was lean and solid under my hand. I wondered if Wren was into scars.

He released a slow breath. "You're completely hilarious."

"Come on, drop trou. Maybe it'll seem funny to you tomorrow."

"Right." He stood, carefully, and growled at me again when I tried to help him unbutton his khakis. Blue boxers. Nice. "Stop staring."

Cocking my head at him, I asked, "Was I staring?"

"Damn, you should do improv. I'm finding this a little embarrassing, if you want to know the truth."

Smiling, I said, "I love the truth. Here's the bad news, speaking of the truth. This cut's deep. I don't think nature loves you as much as you love it. And your pants, well, they're kaput."

"Just get me a wet washcloth," he said, sinking back to the couch. "Sorry. Please get me a wet washcloth."

"That's fine for getting the dirt out, but you're going to have to abrade this, running water, the works."

"What are you, Nurse Nell all the sudden?"

"No, I'm just not an idiot. A deep wound, you have to clean it out, not just scrub at it. Can you make it into my bathroom?"

"I get a sponge bath now?" His smile was less strained with pain.

"I think you're enjoying this as much as I am. No, I just want you to hold it under the tap for a minute while I go get a bandage and antiseptic."

Grumbling, Caleb let me help him up and into the tub. No way would he clean the thing without getting naked or getting the boxers wet, but I decided to let him deal with that problem on his own. As it was, I was collecting images of some damn fine legs to savor later. Not trying to edge in on Wren or anything, but when providence throws damn fine legs your way, you have to pay attention.

"Use soap on it," I commanded as I left him, half-crouched on the rim of the tub, a fresh towel beside him.

Margie's first aid kit had every necessity. I stuck it on my mini-bar and tapped at the door. "You decent?"

Growl. "Come in already."

Poor Caleb was on his ass in the tub, leg sticking up by the window, attempting to get the wound close to the faucet. He'd left his shirt on, but shoved it under his armpits, and wrapped his hips in the towel. More's the pity. He wasn't looking happy.

Probably I was looking too happy. I was getting an eyeful of slim muscled torso as he twisted to position his leg. His feet were bare and his thighs flexed strong and he was basically writhing half-naked in the tub I'd spent a little time writhing fully naked in myself. My next bath was going to be even more stimulating, I could tell.

Caleb's grumbling recalled me. "Fucking water hurts like hell."

"So you didn't use the soap?"

"If the water hurts this much, it's getting all the crap out on its own."

"Nice try. You going to do it yourself, or do I have to lather up your leg for you?"

His hand went back to covering his groin. "Just hand me the damn soap."

I grinned. Clearly, he was going to be fine, so it was time for me to start having some real fun.

"Fuck!" he hissed as the water ran over the wound.

"Poor Caleb." I pat his shoulder and got another towel. "Now rinse it real good and let me help you up."

"I can get myself up."

"You've left me in no doubt about your ability to get yourself up, Caleb, dear. But just this once, okay? The tub's slippery and I wouldn't want your towel to fall askew."

"Now I know you're enjoying this. And it's all your fault. Stop enjoying my pain."

Did I deliberately put my arm around his body so my palm stroked his bare, warm side? Maybe. Was his quick indrawn breath because of my touch or because it hurt to stand on his wounded leg? Only the hardening erection he wasn't managing to obscure knew for sure. "Sure, as soon as possible. Come on, back to the other room. And you'd better let me put the ointment on."

"Are you crazy?"

"Nope. But look what a wimp you were about the soap. The ointment is gonna hurt even more. You wouldn't do it right."

He rearranged the towel carefully as he sat down. "I am not a wimp."

"Course not." I spread his knees so when I knelt between his thighs I could still see the wound. Maybe it was because he'd removed his work vest, but he certainly didn't smell bad. "Now hold still. If you're a good boy I'll get you a sucker later."

"Such wit. Fuck!"

"Be still." I trapped the cut leg between my ribs and my arm.

"Ow, fuck! Ash!"

"Almost done. There." I leaned forward to blow on the wound, the way Gran always did to take the sting away. I swear I didn't mean for my cheek to brush the towel. And I'm confident Caleb's groan was one of pain.

"Do you want me to tape down the bandage, or?" I was a little hot in the face. "Or, you could do it, and I'll try to sew up your pants."

Caleb wasn't looking at me. I think it was the injury. "You'd do that?"

"Sure," I shrugged. "I have needle, I have thread, it's a natural."

He cleared his throat. Twice. "Um, yeah. That'd be great. Thanks."

So I took his pants into the studio, leaving him on the love seat with the gauze. The gash was actually a little large; I'd need to put a patch on it.

"You think you'll walk again?" I called over the low wall between us as I dug for fabric that would match his trousers.

"One day very soon," he confirmed. "Though I guess you do win the turf war—no way I'm hunkering down for photos tonight."

Mentioning his territorial aggression was his tactical error. I shuffled past the muted calico I'd landed on and chose a leftover scrap from a baby quilt. Lavender, with duckies. A nice orange thread to accentuate their little beaks, and the pants were better than new.

Caleb was sporting about the ducks. He quacked when he saw them. I cursorily inspected his bandage, patted him on the knee, and promised I'd stay in my room while he got dressed.

Whew.

I had to flop on my bed hugging on my pillow a little. The man had a mouth on him, in addition to the damn fine legs, on top of the moment in the clearing when his eyes said clear as day, "You, I'll trust." And the heat. His arm across my neck as I'd helped him to the tub had branded me. And the quack.

Timing, humor, communion.

Snap the hell out of it, Ash, he's taken. Or, kinda. He's staked out. Whatever the situation, I needed to snap the hell out of it.

"Ash?" The liquid timbre of his voice did not help me snap. "Ashlyn?"

"Yeah, I'm here. You decent now?"

"Rarely, but my fly's done up."

He edged himself over on the love seat, so I sat beside him. "Caleb, listen, I'm sorry if I was flippant."

"Flippant? I don't think they've invented a word to describe how you were. 'Antagonizing' comes close."

"Was I so bad?" Come to think of it, his eyes weren't pure chocolate; there were some bronze flecks in there.

Little smile. "Nah, you were perfect. I have to admit it was funny."

"Can you walk?"

"You kicking me out?"

"No." Because his staying wasn't in the least a dangerously appealing idea. "Just asking."

"Yes, you are. I can tell." His tone said he could tell many things, maybe some things I wasn't telling myself yet.

A couple of different replies jockeyed for position, but I reminded myself about snapping out of it. The moral she-was-there-first ground was definitely the easier path. "Okay, a little, yeah, I am kicking you out. I need to work on my drawings before dinner."

"You know what? I think you owe me for laughing at me so much. Tell me what this big dyed-cloth project is all about." He didn't act like a man about to vacate the premises.

I shook my head. "It's not that easy, sorry. I have to work it out more myself."

"Come on, maybe talking about it will help."

Why did guys keep trying to force me to discuss my vision? I had a process that worked best in isolation. If I desired their opinions, I was perfectly capable of asking for them. "Nope."

"Right." He stood up, gimpily. Was he actually offended? "See ya at dinner, then."

And off he limped. Through the studio windows, I watched him find the right path to his cabin, stopping to rip the offending branch off the tree. He took it with him.

The sun shone through the indigo cloth like sea glass in a tide pool. Instead of taking pencil to sketchpad, I started to speak to the view about the project. Talking to yourself isn't supposed to be a good sign, but when you're as alone as I am, it comes naturally.

"Okay, *Chains* is about love, it's about Pappa and Gran and how the parts, the elements, the links in their lives all came together. Even though they both started in Ireland, he was a man on his own deliberately coming here from Liverpool, and she was a child in the middle of a family that didn't mean to wash up in Houston. But they went from being two to being one and from being one to being a family. Their three children, and Zach and I, Ireland and Texas and the Atlantic between them." I was pacing, I was gesticulating, I was muttering. Must have been quite a sight.

"It's about them, about how they're the consummate love story, about how they completed each other and made a new life—not just Dermot and Bernadette and Matthew, but a reality of life, a lifestyle, together. Ups and downs, babies lost and stories told and learning to grow crops and picnics by the creek and sleeping on the train to their honeymoon. So, it's a chain. There will be links. A link for me, a link for Matthew, a link for Pad Maguire. Broken links for Berneen and Albert. Broken links for Pappa's family back home. A big link, central, holding them both—or two links, intertwined? Sketch it. I don't know. So, each link is a story, each link is the thing itself but in relation to Pappa and Gran, but there needs to be a consistent style to them all. More traditional? No, yes?" I stopped a moment. "Not traditional. New. They left the old country, moved to a new land, found a new life together. So, new style."

Now I had to stop pacing, had to go sketch. Barely made it to dinner—Caleb had changed into shorts—and afterwards, I took down the cloth and fell exhausted into bed, too wiped to even brush my teeth.

NEXT MORNING, I was up early ironing what would become the base for the quit top, and doe was back in the clearing working the salt lick. I suspected she'd eaten the corn the prior evening. When she started and ran off towards the stream, I wasn't surprised to see Caleb emerge from the path, putting a lens cap on his telephoto attachment. I waved.

"Hungry?" he asked when I came to the porch to let him in.

"No. Give me a sec. I'll grab my shoes."

"Well, I got some good shots before you scared her off today, thanks."

"Ha, ha."

"Do you think Zach'll mind driving us around town a little? I want to get some of the buildings."

"Did you not notice the size of this place when you came in? We park on the far side of the square and walk two minutes to John Henry's and that's all the town there is."

"Oh." He shrugged. "I suppose it's just as well. Suits the idea, anyway."

On the way to the Main House, he told me about it. Wildlife inhabiting human habitations—he was snapping all the animal life he could find in a place, then the structures of the area, and digitally processing buildings with deer and raccoons and whatnot. He bragged on his manipulation skills, on all he did to convey meaningful, elevated messages.

In between ordering me around the kitchen, he waxed what he must have considered lyrical about the destruction of natural habitats, the lack of concern in most municipalities for the ecosystems that had been the basis for their town's founding in the first place, the ways various animals had adapted to civilization. I told him Frank and Bernadette would have been riveted, which made him laugh. Apparently, back at Berkeley he and Zach had bonded over being misfits in their families. Caleb's Silicon Valley folks thought he was still studying computer engineering, and mine thought Zach was still the star of the ecology program.

"You two obviously mixed up your families of origin," I said, remembering the unprecedented eleven days of silence from Frank and Bernadette when Zach finally confessed he'd switched majors.

"Yep. Though I must say I'm glad we weren't switched at birth," Caleb said with what might have been a leer if I'd taken the time to decipher it properly, instead of determinedly ignoring it.

Our first breakfast was a success. Rafael even came in at the end, acrylic-smeared and blurry-eyed, and smiled at the pecan roll we had left out. He didn't say anything, but we were all too startled by the sight of him to try to open a conversation, so perhaps it was more of a matter of him feeling frozen out. Then he yawned, drank some cranberry juice, and left.

"At least he's learned to stack away his dishes," Wren said. "If I accomplish nothing else here, I can go home with that."

"Do yous all think he's just nocturnal?" asked Lizzy, when she turned back from watching him walk down the path. He was living in WestWind, which suitably enough was the most remote of the cabins, the only one on the far side of the lake.

"If so, I'm in trouble again when it comes to making lunch next week," Wren moped.

"We'll have him well sorted by then," Caleb assured her. "Margie's strict conscious won't allow her to let one of the artists bear an unjust burden due to the non-cooperation of another."

Wren cheered up, but I was thinking Caleb's frequent Margie imitations were revealing a secret dictatorial side of him. The bossiness in the kitchen didn't help. It was the same at lunchtime, even though all we made was egg and tempeh salad sandwiches with German fries on the side. When I told Liz and Wren about it later on, as we were waiting for Zach to pull up, Wren just thought it was wonderful to have such a helpful food partner, and Lizzy told me any successful meal had to have someone in charge with as many attentive assistants as the kitchen space allowed.

"As Brandon is about to find out, I can be very attentive. 'Tis a shame you'll miss the first group meal I'll ever prepare by standing back. I did make sure there's nothing poisonous on the menu."

"Can you just make a couple of people nauseous? If I have to watch Theo and Angelica sneak past my cabin to each other any more I'll be sick myself," Wren said.

"You think you've got it bad," I said, "try living next door to him. If he's working, it's all mega-industrial music out of there, and if she's there, I hear even more than I'd like to. If I'm outside it's actually decipherable—'Theo, my God, my deity, my Zeus and Jove!' Don't laugh—I'm not making it up. I swear to Theo, I'm not!"

We'd managed to stop making fun of the other retreaters by the time Caleb came to my cabin. And when Lizzy nudged me as he crossed my threshold, I knew it made three of us who noticed he cleaned up pretty good. It was a simple outfit: khakis and a white button-down, but against his gold-brown skin and dark hair, it worked especially well. And he knew how to buy classy shoes, or knew someone who knew, which was almost as good.

My version of dress-up clothes wasn't as well chosen as Wren's fawn-colored jumpsuit, which made her even lither and more soft-focus than usual (or, as Lizzy put it, '*Tres femme, mon cherie*'). I figured I pulled off the fitted scoop-neck tee with maxi skirt well enough to eat out at what passed for fine dining in a small Hill Country town.

And if I opted to go by the way Caleb's gaze lingered on my curves before he directed his crinkly eyes and dimpled chin in Wren and Lizzy's direction, I looked as good as, if not better than, I needed to.

CHAPTER 4

*L*izzy gave up her spot on the love seat for Caleb, who was shoulder to shoulder with Wren by the time I'd walked Lizzy to the door. Despite their snugness, he was focused on me. "Hey, Ashlyn? What ever happened with Zach and Eva? I mean, I know they split, but I thought they were a sure bet."

So had we all. Most especially Zach, who'd started dating Eva in their first year at Berkeley. "She got into grad school and thought he'd be an albatross so she stomped on his heart," I said. Maybe it had been more nuanced than that, but Zach was one of the essential support beams of my life. It happened when I was in high school, right after Pappa died and that beam had crumbled. I'd taken Eva's decision personally.

"Damn. Poor Zach," Caleb said. We traded sad looks. It was comforting to share my mostly-buried angst over my brother's most depressing period. I knew several of Zach's current friends, but Caleb was the only guy I'd met from Zach's California years.

Tires crunched on the shell road. Caleb stood, stretched, walked to the door. Wren wasn't alone in noting the muscle tone in his chest. She grinned at me behind his back. Or maybe she was grinning about his butt, which also deserved a smile.

"That's him, anyway," Caleb said, turning back to pick up his bag. Wren mouthed, "Be right back," at me vamoosed to the bathroom.

Zach did the Zeke / Ned chest bump with Caleb before he turned to me for my semi-hug. "Show me what you've been up to," he said, and, arm around my shoulders, steered me into the studio.

I unfolded my dyed fabric and went to the table to open my sketchbook. Zach leaned in like he of all people was engaged by my artistic vision, muttering, "So we want the two of them together?"

"It's her idea," I whispered back. "Apparently he's her dream man. Something about the way he smiles."

He shrugged. "Well, it always turned me on."

"You're supposed to slip me some dirt about what he was like at Berkeley, too. Who he dated and for how long and is he some sort of deviant in disguise."

"I'll have to think on that one," he said, looking around as Wren emerged from powdering her nose. "Hi. How're you?"

"Good. Hungry; I get to eat something tonight I didn't cook, and I'm very excited about it."

"Let's go, then," Caleb said from the doorway.

We hit the town.

WIMBERLEY'S not quite typical for small-town Texas. It's a bit more scrutinized, thanks to being in the midst of the hill country, with all the amenities: ground rolling off in all directions, bunnies and does leaping about, roads like someone real tall poured an oversize bottle of dark molasses across green fields, cool streams reflecting canopies of Spanish moss.

Plus, it's just easy enough to get to from Austin and San

Antonio that it's cache of B&Bs stay busy most of the year. So along with the small-town stuff like ice cream parlors and a dearth of national chain stores, you get dusty antique stores stuffed with traditional quilts, extra-high gas prices at full-service stations, and quirky semi-gourmet dining spots. The place we'd chosen was called John Henry's. As I'd promised Caleb, who took a couple dozen shots of town on film, and ten more on his digital, the Square was small enough to see John Henry's from Millie's Hat Shop at the catty-corner end. We paid a few extra dollars at the door for temporary membership. Anyone could eat in the restaurant, but if you wanted bar service, you had to join the club. They fixed us up with some good Texas beer and we crossed the back lawn to Cypress Creek while we waited on our table.

Water lilies flanked both banks, in places so dense the ropy, gnarled roots of the cypress trees weren't visible as they hooked themselves into the water. The management had scattered some benches and picnic tables across the live oak-shaded lawn, and a few other groups were lounging and drinking in the late afternoon sun. One couple was sharing bruschetta topped with something red; as they fed it to each other, they splatted blobs of crimson on their cheeks and chins. If it weren't for that visual, it would have been downright romantic.

We walked a ways up the path. There were some kids fishing off the main road's bridge, skinny little dudes. The ducks backpeddling around the edge of the water right near them probably had a lot to do with why they weren't catching anything. Just to confuse them, Wren tore up bits of her napkin and tossed them at the ducks, which figured out quickly she was toying with them, but stuck around just in case she was hiding something.

"That table's free now," Zach told us, tipping his chin at the picnic table on the far end of the lawn. Caleb spied some fresh patrons edging out onto the patio, handed me his beer, and sprinted to claim the table before them.

"Mine, all mine," he cackled when we caught up to him. I sat opposite him and handed over his Shiner Bock.

"Those people think you're an idiot," I said. They were leaning up against the railing of the covered porch, pretending to laugh at a joke instead of us.

"So?"

Zach slid in next to me, telling Wren, "You should keep an eye on those ducks." She moved around to sit opposite me, facing the water. Already the alcohol had flushed her cheeks; when she'd told me she was a lightweight drinker, I'd figured she could take two or three units before she turned tipsy. But if she was right about her inhibitions, too, maybe the beer'd help her out. Already a couple of times she had flipped her hair in that annoyingly attractive way longhaired blondes have when their pheromones were firing. Having rather flat brown hair myself, the most I could ever manage was letting wisps of it escape from a braid or ponytail, so unless it was humid I ended up looking unkempt rather than fetching.

Zeke and Ned started in talking about other Zekes and Neds out there, and what had happened to them in the prior years. Like I cared. But Caleb started it, and we were all there on the premise of the two of them catching up. So I heard all about Noa, who'd invented an ergonomic keyboard, and Emily, whose group had just been awarded a patent for their Gamma project, and Warren, who had worked on the Atlas URL. Neither Zach nor Caleb brought up Eva, so I was glad I'd given Caleb enough info for him to flag her as a hot topic.

It took me sighing and leaning against Zach's shoulder to get him to shut up about him and focus on us gals. Or more specifically, on Wren, whose eyes were beginning to rim with red. Boredom or frustration about hearing yet another geek success story, I couldn't tell. Either way, she blinked it out of her when Caleb started acting interested in her stories about the agent she'd hooked up with out of college and just recently dropped. His monstrosities ranged from a commission for Wren to make cruci-fixes for a priest who wanted gifts for his mistresses, to selling her bowls to a traveling exhibition of the art of the differently-abled.

"He told them I was mute, so I couldn't interview, then pointed out how wonderfully I'd learned to express myself through my work! He says to me, 'Lauren, baby, this one is perfect—it's no problem for you to fake it, and if you make it big and they come back asking questions, you can attribute it to a miracle! Think of all the poor desperate souls who'll buy up your stuff to try to ride the coattails of your encounter with the Lord!' Well, I called the Enabled Artists and told them my 'miracle' had happened a little sooner than Marty had planned."

As we laughed, Caleb caught my eye. He let his eyes shift towards Wren, smiled, and subtly toasted me with his longneck before taking a swig. He obviously didn't think she noticed, but from the way her cheeks went red right back to her ears, I knew she had.

Dinner itself was a little less flirty and more friendly. There was give-and-take to the conversation, and I was happy to feel a part of it instead of like an inexperienced puppeteer watching to see if my marionettes would go where I'd directed them. Zach ordered a half-pound of fajitas with his salad, making me promise not to tell Bernadette, which brought on the inevitable story of why we were veggies in the first place. How Bernadette said Gran and Pappa couldn't be our caretakers while they ran their co-op store unless Pappa traded in his chicken ranching for organic farming.

"What would they have done if he'd refused?" Wren asked, pecking away at her burger.

"Handed us over anyway, I suppose."

"It's not like they were so successful they could afford to put us anywhere else," I added. "And having Zach at the store for a couple of years before I was born was enough for them. They didn't want to try to keep us both under control while they spread the natural word through the Gulf States."

Zach disagreed. "They'd have kept us there if they'd had to. But Gran and Uncle Matt were pretty set on us coming out every day. When I was ten Frank told me I could come home after school and hang out in front or up in my room if I wanted, but Pappa said I shouldn't."

"Matt was already gone by then." Our Uncle Matthew was a guitarist, and had lived at home throughout early adulthood, until he had the money and reputation to move to LA and make it as a session musician. Our Uncle Dermot, who was stationed in San Diego, was supposed to help ground him, but Matt had spent years wandering up and down the Pacific Coast. The rest of us never heard much from him, but he and Zach had been close since Zach's earliest days, infant ears turning whenever Matthew crooned songs his way.

"Yeah, and Pappa was lonely. You and Gran were so cliquish, us guys had to bond with each other to stop ourselves from pure-dried boredom." He'd unleashed the brogue-y drawl.

I smiled. "I'd never-a guessed."

"It's the God's honest."

"Well, shit fire and save the matches!"

Zach nearly choked on his jalapeños. Most of Pappa's trademark phrases we kept to ourselves, but once we started exchanging them it took no time before one of us was doubled over.

"Careful, there, lady boy, you cut yourself a fat hog this time," I said, thumbing at his over-loaded plate. He coughed again and called for another beer.

"Want one?" he asked Wren and Caleb.

"No, you two go ahead," Caleb said. "Whatever you're having is obviously doing a lot for you."

Wren grinned at him. "I knew there was some sort of backwoods fool in that girl there. All it took was one beer to bring it out."

"I hope it goes back before breakfast tomorrow. I don't want to find myself bellying up to a mess of grits anytime soon."

"You have both been watching too much *Beverly Hillbillies*," I said, primly dabbing at my mouth and folding my napkin back into my lap. "Y'all hush now, y'hear?"

STUFFED, we all collapsed on my sofa and floor for coffee and lingering chat. I was getting to know them both pretty well now. It had bee one of those revelatory nights that draws people together. Caleb's nuevo-environmentalism sprang from spending two weeks hiking Oregon after graduation; he'd been on mini-pilgrimages to many of the sites Ansel Adams had immortalized ever since, and was gradually compiling enough for a photo essay.

Wren told us about the night when she was seventeen and had run away in order to find a home where no one would force her to pack up every few months. Her college fund paid for the bus to Norwich, Connecticut, a deposit on the two-bedroom duplex, and drinks for a guy who helped her polish her resume. She'd been in the same place for the intervening years and had never since traveled further than Cape Cod. GED obtained, she commuted to New London three times a week for five years to get a studio arts degree at Connecticut College. Flying to Austin for FireWind was her first plane ride since her childhood trips to summer with her grandmother in Alaska.

Zach hung around until almost two, long after Caleb and Wren headed out of my den. "You think they're going off together?" he asked when the sound of her flats on the short concrete path had faded.

"Dunno. They weren't being obvious enough for me."

"Well, I think we done good. Did you notice the way I kept bringing the conversation back to her?"

"Yeah, you're a master of subtlety, but I picked up on it."

"What's that mean?"

"Oh, I don't know. 'No, I can't stand watching baseball on TV. Wren, what will you do when FireWind is over?'"

He threw a vegan marshmallow at me from the bag he'd imported for my hot chocolate. "You told me to set them up."

"And you did. Thank you." I ate the mallow. "Don't forget to load me up with dirt on college days."

He groaned. "I don't know anything. We weren't exactly bosom buddies, you know, we just saw each other at the lab."

"Which you were at for hours every day. You know stuff, so spill it."

"I honestly don't remember much. He had some girlfriends, off-and-on kind of things. One of them, this brunette with a ponytail, she and Eva hit it off. We doubled a couple of times." He did the usual brow-crinkling thing, which meant he was pretending to think hard but was just looking for a way to end the stream of the conversation. "Her name was Ellen or Lucy, something like that. Ellen, I think. Helen. Pre-med. They lasted a few months, a year, I don't know. Then she moved. Or got a new boyfriend, or something."

"Was her name Ann and she dropped him after sleeping with some guy she met because y'all were meeting at Eva's place for a movie and this guy lived next door?" I asked.

He sat up and thunked his mug on the table. "Oh God."

"That was him?"

"Oh Mother God. I'd forgotten."

"Zach? It was Caleb, wasn't it?"

He nodded. "Do you think he hates me?"

"Where would you get that?"

"Cause Ann and Shawn..."

"Cause nothing, Zach, Ann was a bitch. She'd have done it with someone else if it wasn't with Eva's neighbor. You just wouldn't have known so much about it, is all."

"Well, I'd hate me."

"Maybe you're more into displacing your emotions than he is. He hasn't acted at all like he's got a problem with you."

"Has he mentioned Ann at all?"

"Why would he? It was like a decade ago. Do you still mention Eva all the time?" Stupid me. Because of course he doesn't. He hasn't dealt with it, which I, the trusted and knowing little sister, am perfectly aware of. "Sorry," I added.

He sat back down. "No, it's okay. Like you said, it was years ago."

"Zach. Come on, it can't still hurt that bad?"

He wouldn't focus on me. He just shook his head.

"You wanna talk about it?"

He shook his head again. "It's not her, Ashlyn. It's me. I mean, I'm worldly enough to know things just don't work out sometimes, and at least she didn't do anything cruel, like Ann. So it ended. Life goes on."

"Well, then?"

"Well, then, she lives in Marin with her law degree and architect husband and baby girl. She's happy, I've moved on."

"So you keep saying." It wasn't the first time we'd talked about love and the way it ends and what happens afterwards. But I'd always let him bring it up before, or else I'd talked to him about my own situations. And he'd never brought up the break-up with Eva, not since he'd told me what had happened.

"I know all the things to say, Ash. I'll meet someone else. It'll be magic. I'll forget anyone like Eva ever existed. We'll be so good together it'll make my life whole in a way she never could have." He looked at me then, and smiled a little. "And when all that happens, I'll be happy."

"You don't think it will?"

"No, I do. Some day. Hell, tomorrow would be good. I'm open for it."

"Well, I love you."

He let me hug on him a while. "I love you, too, sis." Pulling back, he added, "And if it were *Game of Thrones* we could go with that and live happily ever after. Well, not happily ever after. Those guys are fucked up. So it's a bad idea."

"Good thing. Cause I hate to burst your bubble and all, but you're so not my type."

He laughed, finally. "What? You crazy? Look at me, I'm downright perfect."

"You're a little skinny."

"I'm just healthy. Check out these muscles."

"And you're definitely a nerd."

"But a well-off one."

"And above all, that mom of yours near 'bout scares me to death. That is one lady I do *not* want as a mother-in-law."

"Now, that I can agree with." Yawning, he stood. "I should hit the road, gotta actually go in for a lunch meeting tomorrow."

"Poor guy. I gotta get up in about five hours to cook muffins for eight grumpy artists."

"When I get home, before I go to sleep, I'll cry a river of tears for you."

"Thanks." We hugged at the door. "And thanks for coming down and all. Now get the hell out of here."

He headed out into the blackness, his headlights bobbing across the crushed white of the dozed-out road. I sighed. My brother, whisking through the darkness to his hip little stone house in Austin; he'd bought a three-bedroom in anticipation of needing both a study and a nursery some day. I had a key so I could crash in the guest room at a moment's notice, and only four or five times had he asked me to stay away because there'd be someone else there in the morning eating his signature huevos rancheros. I was all about the free accommodations, but for his sake, hoped he would find the woman to make him forget the Evas out there can take all your love and trust and turn it around until you are afraid to give it to anyone else again.

Maybe someday.

Maybe tomorrow.

I closed the door and closed my eyes, sending happy ever after thoughts into the ether for my too-alone brother.

CHAPTER 5

The alarm clock dragged me up through a confusing swathe of fuzzy dream-chatting with a 21st Century Martha Washington. It was 6:30; Caleb insisted I be by his side in the kitchen by seven. He *pffted* at my pointing out it takes only minutes to prepare cereal in a bowl of soy milk.

In deference to my headache, I kept my grumblings quiet as I drenched myself in the shower. I had to wash my face three times to get the sleep rocks out of my eyes and the smell of asparagus-tainted pee out of my nose. It was the kind of morning I most cherished my collection of oversized sweatshirts. I felt almost like myself when I stepped onto the porch of the Main House.

"Hey, sleepyhead," Caleb said over his shoulder as he rinsed potatoes in the sink.

"How long have you been up?"

"An hour, I guess. Zach got home okay?"

"I suppose. He'd sobered up before he left, and he's used to late nights, so I'm not worried."

"Here, grate these," he said, passing me a chopping board loaded with peeled spuds. "We're making latkes this morning."

I looked around. "Isn't there a food processor or something?"

"It makes it too fine. Latkes need texture. Use the coarse end." He gathered up all the scraps of peel. "Have you seen a compost?"

I shook my head no. "Haven't looked. She shoulda mentioned it on the tour, though. Just feed them to the electric pig."

"The what now?"

I stifled a yawn in my collarbone before looking up at him. "The disposal."

"God, you've gone all Texan on us again. Zach never did that."

"He says the only thing anyone ever asked him in California was why he didn't have a Texas accent. So he dropped it all, just told people he was from a little town called Spring and they assumed it was off I-5 somewhere. But ever since he moved to Austin, he grew more of a drawl than ever."

"Doesn't explain yours."

"The beer explains mine. Pure and simple."

Caleb smiled those crinkles again. "Well, it's cute, you should drink more often."

"I'm glad you enjoy it. Damnation!" I shoved him away to wash the blood from my knuckles where I'd grated them. "You're sure I can't use a food processor?"

"I'll do it. You oil the skillet and put the sour cream and preserves into serving bowls."

"Yes, sir." I didn't mind his being in charge so much, but surely he considered me capable of doing more than menial kitchen jobs. My silence was resentful enough to stop him issuing more orders until he had the first batch frying.

"Ashlyn, would you mind watching these so I can finish up the fruit salad? Just flip them when the edges brown up a little."

"I've made potato pancakes before, Caleb."

"Oh. Sorry."

"I also mix up a damn good black bean burrito, a zesty western omelet, and my home-toasted granola will knock your socks off."

He stopped chopping to look at me. "All your talk of sleeping in had me fooled. I had you pegged as a toasted bagel and out the door type."

"Breakfast is my main meal when I'm working. I don't feel like going through a lot of trouble for lunch and big dinners for one are depressing, so I sleep late, make myself something yummy, and get to it. But the key is sleeping late."

"Well, remind me to give you a choice in what we make this week. Sorry if I've been a little pushy."

A little pushy? He'd been the most militant cook I'd ever met. I hoped Wren didn't mind being submissive.

As if summoned by my brain, she walked in, apparently scrubbed to freshness and vitality by her own morning shower. I would have snoop in her bathroom to see what product she used. "Morning, all!"

Caleb turned to smile at her. "Hi. Sleep good?"

She rose up onto her toes a moment. "Like a log."

"You seemed so tired."

I threw a questioning look Wren's way. She just batted a hand at me as she reached for a coffee cup. "You all need any help?"

"No, we're fine."

"You can watch me set the table if you want." I reached for a pile of plates and nudged her towards the dining room.

Seeing my raised eyebrows, she shrugged. "It's not what you're thinking, unfortunately. He's not alluding to anything."

"Well, did he walk you home?"

She nodded. "But that was it. A little good night hug. We just kept talking about how sleepy we were after the big meal."

I glanced back through the transom to see if he was watching us. "It sounds good, though. He seemed pretty happy to see you this morning."

"I know!" She hid a giggle in her coffee cup. "I'm not saying I'm not encouraged."

Lizzy came in. "God, you're really a couple of early birds, aren't you?"

I yawned again. "No, but the latke-miester in there runs a tight camp."

"I hope they're as good as they smell. Brandon came up with pan-fried chicken and a side of canned green beans for us last night."

"Goddess, what did Angelica eat?" She was the other vegetarian, with Caleb and I. Which hadn't stopped her from letting Theo make bacon or sausage every morning, of course.

"I scrounged around and made her a rice pilaf to go with the beans. Had some of it myself, actually, and it was pretty tasty."

"I hope you're willing to recreate it if he's planning on serving those pork chops in the fridge tonight," Caleb said, coming in with the first platter of pancakes.

"Don't worry, I'll look after you," Lizzy promised. She waited until Caleb went back for the applesauce. "Did you get some dirt on him? How was dinner?"

Wren leaned in to us. "Your cabin after breakfast, okay?"

I nodded. "And yes, I've got dirt. Boy, do I ever." I straightened up as Caleb came back in. Poor guy. I could just imagine his expression that night, coming home late to hear Ann. Maybe some of those smile lines were from tension and tears. Our gazes locked for a while over the table as I contemplated him, then I retreated to the kitchen to bring out the juice and coffee.

As we ate, Caleb passed some of the credit for the latkes to me. Rafael didn't show. Neither did Angelica, though Theo came in to load up one plate for the two of them. Lizzy, Wren, Caleb, and I chatted easily, while Brandon made obnoxious comments. We all relaxed when he shut up and headed to the computer room with his second cup of coffee.

"You know, I'm almost sorry for the guy."

Lizzy looked at Caleb. "Don't. Have you not seen his stuff?"

Caleb winced. "Well, there is that."

"He needs all the working time he can get. Sitting here with us won't make him any better."

"But will sitting in there on the computer help?" Wren asked. "The man needs to develop a purpose, then develop some pics to go along with it. What is he trying to do?"

"You know what?" I stood. "As long as you don't ask him when I'm around to listen to the answer, I don't care. I think an artistic mission statement from him would be more than I could handle." Gathering the rest of the plates, I went to the kitchen. "You'd think a dishwasher wouldn't be too much of a convenience, wouldn't you?"

Caleb, following me with the empty pitcher and a tub of cups, told me Margie and the founders' philosophy about hand-washing building community spirit while discouraging any one team from leaving a half-load of dirty dishes for the next to deal with. "Which is not to say we can't leave this until lunch time, if you want."

"No, we'd best to get it done now. Like I said, I don't like to spend a lot of time cooking in the afternoons."

"I'll do it, then, you go on to work."

"Why? That's not fair."

"It's fine, I think well when I'm cleaning. And I feel bad for underestimating your kitchen prowess." I glanced back through the transom, where Lizzy and Wren were whispering and obviously waiting for me to spill the beans.

"You sure?"

He wrapped a dishtowel around his waist. "Sure."

"I'll make it up to you later."

His eyes locked with mine again. "I'll count on it."

"So, I take it you've heard the high points of dinner," I said, flopping onto the sofa beside Lizzy.

"Pretty much so."

"Dinner's nothing. Tell us what Zach said," Wren insisted as she came out from the bathroom.

"You pee more than anyone I know."

"Shut up. I have a weak bladder, I don't like to take medication."

"Okay, as long as you're aware of the situation," I said.

Lizzy nudged me. "We don't care about Wren's toilet habits. Tell us what Zach said."

"Yeah."

"Well, as it turns out..." I watched them to see who would choke me first. As Wren lunged at me I added, "Zach had told me this when it happened, since it was so awful, and neither of us remembered it was Caleb until we started talking about things last night. Zach feels terrible now, but I told him Caleb wasn't going around blaming him or anything."

"For what, for God's sake?" Lizzy asked.

"Okay, here it is. First, Caleb and Zach mostly just saw each other at the computer lab, so he didn't have much intel on casual girlfriends. Just, he seemed pretty relaxed about dating, you know?" They nodded. "But then there was this one woman, Ann, who got kinda tight with Eva, so they all spent more social time together."

"And?" prompted Wren, when I broke off to drink water.

"And they doubled a few times, went into San Francisco for concerts, stuff like that. It had been going on between them for most of their junior year, and she was pre-med so she was talking about where she'd end up, and he was saying maybe he could go along, since he wasn't going to get an MFA right away. Oh, and her last name was Kym, and there was some joke about her being Dr. Kym-Kendall, so it must have gotten intense between them. Then one night they were all meeting at Eva's for a movie, and Caleb was late, so they missed the beginning and decided to just skip it."

I sipped again. Talking after eating makes me thirsty. "There was a party in Eva's courtyard, some of the residents were doing, like, a potluck social or something, so they went there instead. When Caleb showed, all apologetic, Ann gives him the cold shoulder, so he talked to Zach a while then headed off alone."

"She didn't come home?" guessed Lizzy.

"No, she did. Zach dropped her off on his way back to his dorm." I snorted. "Not that he slept there much, unless he had an early class. But Frank and Bernadette were paying for it, so he popped in once in a while just to confuse his roommate and check his messages."

"Then what was the drama?"

"She slept with Zach?" asked Lizzy.

"No! You're terrible at this game," I told her. "Zach and Eva were joined at the pelvis. He wouldn't, anyway. No, this was a few weeks later. Eva had started wondering why Ann kept coming by just to say a quick hello, as she put it. Then one night she's headed out to the library and sees someone down the hall with a suitcase. She knew there were a couple of empty units on her floor, so she didn't wonder much. After the library, she goes to the computer lab. The usual crowd of geeks is there, including Zach and Caleb. They invite Caleb to go for a late-night latte with them, but he says no, he's headed home. So Eva and Zach go on their own."

"Ann was gone?"

"I told you to stop guessing, you're horrible. Besides, it's worse than anything you'd think up." I wished there was room to pace in this den, or we were all in my studio, or outside. The whole thing made me restless. "Caleb goes home at his usual time. Everything's dark, so he thinks Ann's turned in early. She'd been acting a little stressed with microbiology, or something."

"She was hacked up, right?"

"Ooh, yuck. No!"

"Well, you said it was bad."

"It was. Shush. Like I said, it was dark. So he's quiet, not wanting to disturb her. He sits on the sofa to take off his shoes. As he bends over, he hears it." I looked at them one at a time. "Sex. People coming. And one of them, he knows for sure, is Ann."

Wren let out a sad little chirp, and Lizzy gasped, "Who else?"

"Eva's neighbor, a guy named Ted. They'd been at it since the night of the party. But apparently Caleb was such a sweetie she couldn't stand to tell him it was over. So instead, she staged the overheard sex act. Ted didn't even question why they were going to her place for once. She timed it all so Caleb would be home when they climaxed."

"What did he do?" Wren's eyes were moist.

I shook my head. "This is what kills me. She obviously thought he'd storm in there and have it out, but instead he just got up and left. He went to the cafe where Zach was, actually, but he didn't tell them anything. Just sat there, not drinking his soda, and pretending to listen to the conversation. Around one they all leave and he goes back to the apartment to sleep on the sofa. Ann's still in the bed, but Ted is gone. He checked.

"She got up early and showered and left, not even a note. He was awake but pretended not to be. Once she was gone, he goes to pack up her stuff, and it was all gone."

"The person with the suitcase?"

"You got one right, yeah. That was her, moving everything into Ted's place. She'd figured after they were caught and had the fight, she wouldn't want to stick around and pack. Pretty practical, if you ask me. Pretty nasty, too."

"Then what did he do?" Wren again.

"Called a locksmith. Had the doorknob changed and took the old one, along with a couple of things like barrettes she'd forgotten, and bundled it all up in the sheets she'd fucked Ted on."

"They were never still on the bed?" Lizzy's face was aghast.

"No, they were. He stuck everything in a box and left it at the campus mailroom for her." I couldn't stand to sit anymore, and went to the front door to look out. "They never fought at all, never talked at all, according to her. She told Eva most of it, and he told Zach a little. It was pretty close to the end of term. When they came back senior year they acted like it never happened. Zach saw them around each other a few times and it was as if they were strangers."

We all were quiet for a while. I sighed. "I don't know. I mean, I thought it was horrible when Zach first told me about it, but now I know him," I turned back into the room, "it's just bad, is all."

"Bloody hell," said Lizzy. "And I thought Moira was a bitch."

"Poor guy. Did Zach say anything else?"

"Nah, he hadn't even remembered it was Caleb it happened to until I asked him about it. They've pretty much been out of touch for years now."

"Never mind," Lizzy told Wren, "that'll give you enough to work with. He's cautious, dislikes cheaters, and finds long hair attractive."

I rolled my eyes at her. "Where do you get the part about the hair?"

"You said she left behind hair clips, obviously she had to put them in something. I doubt they just marked the pages in her textbooks."

"Well, I hope it's true, cause it's the one thing I know I've got going for me."

"Yeah, I noticed you flipping it all over the place last night."

"Did you?" Lizzy laughed. "I guess we're not quite so shy after all, are we?"

She turned red. "Was I obnoxious?"

"No, you were fine." I smiled and ruffed my own head. "But since I don't have your advantage I can't help but notice it in others."

"Do you think he noticed?"

"Well, he doesn't have long blonde tresses, either, besides which I think you hit him with it a couple of times, so I'd say so, yeah."

"Go Wren, you got it, go Wren, you work it." Lizzy did a little dance to accompany herself. Wren doubled over, but I felt I had to put a stop to it.

"Elizabeth, I must say, your hip-hop American accent is even worse than your regular one. I tell you this only as a friend."

"Aisling, if you won't call me that, I'll try not to offend your Americanized self."

"Girls, girls, settle down! We don't need no internecine wars here. I thought we were all united in a common goal."

"Getting you in bed with Caleb is our mortar?" I asked.

"Hey, whatever works," Wren replied.

Women artists searching for ways to express their unity or lack thereof with the world, meeting for two months of soul-searching and sharing, and what we had going for us in the way of bonding was gossip and plotting to catch us a man. Fantastic.

Wren poked at me with her toe. "That, and the fact I really like you. Both of you. Wipe the pout off your face."

I stood and stretched. "I know. I was just thinking of the time. If I'm going to get anything done before lunch duty hits, y'all need to get going."

"Can't believe this woman. Comes to a retreat and actually wants to work while she's here. Have you seen the like?"

Wren shook her head. "Never. Come on, let's go play and let Ms. Dedication here get her quilting done. We don't want to stand in the way of progress!"

They gave me hugs and headed out. Alone at last, first time since Saturday afternoon. I was a lot more used to personal space than I'd realized, back when I kept complaining about the solitude of living on my own. Taking the tools I'd snatched from the Main House, I hung some display hooks I'd brought to FireWind, and stretched what I had of *Chains of Love* on the studio wall. The patch portrait of Gran was done, and I'd tacked it to a piece of muslin with the strips for the chains weaving their way across it.

Standing ten feet back, I decided to bring the Gran patch closer to center left, the radiant locus of the design. One broken chain for Berneen and Albert would head towards the top left, and the one for Pappa would be smack in the center, the link actually connecting them broken, but the ones surrounding them and their life together keeping them always close.

I didn't like the prevalence of gray tones in the chains. They needed to be more vibrant, with some reds and oranges. I sifted until I had floss in the right tones and moved forward to braid them around and through some of the chain strands—the chain would be the last element actually pieced, overlaid on the rest so the links, rather than forging the connections, reinforced them.

Nodding, I stepped close to work on their construction, but was stopped by coming face to face with my stitched version of Gran.

She'd become increasingly wrinkled the last few months, and I knew my moving out was more of a strain than she let on. Pappa's death a decade earlier had slammed home Gran's own mortality, and she'd become older and frailer almost overnight. From the time toddler me had analyzed and memorized her, until that mournful March day when his heart failed, she'd changed only subtly.

But with Pappa gone, her arthritis constricted more, her insomnia took hold, and her thirst to always be doing something new turned into more of a sipping acquaintance. She'd gradually stopped resisting when Bernadette and I took over household chores. Bernadette's biggest relief came when Gran agreed to her escort to doctor's appointments. Mine was when Gran admitted that listening to audiobooks was easier on her thin, curled fingers than turning pages was, and let me show her how to browse and download titles.

I didn't think about the time, or my tears, until the knock at my door heralded the gazpacho king. Tracing a finger down the painted Gran's cheek, I set aside my art and prepared for the crucial work of slicing and dicing.

CHAPTER 6

*L*izzy pulled me aside after lunch the next day. "I've had an email from my parents. They're coming. They figured out how fare alerts worked, just so they could show up here unannounced."

"You don't seem very pleased."

"Ashlyn, they'll be here at the weekend. They want to see my rural Texas home, they want to meet my friends, they want to tell agonizing stories about my infancy." Her brow compressed. "I need your help."

Another one. I adored them, but my FireWind friends weren't the most self-sufficient bunch. "What can I do?"

"Tell them all about your grandparents, distract them with questions about the old country. I can't have them talking to Brandon about my first fallen soufflé."

"They'd hardly do that."

"They would. You don't know. My parents turn me into a girl with a whimsical fondness for big rocks. I may as well not be talented, or adult, or anything when they're around."

Lizzy was scraping the toe of her Doc Martens back against the edge of the porch. Her callused hands were buried in the spikes of her hair, her eyes had rounded and gone moist. I got over myself, gave her an understanding smile. "How long will they be here?"

"A day, they've said. Saturday morning they're driving in from Austin, and I have dinner duty that night so I told them they had to leave by five."

"Why not just go up to Austin to meet them?"

She shook her head and pushed up her glasses. "If only. They have an agenda. They're connecting to Dallas and picking up the car, driving past the grassy knoll, stopping in Waco to take pictures of the Davidian complex, and will be in Austin for just long enough to tour the capital and have dinner. That's all they want out of this state, other than to see me and the artistic little world they've sent me to."

"They paid?"

She nodded briefly. "For the flight, yeah."

Wow, the tug of the financial apron string. I'd seen many people hung from it, but never thought someone as resolute as Lizzy would be roped in. "I still don't know what you're so afraid of."

"You may never will. But you're my friend, you're half-Irish, and you're another artist, so if they can corner you for an afternoon I can distract them from everything else. Please give me this time."

I supposed there could be worse things. "Saturday?"

She nodded.

"I'm still on lunch."

"I know. But if I help you make it early, maybe you could ask Caleb to serve and clean up?"

"You've got it all figured out."

She smiled at me. "Desperation brings out the best in me. You'll do it?"

"Yeah. You explain it to Caleb, though; he's got the week's menu planned from some sort of brunch food pyramid, and whatever we make Saturday had better not interfere with his master plan or we'll never hear the end."

She agreed, and I headed back to ValeSong for a nap. I'd been up late finalizing the layout of *Chains* and piecing together the top layer, and now was blinking moisture back into my tired eyes every second they weren't scrunched closed for a yawn. I didn't even look at it hanging on the north wall of the studio as I zombied towards bed.

In early twilight I woke up, stiff and disoriented and still in my jeans. My left leg tingled as I straightened it, so I staggered to a hot shower. A bit clearer, I plopped myself, towel-draped, on the studio floor.

Outside was dim and my lights were off, which was just how I needed to view *Chains*. The detail faded to dark and pale patches with a hint of hue, and the beads I'd stitched for hours glinted across the cloth. Viewed as a starscape, the predominate feature was the strands of silver I'd stitched into Gran's hair, echoes of the same thread dancing in and out of the chains. The black beads in the Irish Sea were ominously broken by the spirits of Gran's siblings rising from it. The patches from the farm, which were light enough to largely conceal the shining elements, surprised the viewer with the hints of a snail trail up the pear trees and a couple of beetles in the chicken yard.

I used stickers to mark a few places to add beading, then went to get dressed. I hoped to finish the piece by the next day; I had two other projects lined up and had already spent a week and a half of my eight retreat weeks on the first one.

I was late for dinner—not a great loss, since Brandon's signature dish was turning out to be fried chicken with a side of mac and cheese for the vegetarians. Margie made an unexpected appearance over coffee and a tin of cookies. After raising a suspicious eye at the preservatives in the butter wafers, she sat between Wren and me. The sandalwood musk was an unexpected touch; I wasn't expecting her to be so formal.

She gingerly set down the coffee mug Brandon had jumped to fill for her when she came in, and reached for the sugar bowl. "Thank you. I hope I am not interrupting anything?" As she looked at each of us in turn, I noted the way Wren brushed her hair back, Caleb sat up straighter, and Angelica took her elbows off the table to link her fingers across her dessert plate. By the time Margie's gaze turned to me, I had wiped the smile off my face and crossed my legs at the ankles.

"Well, I wanted to bring up a few things at this juncture, and give us all a chance to discuss them. First is a general note. There have been a number of occasions on which I have used the laundry facilities only to discover a large build-up of lint in the dryer trap. Now, as we know," she paused to stir her coffee, "this not only wastes energy, but it adds considerable time to the drying cycle. I've posted a notice on the dryer lid, but I wanted to bring it up in person to reinforce the point. I should hope time, for each of you, can be more valuably spent pursuing your art."

"I've always found white noise like the dryer makes helps me think," Theo said. "I mean, not that I won't be careful about lint. Just so you know I'm not, I mean we're all not, just sitting waiting for our stuff to dry and not working."

Angelica smiled at him. "That's true. About Theo, anyway. I've seen him working in one of your sketch pads while he was doing laundry."

"Yes. Well. Despite what you and Theo have experienced in the laundry room," I stifled the laugh until Lizzy caught my eye, "or elsewhere for that matter, thank you Lizzy and Ashlyn, may I continue?"

We managed to stop, but not before Wren had let out a squeak.

"Thank you. Despite Theo's white noise theory, the founders did not intend this to be a place in which you spend more time on domestic chores than on creativity. Therefore, please help to keep our operating costs down and our lint traps clean."

The seven of us nodded dutifully. I couldn't even look at Lizzy, and was unbelievably glad Margie had Wren and I separated. If she was as canny as she was strict, she'd planned it.

"Now, the other thing concerning me is the social interactions I have observed. There has never, in the short history of Fire-Wind, been such factionalism and rejection of the group's fellow artists. Personally, I don't understand it. You were chosen from a large pool of applicants, based not only on the artistic merit of your projects, but also on the perceived ability for the eight of you to exchange insight into each other's work and the very meaning of art." Again, she looked sternly around the table and we fiddled with our napkins and chair placements. "What I see with you eight—no, let me correct myself—with the seven of you who are here, is an unprecedented level of separatism. The very fact one of you does not feel comfortable enough to sit with the rest of you at meals is an indication."

I was going to fall out of my chair if she used a contraction. My high school English teachers never spoke with such careful syntax.

"It seems to me you have driven one of your member away, been prone to pairing off and forming other small, exclusive groups, and shown a remarkable lack of interest in each other's visions. Other groups by this stage in their retreats have staged small shows of works-in-progress, held all night long sessions to discuss the history of art and how it applies to their ideas, and organized field trips to galleries in Austin and San Marcos. I have not seen the eight of you together since the night of orientation, once Ashlyn arrived."

Of course she looked archly at me. Of course my face burned.

"Why is it bad if a few of us want to do things together and others don't?" Caleb asked.

"Right, I don't understand this. Do you want us to stay in our studios and create art, or go gallivanting off on a bus together?" Lizzy added. "And Rafael hasn't spoken three words to any of us, so it's not as if we offended him. He's welcome anytime."

Wren mumbled, "He was especially welcome last week when I was cooking and cleaning on my own."

"That's another thing!" Lizzy leaned forward and flung an arm towards Wren. "No one heard you telling Rafael about the spirit of togetherness when poor Wren was left without a food partner. The rest of us get on fine, but we wouldn't exactly go arranging slide shows together without inviting him and he's never around to make us feel as if he cares one way or the opposite about our work, now is he?"

Margie's coffee whirlpooled for a moment as she set down her spoon. "I am not under the impression you are seven souls eagerly awaiting an eighth to make your union complete. I grant Rafael keeps odd hours, and I am aware of the bind in which he left Lauren, but my point about your unusually anti-social behavior still holds. The founders and I cannot force friendship upon you, but we can make you aware of the need for greater and more productive interaction and strive for it. I am going to speak to Rafael tonight, and want you all to know I am available to answer your individual or group concerns whenever you see fit to bring them to me." Pushing back her chair in some magic way that didn't make the leg scrape against the wooden floor, she stood. "Does anyone have any other questions for me at the moment?"

We shook our collective heads.

"Very well, then. Good night."

It took a good two minutes of listening to her take the lake path towards Rafael's before anyone spoke.

"Well, I want to know who's been leaving lint in the dryer," Lizzy said. "My jeans took at least an hour to dry the other day."

"I vote we have an exhibition in the laundry room," Angelica added to the laughter, "We can preview each other's work, and figure out who the culprit is at the same time."

"Oh, I know who it is," I said.

"Who?" Theo and Angelica asked together.

"Who else? Our recluse. He spends his days wandering the

abundant lint-forests of central Texas, and stays up all night eating our leftovers and fluffing things."

Caleb reached across and took my hand, kissed the big knuckle. "She's hilarious," he told Wren, who sat across from him. "Aren't we lucky?" He squeezed my fingers and let them go.

"I wouldn't mind an exhibition of sorts, actually," Lizzy said, standing to clear the coffee mugs. "If that's not falling too much for the party line. I'd be interested in what yous all have to say about what I've just finished."

"You finished it? You rock. I still have hours more work on *Chains*."

"Technically, it's half done. But before I start on the other half I'd take some good critical reaction."

"I have some things I could show," Caleb volunteered. "You do, too, don't you, Wren?"

She nodded.

"I'm almost to that point myself," Brandon said.

"Theo's done wonders." Angelica put in.

"Thanks." He gave her an absorbed smile. "Your stuff, too. Don't be modest."

"Right. So, we're almost all ready. How about this? We do a door-to-door thing, each day, say after lunch? We visit one person's studio and talk about their work. We can start with Angelica's, then mine, Wren, and so on. Would that give you enough time?" Lizzy asked me. I nodded.

"Brandon?"

"I could swing it. That's a week for me."

"Eight days," she corrected him. "Saturday Ash and I will be out."

"Do we invite our silent member?" I asked. Quite admirable, the way the woman who earlier implored me to spend a day saving her from direct contact with her parents had become the ringleader and swept the issue of their arrival aside as if it were no more inconvenient than an annual check-up.

"Does no harm to ask him. He doesn't have to come, doesn't have to say anything, doesn't have to let us into his studio."

"Okay, but please don't ask Margie," Wren said. "I couldn't take what passes for critique from her."

"Absolutely. Are we agreed? Angelica, will you be ready on the morrow for an invasion of artists into your world?" Lizzy looked at her as if anything but agreement would be ridiculous.

"After lunch," she confirmed.

"Great. Brandon, finish this washing up, will you? I'm bushed. Night, all." And with that, she left.

I DON'T KNOW if our first meeting about Angelica was stilted because of her work, or the way Theo wouldn't let us say anything negative, or because despite our growing ease with each other, we hadn't yet experienced many group discussions about our art, and didn't know where each other's biases lay.

She started us off on a porcelain rose, glitteringly beautiful, with had three oversized and rather fierce aphids crawling up its interior petals. "I'm exploring aspects of loveliness," she said, and I couldn't gauge whether or not she realized how discordant the piece was.

We all stammered vaguely, until Theo said, "I think it's all about the ephemeral nature of beauty and the fragility of life."

"It's remarkably realistic," I ventured, meeting Wren's gaze and quickly averting my eyes.

"And the shock effect is genuine," Caleb added. "Not like a lot of stuff people do just for effect. It genuinely surprises."

"I like the combination of brass and porcelain. It's both brittle and enduring," Wren said, taking it back from Angelica. "They must have been hard to combine."

Angelica grinned. "It was. God, I'm glad you all like it. I was so nervous, being the first one under the microscope, so to speak."

"I kept telling her she didn't need to worry," Theo said, taking her hand. This was new, their holding hands in front of us all. For several painfully obvious days, they had pretended to be just pals when anyone else was around. "Everyone can see right off how talented you are. Show them the sketches of the heron."

We had seen the white block on the way in, cleaned and formed but not yet detailed. She gathered us around her easel and drew back the cover page.

"Is it, um?" I asked.

"Dead?" finished Wren.

Angelica traced the neck lightly. The heron was apparently asleep, but in some of her sketches we could see the bare patches of feathers carried away, the lack of eyeballs, the fact one of its legs was actually in three separate pieces.

"I want him to look as peaceful as possible," she explained. "He'll be large, of course, so I can get all the details right. It was taking up so much of my energy, I had to step back and regroup by finishing the little rose."

"I do that all the time," said Brandon. "It's like, certain projects are so intense we can't focus on the big picture, as it were. So we have to let it drop for a bit and just take study snaps of trees, which is what I do."

Of all of Brandon's work I'd glimpsed in the computer lab—he left it on screen a lot when he stepped out to the toilet, it's not as if I was snooping—every shot had been a tree. Mostly the tallish pine near the main entrance to FireWind.

Happy to get off the subject of her work—did she not find it in the least macabre?—I talked about the way I'd been stuck at home, how this retreat was exactly what I needed to refresh my mind. Everyone had a similar story, except Theo, who was, according to him, merely a funnel of some kind. His inspiration came from outside himself and he was the hand holding the brush. Angelica stroked him from shoulder to elbow as he said this.

Caleb, Lizzy, and I stopped at Wren's cabin on the way out of Angelica's.

"I'm all for twisted art, but am I the only one who thinks she doesn't get the impact of her work?" I asked. "I mean, she's talented as hell, but there was, like, no awareness death and destruction can be disturbing. She could be sculpting bluebirds and rainbows for all she reacts to it."

"If eight year old boys could buy art, she'd have a big market," Wren said, scooting over so Caleb could sit on the arm of the sofa next to her.

"Maybe that's what she's going for." He leaned back so his arm was along the back of the sofa, behind Wren, and Lizzy, and Wren's bright face. "Of course, I'm not saying anything bad. I don't want anyone retaliating against me next week."

Wren grinned up at him. "You have a lot of maggots and decomposition in your compositions?"

"Not so much."

"Then I'm sure we'll love it."

"Ah, you're just saying that. Make me feel all confident so I'll be crushed on Tuesday."

I stood up. "I'd best to get going if I'm going to have anything presentable myself. I haven't had this tight a deadline in a long while."

"I'll walk you out," Caleb offered, standing. "I forgot to order the groceries after lunch."

"Give you one simple job," I muttered.

"Hey, not fair. I'll get them in time."

"Barely."

"Shuddup," he said, nudging me with his elbow. "See you later, alligators," he added to Wren and Lizzy.

"Bye," they chorused. I winked at Wren, who suppressed a giggle.

～

LIZZY AND WREN'S shows were a lot smoother. Rafael even wandered up to CypressWood when we were marveling at the half-completed *In Sickness and In Health*. Lizzy stopped talking about how she would interlink the soapstone with the granite when he walked in, and we all turned to gape. He'd grown a goatee. He didn't say anything more than 'hi' before kneeling in front of the sculpture to examine it, straightening to shake Lizzy's hand with a formal little bow, and leaving.

"That was praise, I think," I ventured after he'd left.

"I guess. He wasn't exactly moved to tears."

"Maybe he was holding them back until he got outside."

She shook her head at me. "Well. As I was saying." She looked around. "What was I saying?"

Wren let rip with a belly laugh. "He just did it for effect, hon, snap out of it! You were telling the assembled crowd of admirers about fitting *Sickness* over and around her," she reached out and played her fingers over *Health's* muscular back.

Health was a granite woman half-kneeling, her face towards the ground and her hair pulled loosely behind her. Her calf muscles were flexed and her hands reached behind her to cup the empty air above her hips. Her smile was so strained it was hard to decide if she was actually grimacing or not.

Sickness would be a soapstone woman resting on *Health's* back. Lizzy wanted to wrap one of her arms around the granite waist; the other would be supporting her head as she leaned her elbow into *Health's* back (which explained the twisting of her left shoulder blade.) Lizzy had started the sculpture months before, when she was still in Ireland, but once she had shaped the granite, she'd found she couldn't concentrate on it long enough to get anything substantial done. The break-up with Moira had further complicated things, since she couldn't contemplate the work without also facing her emotions about the end of her relationship.

So she'd applied to FireWind and a few other retreats, and

shipped the stone ahead of her once she'd been accepted. The founders had provided all the pneumatic equipment she and Angelica could use. Their studio was outfitted for the heavy work of sculpture: built-in compressor cabinets, hoseable studio floors, hydraulic work tables that could elevate to five feet, two- and four-wheel dollies. She's bought a good block of soapstone in Austin when she'd arrived, and concentrated since her arrival on drilling *Health's* features.

"I've been vacillating so much on the expression of *Sickness*, I suppose it's my main problem at the moment," she told us, moving to her easel. "Her form I know already, as you can see, so long as I can handle the logistics of fitting them together. But her face leaves me cold."

She flipped to a page with five sketches of a face. They ranged from nauseated to lugubrious. "What do yous think? I don't want her too much, you know, in need of antacids. It's more of a mindset thing."

"But aren't you going for the problem between the two?" Caleb asked. "*Health* is carrying *Sickness* even when she shouldn't?"

"Even so, the way these things work, or at least how I've seen them, is the *Sickness* one will play up the problem with her weakness," I said. "So she can't look all happy or anything."

"I know, but look at the way Lizzy has the posture," he said, turning back a page to indicate the lax muscles. "She's just flopped up there on top of *Health*, it's not like she's so sick she can't even sit up a little and look around and enjoy the ride."

"Codependency goes deeper than that," Angelica told him. "Both partners become so tied to their roles they can't help but adopt them when they're together. Isn't that your message, Lizzy, at least a little?"

"That's what I see," said Theo.

She smiled at the two of them. "That is how I put them together, yeah. So you know what I mean about her face, right? Not too ill but believing she is?"

I turned back to her sketches. "So here, maybe, along these lines?" I pointed to a face with sad eyes and drooping mouth, but a slightly raised brow. "She's feeling down and yet enjoying the vantage point, maybe just a little bored, too."

"I don't know," Wren chimed in. "It's close, but maybe a little too, calculating, I guess. Can you work from here and maybe add more furrows, more pain?"

Lizzy considered it. "I think...you mean along here?" she asked.

Wren nodded.

"And if I thin out the hair a bit, let her grasp a handful of it with her left hand?"

"But leave her body like it is," Wren told her, "so we know it's coming from her mind, not so much physical."

"That's great," Caleb said to Wren. "You've got a fantastic eye."

"You're telling me," Lizzy said, kissing Wren's cheek. "Thanks. Thanks a million."

Wren blushed. "Aw, go on."

"No, really," I added. "That was inspired. Let's skip doing you tomorrow so you can come tell me how I'm doing."

"Now you all have to get out of here so I can work on this before dinner," Lizzy said, grabbing pencils from her desk. "Brandon, I'll be late for k.p., you get it going and I'll set the table and wash up."

I laughed. He'd spent the whole time at Lizzy's silent, even less of a presence than Rafael. It seemed he was afraid of his food partner.

Caleb headed for the door. "Let's go, people, the artist is at work. Nothing more to see here."

ANOTHER VOLLEY of pebbles woke me the next morning. Wren half-waved when I sat up to squint at her. She threw herself down on my still warm, still comfortable bed while I shut myself in the bathroom.

"You're up before Caleb."

"I'm sorry, I know you wanted to rest."

"Uh-huh." Wetting my hand in the warming shower spray, I rubbed at my eyelids and forehead.

"I tried Lizzy but she had her curtains drawn and wouldn't stir."

"Lucky Lizzy." I brushed my teeth while leaning against the tub.

"My showing is this afternoon."

"Uh-huh."

"Maybe you've noticed I haven't been talking about the houses much lately."

Sighing, I wrapped a towel around myself and stepped out to kiss the top of her head. "I know, sweetie, but some people are just like that. Give me a minute to get clean, okay?"

She nodded and I went back to my shower. The peppermint castile soap slowly but sweetly opened my senses to the day, and just to bring myself wholly awake I exfoliated my face. Wren had a cup of coffee sitting on my dresser when I opened the bathroom door, and she'd made my bed.

"Thanks," I smiled. "Caleb knocked yet?"

She shook her head. "It's not late."

"So why are you nervous? It's just us."

"Doesn't matter. I hate showing my stuff even when it's done."

"Everyone does."

"No, not...not for validation." She flopped on the bed again. "Well, yes, for validation, but more for my own sense of purpose. I can talk about it in advance, because I'm just telling you what I intend the finished product to be, but half the time even when I think I'm done I realize there's another angle I haven't explored yet, another way to re-examine and re-focus—I don't know if I'm saying it right. It's like, I think I know what I'm doing, I put a lot into development, but the second I show it to someone, they say something that isn't even necessarily what I'm trying to accomplish, but it suddenly points up some major flaw in execution which means I have to almost go back to square one."

"You don't have to listen to us. You can even tell us not to talk."

"I know. But nothing's going to stop you thinking, and I'll be trying to read your minds and second-guessing myself anyway."

"Well, then, if you know you're going to be re-thinking the project when we're done today, just accept it and give yourself the space you need to dwell on everything."

Wren laughed, dropping the hair she'd been idly braiding. "Sounds simple, doesn't it? But I'm not sure I want anyone else causing me to re-think this. I've been dwelling on these dwellings for months, and now I think I have the key to the right execution, and the second you squint to take in a detail, I'll be convinced I've done even this all wrong."

"I know what your problem is."

"Oh, good." She sat up a little.

"Your internal critic is far too astute. You did it to Lizzy, and you've done it to me, too—swept in and in thirty seconds seen what we've been completely blind about, and told us exactly how to fix it without taking anything away from our own ideas. It seems like no big deal to you when you do it to us—and believe me, I've appreciated it—but when you do it to yourself it's complicated by the ideas the artist side of you has about the work, so the critic side of you ends up giving you grief."

She raised an eyebrow at me. "So the fact I'm multifaceted makes it hard for me to be an artist?"

"In a nutshell."

"I'm not sure I feel any better."

I wasn't sure I would, either, in her place. Internal critics can be so loud, even in the face of external praise. I did have one easy distraction to offer. And I was all too aware that I'd been hoarding that distraction to myself instead of pushing forward Wren's agenda. "Come on to breakfast with me; you can take your mind off this afternoon while you moon at Caleb. I'll try to get him to bend over a lot with his backside towards you."

She linked her bony arm through mine. "What a pal."

RAFAEL, oddly enough, showed up at Wren's studio with a handful of wildflowers—the bluebonnets were just beginning to bloom and he'd mixed them with some vivid Indian paintbrush to form a startling and cheerful bouquet. I decided not to mention it was illegal to pick our state flower. Wren stuck them in a glass of water while we looked at her houses.

They were small-scale ceramics, none taller than five inches, and an almost random mixture of crude construction and minute detail. The walls of her San Antonio barracks house didn't meet at ninety degrees, but the mission architecture style was richly formed at the windows and doors.

"It's baby blue because it's where my brother was born. I was eight, and my mother drifted into a post-partum depression that kinda changed her forever. It was a very disjointed time in my life."

She also had finished the ranch house where they'd lived when she was twelve and got her first period. It was glazed in blood red, streaked with iron. The vines climbing up the side wall looked enough like the shed uterine lining to make me shiver.

Rafael loved it. At least, I can only assume he did, since he discoursed so long about it. "It's, like, so sensual—almost inviting but thorny at the same time," he said.

"Um, thanks," answered Wren, glancing nervously at Lizzy and I.

"Thanks for sharing," he added as he turned to go.

"Bye, man," Caleb called after him.

"He spoke, like, a dozen words!" I turned to Wren. "Wow. I wonder what Margie said to him."

"Whatever it was, it seemed to spark the spirit of togetherness in him," Angelica sneered. "Wonders will never cease."

Wren had four more houses planned in her *Military Brat* series. As she told us about them, outlining the general trend of mono-chromatic structures and their personal significance, I wrestled with my own fears about the creation of a very personal art. She's said she was trying to define 'home' with this series, but the dwellings didn't meet my definition of 'homey.' They were houses, distinct in style but the impact grew from the chronology of Wren's life. Even the way we determined she should name them—descriptively (*12th year—menstruation*) rather than geographically (*Ft. St. Helen*)—pointed towards their being more about autobiography than about a global sense of home.

Of course, I had never been moved from place to place like her; perhaps to another military kid her work would resonate. But why should she be forced to universalize it if it felt right to her?

Looking at my *Chains of Love*, I had to admit it was about nothing more cosmic than my relationship with my mother's mother. Would anyone other than Gran and I 'get' it? Zach or Bernadette, maybe, at least for the artistic merit—I knew it had that—and the hints about them it contained. Caleb and Wren and Lizzy and the rest, instead of discussing the meaning, might only comment on the stitchery, the combination of elements, and other externals.

I walked throughout dinner, up the road away from town and circling back through the woods as it got darker and I worried about the cars. Not many passed, but those that did drove the country road as if it were an enclosed track, and I didn't trust their headlights and their common sense to keep me safe.

Hunger finally drove me to the Main House, where I ate in the computer room after making sure there were no signs of life from early-to-bed Margie. Email from Zach alluded to some hot news from him, but I knew it was pointless to try to drag it out of him ahead of schedule. I hoped he'd met someone.

Caleb was dishing himself some ice cream when I went in to wash up. "Join me?" he asked, scoop halfway into the chocolate chunk.

"Why not," I agreed, and put the kettle on. Nothing like ice cream and green tea.

"Why weren't you at dinner?"

"Oh, I was just walking around, thinking. I grabbed a late sandwich instead. I miss anything?"

"Not food-wise. Pork chops and canned green beans. Margie stopped by to pat us on the head while we told her about our workshops. Wren..."

We traded places as I moved to the pantry. "What?"

"Nothing, I guess. Did you see her earlier?"

"No. Did something happen?"

He was quiet for a moment. "No. She just seemed to be kind of down. I've never seen her depressed like that, and I thought things went well today, you know?"

I nodded, getting out spoons. "No one was mean or anything. Do you think we offended her?"

Caleb leaned through the pass-through to identify a passing noise. He was wearing jeans, a distractingly nice pair of black jeans. "Just Brandon going to the computer," he reported. "Anyway, I was thinking, you know, her house thing is so, well, private. Maybe we didn't give her the kind of reaction she was hoping for. We weren't drawn in as intensely as we should have been."

Opening the freezer covered my little shiver. "Uh-huh."

"So you think we upset her? She was kind of, I don't know, quiet at dinner, hardly even laughed at Margie."

"I don't know."

"Ash?"

I just glanced at him.

"Hey, Ashlyn, what's wrong?"

I blinked. "Huh? Nothing. Thinking."

He shook his head. "No, really, what's wrong? You tired?"

I smiled. "Oh, hush, Caleb. I'm just preoccupied. My mind's on Sunday."

He furrowed, then released, his brow. "Oh, your big day under the spotlight. You shouldn't worry, it'll be great. We'll love it."

"You've never seen it."

"Doesn't matter. I can tell just from knowing you." He gave me a bear hug and stepped back without taking his hands from my shoulders, which he began kneading. "Look, Ash, I know it'll be fine. And I promise to love it myself, no matter what." He grinned.

I shrugged my shoulders. Did he think I was a piece of dough? "Caleb, you idiot, you can hate it or love it or think it's nothing more than child's play. Just be honest. No one can say anything about my work I haven't heard before, probably from myself."

When I'd called him an idiot he'd let go of me. Now he reached down and took my left palm with his right fingers. "Guess I am being stupid. Sorry, I shouldn't have said anything so asinine." He kissed the back of my hand and smiled. "Come sit outside with me, okay?" There went those crinkly eyes, the ones forcing me to smile back. I took my mug and followed him out the door.

"So, are you ready for your exhibition?" I joined him on the swing.

"I think so," he said, putting his bowl down on the porch. "I like what I've done so far, anyway, I'm just going to work on mounting it tomorrow while you're playing old country roots."

"Be nice."

He grinned and pushed the swing back swiftly, which tilted me into his side as I tried to hold my mug up and away from my body.

"Thanks."

His arm wrapped around my shoulders. "Sorry," he said with a squeeze. "Did you spill?"

His fascination with my shoulders was beginning to worry me. "No, it's almost empty anyway."

"You need more? I'll make it."

I shook my head. "I'm good. No more caffeine tonight, anyway, I need my beauty sleep."

"Hardly."

"Huh?" I looked at him.

He winked. "Nothing." His arm was still around me. I hoped Wren wasn't feeling restless tonight.

"I should turn in, too. Let's leave these until morning," Caleb said, nudging his bowl with his toe.

"I'll just carry them in," I said, standing. The back of my neck felt chilly.

When I returned, he was looking out towards the lake. His t-shirt was tight across his upper back. He fell into step beside me as I started down the porch steps.

"I'm going to miss your cheerful morning smile after tomorrow," he said.

"Don't worry, only three more weeks until we flip pancakes together again."

We were at the footbridge. Caleb turned towards me dramatically and grasped my hand between his two, drawing it to his chest. "Promise me you won't flip pancakes with any other man until then."

I couldn't resist giving him a sultry voice. "I didn't realize my spatula was so important to you."

"Oh, but it is. It truly is."

"In that case, I promise."

He kissed my fingertips gallantly. "You have made my month, madam." And when we started walking again, he forgot to unlink our hands. I figured it would be rude to do it myself, so I left my hand in his until I needed it to enter my door code.

We just looked at each other for a minute while I stood in the half-opened door. Somehow, even though he wasn't smiling, the wrinkles around Caleb's dark eyes were still there.

"Good night, then," I finally said.

"Sweet dreams, Ashlyn."

"Visions of maple syrup will dance in my head," I assured him, and before he had quite started the motion to turn and walk away, I put my hand on his shoulder and leaned in to kiss his cheek. His hand grazed my hair when he kissed mine in return.

"Sweet dreams, Caleb," I said quietly, and went slowly in to bed.

CHAPTER 7

A volley of pebbles woke me. They fell skipping off the roof, window, and wood of my cabin, and I let out a little scream when I saw Lizzy's face at the pane.

"If you'd just set an alarm we wouldn't have to resort to this," she said, throwing herself onto her favorite spot in the corner.

"Every one of you people is far too bothered by my dislike of clocks." I turned to shower. "At least Caleb has the decency to knock loudly on the door and leave. I'm too much of a city gal to like seeing faces at my window."

"Grump."

I shut the bathroom door on her. Here I was devoting my day to her and she was criticizing.

When I came out of the shower, she and Caleb were sitting on my bed. "Make yourselves at home."

He stared at the towel covering my torso, started to speak, then stopped. She didn't. "We were comparing this quilt to your stuff."

"Well, do it outside. I'm not in the mood for an audience."

They rose and Caleb took a step towards me. The pad of his

forefinger was tracing my stitching on the duckie patch of his pants, as if I needed a reminder of his being the naked, towel-wrapped one in my cabin. Lizzy shoved him towards the living area and handed me my wet-hair comb. "I sure hope you get nicer before my parents arrive. They're hardly going to be charmed by this sort of thing."

"Go away." Again, I shut the door on her. Some retreat.

THEY PRETTY MUCH LEFT ME alone to make the coffee and juice once we got to the kitchen. He started to grate the carrots and she showed him her method of separating eggs. She launched into a rant about poppy seeds and he opted instead to add walnuts to the muffins. They both eyed the way I was slicing oranges for the juice until I glared them off. I almost didn't remind her to wipe the flour off her forehead before Brandon came in for his early cuppa.

After breakfast, as I washed the dishes and Lizzy taught Caleb how to dress up a lime marinade, a car came crunching and honking up the oyster shell road to the Main House. "God almighty, they're early. They're never early," Lizzy said, wiping her hands on an apron.

I looked out. A large silver sedan with more than its share of mud streaks at the wheel wells was rolling to a stop. The driver was not as short as she looked slumped back against the headrest, but the passenger was every bit as tall as his hair brushing against the roof led me to believe.

"Elizabeth!" he called, unfolding from the seat. She walked off the porch and into his arms. "Say hello to your mother."

"I'm on my way." She wrapped one arm around her mother's softly framed body. As hard-wired as Lizzy was, they still looked alike. Images of Lizzy with fuzzy dove-colored hair and a cardigan didn't come easily to mind, but it was suddenly easier to predict her features mellowing with age, her muscles plumping and her gold rims framing bifocals.

She led them back up to the dining room, which I was clearing while pretending not to watch the reunion scene. Caleb picked up the drying towel and busied himself with passing in front of the kitchen door as often as possible.

"And this is Ashlyn May and Caleb Kendall, Mum," Lizzy said, steering her parents towards us. Wiping our hands dry, we smiled. "Aren't they just the picture of lovely American co-artists? Ashlyn's grandpa is from Dalkey, remember I said to you, Dad? She wants to ask you about the old days."

"Would either of you care for tea or coffee?" I asked.

"After our drive down, anything is appreciated. Coffee if you have it. Tea for Agnes."

"Coming right up," Caleb smiled, putting on the kettle.

"Sit down, please, we'll bring it right in."

"Thank you, dear," Agnes smiled.

Caleb raised an eyebrow at me as I pulled out clean mugs. "Very upper-middle-class, no?"

"They're cute," I whispered back.

"Cute, sure, but come on—are they how you imagined the hotbed of Lizzy's origins?"

"Sssh." I arranged the cookies and glanced through the pass-through, where everyone was all settled in at the table. Caleb and I were alone for the first time that day. For a second we just breathed next to each other's stillness.

"You want tea, too?" he asked, pulling out my favorite ceramic mug.

"Peppermint."

He set the coffee plunger and teapot on the tray, and then joined me leaning against the counter as we waited for the water to boil.

"Ash?"

"Yeah?"

"Can I ask you to tell me something honestly?"

I looked up at him and put my hand on his arm, thinking both of Ann and of the almost-tearful shock of my fingers on his tan skin. "One thing I'll tell you about me today, Caleb Kendall, is you can count on me to always be honest."

"You're something else, Ashlyn May. Look, I need to know if your pal Lauren is, well.... God this sounds vain and stupid." He drew a breath. "Does Wren want to, you know, be with me?"

The kettle boiled.

"Do you want her to?"

"Don't. Just tell me."

I filled the cafetière. "She does. She's liked you since the bus ride from Austin. She's the one who pointed out how bright your face is when you're feeling spirited."

"When what?"

"Never mind." I shifted all the mug handles so they faced the same direction. "Why do you ask?"

He rubbed the back of his neck. "It's a little bit of a long story. Maybe we can talk later?"

"I don't know how long I'll be with Lizzy...."

"But back by dinner, she has to be here for dinner?"

"She does."

"So after?"

I took up the tray. "You've got a date, partner."

He and the plate of cookies followed me into the dining room.

DUB AND AGNES were quite the couple. He had been a banker for most of his career, before that a delivery driver for a woolen mills. She had been a secretary at the woolen mills who'd gotten obsessed with travel and history after her marriage. She'd taken Dub and Lizzy and her brother Stephen to as many famous battle sites as they could pack into two-week holidays in Ireland,

Britain, and France. When they left Wimberley, they were headed for a day at the Alamo, flying home from San Antonio via New York.

Dub talked about the good old days of Dalkey for a while; the big hotel where everyone worked at some point or another, the frequent trips out the island for picnics, and getaways to the surrounding hills. Pappa's tales had populated the same scenery, but Dub's Dalkey was so much more modern.

Pappa never returned to Ireland; whenever his fond recollections of the place prompted curious questions, he said, "It's where my children and my wife are that's my home, not some distant green memory of a place." Pappa insisted he had no desire to leave even after his kids were grown—he wanted to keep a warm place with a snug bed available to his children wherever they were. And he did. He spearheaded the campaign to bring Bernadette and Frank back to Texas before Zach's birth, though Gran was of the same mind about it.

All he ever wanted was his children around him. They grew up knowing it, and when he died they still knew it. Uncle Dermot at the funeral said, with the simplest truth of the day, "Being our dad was the thing Niall O'Connor prioritized above anything else in his life."

It was interesting to hear what modern-day Dalkey was like, though, and to imagine Pappa's life if he'd never left.

The Murphys wanted to see Lizzy's cabin before we headed to town for a through investigation of all the quaint shops Wimberley had on offer. As Caleb stacked the mugs back on the tray and said his farewells, he brushed his fingers against my nape. It was small, but Lizzy gave me quite the arch look. She cornered me in town while her parents took pictures of the split-rail fence lining a park by the water. "And what was the touching back there all about?"

I grimaced. "Don't know yet. Can I tell you later?"

After peeking in at the milliners and the curiosity shop,

where Dub debated between some knobby walking sticks before settling on an easier-to-pack garden chime, we settled down with sandwiches outside a cafe on the river. Thus far the talk had mostly been of Lizzy's brother Stephen and his family, along with various aunts ("she collapsed on the bus to Rathgar and was sent to hospital with a kidney infection. They read her last rights before she got better. Desperate business"), cousins ("separated from Aoife, they just told us"), and neighbors ("can you believe it, drug addicts stole the vases from her brother's grave").

Then they started in on Lizzy. I was enchanted as Agnes recounted her first school dance experience, and grinned openly when Dub told, not the soufflé story, but the special anniversary tea she'd made them at age eight, which was soon followed by her first cooking lesson. Lizzy kicked me under the table—kinda hard —before I recollected myself, and my mission.

Watching a jay flash out over the water, I asked Dub, "Would you have known or heard of any of my Pappa's family? He was Niall O'Connor, and he emigrated in 1937, when he was eighteen."

"Well now. There were the O'Connors that ran the boats and the O'Connors further up towards town that were old Dr. O'Connor and his lot. But I don't recall either family having a boy gone to America. '37, you said?"

I nodded. "'37. And his father was a doctor."

"Dr. O'Connor never had a boy off to America. Three girls in his family, young Kitty was a great friend of my oldest sister, Elizabeth." His eyes narrowed, then he shook his head.

"What?" asked Lizzy.

"Must be a mistake. Never mind," replied her dad.

"Never mind what?"

"Nothing, pet, I'm sure it's naught to do with your friend's granddad."

Agnes was looking at him sharply. He wouldn't meet her eye,

though. I was embarrassed, but I said, "Go on, Mr. Murphy, you can tell me. I won't mind. Whatever it is."

"Well," he sighed. "I'm sure it's nothing. Young Kitty just had a nephew, named Matthew after the doctor, born around then. The mum was a widow, I always heard, just married to the doctor's son but he was kicked by a horse on their honeymoon in England, and killed."

Agnes gasped. "You're talking about Alice O'Connor and her boy?"

Dub nodded.

"She's Alice Magill as was. My da's cousin. Why didn't I think of her?"

I looked from him to her. "But this must have been Pappa's brother, surely?"

Dub cocked his head with half a shrug, but wouldn't elaborate. Agnes, however, said, "People always said, poor Dr. O'Connor, his only boy lost so young."

"And was his name Niall?"

Before Agnes could answer the table shook gently and she veed her eyebrows at Dub. Looking back at me, she patted my hand and said, "I couldn't say for sure, dear."

I sat back, not quite able to focus. It was too much, not credible. My thoughts were a tangle, looped like a bobbin thread when the machine tension is all wrong.

It had to be a mistake.

Lizzy glanced between us all, then watched my reaction as she asked them, "So what ever happened with this Matthew O'Connor?"

"I couldn't say," replied Dub.

"Mum, he's your cousin. I know you could say." Agnes pressed her lips together, but Lizzy kept at her. "Go on, Mum. I'm just going to keep asking."

She nodded, as did Dub. "Well. He's living in Dublin now. He took early retirement a few years back from RTE. He's got grandchildren now. I remember his oldest girl married a Dutch man."

"How many kids?"

"Two girls. They'd be in their forties now."

I licked my dry lips. "And his mom? Alice?"

"Dead some few decades now, God love her. Cancer."

I closed my eyes and rubbed at my temples. My own—my American—Uncle Matthew was in his forties, living in California touring with a semi-successful jazz band and acting bit parts when he could get them. Zach and I had gone to a dozen bad movies over the years to catch twenty seconds of Matthew delivering take-out or being shot by crossfire.

"You okay, Ash?" Lizzy's worried look was such an echo of her mother's more gentle one I had to smile.

"Uh." I sighed. "Okay, yeah. A little, how do I describe it? Taken aback?"

"You wanna go back? Be alone?"

"No. I mean, I guess so, yeah, I'm not likely to be good company now. You three would do better without me. I can grab the bus, it stops just down the road." Or somewhere. Margie had hung the laminated bus schedule in the laundry room. I would figure it out.

Dub stood. "Don't be ridiculous. We'll drop you back. Agnes would like a walk in those woods you have anyway, wouldn't you?"

"Of course. We'll all go. Come on, dear." That was directed at Lizzy, who was still sitting.

As we buckled our seat belts, she asked, "Mum. Is this the cousin Alice who Crazy Uncle Corneilus dropped all those hints about?"

"Goodness, child, your Uncle Corneilus has been—you haven't seen him these twelve years. How do you remember that?"

"It is, then?"

"What hints?" I asked.

Agnes signaled her turn. Once she'd taken her lane on the main road, she said carefully, "No one was invited to the wedding, except Alice's sister, they said. We never heard about it in advance, just one day she was returning from England a widow, and the baby born not seven months later. In those days, girls went suddenly to England for reasons we didn't discuss."

Lizzy looked at me and mimed a pregnant belly. "But no one ever claimed they weren't married, right?" she asked the front seat.

"Not in so many words. It was a tragedy, his dying. The O'Connors were just happy to have young Matthew to love. That boy was the image of the doctor."

Pappa had come to Galveston from Liverpool. And many of the places of Dalkey he'd described were mirrors of Dub's stories; people, too. Still, there surely could have been another Dr. Matthew O'Connor with a son last seen in the late '30s. Or would Pappa have assumed the dead man's identity? No, that was a worse tangle than deserting his pregnant girlfriend. I sank back into my seat, eyes closed. In what possible twist of fate's knife could my Pappa be a man who'd left a pregnant girl behind and run away to Texas, letting his own parents think he was dead?

No one spoke until we'd pulled into FireWind, though I could see Dub and Lizzy both silencing themselves. As Agnes pulled up in front of the Main House, Lizzy started to give her directions to my cabin. I stopped her, said I'd like the walk. Summoned up thanks to her parents for lunch.

"Well, it was lovely to meet you, dear," said Agnes as she got out of the car. "I only wish...."

"I know, it's okay. It's not what we expected to happen." I gave her a little hug. "Have a good trip back. Thanks for everything, Dub," I added, turning to shake his hand. He leaned down to kiss my cheek.

"Thank you. And if there is anything you need, other questions," he paused. "Well, our Elizabeth will pass it along, I'm sure. We're happy to help if we can. After this."

I nodded. "See you later, Lizzy."

"You're okay back?"

"It's a hundred steps. I'll be fine." I was already walking towards ValeSong.

Climbing my porch, I caught motion out of the corner of my eye. It was Caleb, saddled with a couple of cameras and in the process of adjusting a lens as he walked through the trees. He turned my way as the keypad beeped with my entry code, but without looking back, I stepped over the threshold and shut the door.

CHAPTER 8

Someone knocked on the cabin door around dusk. Sounded like Lizzy. I stayed in my studio; I had unhung *Chains* and folded it away, and was sitting at the drafting table scrawling random patterns, detailing each one more and more until the gray lines of the pencil obscured the design, then starting over on a new sheet. I switched to colored pencils, but every sketch devolved into brown mush, until I finally stopped and just sat, rubbing at the accumulated graphite on my fingertips and along my palm's Mercury line.

Time for a bath. Or a shower. But the shower head didn't have the obliterating pressure the situation required, so I poured a mug full of white wine and a capful of bubbles, and sank into the moist heat.

I emerged after giving in to the steam and a good cry, and went to pour the rest of the wine into my mug. On my counter sat a plate of pasta salad and a bowl of dried fruits and nuts in strawberry yogurt. There was also a note from Caleb: 'You promised me a date tonight. Come by later?' Except instead of the word 'date' he'd taped an actual date to the paper.

I sank onto the sofa and picked at the food. Before I could decide whether to go see him, Lizzy knocked again.

"Can I come in? I saw your studio light was off now."

"Sure." I stood back. "Did your parents make it off okay?"

She nodded. "They said to tell you of course they'll be discreet back home, not tell anyone or anything."

"Oh crap, I hadn't even thought about that."

"It's not a problem, them being quiet about it, you know. Yous all laugh at me for being a gossip, but I didn't get it from them."

The rundown of news from home earlier kinda belied her statement, but I let it go. There wasn't much I could do about it regardless.

"You know," she started carefully, watching my face, "it has such a stigma even now, abortion. Even out of wedlock births— not so much in our generation, but we all grew up hearing how shocking it all was. Even my friends with younger parents than mine, it was practically top story of the news if someone they knew had an early birth. It would have been a lot for them to face."

I let her talk, unsure why she thought some sociology would negate this total inversion of Pappa.

"I could do some research on it, if you want."

Now I shook my head. "Thanks, Lizzy, I know you're trying tot help, but I don't even know what I want right now, I couldn't begin to tell you how I feel about it all. I should sleep on it, I guess."

She started. "I should let you go, I'm sorry."

"No, no. I just meant later."

"But you obviously don't want to talk about it."

I shook my head again. Sitting down, I noticed my plate and bowl next to the sink. "Do you want a drink?"

"No, I'm just after cleaning up back there, I don't want to see any more dishes for a while."

"It'll be strange to have all this free time again, I think I'll appreciate it more. And I know I'll appreciate being able to sleep in. Finally."

"Uh-hum." She toed the note, where I had left it on the coffee table. "And I, well, noticed your food partner was looking out for you tonight."

One of those moments—should I leave the note, or stuff it into my pocket? It was folded over so just my name showed, so I left it. "Did...? Did Wren notice, too?"

Lizzy stared me down for a minute before pushing her glasses back up her nose and answering, "No. He got the food after she'd left." She paused. "But I did."

"Yeah." I went to make myself some tea. "He wanted to talk to me tonight. I guess he was just trying to wile his way into my den with food, but I must have been in the bath when he came."

The coffee maker heated the water. Lizzy still didn't say anything. "I ought never to have told any of you my door code," I added.

"You're bluffing. Or at least covering. I get your point; it's none of my business. Just that, you have to remember I'm not dense and I don't think Wren is, either. And you're both my friends. Don't expect me to cover for you if it comes up. And knowing Wren, the subject of Caleb Kendall is going to come up, soon."

I put out my hand to stop her standing up. "Oh, Lizzy, don't. I'm not trying to deceive you, I just don't know the answer to the question you're trying not to ask."

"What question?"

"Do Caleb and I have something beyond friendship going on."

"And do you?"

I shrugged. "No. Not, well, explicitly, anyway. And between Wren and my Pappa, I wasn't going to go over like he asked to find out." She simply looked at me. Well, I was pretty sure I wouldn't have gone over. It wasn't a complete lie. "He wasn't asking me so we could start something. He had a question. Something related, I think, but not about us. We haven't either of us said anything about us."

"But there's been enough, shall we say, non-verbal communication between you to hint at it, hasn't there?"

I thought of the note, and the gesture with my hair this morning. Other moments, other touches. Other looks. "Yeah."

"And this thing he wants to talk about?"

I shook 'no' at her. "It wouldn't be fair to him to tell you. I've probably already said more to you than he would like me to say."

She nodded. "Okay. I'll just say this—if you're to the point of protecting his feelings when he's not here, and hedging around your friends, I'd say you have a better idea of the nature of your relationship, or your intentions, than you're letting on."

Sinking back and closing my eyes, I said, "Lizzy, don't be hurtful. He's my friend—our friend—first and foremost, so if I won't betray his confidences you should take it as a good sign of the kind of friend I am, not some indication of a plot we've cooked up. I've admitted there's something, maybe, in the wind between us. And that I'm trying to keep it from Wren for now. What am I supposed to do, go to her and say, hey, I may be interested and he may be interested in me but neither of us knows for sure so I'll fill you in later? For all we know, what he wants to tell me tonight is he thinks I'm sweet but he's more inclined towards her and am I terribly disappointed?"

I flushed a little as I said it; before, I hadn't realized I was half-fearing that would be his message. Lizzy didn't seem to particularly notice—she was getting up and making for the door.

"Okay, Ash, I'll try to just stay out of it. I suppose I'm a bit curious, and worried for Wren's sake."

"I'm not setting out to hurt her."

"I know." She stood by the door. "Are you headed over there now?"

"No. I'm not planning to." Not definitely.

With a hug she said, "You're a good girl, Ashlyn. You please yourself, now, you've had a rough enough day without my meddling."

I laughed. "You're a good girl yourself, Lizzy. Thanks. See you tomorrow."

"See yas." She left.

THE PERSON I most needed to talk to was Gran. It was always Gran—even when I had to weep out my fears about Bernadette's comparative lack of interest in me, it was to Gran I talked. She taught me about the Bernadette whom I, being her daughter, couldn't see. But I couldn't return the favor, try as I might. Not that Gran was a know-it-all, just that she perceived the whole dynamic between my mother and myself. I had a tendency to misappropriate all of our difficulties to my own personal failings, where Gran saw them in a much more complex light.

Bernadette had always been a tomboy, had always and forever been Pappa's girl. She loved Gran, but wasn't the kind of daughter who was dependent upon her mom. I, by a long shot, had never been a tomboy. Bernadette tried, but couldn't share my pride in the things I was good at—my drawing, my sewing, even my nascent cooking skills. And I never could get interested in playing ball with her and Frank and Zach, or their heated political and social debates, and I hated camping. We were just coming at each other from the wrong angles. With Gran's help, I'd learned to not blame myself for the lack of a bridge across the divides.

So I've always and forever been Gran's girl. The one she'd never truly had, with her two boys and her tomboy. She named me. Held me in my first hours, the first ones in which I didn't wail, and called me her 'vision of babyness' and gave me the American version of the Irish for *vision*. Bernadette relinquished me to her at an early age, which to Bernadette was the happy medium between loving me but not 'being on the same wavelength' as me, as she often put it.

In many ways, it was. But I still missed my mommy at times.

Now would be a very good time for me to have my mommy. I needed someone to tell me if I should tell Gran about Pappa. I needed someone to tell me if I should believe it was true, if I should somehow verify it first, if it would break her heart, or if she'd probably known for years but kept it secret.

However, Bernadette was still her daddy's girl. We were all crushed when he'd died, back when I was sixteen. But for Bernadette, the grief stopped with her. Zach and my uncles and I were devastated at losing Pappa, but also concerned for Gran and how she would manage to live on her own for the first time in her life. I spent days sitting, her arthritic hands in mine, talking about their life together. Talking about how they met, and the mistakes they made when they first bought the farm, and the tales about two trouble-prone giraffes Pappa spun for his children. Only Bernadette didn't commiserate with Gran, at least not that I saw, and I would have seen.

So here I was again in my life, wanting my mother, and realizing again the mother I had was not the mother I needed. Gran, who had such insight into people and the knack of delving right to the heart of a problem, was who I needed to talk to. I'd never had much call to talk to her about her problems, though. I wasn't eager to start with this.

I sighed and stood and stretched.

It was full dark out. I figured I could safely wash my dishes without running into anyone, so I headed to the Main House. The computer room was deserted. I skimmed my new messages. Some nice seller feedback from my online store. A cheerful note from Zach, with more hints about his upbeat mindset. It must be a woman—he wouldn't bother dropping hints about anything else. Also, the e-invite to Bernadette's birthday party, which credited me as a co-host. Sweet Zach, though Bernadette and Frank wouldn't be likely to credit me just because he did.

I surfed around for an online phone directory for Dublin. There were eighty-four M O'Connors, three Matts, and a Matthew. Hardly surprising, or helpful. For confirmation of Agnes' story, if that were what I needed, I'd have to talk to this purported Matthew O'Connor, or his daughters—my half-cousins —or get ahold of birth and marriage certificates somehow. I wondered which would be easier, logistically and emotionally.

When the door opened, I flinched.

"You're going out of your way to avoid me, aren't you?"

Caleb sounded lighthearted, but his eyes didn't join in on the smile as he sat in the revolving chair at the next CPU. "What's up?"

I gestured at the screen. "Trying to decide whether to break my Gran's heart or not."

"What?" He leaned in to read the monitor. "How exactly?"

"Never mind. Just had some strange news from the old country today, and I don't know what to do with it."

Sitting back, he asked, "Is that why you're not coming to see me?"

God he looked gorgeous. Khaki button-down with those black jeans, hair brushed back, just a hint of after-shave. I had a little private shiver wondering if I merited such careful grooming. Less glum now, I reached for his hand.

"I'm sorry. I should have come by to explain to you—it's just such a long story, and it's—it's family. Personal, you know? I'd tell you everything if it was just to do with me, but it's a bit much to be dragging you anywhere near this mess with my family."

He squeezed my fingers, then stroked the back of my hand with his thumb a while before he answered. "Don't you trust me?"

I squeezed back, and then took my hand back to shut down the computer. "Yes, I trust you. It's not that. It's just complex and I don't know where to go with it and I know you have other things on your mind besides my grandparents."

"Okay, don't get mad."

"I'm not mad."

He had walked almost to the door, but he turned and listened.

"Caleb. I'm not mad, relax. I'm confused and I'm stressed and," I sighed, "on top of that, if I come to you and talk about this, it's presuming."

I stopped and crossed the room to him. "It's presuming you want to be in the position of hearing me out and helping me with my confidences, and until I'm a little clearer about what's happening here I don't want to presume anything."

He stared down at me, started to say something but stopped, and took my hands again. "Ashlyn."

"Yeah?"

His lips barely moved but his eyes broke out in crinkles. Crow's feet my hiney, Gran, these were something else. "Can I presume something?"

I closed my eyes and nodded.

As he wrapped his arms around me, I looked up at him and smiled. A brief smile, because within seconds my mouth, and mind, were more happily engaged than they had been in quite some time.

CHAPTER 9

*R*eluctantly, I stepped back. "This—we should stop."

He looked pained.

"No, just—not in here. Let's go talk, okay?"

And he gave me his crinkly smile, which had gained the ability to send a blush up my core. I stroked his smooth cheek, and he kissed my palm, then held it as he led the way out of the Main House.

"Your place or mine?"

"Yours," I answered quickly, adding, "I seem to get a lot of unexpected visitors."

He nodded and we turned south along the little road, the crunching of crushed shells and a horny bullfrog the only sounds until we reached his cabin.

"Okay," I said, taking the glass of water and scootching a bit closer into his warmth as he sat down, "I think we have a lot to talk about."

"Can't we postpone a little bit?"

I had to seriously batten down my hatches as I shook my head. "I'd love to. But I think not. You could easily take advantage of my state of confusion tonight, and I think I'd like that very much," I ran my cheekbone along the soft cotton of his shirt, aware of the rise and fall of his chest within it, "very much indeed. But I need to deal with things before I go making them much more complex."

He laughed and swept my hair back from my forehead. "You are definitely off your rocker, Ashlyn May. And I don't believe you have the soul of an artist, either. A proper artist would let herself be swept away by passion."

"Now you're hitting below the belt. Be good," I stopped him from tugging at my belt loop, "and talk to me or say good night."

With an exaggerated sigh, Caleb heaved himself up to sit on the desk chair. "I'll be good."

It felt great just to look at him, watch his body move, meet his gaze without wondering what he was thinking about what I was thinking. The stranglehold the tension had on my forehead eased for the first time since lunch.

"So, what do you want to talk about?"

I suddenly felt self-conscious, and arranged myself so I was sitting with my legs folded under, tucking as deeply into the sofa cushions as I could go. The subtly different layout of his cabin from mine put me slightly off-kilter. I didn't own the space the way I did ValeSong, and had to blink a couple of times with the oddness of sitting on an identical sofa but speaking towards the chair now on my left.

I refocused on Caleb. "Okay, starting at the beginning of this long bizarre day, tell me what you were talking about in the kitchen this morning, about Wren."

He squeezed his eyes shut for a moment. "You would start with that."

"It's easier for me." I sipped the water. "Although it presents a whole range of new problems I'd rather not face."

"So she does like me, then?"

"We all like you, Caleb."

"No." Smiling. "She's—she's had ideas about being the one I kiss in the computer room, instead of you?"

"I didn't realize the computer room was integral to your plan. You can take this Zeke and Ned thing too far, you know."

"You're just glad I have problems and concerns of my own now. Answer the question."

I sighed. "I wasn't going to tell you this earlier today, but given the circumstances. Yes, Wren has been interested in you from day one, and has been asking Lizzy and I advice about what to do since, well, since day two."

"Is that why Zach wanted her along at dinner?"

I frowned my eyebrows at him. "Yeah, of course. What did you think?"

"I thought Zach was into her. I mean, she's his type, isn't she, and then he kept on asking her all kinds of stuff about her work and her life—he barely talked to either of us at all. I was sure he was into her."

I shook my head and sat forward. "No, he was trying to keep the focus on her so you'd realize how great she was and pursue her."

"God, and there I was, thinking—isn't this great, Zach'll come up here and pretend he wants to see Ash and me and he'll really want to be with Wren, and I'll have all this time with Ash practically all to myself."

I suppressed a grin. "You thought that?"

"Yeah. I couldn't believe my luck when we were made food partners, and then when I knew your brother...."

"It was like destiny, baby."

"Stop making fun of me."

"Don't sulk."

"I'm not sulking."

I moved to his lap and traced his lower lip. "What's this, then?"

His arms came around my back. "Why don't you come a little closer and find out?"

I did.

~

"YOU ARE JUST no good at talking," I accused, sitting up and moving a cushion away from him. We had made it back onto the sofa.

"Mmnh."

"I mean it."

"I know."

"I think you're only interested in one thing."

He sat straight and faced me. "Ash, no. That's not true." His eyes locked onto mine. "I swear. Of course I want you. So much. But that's not the only thing. It's not."

Running my fingertips through his wavy hair, I said, "I believe you."

"Do you? Honestly? Because I know I'm being a pig and you were so upset, you weren't even going to come over here, while I've just been wishing I could kiss you some more."

I bit my swollen lips. "I honestly do believe you. But maybe I should get going. I mean, I just want to kiss you, too, but I also need to sort all of this out, and I'm just taking any excuse to avoid it."

All he did was look at me, with a shadow passing across his eyes.

"You're not just any excuse, Caleb." It was such a relief to get my hands on him, to know whatever else was waiting in the wings, this connection between us deserved center stage.

He feathered kisses up my arm. "We've only known each other two weeks."

I sighed. "And we're only here six more weeks, and Wren is

here, too, and Lizzy is already mad at me because of you, and then there's all this stuff with Gran."

"Which I haven't even asked you about." He groaned. "I'm such a pig."

"No, you're not."

"You'll tell me if you think I am?"

"Oh, I'll tell you all right."

"Don't laugh at me," he warned.

"Man, you sulk easier than any guy I've ever met."

He sank back against the sofa and wrapped his arm around me. "I'll stop, I promise."

"Okay, then." I leaned into him. "Going back to Wren."

"You're relentless."

"You'll live." I kissed his knuckles. "So, have the two of you talked about it at all?"

He shook his head. "I just, I don't know, picked up a vibe?"

"Yeah."

"So?" He raised his eyebrows. I traced them with my thumbs.

"I don't know. It's not much good telling her I didn't want for this to happen."

"You didn't?"

"Hey, relax. I do. I want it—this—whatever. You know what I'm saying. I'm glad."

"But it hadn't been your intention?"

I dismissed that first twitch of interest before I knew any dynamics, that first day. "No—she told me from the start she wanted you, and I wasn't looking to hook up with anyone, so I never thought about it. Not until recently, anyway."

"Every morning when I knocked on your door I had to stop myself from going in to wake you with a kiss."

I kissed him then, to make up for it. And then again, for good measure.

"Do you think she'll be angry at you? Or me?"

"Not at you. Hurt. Maybe, I don't know, pissed off. At me,

she'll be angry." I sighed. "I'll have to talk to her before Lizzy spills it."

"She wouldn't, would she?"

"She's a wretched gossip."

"True." She loved to regale us with slanderous tales about Theo's visits to Angelica's cabin. "Does she know, then? What could she know?"

"She noticed a few things. She doesn't know this."

"So, if we just, I don't know—keep a low profile?"

I nodded. "At least until I talk to Wren." I looked at him. "Why weren't you interested in her, anyway? I mean, she's gorgeous and all."

"You're fishing."

"No. Really."

He shrugged. "I don't know. I did think about it, I mean, once I'd kind of noticed her looking at me and all."

"And?"

He shrugged again. "I guess, I just thought she was a little—a little too wild? Too uneven, in a way."

I rubbed my brow. "I'm not sure I get what you mean."

"It could just be my perception. She laughs erratically, then goes quiet. Her pendulum's off kilter. It's not like she's unbalanced, it's just you're so, you know, balanced."

The last thing I felt was balanced. But it didn't matter. The thing was, frankly, I wanted to make sure he wasn't at all interested in Wren, so I wouldn't feel guilty at having been chosen just from being in the right place at the wrong time. Of course, odds were he wouldn't admit to wavering between us, but I decided to take him at face anyway.

"So. What else did you want to tell me this morning?"

Shaking his head, he said, "That was it."

"You said it was complicated."

"Well, it was. Explaining it all would have been. Now I don't have to try to find out about her without telling you why. You know why." He squeezed my shoulders. "But we can talk about all this later. Tell me what happened today?"

"I don't know. It's—it's hard to explain."

"Come on, Ash, give me a shot. I'm perceptive."

"I know. I'm not doubting you. But you're not family and it's extremely personal and I don't think I can even talk to Zach about it, so how could I talk to you?"

"Why not Zach?" He knew by now I told Zach pretty much everything.

"Because," I sighed, "he'll want me to talk to Bernadette and Frank first, instead of Gran. And Bernadette won't hear anything against Pappa, any more than she would against Zach."

"Okay," he sat up. "So why do you have to tell any of them?"

"Because I do."

"You know," Caleb said, "this would be a lot easier to discuss if you told me what it was."

I rotated his wrist so I could read the time. Ten to ten. My eyes were burning dry and tired, but the tips of my fingers drew fire out of his forearm and shot it up my veins. "Okay." I stood and twisted my spine until it popped. Caleb winced. "I'm just going to be blunt. I've had a long day. I've been looking forward all week to sleeping in tomorrow. And I like you, but there's some things about you and me we still need to talk about, especially so I can face Wren."

Caleb arched one eyebrow. "Such as?"

I could feel my blush, but gulped down nerves and continued. "Things. Things like, what are your intentions. Things like, are you just hoping to sleep with me for the next month and a half and then move on back to whatever awaits you in California. Things like, are we going to make whatever this is clear to the rest of them, or sneak around and try to cover like Theo and Angelica did at first."

"They weren't any good at it."

"Be that as it may be. What concerns me is, if I stay here

talking to you about Gran and all, late into the night, I'm going to be too tired to go home, and you're going to wake up early as usual and disturb me. Besides which, you may be the most gorgeous guy here but that doesn't mean I'm just going to go and hop into the sack with you instantly."

He tilted his head. "You are a chaste and good woman, Ash."

"No, I'm not. I'd love to sleep with you. I'm practically aching to sleep with you."

"Not helping," he groaned.

"Well, it's the truth. I said I'd be honest with you."

"I know." His eyes softened as he regarded me. "I guess there's a couple of other things I want to talk to you about, too. Ask you about, I mean."

"We will."

"Good. Can I proposition you, for tonight?"

"Haven't you been listening?" I felt like such a hard-ass. Or a tease. Something not appropriately demure and feminine, anyway.

"I have, darling. That's the point."

I smiled. "What is it, then?"

"No hard feelings if you don't like my idea."

I nodded.

"Okay. Can I grab a change of clothes and accompany you to ValeSong, where we can lay like chaste spoons in the dark and I will listen to you talk until you fall asleep. And in the morning I will slip out without waking you, and go to breakfast alone," he pouted comically, "and when you are ready for company you can come by and I'll make you coffee and we can talk in the light of day."

The man had me almost in tears. He was so sincere and so sweet—and he may have been a photographer but he painted a beautiful picture. I decided it was a fair compromise between heart and mind, and we set off.

It was a warm, breezy night and I cracked open the window—

not much of a habit in Texas where the skeeters take any chance they get and the heat is positively anthropomorphic. But the wire screen was tight against the sill and the air under the trees carried the river mist past my rooms. The katydids held a little concert, with only the occasional babble of water as an accompaniment.

I carried my flannel pajamas into the bathroom to change after Caleb washed up. I decided my face was entirely too red as I scrubbed at it, but it was ignoring my instructions to fade away. My heart, for all the fluttering it was doing, seemed to be over-throwing my brain. I took a deep breath and went back into my room.

Caleb was in bed. He grinned up at me—not looking nearly as shy as I felt—and complimented my red plaid before lifting the covers so I could slip under them. He smelled of my face soap, and he felt warm and gentle. Lying next to him was a delightful agony.

"Okay," he said, reaching to turn off the lamp. "Talk to me."

"Mmmnh." I stroked his face. "You aren't helping my motivation any, being this close."

"Come on." He wrapped one arm around my waist and put the other hand on my shoulder and I let him pivot my body so my back was to him. He used one hand to stroke my hair smooth on the pillow, but left the other resting on my stomach, which I forced myself not to clench tight. Let him feel from the start how soft it was, dammit. I felt his lips graze the back of my neck and his head rest on the pillow. "Now, pretend I'm not here, and talk. Tell me what happened today."

I took a long breath. I couldn't think where to begin, so I linked my fingers with his and just started talking. I told him what Dub and Agnes had said, and about Bernadette and Gran and I, and Pappa with his children, and Gran after Pappa died. When I cried, which I did silently so I could pretend Caleb didn't realize, I cried not just for Gran and my confusion, but also for the calming joy of Caleb's squeezing my hand just when I needed him to, and gently bending his head to nuzzle my shoulder when I was tired and unwilling to go on.

Our kisses had all been electric, far more startling and vibrant than first kisses I'd known in the past. I was still in a bit of shock about it all. But his attentiveness and gentleness as we lay there demonstrated everything that was more than carnal between us. I was with a man who cared about me, who was listening to me, who wanted little more at that moment other than to help me. He didn't ask me much, just let me talk. As I wrapped up my story of the day, I descended into mumblings and long pauses. My body sank into the mattress and back against Caleb's broad chest.

I felt relaxed. It wasn't what I'd expected.

At some point, I fell asleep. I didn't realize it until hours later when I started to roll over and came up against the wall of Caleb's body. Holding my breath, I eased around until I was lying on my back, and studied his face in what moonlight there was. At least he didn't drool in his sleep or snore, both of which had been afflictions of a previous boyfriend.

Boyfriend. Was that the right word? How could it be, when we lived in different states and were only together now because of the rarefied atmosphere of this retreat?

Curious, I snaked my hand down the sheet and touched his thigh. He was wearing a pair of drawstring shorts, blue if memory served. His head rolled towards me and I slid my hand back to my waist. His hand found it there and squeezed it as he smiled, eyes still closed. Again my cheeks flamed a bit, but he didn't move, and soon we'd both fallen back to sleep.

CHAPTER 10

As promised, Caleb stole out in the morning without my realizing it. At one point, I woke up enough to stretch, realize he was gone, and snuggle myself more comfortably into bed, but my eyes stayed glued shut. It was well after ten on that annoying bedside clock when I finally stretched and yawned. The first thing I saw was a tray on my dresser, holding a muffin and a glass of orange juice bracketed by sprigs of rhododendron.

First, I started the bath, overloading on the bath salts. Everything lavender-derived I could find went under the rush of hot water. Then as the coffee brewed, I did some stretches and crunches—not enough to sweat, just enough to limber up my muscles. Putting the coffee on the windowsill, I slipped off the robe.

By most people's standards, it was warm out. To my Texan toes, it was still sock weather. My feet were so icy I couldn't at first register the heat of the water. Dipping them in gave me a rush of relief at escaping the cold. Seconds later, I had to yank my scaled feet out of the bath.

For a moment, I perched naked on the rim of the tub. Then I

stretched my feet across to turn off the faucets with my toes. The silence after the rush of water was an absence, and I granted that much more credence to Theo's white noise theories. I sank under the bubbles, held my breath until I felt tense, then blew out as I lifted my head and settled back, sweeping my plastered hair behind my ears.

Sunday. My morning of rest. After lunch was my studio. I could barely credit the idea of the six or seven of them traipsing in and judging the links of *Chains*, the pictograms of Gran's life as a daughter, a wife, a mother, a soul dedicated to others. I just lay there in the steam, feeling hollowed out by the tears and the impossibility of this deliberate stripping naked of my love.

And worse, I still had to factor in talking to the girls. About Caleb. Caleb, who I wanted to go see immediately, but only because he felt like a sanctuary to run towards. It wouldn't accomplish a thing. I should get up and go talk to Lizzy, though I didn't want to, and I definitely didn't want to talk to Wren.

I flexed my shoulders and wet the loofah, pouring body wash into its pores. My toes and nipples and probably cheeks were red from the heat. And from thoughts of Caleb. I let some water out and scrubbed away and turned on the cold full force to feel it gradually taking over the temperature of the bath before I rinsed out the shampoo and emerged.

Slipping into a t-shirt, I clipped my damp hair up in the broad unattractive pink clips that were the only things I could find to keep it out of my way as I hunched over my work. The studio, at least, was warm enough for me to wear shorts and sit cross-legged in the rolling chair. I had re-hung *Chains of Love*, and swiveled my chair around to face it.

Artistically, I was satisfied. Even pleased, proud. The yellows and greens were mood lifting, if I'd been in the mood to let them, and there was a fine sense of balance. I hadn't used a middle layer on this one, except for a tight roll of batting as a frame, which helped give it shape so the chains lay properly across the piece. I could handle their comments about it as art.

Emotionally, I was shaky. There seemed suddenly to be an irony in the way the links between Gran and Pappa were broken, and seeing this graphic representation of how central he was to her world, I had to wonder how strong those links had been in the first place. Had she known? Had she felt it, his deception? Was he innocent, or a hypocrite? Now both Caleb and Lizzy knew this unexpected bit of my personal history, so how would their knowledge inform their reaction to the piece?

I growled, a primal growl, and started to move. My sock-clad feet slid pleasantly across the wood floor as I padded into the bedroom to read the time. Noon. Wren would be starting lunch prep. Probably alone, and grumpy because Rafael was getting away with another absence. Maybe Lizzy was with her. I didn't want to be ambushed.

I tied up my Keds and went north to Lizzy's cabin. She wasn't there.

The shortest path to Caleb's was past the Main House, but there was no way I was going there. I took off through the cypress and juniper until I hit the stream, found the shallow part where I could cross a series of well-placed boulders, and skirted the other side of the doe's clearing until I reached the little path to his door. The day had turned muggy and the bands of sweat across my waistline and under my breasts annoyed me. It made me imagine my face was red, and imagining it, heat fired my cheeks.

I knew he'd been expecting me earlier. He wouldn't think I'd spend a couple of hours alone in the morning when we could have been talking and kissing. However, I had my reasons, not all of which were related to safeguarding my actual work time while at the retreat. Most were, but not all.

I didn't know whether or not I was starting a new relationship here, but if I was, it certainly wasn't going to begin with his assuming his time with me was more important to me than my time with myself. I'd made that mistake before, and it never ceased to amaze me how readily men will forget there is anything more vital to me than them. I'd vowed after college I was going to be far more 'masculine' in my future relationships, if by 'masculine' I can mean 'selfish' and 'presumptuous.' Caleb, I knew, would still be there after I'd gotten my studio ready, and if it offended his ego when I put my work first, we were definitely not going to get much further than FireWind together.

Not that I was assuming he'd even want to stay with me, or that we could work out a way for it to happen.

But just in case.

Turned out Caleb had gone on a photo shoot down the river after eating breakfast and sneaking in my muffin tray, and had only been waiting for less than an hour. Which annoyed me to no end, of course—he had invited me for coffee, and should have found things to do around his cabin to keep him busy until I showed up. What typical male behavior. So I told him I'd gotten so absorbed I'd lost track of time, gave him a brief kiss on the cheek, and asked how he'd slept.

"Peacefully," he smiled, holding my hand. "But I have to tell you, at breakfast, Lizzy gave me this—well, this Look—and asked, 'does anyone know where Ashlyn is?' and I'm pretty damn sure I blushed. I know I looked away too fast. Wren didn't seem to notice. She was busy giving the dirty dishes to Rafael. All of them."

"Rafael showed?"

"Under duress—Margie went out there at seven, and when he wouldn't answer her knock, she yelled she was going to count to five and then go in, and on 'four' he opened the door and asked her what the hell she was doing. Wren said Margie was still furious when they came back up, and Margie told Rafael he was doing half the prep and serving and all the clean up for both meals all week."

"Whoa."

"Yeah. Wren was in a good mood when he went to the sink and

she sat with another cup of coffee. She used a new mug, too, instead of the one she had earlier."

"Oh, vindictive."

"That's our Wren."

"Which is exactly what I'm afraid of."

Caleb stroked my cheek with two fingers, then pulled me in for one of his all-encompassing hugs. "I know. I know. Tell me what we should do. You haven't seen anyone yet, have you?"

I shook my head. "No, Lizzy's not home now. And I think we should tell Wren first, anyway." I pulled him down onto the sofa next to me. "If only I knew exactly what to tell her."

"Mmm." He tasted pepperminty. "That's easy. Say I swept you off your feet, you resisted every step of the way, but I was just too charming for you."

"I don't know if this situation calls for such strict adherence to the truth."

He raised his eyebrows. "I wasn't aware it was that true."

"Well, it depends on your perspective."

"Okay, I'll buy that."

I sat up and hugged my upper arms. "Yeah, but it's not a question of what you'll buy. I'm not going to lie to her or anything, but I don't know how to present this without pissing her off and screwing our friendship."

"Wouldn't it be easier if I told her?"

"No. I don't think so; I think it would make her feel almost laughed at, to have you say we're together or whatever without her putting her cards on the table to you first. I wouldn't mind if you talk to Lizzy? You could deal with her while I talk to Wren."

"Okay, fair enough." He checked his watch. "Time to go eat. Are we going to just not—well, not kiss again until after these summits?"

I nodded. "Guess so, sadly enough. As soon as Wren and I are done, though, we can make up for it?"

He leaned close enough for me to smell the peppermint. "Can't we start to make up for it now?"

I licked my lower lip just before his mouth touched mine.

~

I ATE QUICKLY and left the others munching their fruit, berating myself all way to my studio—*snap out of it, Ash, they say what they say, they like what they like. Life goes on.* The usual combination of pep talk and self-loathing.

I picked a few loose threads off *Chains* and myself, and directed a light at the ceiling above it to lend a little more brightness.

They came. They looked. I talked.

It was fine. No big deal. Wren told me she could tell how strong my love for my subject was, and seeing the quilt, she loved Gran, too. Theo praised my use of color and texture; we talked a little about incorporating texture like that into a canvas and things he'd experimented with in his work. Lizzy asked if she could touch it, and ran her fingers over the bead work, while Angelica told me about an article she'd read on gallery shows for the blind, where the artists created tactically as well as visually aesthetic work for those who could only experience art they could touch. Caleb smiled when he asked if I wanted his honest opinion. I nodded.

"It's gorgeous, it really is. And you can tell how skilled you are at sewing and all; you don't even see the stitching except where it makes an impact, like this." He pointed to the breaking chain of Berneen and Albert drowning.

"But?"

"No 'but', just what we've already said about universal appeal and all. You make stunning art, Ashlyn, but I don't know if a piece like this will ever make you a gallery headliner."

"She already said this piece is meant to be a personal one, a gift to her grandmother," pointed out Wren, defensively.

"I know, but it's the only one of hers I can base my assessment on. If she makes something else less personal, I'll revise my opinion. I'm just saying, based on this one thing, I see this one drawback."

Wren opened her mouth but closed it when I spoke.

"No, it's fine. It's a valid enough point, in its way. But of course every museum in the world has its share of very personal art. What are portraits, generally, other than a form of homage?"

"So this is a portrait of your grandmother?" Caleb asked.

"Yes. A portrait and a story about her, and a tribute."

"I'd buy it," Lizzy said. "I see a lot more to it than you do, Caleb. And I like how it's personal, I like being let in on this life in this way."

"It's not that I don't like it," he protested.

"Okay, relax, I'm not offended, I know what you both, all, are saying. And thanks, all of you." I grinned at the ring of my fellow artists. "I'm glad we did this."

Truth, or being polite? Some of each, I thought, as they walked away in ones and twos. I needed to have someone else look at it, and to see them seeing it for the first time, but not all of the conversation was useful. Nevertheless, I jotted down their comments to look at in the morning.

In a week Zach was picking me up and taking me to Houston for Bernadette's birthday dinner, and I was taking *Chains* with me. Margie didn't approve of my leaving FireWind overnight, but she couldn't stop me, and Bernadette was unforgiving about attendance for her milestones.

I'd quilted for Bernadette, too. What she called a 'real' quilt, not for hanging but for warmth. No matter how often I spread it across various surfaces in my cabin, I couldn't guess if Bernadette would love it, be upset by it, or, simply, not be touched. It burned with campfire colors, shadows in the upper left banished by the flames, and a protective hollow of light in the lower right, behind which I would affix my sewn signature.

The quilt had been done for days, but I was having trouble getting around to sewing the title patch onto the back. Putting my name to it, in offering.

I smoothed microscopic wrinkles out of the patch, which I'd already ironed and hemmed and ironed again. Crimson thread gleamed against a bark-brown calico, spelling out 'Mama Bear, for Bernadette's 60th, with love from Ashlyn.' All I had to do was baste it to the backer, but every time I picked it up, I remembered the last time—the only time I could remember—I camped with my family.

I was maybe nine. They hadn't taken me since I was tiny—papoose board tiny—other than once when I was four and cried the whole time. After that, I went back to spending family camping weekends at Pappa and Gran's. This trip, Frank argued I'd reached the age of reason, and corralled me into the spelunking trip. Bernadette beamed, describing the magic of the caves, trying to fire me up. So I rolled up Zach's old sleeping bag and went with.

Can we say cold, and damp, and dangerous? I slipped on the uneven path every ten feet, while Zach laughed and Frank told me to buck up and walk confident so I wouldn't fall. Bernadette was in front, with the flashlight. Every few minutes she'd pull our only light source away from its vital job of giving me some glimpse of the trek ahead, to skitter rapidly over some slimy limestone walls and the occasional glint of mica or something. I kept agreeing when she asked, "Isn't it just amazing, Ashlyn?"

Later at camp, as we admired the brilliance of Zach's A-frame fire building, I said I liked the stalagmites and Frank tousled my head and told me, no, there were only stalactites in that cavern, and Bernadette reprimanded Zach for laughing at me before I could get glum about her favoritism. I suppose she thought it was a good idea to distract us with the scary stories, like it would be fun or something.

She was wrong.

We sat there, the back half of me cold from the dark air, eyes stinging from smoke that wouldn't stay away, and Bernadette leaning into the fire's glow for peak eeriness.

She told us one about a soul who'd died in an industrial accident, leaving it's armless body to haunt the earth. Unable to do much damage without biceps, it had affixed an axe to one shoulder and a machete to the other, and roamed the woods, seeking anyone who resembled the foreman who'd failed to save it, and killing them. Creepy, but even my young heart didn't race much.

Then, as the fire crackled and Frank hummed a haunting tune under his breath, she lowered her voice until we strained to hear. "That, dear children, was just a story, a fiction. You suspected, of course. But what I'm going to tell you now, I can swear to you, as your mother, is true." She glanced between us, but my eyes never left her face. "We know most of the wildlife has left these woods, thanks to the encroachment of man. But there are places, pockets of the forest so deep and dark no city dweller dares to enter, where the wild creatures still reign over this land. Even in the very caves we visited today, through tunnels that may have looked to you like depressions in the rock, or the shadow cast by a stalactite," Zach chortled but quieted quickly, "even there, the wild creatures live. I'm sure they watched us today, creeping stealthily to the edges of their hiding places, their eyes glowing in the dark but looking to us like just another flash of quartz. Noting our intrusion into their world."

She grew silent for a moment, and I shifted a couple of inches closer to the smoky flames.

"One creature, in this ferocious kingdom, is revered above all of the others. Her thirst for human blood is legendary, to man and beast alike. For though urban people like us are scared to venture past these well-marked trails, enough brave, or foolish, hikers have been through the dark woods, and survived to share the details about her wrath."

Frank's tune dropped an octave, and the metronome of his swaying accelerated.

"Much of the time her life is much like that of any other bear—oh, yes, she is an ursine foe, though she is twice as big and ten times as strong as the grizzlies living here a hundred years ago—but there are nights when the rage in her awakens, and her keen nose seeks out any human within eighty miles. And what, you ask, awakens her rage?" Frank abruptly stopped moving, then looked past me into the night. Bernadette leaned in closer. "Maybe you've guessed. It's people doing exactly what we are now. Driving into her forest, burning the wood of her trees, desecrating the land where she and her fellow wild creatures are trying to live and survive. And when she scents these intruders, nothing will satisfy her except their complete and utter elimination!"

An opportune log fell, snapping with a jolt we all felt. Frank howled like a rabid wolf, I screamed, and kept on screaming, while Zach convulsed with laughter.

Bernadette just looked at us and shook her head slowly, smiling.

It wasn't long before I was in tears, and though Frank patted at my back and said, "Oh, Ashlyn, you know it was just a story," and Bernadette gave me a little hug but growled her way into a laugh in the middle of it. I couldn't stop. I curled up with my tears all night, balling myself tighter and tighter with each rustle and whistle from the wide-open world around me. It was the last time I ever agreed to go camping, with them or anyone.

It's not, as Frank and Bernadette assume, the dirtiness or the discomfort or the bugs stopping me. I don't mind the woods at all, for a day hike. As dusk falls, I can't escape that feeling, the one of being a stranger in a land with hostile hosts, and not having a friendly soul to help you along.

Even worse: it's having the soul you thought was your protector turn to you at your most crucially exposed, revealing her utter triumph and delight at your vulnerability.

A vulnerability against which no tent or lamp or Swiss army knife can offer protection.

I placed the *Mama Bear* patch next to my machine. It was a double-tipped needle of a gift: the beauty and strength from hours of my work, all to deliver my fantasy about being protected by a mom I'd dreamed up out of whole cloth.

*B*efore breakfast on Monday, before coffee could kickstart synapses I was better off leaving uncon-nected, I slipstitched the *Mama Bear* patch to the back of Bernadette's quilt. It was only post-caffeine that I noticed I'd put the title behind the menacing shadows of the upper right, instead of the safe haven of the lower left.

Well, I wasn't going to change it.

I took the time to be precise with my corners as I folded away both *Mama Bear* and *Chains of Love*, clearing my workspace in anticipation of new energies coming in to accompany my new projects. I didn't have the emotional or intellectual vigor left for any of the pieces I'd conceived of earlier at FireWind, so I decided to make something lighthearted. The dark sketches from before were still on the drafting table, but I had a fresh pad ready to go.

Lighthearted. Light of heart. A heart seeking light. Down the left-hand side of the paper, I listed my ex-boyfriends, names sepa-rated by a couple of inches.

There weren't many. I'd dated infrequently in high school, not that I wasn't asked out, thank you very much. I just never did find anyone in Spring I wanted to hang out with, and I'd been stung by the way my best friend had deserted me for the love of her teenage life. It made the whole idea of steady boyfriends less than charming. She did come back to me when they were picking their wedding party, and bonding over bridesmaid dress fabrics and patterns repaired our friendship. But back in school it had colored my opinion on boyfriends.

So there they were: Carlos, Daryl, Shawn, Eric, Jason, and Wig. What the heck was Wig's real name? Something less bizarre but less apt: Eugene. Right. Anyway. Six men, a good third of my life, and what did I carry away from them? Carlos was the one who drooled and snored. I sketched a generic male head, prone, with spittle collecting at his chin. Then I flipped over to a new page and drafted a three by three grid, filled in the center section with the logo, 'The Trouble With Men', and put Carlos's head in the top left square. Next went Daryl with a bottle of superglue trying to attach me to his side, then Shawn holding my hand but leering at a group of women. At the bottom went Wig standing on his head and juggling with his feet—which he never perfected but persisted in trying—then Eric with suitcase in hand and globes in his eyes, and finally dear Jason with me on a pedestal and shrines all around.

I erased myself and drew me back in as an outline, transparent. Then I added myself awake and staring into the night next to Carlos, and leaning against the wall rolling my eyes at Wig, and half-waving goodbye to Eric as he headed for the exit sign I sketched into the top corner of his square.

Breathing deeply, I stood. After a couple of minutes pacing and glancing out into the empty clearing, I went back to the sketchpad.

I smiled; I still liked it. I would play with the proportions, make the center section shorter, play with the letter style a bit—I was thinking of fashioning them like cut-outs from newspapers, *a la* ransom notes, though I hadn't really delved into why. At any rate, I liked it.

EVERYONE WAS relaxed and chatty at lunch. Wren didn't notice we came in together—Lizzy did but Caleb sat on one side of her and I on the other and the only thing she did was scooch her chair forward so we would have to lean around her awkwardly if we were going to make eye contact. So we didn't, which seemed to please her.

Angelica showed up without Theo. When Wren asked if he was coming to lunch, she tossed her head and said, "Oh how should I know? I'm not his damn keeper." When we were done with our sandwiches and headed to Theo's cabin for the showing, Brandon asked Angelica if she was coming along—she was headed out into the hall instead of towards the porch—and I learned what it meant when someone was said to 'bite your head off.'

"No, I have to go order dinner since his Divinity is busy preparing the unveiling of his supposed masterpiece."

To his credit, Brandon just nodded and said, "Right, see you later."

Lizzy, Caleb, Wren, and I headed out. "What the hell was that all about?" Wren muttered as we descended the porch steps.

"Beats me," Lizzy replied. "Last night she was giggling and telling him she wanted to worship at his altar."

"Well, something obviously went wrong in the temple of love," Caleb shrugged.

"I think it's proof these impetuous retreat romances never work," Lizzy said, pointedly turning to look back at me.

"I think," Caleb countered mildly, "it depends on the people."

WE SOON EXPOSED the root of her problem. Theo's studio was cleared of everything but one covered canvas on his easel—the desk was bare, the sinks empty, the brushes all cleaned and put away. He couldn't stop pacing as we formed an arc around the painting.

"Okay, you know I've talked about the spirit of my work, and how I always just channel the divine inspiration I'm sent, right?" We nodded but he barely glanced at us. "So that's what I do. I'm, well, I'm like a conduit, that's the best way I can explain it. I never fully understood where the ideas come from, you know? I just take up my brush or my pens or whatever and suddenly, it's just, well, There."

He stopped briefly and scanned us, silently counting, one two three four five—Rafael was still doing the dishes or just plain not coming—and again mouthed 'five' before continuing. "So I've had people tell me I should plan things out more, should think about the overall intent or statement of my art, should somehow consider more, or be more considerate, or something. But it's not like that. It just is the way it is, I can't change it and still be an artist. I don't control it or I would destroy it. Do you understand?"

Again we nodded; this time he saw us. "You do. Good. It's not something I can argue. It just is. I'm not in charge of what I produce; you can try and argue that I am, but you'd be wrong. Plainly wrong. That's all there is to it. So. You said you understand that. You can't argue it. No going back once I unveil, right?" A few shaken heads convinced him. "Right. Okay, then. Here we go." He drew a deep breath and pulled off the covering sheet.

Frankly, I was moved. It was beautiful. The colors, the balance, the chiaroscuro, the skill of the brush—they all worked in such harmony. "Wow," I said, and Wren added, "Yeah. Wow."

Theo grinned like a kid with a new scooter. "Good wow, right? Thanks, great. Its title is *Angel by Starlight*. Tell me what's good. And bad. Just be true to yourselves, to what you are inspired to say."

I looked at Wren and Lizzy and they looked back at me and we all knew that we each knew what had pissed off Angelica Starlight. The painting—it was gorgeous. But it was a nude, for starters, which are a bit tricky to create only a week or two into a relationship. The composition was of a naked woman sleeping facedown on a double bed. She was relaxed, peaceful. Silver wings sprouted from her shoulder blades, folded in rest and coming to a point just at her tailbone. Beside her, the window was open to the night sky—a few treetops and about half of Orion were gazing down on her. The light in the painting radiated from the stars and her wings, so the far corners of the room were almost pitch black but the intricate weave of the bedspread and the stones of her earring were finely detailed.

If I were Theo's lover and had been for weeks or months or years, and he'd told me my beauty and care were this inspirational, I would have been flattered. I would have been dancing with the moon and performing sexual treats he'd only dreamed of. But if I were Theo's lover and had only known him a couple of weeks and he'd told me I had nothing to do with his creation of something so deeply stunning, that my relationship with him was divorced from his relationship with his art, my so-obvious presence in his canvas nothing more than coincidence, I'd have railed. I'd have argued. Maybe it was true with other paintings, maybe it was conceivable that his technique or his choice of layout was ethereal, but the use of my body, my name being transformed to idea, was a tribute to me. I'd have insisted that at the least it was an idea he'd grown himself, thanks to my presence.

And when he'd denied it, sworn I wasn't involved, put my kisses and my jokes and my confidences and my name and my spine firmly into a different realm, I'd have been furious. Utterly, unutterably furious.

But this wasn't relationship school; we were there to talk about the art. The girls, I noticed, were as careful as I about their comments—nothing to do with subject or meaning, only style and color and view. Brandon wasn't as cautious and got us subjected to another inspirational rant when he asked about the pose and referred to her as 'Angelica.'

Tense as the whole thing was, I didn't want to leave. I didn't know how to draw Wren aside, engage her in friendly chat, get her alone, and confess. It made my brain hurt. It made me wriggle my toes in my tennies. It made me want to lean against Caleb for fortitude.

So I took it as a happy little miracle in my life when we left Theo's studio, I turned to Wren, and Lizzy said, "Let's get going while the sun's still out. I need a diversion."

"Go where?" Caleb asked after shooting me a quick glance.

"Lizzy's going to teach me to row down on Hester's lake. Did you know she was on a crew team in university?"

"It was just a society," Lizzy amended. "They wouldn't start a woman's team because we didn't have enough competition. Jerks."

"Wow," I said. "Well, have fun. I guess I'll go check on Angelica, she could probably use some company."

"Yeah. Poor thing. Tell her I think Theo's full of shit, okay?" I nodded and Lizzy took Wren's arm to pull her down the path to the lake.

I sighed as they went. "Can't say I'm not glad, but what're they up to? Or, what's she up to, more like?"

"I don't know. Are you really going to see Angelica?"

I winked at him. "In a minute. Got a little detour to make along the way."

He grinned. "Good."

I WAS FINDING Caleb terribly easy to talk to. He was funny, too, in this fetchingly quiet way—understated, but right on cue. I had to explain a bit of the reason Angelica was mad at Theo—he thought it was embarrassment over the nudity—but once I pointed out the obvious, he caught the nuances right away. Throw in the hot body, and the emotions in his eyes, and the timing of his touches, and the kindness and even vulnerability I could read into his history, and I was finding myself hooked. More than hooked. Verging on ensnared.

But we hadn't talked past the next month. We hadn't even talked much past the next couple of days. As we lay on his bed chatting, kissing, copping feels in a delicate, delicate way, I decided it didn't matter. Not really.

I wanted it to matter to him; I wanted him to fall deeply in love with me and be my soulmate and support my work and help me follow my dreams and do all the vacuuming for the rest of our lives, but I decided to proceed as if it didn't matter. I would follow my impulses and enjoy the moments and if it came down to us never seeing each other after May rolled around, I'd be satisfied I hadn't denied myself pleasure on questionably moral grounds. So I sat up and planted a big ol' smooch on his cheek.

"Here's the plan, Caleb Kendall. I'm going to talk to Angelica, then if there's time I'm going to work some more, and I'll see you at dinner. Before you go eat, stash some clothes for tomorrow in my room, and we'll forget about talking to anyone tonight and finish off that bottle of wine instead. Deal?"

"Oh, most definitely."

"Great." The next smooch was a bit deeper and awakened some sort of gravitational pull between our pelvises. But I left it at that and hit the woods again.

Angelica and I hadn't spent much time together, but she'd always seemed nice, in her macabre way, and to be frank I figured I could use an ally of sorts if I was about to alienate Lizzy and Wren on Caleb's behalf. I hoped that wasn't going to happen, but if it did, I didn't want to be dependent on him as my only friend at Fire-Wind. And even without that, and although this was a retreat not relationship school, I couldn't just let her sit there knowing we'd all seen it and not tell her what the consensus on Theo was.

She was in her studio, drawing with heavy black lines. I almost laughed at the coincidence. Our mediums and artistic goals were yards apart, but turbulent emotion brought the angry sketcher out in us both. Instead, as she rubbed graphite off her fingertips and looked warily at me, I said, "I can't believe what an idiot he is—we all agree. What's all this crap about conduits?"

"You all agree?"

"Well, Lizzy and Wren and Caleb and I all agree you're obviously the inspiration, and he's deluding himself to think otherwise."

"Not Brandon or Rafael?"

"Rafael wasn't there. I didn't talk to Brandon about it but he did talk about the painting as if you were the subject and Theo went off on him."

"What an asshole! Poor Brandon."

I just nodded—I figured it was Brandon's stupid mistake. But Angelica had perked up, and she grinned at me. "So what else did they say?"

"I don't know, it was a great painting and all, very stunning, all of that." I wouldn't disparage the painting—it was marvelous—but she didn't want to hear it. "But he also gave us this huge lecture about cosmic inspiration and divine intervention and I don't know what-all kind of crap."

"Basically saying I'm not in the picture?"

I nodded. "Basically."

"Bastard."

"May lightening strike him down on a sunny day," I said, regarding Angelica. She was starting to vibrate with anger again, but I sensed a more self-righteous rage. It definitely made me a bit antsy. "Are you going to be okay with making dinner?"

She growled. "After this morning with Margie I don't see a lot of options."

"Maybe if y'all don't work something out you can trade partners."

"Will you let me have Caleb?"

I laughed. "Not a chance, sorry."

"Didn't think so. You lucked out getting paired with him, you know."

"I know." She seemed calm again. "I kinda need to get back to work. Are you okay?"

"Yeah, I'm fine. Thanks for coming by with the report; I'm glad I'm not deluding myself by refusing to see things his way."

"You're not, not by a long shot." I stood. "Let me know if you need something."

"Cool." She opened the door for me but hesitated, not knowing, I think, whether to make some gesture like an appreciative hug. I bobbed in with a quick squeeze, which she returned, saying, "See you at dinner," before heading back inside.

THERE WASN'T ACTUALLY much time before we had to go eat, but I flipped to a new page and started to redraft the nine-patch of men. *Nine Patchy Men*—I liked it. I liked it enough that I nixed the central logo and came up with three more guys from my past to add in: Byron, the high school flirtation who'd lost me by spending all of our study date time together mansplaining Duke's final four match against Kentucky; Doug, who'd agreed to our blind date because he was still keeping his orientation from his extended family, and could I please not tell his cousin who worked with me; and the one who really made me mad. The one who I didn't like to think about, much less turn into art—X, who fought with me about ordering extra fried rice, because he was paying and was low on cash, and he hit me. Hard. Right in front of the damn waiter and everyone, and kept yelling damn bitch as they—they, the random strangers whose faces I can't recall— stepped between us to stop him hitting again and maneuvered him outside while I took cover in the kitchen.

Luckily, Zach was in town for Christmas and could come get me. I kept telling him other women had it worse—way worse—and the last thing I needed after X was to fight with Zach and his infuriating macho 'I'll beat the crap out of him' instincts. But truth to tell, Zach's instincts were no where near as infuriating, or as frightening, as what X did to me. And horrid as the process was at the time, I'm glad now he hustled me to the police station to file a report, on the off chance it would help stop X from hurting someone else.

And like that, my lighthearted vent session about the general inadequacies of men had turned itself into a statement.

I hated it when that happened.

My art has plenty to say about darker subjects. I'd entered three pieces from my *Sheltering Arms* series in a juried exhibition about reframing domesticity, and was hoping to hear they'd been accepted soon; those quilts had grown from a footnote about a mid-1800s quilting club whose members helped battered women find advocates. I'd enjoyed delving into the idea of turning a woman's craft into a network for comfort and protection from male violence.

In general, I strive to stretch my work beyond entertainment and tradition—to have meaning, to make a strong statement, is for me what separates my true art from my commissions for wedding and baby quilts. Those are skillful and original and in general just lovely. And they pay for my fabric and thread, but they stop short of self-expression.

Shaking off gloom at the turn the piece had taken, I focused on the issue of balance. *Nine Patchy Men* were well and good, but how did Wig's goofy self-absorption reflect against X's fist coming at my jaw? I couldn't put X either in the middle or the lower right corner—he was neither the conclusion nor the locus. Similar problem with Wig—he couldn't be next to X, or in the top left as a low-key start. It wasn't a progression. X didn't sit well next to anyone, so I put him in the bottom left and Wig in the top right and Daryl with his superglue in the center. Jason's shrine next to X worked out well—point, counterpoint—and Eric was exiting through the lower right square.

My sketchpad was beginning to resemble a bad succession of tic-tac-toe games. And I felt sad. And mad. And bad and glad and probably plaid as well.

X churned me up. Not even him, more me and the fact I'd let myself get into a relationship with someone who would so readily both hurt and humiliate me. I couldn't even say why we'd dated so long—a couple of months, and I wasn't positive at any point during it I genuinely liked him, or if I kept dating him because there was no one better around. So I was eternally pissed at the person I was then, who wouldn't leave an unsatisfactory situation just because I had nothing else to do. As impatient as I got with Zach and his expectations about his perfect woman, I know I'm prone to being equally insecure and screwed up about love. He'll avoid going out with anyone who seems to have even the most minuscule flaw, and I'll go out with anyone who asks, just so I have a date.

Technically, neither of us were as bad as all that. But we had tendencies, for damn sure. And the ease with which I could trace them to the obvious differences in our relationships with Frank and Bernadette just irritated me further.

Still, knowledge leads to change, and after college I'd spent some time ruminating about X and Daryl and Eric and all, so each relationship felt like baby steps towards improvement. And here I was, starting again with Caleb.

Caleb, who I was kissing because he asked. And because there was no one else around.

There had to be more to it. I had reason enough to avoid his advances, thanks to Wren, but—I hadn't. I hadn't been looking, but look what I'd found.

To elevate my mood, I threaded the machine with a rich Bordeaux spool and picked a scrap the color of dark Godiva, and free-embroidered '*Nine Patchy Men*, by Ashlyn May', then tacked it up on the wall above my desk.

I was just washing my face when Caleb arrived with a suspiciously dense camera bag.

"Is that a wide-angle lens in there or are you just happy to see me?" I wrapped my arms around him and melted as he played his fingers down my spine. He reached my lower back, and forgot to answer. "Mmmm. I suppose it's time to head to dinner already?"

"Yeah."

"And it would be bad if we both showed up late?"

"Yeah."

"Or didn't show?"

"Oh, yeah."

I sighed. "Damn. You better let go of me, then, cause somehow I'm losing my appetite for food."

He gave me another minty kiss and stepped into the bedroom to put down his bag. It struck me again I didn't know what we were getting into. Then I remembered that I didn't care. It was my desire, and sometimes you just have to let desire reign supreme. Or such was my prevailing theory. We held hands until we got to the footbridge and I actually giggled, a sure sign I wasn't in full possession of my faculties. What the hell was the point of having convictions, of making resolutions, if they flew out the window the second a man's gaze lingered a loaded second too long?

Lizzy and Wren were good at pulling me out of my starry-eyed dreams and into a reality where I shouldn't be contemplating anything romantic with Caleb. They had us all in stitches as they relayed their Canoeing Catastrophes, which included being drenched not once but thrice, and a swift but stumbling run from a very agitated Hester the Peahen, the retreat's unofficial, and territorial, mascot. Clever Lizzy managed to turn even that recount into a pointed stick for me, saying she didn't blame poor Hester, who had staked her claim early on and had every right to defend it. All while looking directly at me. Very subtle.

Angelica was in a fine fettle, chatting away at Rafa and Brandon, who settled quite comfortably into Theo's usual seat. Rafa was as taciturn as ever, but Brandon unctuously declared he had a new appreciation for Angelica after viewing Theo's painting. A clear implication, but Angelica seemed pleased. Wren caught my eye and mimed a retch, and my stifled laughter was edged with relief Lizzy hadn't yet blown our secret.

Wren said she'd come by and have a look at my new layout after dinner and Caleb drew Lizzy into a discussion about his showing over coffee. It took his leaning over to whisper to her—later he told me he'd said, 'don't be a bulldog, she won't hurt her'—to get her to sit back down as Wren and I left together.

"So you've already got the next one planned?"

"Yeah, I think. It was going to be playful, but it's taken a turn. I think I'll end up liking it better now, once I get comfortable with it."

"Great."

"Yeah. Hey, have a seat. It was just a ruse."

"Eh?"

"To get you alone to talk. I mean, if you still want to look at it that's great, cause you've got an incredible eye, but I just needed to talk to you."

Wren looked perplexed. I was being too serious. "Okay.... About what?"

I sat next to her on the sofa. "About Caleb."

"Geez. Did he say something?"

"Not exactly."

Her lips were set tight. "Out with it. I'm not blind enough to think he fancies me. Lustful, but not blind."

"I know. I just hope you're not vengeful."

"Man, woman, you're so on edge. What could be so bad?"

I forced a few deep belly breaths and tried to lighten up. "Not bad. But you're right, he's not interested in you. Never has been, really."

"Well you don't have to rub it in."

"No, I'm not. I just wanted you to know, so the next part isn't so bad."

"There's a next part?"

I nodded. "Afraid so."

She tried to read my face a moment, and then gave up. "What?"

"He has had an interest here, he says since he got here. All along, I mean."

She arched the one eyebrow. "And?"

I shrugged. "You remember that first morning?" She nodded. "We were walking the paths, and I told you, not my type, I'm not interested?"

One more glance at me and she stood up. "Well. Obviously things change, don't they?" It wasn't a dagger in her voice, but certainly a sharp kitchen knife. "When?"

"It's not like we—well, like we're consummated or anything," I protested, hoping his bag in my bedroom was well out of sight. "But Saturday we started talking, and it became obvious, and when I realized he...well, when he said it, I realized I was interested, too. I hadn't given it a thought before then." Mentally I blocked the image of us on the porch swing, praying it wouldn't betray my half-truth. "But I'd like to pursue it. And I can't unless I, I don't know, clear it with you first. I don't want to screw up our friendship."

Wren rubbed her eyes and forehead with her palm, and then raked back her hair, looking square at me. "Well, frankly, Ash, I don't know what to say. It's not like I feel up to giving you my blessing, is it? I don't even know if that's appropriate, anyway. What do you want me to do?"

I felt like a beach ball in storage, gritty and deflated. "I don't know, Wren. I just find myself in this situation, and I love our friendship, and wish it didn't have to make a difference if Caleb and I want to kiss. But like it or not, it does. At least, it makes enough of a difference I have to talk to you about it. Beyond that, it's up to you."

She sat on the arm of the chair, balefully. My sub-conscious slapped at me and reminded me it wasn't fair to leave it up to her, so I added, "I guess what I want, what would be ideal, is for you to say you are happy for me, or for us. And mean it."

"Yeah," Wren sighed. "That last part's the hard one though, isn't it?"

I nodded.

She looked out the dark window. "Ash, I wouldn't let a man come between myself and a friend. It wouldn't seem worth it. Since you're a friend, I have to stick with that and not mind. And yes, even be happy for you." She glanced back at me, then turned and walked for the door. "But just for now, don't go expecting me to listen to all the details, okay? I'll work on the meaning it part, if you keep working on the being my friend part. Deal?"

"Deal." I hugged her, which she didn't want, but I did anyway. "Thanks, Wren. Thanks for being honest."

"Yeah, you too, I guess. Good night."

I watched her walk up the path to her cabin, catching the peripheral motion of Caleb coming towards me the back way. When she was far enough from ValeSong, I turned to him, and opened the door wide.

CHAPTER 12

It hadn't gone smoothly between Caleb and Lizzy. Lizzy thought he owed it to Wren, as a friend, to find out if there were sparks. Caleb told her it wasn't feasible, he'd thought about it, and had decided it would be leading her on, which he wouldn't do. "I said how even when I didn't know if you were into me, I still wanted you."

He grinned like my blushing had to do with his lascivious intentions, but I was kinda busy being embarrassed at how, unlike me, he didn't just take the easy path of going with whoever indicated an interest.

Mid-kiss, I decided I was just being down on myself and I wouldn't have been standing there with Caleb if he'd been somebody else—if he'd been Brandon or Rafa or whoever, I would have just said 'no thanks.' Actually, if it was Brandon, more like 'get real, you idiot.'

But Caleb was my friend. We were knowing each other better and liking each other more by the day. And he had been subtle enough I could have missed his point. I obviously hadn't wanted to.

And there we were.

Alone.

Trading stories.

Trading kisses.

Sharing electricity.

His bag in my room. He'd gotten ahold of some condoms, and I did not intend to ask how, when, or why.

I didn't expect interruptions, but slid a chair in front of the door as a warning system, just in case. It didn't take long for me to stop thinking about relationship motives and other people and even to put aside those persistently lingering thoughts about Gran and what I would have to tell her.

WE STARTED in the sitting room. But the lamp was on and there were no shades to keep anyone passing by from viewing us like an R-rated movie. Or PG-13, but moving rapidly up the MPAA rating system. Every time I heard a noise outside my body did a little hop-skip away from his, until we were doubled with laughter.

"Let's lock up this place, shall we?" I asked, and stood to take our wineglasses into the other room. He followed me to the door of my studio, where I had more lights to turn off.

"May I?" he asked, nodding in.

I shrugged. "If you want."

"I just like looking around in here, seeing where you work. So I can imagine you better when we're apart."

Something in me melted at the idea of his envisioning me at work. I felt liquid, watching him, in his marvelous black jeans, swiveling slowly in my desk chair, running his strong hand across the top of my sewing machine. He stroked the thread lightly, felt the sharp point of the needle, half-stood to lean forward and examine the title patch I'd hung earlier.

"Am I one of them?" He didn't turn around.

"The patchy men? Hardly." He sat and spun the chair around in one motion. He was grinning—he'd been teasing. So I added, "Not yet, anyway. We'll see."

As he walked towards me, towards the bedroom, I turned off the light. He protested. "You'll just have to feel your way," I said.

"Mmmm." He did.

Once his palms had cupped my hips and his head was brushing lightly over mine, I glided backwards into the dark bedroom. The back of my thigh found the mattress; my hands found the table to set the glasses down; my fingers found the dimple of his chin.

Caleb's head turned, his mouth ravenous for my fingers. My other hand was on the back of his neck, my lips were traversing his earlobes, his hands lifted my butt and scooted me onto the bed, his body pressing close after mine.

As his mouth moved down my throat, his hands up my ribs, I don't know what I did. I remember the feel of his vertebrae and muscles, their contours under my fingertips and the stretch of his cotton t-shirt across the backs of my hands. I'll know when I'm eighty the electricity of our thighs touching through my jeans and his, the muscles contracting for each other as if transmitting some sort of code. Which they were, a message of tender urgency, a need needier than just need: it was demanding, but solicitous. My shirt didn't last long; his fly flew open. We were talking but not listening to each other, or ourselves, just touching: flesh, tongue, cloth, and mind to mind.

He sat up enough to pull off his shirt. We rolled so I hung over him. As I tasted his chest, he swept my hair into his hands, and my breasts brushed his skin, nipples crinkled hard through their restraining cotton. My crotch slid down his thigh, encountered his kneecap, stayed for a ride. One half of me was flitting over him like a butterfly, agonizingly light, while the other half dug in, desperate to meld.

Each stretch of skin he touched radiated chills to my nerve endings. All my favorite romance novel descriptions kept flying through my head: hot loins, pulsating desire, searing flames of passion. I giggled, trying to come up with a definition for 'loins'— was it a gender-specific term? I decided if I had them, they were somewhere between the belly button and the actual genitalia, because that's where I was throbbing. Eventually Caleb paused long enough to ask if I was ticklish, his hand playing gentle sonatas on my abdomen, which, I was embarrassed to note, quivered with delight.

"You? Want me to stop?" he was reluctant to ask.

"Oh Goddess no." His flushed face in the half-dark was even more gorgeous. I was becoming quite fond of his jaw line and the faint 'hmm' he often breathed before speaking. It was so deep and low in his throat, you hardly noticed it, unless you were close to him. He hummed it a bit while he was kissing me, too.

His eyes scanned my face, searching for latent reluctance. I grinned at him. "You know what I am? I'm giddy." But he didn't look any more reassured. "Happy," I clarified. "Giddy. Pleased to be here, to be with you." I kissed his cheek and whispered, "Excited."

A hmm-groan. Woah. I was going places on his voice alone. Then there was his warm breath on my nipples, making me want to cry every time he moved his mouth from one to the other. And the sheer solidity of his torso, the grace and ease with which he moved his body over, under, around mine, as if we were the two parts of a lava lamp sliding and curving around each other, fitting, our shapes defined by each other—sinuous oil and water dancing, always moving but never parting.

It's not like I hadn't had good sex before. It's not like I hadn't had shit-hot sex before. But frankly, it had been a while. And there was an electricity with Caleb which, if I'd felt it before, I didn't remember.

He was so tender, then. So damn tender I did cry, and he kissed my tears, and we were carried away to some salt-water world where we were each other's life rafts, and we clung to each other, buffeted by the waves, and it took us a long time to arrive at the shores of our own personal desert island together.

When I could breathe semi-normally again, I pulled the quilt up over the drying sweat of our limbs, rolled into his embrace, and just said, "Cool."

He burst into laughter. "Ashlyn May, you are the queen of understatement."

"So shoot me."

"Okay." He rolled over and leaned off the bed a minute, then came back up and pointed his loaded Canon at me. I dove for cover under the quilt but he took his pictures anyway.

"My hair's a mess," I squealed, and twisted then pinned him down so I could snatch the camera and take one of his mock-horrified face bleached by the flash bulb. Then he chased me into the bathroom to get it back, which was an amusing sight since he still wore the spent condom.

Soon enough we were naked as jaybirds in the shower together, where Caleb proved to have quite the back-scrubbing arsenal. I'd never felt anything like it. I was putty—not boring putty-colored putty, but Aegean Sea turquoise and teal putty, as smooth as the sand at low tide, as relaxed as a day in the sun listening to the waves. As willing to give in to his natural force as a dune in the wind. Whatever else, if the time came I would be making spiteful quilts about him, I held myself to being glad I—we—had decided to ignore any reservations and just go for it.

When morning came I felt the same. Caleb was a peaceful sleeper and he didn't rumble or start or, blessedly, drool. Like a sexy log to curl up against, with a gentle radiance keeping my feet warm and my heart warmer.

I don't know if we were stealthy going to breakfast, but we didn't leave together, since Caleb had to spend the morning setting up his exhibition for us. I had seen a few prints and we'd talked plenty about our respective projects, but I was curious— even trepidatious—to see the finished products. He had a good eye. The photos were sharp and original, somewhat nervy in the way they got into your visual field, but I couldn't imagine the message coming together the way he'd enthused about. I was afraid the brashness of the image quality wouldn't gel with the natural theme.

But that's what the artist does, is make his or her mind's eye apparent in unexpected ways. If it were beautiful but expected, it'd be design, not of art. Or so a theory went, anyway.

And Caleb pulled it off.

Fearing my lack of objectivity would lead me to talk over his work in an effort to 'make' everyone like it and praise Caleb, I winked at him and held my tongue. But it was exciting to see my pregnant doe grazing on the porch of the ice cream shop, and the woodpecker who hung out in the glare of the afternoon sun outside the computer room instead attacking his reflection in what looked to be the men's room of the Austin airport. He had images from California, too—a tumble of ice plant growing down the windshield of a Porsche. A blue jay, presumably as naked as we were the night before, fussing at the squirrel who sat at the desk opposite. The edginess of the photos kept them on the provocative side of kitsch.

Overall, the group was pleased. A couple of the shots fell flat, and after some discussion we still couldn't pinpoint why, but Rafa went so far as to give him a nod and a slap on the back at the same time, and Wren, who had been rather sullen going in, got down-right chatty about his use of light enhancing the blended truth.

No one had much to say to me. Wren and Lizzy took off together, not shunning me but not going out of their way to ask me along. Or Caleb. So we were left to entertain each other.

We spent the night at ValeSong again, and decided to switch to LakeFire the next morning, for a change. I went back to my studio to work on *Patchy Men* after breakfast then packed a duffel with extra underwear and socks and other essentials, and left it at Caleb's. He was shut away in the darkroom. As I was coming out, I thought I heard a noise at the door, so I paused to wait for him. Instead it was Angelica at Brandon's door, and we were face to face coming out of cabins not our own.

"Hey."

"Hey."

I paused. "Lunch time?"

"It should be. I was just helping him set up his studio."

"Oh," I nodded. I'd forgotten we had to look at Brandon's pics soon. Guess I couldn't worm my way out of it anymore. Opting against explaining my own presence, I said, "Well, that's nice of you. Should be fun to see his stuff."

"Yeah, it looks great. I think it'll be a hit."

I suppressed my smirk mid-way and tried to model a grin. "I'm sure."

"See ya at lunch, then," she said, since I hadn't moved off Caleb's porch. This time I knew the sounds were from the dark-room door.

I nodded again. I was beginning to feel like a bobble-headed doll. She walked off, but turned at the sound of Caleb's emergence into the light. I smiled at him but didn't say anything, inclining my head towards Angelica turning back towards the Main House.

"Hi. You ready to eat?" he asked, nibbling at my neck.

I tasted his warm skin. "Starved. You?"

"Oh, yeah."

Sometimes his laughter vibrated out of him, as if from some earthquake-prone core of his being. It was fabulous.

randon's work was about as derivative and uninspired as, well, Brandon himself. He'd even included some of those dumb tree prints digitally tinted mauve and orange, and didn't even try to justify them. I mean, even a blind pig will occasionally snuffle up an acorn, but this stuff was unredeemed.

Rafael didn't bother to show—I was beginning to respect his judgments. Angelica, meanwhile, was fluttering around straightening things and Theo was standing against the back wall as if Spackle pasted him to it, arms across his chest. And then it happened.

Brandon, mid-drivel about how he'd started out because of rave reviews of his sister's wedding portraits, turned and said, "Where is my shot of the bride and groom by the cake, Angel?"

And Angelica said, "Oh I think you left it on the bed after you showed me. I'll get it." She darted through the studio door.

Theo, I don't know how to say it. He imploded or something. He had a bowling ball to the gut look, arms unhinged at his sides. Returning, Angelica gave him a long stare then pointedly turned away and handed the photo to Brandon. Theo nearly fell. Caleb caught hold of his arm and, hand on his back, walked him outside, Lizzy at their heels.

Angelica just stared after him. "What is his problem, anyway?" she shrugged at Wren, and Wren shrugged back. We glanced at the wedding photo—sharp focus on icing flowers, blurred bejeweled hand feeding mustache-framed face—and fumbled out farewells. Angelica stayed behind.

"Okay, I know Theo was a jerk with his painting and all," I said to Wren as we hit the back path to my cabin, "but did she just pull a stone cold move or what?"

"No shit." She sounded stunned, too.

"What a pair."

She barked a laugh. "What a *ménage*. Can they suit each other less and deserve each other more?"

Then we were both laughing in the clearing and I hugged her and asked, "You will tell me if I piss you off, won't you?"

"No."

I stared at her, unable to figure if the laughter had washed clear the air between us, or if it was just a break in the storm.

She squeezed my arm. "Well, maybe. Only if it's enough to make a difference."

It felt sincere. "Fair enough. But you have to promise."

"I promise."

"Good."

I brought her in and showed her the sketches for *Nine Patchy Men*, which she was, predictably, very helpful about. By the time we'd rearranged the layout and tightened up the lines, she had to go make dinner. I offered to help, in case Rafa was MIA.

Caleb came up behind us on the path and put an arm around both our shoulders. The barometer spun as happy warmth at his touch collided with the cold front of Wren's reaction to his peck on my cheek. Men can be so stupid.

She joked it off, but didn't make us welcome in the kitchen, already crowded with Rafael in there, wrist-deep in some dough and muttering something about stirring the tomato sauce before it scalded. Caleb and I headed to the computer room.

Zach finalized our plans for Friday—he would pick me up at the May-family version of bright and early, which put us in Houston in time to have a visit with Gran before the birthday party. Frank was in on our attempt at surprise, and would bring Bernadette to their favorite Tex-Mex joint, where we'd arranged for candles in a tray of spinach enchiladas, since Bernadette wouldn't eat the refined sugar in a cake.

Zach replied to my reply right away—he must have been frustrated or bored with his current project, 'cause normally he won't stop what he's doing for fear of losing his groove—and asked why Caleb and I were both in the lab instead of working.

"Hey, quit writing my brother."

"Quit writing my friend," he countered.

"What did you tell him? Did you tell him about us?"

"Oh, you're ashamed of me now?"

"No."

"Then what's your problem?" He grinned and muttered as he hunted and pecked with the hand not resting on my leg, "What is your sister's problem? Send."

A moment later, from Zach: "What is your problem? Is there a problem all the sudden?"

So I copied Caleb on my reply: "The only problem is people trying to interrupt my creative juices."

From Caleb: "I'd never interrupt your juices."

From Zach: "I think I don't want to know."

From me: "I give up on you both." I logged out.

When Caleb and I looked at each other, we broke into giggles, just in time for Wren to pop in and announce dinner. By the time we closed ourselves in Caleb's cabin, I was shy again. His turf continued to disorient me, despite the stern talking-to I gave myself: why was I having mini anxiety attacks when we'd had a couple of nights together and he had yet to reveal latent axe-murderer tendencies? Being in LakeFire was hardly a step too far from home. And ValeSong wasn't even my real comfort zone; it was just a place I'd been sleeping for a couple of weeks.

Caleb, though, was a doll. A big sexy doll. He didn't even ask me why I was so jittery, just wrapped me in a bear hug, and suggested we take a shower to relax. A brief *Psycho* image phased out to the rhythm of his fingers across my shoulder blades, circling and testing the knots, gradually convincing them—and me—to relax.

Once we were clean, calm, dry, tense again, wet again, dirty again, and dry again, I was feeling at ease. The endorphin buzz and the way Caleb's hand moved up and down my spine like it was frets on a jazz guitar had me at maximum zoned out.

That, of course, is when it happened. It could have been twenty minutes earlier, and neither of us would have cared, but in the quiet, it made quite a racket.

"What is that?" Caleb asked me, sitting up. "Who is that?"

I listened. It was eerie enough that I tucked the sheet protectively around my torso—*Psycho* visions again, perfect—but I eventually deciphered it. "It's Theo. He's calling for Angelica."

"Why?"

"I guess he misses her." Obviously.

"No, why here?"

"He's probably at Brandon's, not here."

He rubbed his brow. "Theo said there was something with Brandon and Angelica, but I thought he was paranoid."

I got out of bed and found some of my clothes. "It started just in the past couple of days, far as I can tell—but I guess Theo figured it out at the studio visit today."

Caleb dressed, too, following my lead instead of questioning me. Points to him.

Theo, meanwhile, continued sobbing. By the low gold light of the moon, we found him right at the edge of the woods, staring in

Brandon's dark bedroom window. "Hey, Theo," Caleb started, but it didn't do much.

I sat next to him in the pine needles. His flannel shirt didn't hide the way his arms trembled. "Sweetie, I don't think they're in there."

He just looked at me. His eyes were freaky-shiny and unfocused.

"I don't think they're in there," I repeated, channeling patience, a calm palm on his shoulder. "Do you want to come inside?"

"Uh," Caleb began. Shrugged. "Let me help you up." He offered his hand.

"Am I at your cabin?" Theo asked me, slowly.

"No, sweetie, I was visiting Caleb. Will you come in?"

"Where's Angelica?" It was hard to make out his words, what with the mucous drain and all—but every syllable compressed the available space in my lungs.

I worked on keeping my voice smooth and focused. "I don't know. She's probably at home."

"I went there!" He stood and threw his arm towards the north. "No answer."

"Come on inside. We'll figure it out."

Finally, he started nodding, and Caleb led him inside. I got him some tissues and a glass of water, and he swabbed at his face. A couple of ragged breaths later, he met my gaze.

"You okay, sweetie?"

"You don't know where she is?"

"Uh-uh."

"You promise?"

"Uh-huh."

"But she's with him?"

I nodded. "Probably."

"I guess it's okay, then."

Caleb looked quick at me. "What did he say? What's okay?"

Theo just sighed. My own breath wasn't coming so readily.

"What's up, Theo?" I asked, rubbing his upper back. "Tell us what's going on?"

His eyes were totally bloodshot, the rims shadowed. "I thought she'd come back, but she didn't. And then she went with him. Him! Of all people; he has no soul. We laughed about him." Theo closed his eyes and slumped against the back of the chair. My hand was trapped. "I took some pills. Aspirins, a lot. I didn't want to tell anyone but Angelica, but she's not there, and I think I need to tell someone."

"My God."

"You what?" I pushed him to sitting, felt his cheek—why, I don't know, but I did. It was clammy. "Theo, are you serious?" I knew he was. He'd gone beyond tears and into some interior whirlpool of depression.

Caleb crouched at his feet, shook him. "My God, you idiot. How much did you take?" Theo didn't look at him. "Can you throw up? If I help you, can you throw it up?"

He shook his head. I said, "I don't know if that's safe. Is it safe?"

"I think he should."

"I don't think he even can."

Theo tried to slump again, and together we pulled him to his feet. Squeezing Caleb's hand, I scanned the cabin, as if its amenities would suddenly include a paramedic where none had been there before. Focus. I gripped Caleb tighter, dug my fingertips into his Mount of Venus. Found a plan. "Look, I'll run to the Main House, call 911. You walk him over there. Can you?"

He nodded.

"Okay. Theo. Theo! You walk with Caleb, okay?"

Theo gave his head one sharp shake.

"No, listen. I think you can find her. Walk with him, he'll help you."

"You'll help?"

"Yeah, sure, man, I'll help. Let's go." He nodded to me. "Go."

I took off, damning the low path lighting. I pounded on

Margie's door first, buzzed her intercom, and went to the phone. She came down as the operator was asking for the address, and when I had it I barked at her to go help Caleb with Theo.

911 kept me on the phone while the paramedics were dispatched, and made sure Margie and Caleb got him into the den okay. At first, Theo refused to talk to them, but I promised they'd help him find Angelica. He told them what he'd swallowed—most of a bottle of extra-strength aspirin, something like seventy caplets. He told the operator it had started with a headache and he just kept going, waiting to feel better. He asked three or four times where Angelica was, and they seemed to take it in stride. I was glad. I felt like shit for lying to him.

Caleb explained to Margie how we'd heard him outside, and she gave me the briefest of looks as she glanced at the grandfather clock—almost two a.m. I heard the siren, went to turn on the front porch lights.

Margie stopped me in the hall. Her hands were fluttering as much as my heart. "Do not let them leave without me, I am just grabbing his file. And put a note on my door for me, in case anyone else comes looking, let them know I'll be back in the morning. If you have any problems, call Fred Lynn, he helps here sometimes. His number is taped to the bottom of the telephone."

I nodded, slightly startled by this trusting side of Sargie Margie, but people get unexpected in a crisis. Like swallowing too many pills, for example.

"He will be fine." She turned up her stairway. "You did well, you two."

I sighed and went back to the sitting room, straightening my clothes. The ambulance crew had the gurney inside already, working fast and calm, and Theo was crying again. "He thought 911 would tell him where she was," Caleb murmured, "and he's upset they hung up."

The paramedic looked at me. "I take it you're not Angelica?"

"No, I'm Ashlyn, I called."

"Okay. Well, Theo, I think we'll find Angelica at the hospital, so why don't you hop on up there and we'll get going."

The other medic was wrapping up some equipment and stating stats, a lot of which were presumably meant to reassure us.

"Margie wants to go with you," I told them, and fortunately by the time they all were outside, so was Margie, halting my fumbled explanations. I seemed to have lost all coherence, and only stopped myself from sinking against Caleb when I saw Rafa and Wren standing on the porch, taking it all in.

The four of us went back into the dining room after the ambulance pulled out, and I left Caleb to explain while I wrote the note for Margie's door. Rafael worked late hours and would have heard the sirens past his room, but Wren was far from the road. Still, sound carried and she'd said she was a light sleeper.

After posting the sign I double-checked for Fred Lynn's number and headed back to the others, noting the extra mug next to Caleb. If he was really, really good, it would be chamomile tea.

It was. The height of my gratitude was stellar, as I sat and sipped. It turned out Wren had been midnight strolling by the lake, with a peace offering for Hester of leftover croutons. She heard the activity and came to investigate. Now she was watching Caleb and I with definite suspicion. Since I didn't want her asking how we came into the situation together, I turned the conversation. "So do we know where they are?"

"Who?" from Rafa.

"Angelica and Brandon," I said. Caleb's half-hmm told me he hadn't mentioned that part. But it's not like it would have remained in any way discreet. "Apparently they're missing together. Theo was looking for her, at his cabin."

After I recapped Angelica's FireWind relationship history for him, Rafa laughed. I'd never heard him laugh before—it was both deep and sardonic. "Guess you're next," he told Caleb.

"Huh?"

"Three down, one to go. Unless she picks Lizzy, too, and she just might."

"You have got to be kidding me."

"Why, has she already made her nocturnal visit to you?"

To his credit, Caleb recoiled. "God, no. But," he glanced at us ladies to see if our delicate constitutions could handle more information. I crossed my eyes at him. "But, when, man? She and Theo were joined at the pelvis."

"Not the first night they weren't."

Okay. Interesting dynamics.

Wren was shaking her foot rapidly against the chair leg. "Are you just fucking with us?"

"No. I wish I was."

"Well, you mind me asking what the hell? Does Theo know?"

"I doubt it. I shouldn't have mentioned it. It was obvious she thought she'd moved on to better things. She didn't miss a chance to flaunt it in front of me." He leaned back, taking the chair onto two legs in a way that would have given Margie a nervous fit. "Why did you think I never stuck around when she was around?"

Wren looked as red as I felt. Caleb, however, shrugged. "Just thought you had your own shit going on."

Wren smiled sweetly at him. "And you wanted out of k.p. duty."

He laughed again, less sardonic this time. I was in danger of liking the guy. "Fair shot. That was obnoxious of me. But you sure as hell put me in my place, siccing Military Margie on me."

I grinned. "We call her Sargie Margie."

"Good one." Rafa stood and bussed our mugs. "I'm gonna get back to it."

"Night." I paused. "Hey, are you gonna show us your stuff tomorrow or not?"

"Not."

I nodded. "Okay."

"See ya." He left.

"Well, a night of surprises," Caleb stated obviously, as the three of us headed down the porch steps.

"You're telling me." But Wren didn't sound so at ease. The dark night hid her expression.

"Wren?"

"You want me to walk you two back to Caleb's place?"

"Wren, come on."

"You come on, Ash. You're the one so full of this honesty shit."

"I never lied to you."

"Two in the morning! You weren't exactly a hundred percent, were you?"

"You didn't want to hear it."

"I didn't want you to fucking play me, either."

"Hey Ash, Wren, don't," said Mr. Congeniality.

"I'll say what I damn well want." She stopped her furious fast striding at the fork. "You asked me to be up front, I'll be up front. You two can go off and screw each other every night until dawn if you want, but you can't explicitly tell me there's nothing like that just to appease me, when there is. You're not lying to be kind; you're just trying to make it easier on yourselves."

"I didn't lie."

"Shut up for once, okay, Ash? You were not truthful, and I could give a damn about you, Caleb, no offense, but you can screw whoever you want, it's up to you. But if the two of you are honest about being my friends, you don't pretend there's nothing happening when there clearly is. It doesn't give me any credit whatsoever for being able to handle things like an equal and an adult. I am not going to break down in tears over some guy, but I am going to be pretty damn annoyed if my supposed friends aren't letting me make my own emotional realizations, instead of making them for me."

By the light of the low path lamps, I stared her down. "You done?"

"Is that an apology?"

"No, it's a question. Are you done?"

"For now."

"Okay. Then listen to me?" I drew a breath, hoping to soothe the stings running rampant in my chest. "I didn't tell you this was going to happen, and we knew it would. But I didn't lie. And I'm sorry, okay? Take it or leave it, but I'm sorry we pissed you off, sorry you feel mislead, and sorry you found out like this instead of through us talking about it."

I took another breath, while Caleb muttered, "Hey, I'm sorry, too."

"But I think we should just not talk more tonight. I don't mean to put you off, but this whole Theo thing has me wiped out, and yeah, you're right, I am going back to Caleb's for the night. We can talk all you want tomorrow, okay?"

"Maybe. Maybe we will. I damn sure don't want to tonight." Her tone wasn't quite enough to put my heartbeat back to normal, but it wasn't nearly as sharp.

"Okay." I nodded. "Okay. Do you, um, need anything?"

"No, I'm outta here. Good night."

"Night, Wren," Caleb said, and I echoed him.

She headed up towards RiverSong and I finally slumped against Caleb. Mighty chivalrously, he exuded solid security as he wrapped his arm around my shoulder. I never think of myself as needing protection, but I didn't mind, walking pressed up against him, that I felt very safe indeed.

We collapsed into his bed—my eyes were void of moisture. I felt like a sandbag. It was an unpleasant counterpoint to the silky beach he'd had me envisioning the night before.

"I'm wiped out," moaned Caleb.

"Yeah." After a moment, I managed, "Did I screw up? With Wren?"

"Uhmm. Honestly, I don't know. I don't think you handled it badly, though."

I rolled over and tucked myself against his side. "Yes, well, you have to say that. You're my boyfriend."

His silent laugh brushed against my nape. "Oh, am I?"

"You are."

"Mmm. Good." He kissed my hair, softly. "Very good." He might have continued, but I was too asleep to notice.

WE MISSED BREAKFAST, and before we got to lunch, Wren had provided a less than gentle answer to Angelica's 'I suppose Theo's going to leave me with all the cooking again tonight' whine, which left us basically fending for ourselves that evening. Angelica and Brandon set a platter of sliced veggies on the sideboard, along with the bread and peanut butter, and then left together. Since Rafael didn't show, we shared his revelation with Lizzy, the better for the four of us to gossip. Wren wasn't speaking directly to me, but she did participate in the conversation, and stopped herself from sitting in the chair next to Caleb as I moved to the table with my sandwich.

"And Sargie's not back?" Lizzy asked.

Caleb shook his head. "She went in the ambulance, so I'm sure she spent the night there and will have to catch a ride back."

"Talk about freaky."

"No kidding."

"Don't tell Brandon or anyone about Rafa, though," I cautioned Lizzy, who snorted. "I know, but it's better I say it."

Wren harrumphed a little, which I chose to ignore.

There were so many soap opera permutations, it was hard to know where to start—the break-up with Theo, the sleeping around, the ickiness of actually going to bed with Brandon and his greasy dusty white-boy dreadlocks, and of course Theo and his need to react to it all with a bottle of analgesics. We barely touched on Sargie and her potential relationship with this Fred Lynn guy.

Brandon stomped past us, on his way to the computer room. "Where's Angelica?" Lizzy demanded, and he just glared and tossed his head.

"Lovely," Wren shot at his departing back.

Margie made it back before we were done eating. "Theo will be okay," she reported. "They will keep him another night, for monitoring, and evaluate his release in the morning. I am not sure if he will return to FireWind, though. It will not be decided today."

She didn't elaborate on whose decision it would be, and told us she hoped we'd all keep the will to live for the next several hours, because she was going to get some sleep.

"Lovely," Wren muttered again as Margie slammed the door behind her.

Caleb laughed as he volunteered to wash up, and then we were three.

Lizzy glanced between Wren and I. "So you had words?"

I smiled. "You're just a terrible gossip, my friend."

"I know. But I want yous to get along, so I'm being presumptive."

Now Wren smiled. "Okay, okay, I forgive her. And I admit I'm jealous. But not envious, if that makes sense."

I nodded. "It does. And I know I need forgiving." I added, "Thanks."

Lizzy took our hands. "Good then. We can go back to usual."

"Thank the Goddess," I said, "cause if I didn't have you two I was gonna be stuck being pals with Angelica, which, nothing personal, just didn't quite work for me."

Lizzy snorted. "I can imagine."

And we digressed into chat about Angelica again, and about her twisted work, and about our work, and my quilt of Gran. I had to explain the news about Pappa to Wren, who looked at it from a different direction, namely: what value would it add to anyone's life to learn about this Irish half-uncle of mine?

It made me think.

I had planned to tell Gran, and was debating how to do it. Could go over it with Zach first, or would that be a betrayal, to not give her a chance to dictate who else would know and when. Wren's question stopped me cold.

"I don't know," I finally concluded. "The reasons keeping quiet most appeals to me are all to do with sparing me the discomfort of laying it all out for her. I don't know if that's making me like your idea too much for the wrong motives."

"Look at it this way," said Caleb, who'd rejoined us mid-conversation. "Pretend it's not you who has to tell it, or you know Gran wouldn't care, or something. Remove the painful telling factor. Do you see the logic still? Is anyone gaining by knowing, and if so, what?"

"I don't think it's a matter of 'gaining' really. Unless knowing some more relatives is a boon, which is debatable—I mean, how much contact would we reasonably even have with them, supposing they do accept us as family?" I sighed. "I sure as hell haven't gained anything by knowing it, except for my elevated blood pressure."

"But do you wish me Da hadn't told you?"

"No," I answered instantly. "No, I'm actually glad he did."

"Why?"

"That's it, isn't it? I've no idea why. It doesn't make sense."

"I suggest," suggested Wren, "it's because if the knowledge is there to be had, you'd rather be with than without."

"That's the human impulse," added Caleb.

"Yeah, but, that leaves me telling Gran, doesn't it?" They nodded. "Well, this'll jar my preserves for damn sure."

They laughed, but Lizzy wanted to know how come I was so sure Gran didn't already know. There wasn't a chance. "Gran can't abide deceit. If she knew, she'd never have let Pappa tell the stories about Ireland the way he did. She may have let him hide it, but his background would have had to fit a little better with this truth." I closed my eyes and they immediately welled with tears.

"Poor Ashlyn." Caleb rubbed my back. "Do you want me to go with you tomorrow?"

I shook my head. "I'll have Zach. But thanks. It's just not gonna be great." Wren was watching my body sinking towards Caleb's hand. I sat up. "And Bernadette's sure to complain about my ruining her big birthday surprise, thanks very much. Always growing older but never growing up."

CHAPTER 14

Zach pulled up by eight on Friday morning, which I recognized as being a remarkable feat by actually having my clothes on and overnight bag packed.

Caleb wandered outside to greet him, and I chose to double-check I had Bernadette's quilt rather than watch Zach wonder why Caleb was at my place so early. Caleb, obviously a man never overprotective of a little sister, slipped an arm around my waist as I joined them. Maybe Zach was tired, but he resisted pulling me out of Caleb's grasp. He just slammed the trunk on my bag and said, "Hey, let's hit the road while traffic's light, 'kay?"

"Hasta," I kissed Caleb—what the hell, the gig was up—and he smoothed my hair before telling us to drive safe.

Zach's car had crunched down the driveway and spat the last of the shell bits onto the blacktopped main road before he managed to give me a glance and say, "So?"

"So indeed. So Caleb and I are in couple-land. What's new with you?"

"And I guess you're happy about it?"

"No, it's torture, whadaya think?"

"You know, he's going back to San Jose in a month."

"Five weeks, we're aware. I'm neither an idiot nor a child."

He slowed to turn onto the highway. "God, Ash, chill. Did you think I wouldn't ask?"

I rolled my eyes at him and he laughed. "Okay, okay, Mr. Need-To-Know. Here's the scoop. We were just friends, you know the whole Wren thing, and I finally figured out he wasn't wearing the aftershave for her benefit. And I thought about it and we kissed, and it was one of those rom-com moments, fireworks and jubilation, and here we are. And no, we haven't talked much about the end, and yes, if it keeps going like this, it'll be an issue, and no, I have no idea how to resolve it. Anything else?"

"You want to stop and get some coffee?"

"Yeah, but if you can hold out until Luling we can hit that bakery."

He shoved towards my head and I ducked. "You're so damn bossy. Remind me to tell Caleb."

I laughed now. "Give me your phone, I'll put it on your calendar."

It wasn't until we'd returned from our bathroom breaks and broken open the package of pecan rolls that Zach quit holding out on me. "I've a little romantic news of my own."

I squealed like a Beatles fan in the front row. "You dirty dog! Out with it. I can't believe you just drove forty miles without saying a word."

"Humph. I thought you cared about my Rick situation." Rick was a co-worker who kept weaseling credit for other's work and getting away with it; we'd discussed him *ad nauseum* for months now. I did care, but not that much.

"Yeah, yeah, yeah. Who's the dame?"

He confessed all. Her name was Rebecca but she hated being called Becky and she was a fellow techie nerd who he'd gravitated towards at a cafe one poetry night. They had approximately a jillion things in common including the desire to learn aikido, so they were taking a class two nights a week and going to the movies, book stores, or work-type functions two or three other nights a week.

"Why didn't you bring her along?"

Zach didn't even bother to do the sarcastic snort. He just looked at me. "Hi, Mom, happy birthday, here's the love of my life and your future daughter-in-law."

"Oh, Zach, do you mean it?"

"What?"

"The love of your life thing."

He actually blushed. My very own big brother blushed. "Yeah, I do, I think." He cut off my delighted babbles with, "And not a word, Ash, it's early days. Anything could happen, and the last thing I need is Rebecca getting the Frank and Bernadette May Third Degree Experience sooner than she has to. She's going to have to turn out to be completely perfect before I subject us to that."

"You just said she is completely perfect."

"I know, I know. And I'm right, just terrified it won't work out cause she's either hiding her past as a con artist or hiding her present revulsion for me until she can find the 'right time' to let me down gently." He grinned. "And if it's the con artist thing, if she's repentant I may just be able to live with it."

I grinned back. "Can I tell Gran?"

"I don't get to tell her myself?"

"If you must. I suppose that'd be better, I just—oh, never mind."

"What? What's up with Gran?"

I stared out the side window at the passing fields. "Nothing, nothing. I just have to talk to her about something and it maybe kinda tough, so I was hoping to use your news as, like, an icebreaker."

"Since when do you and Gran need an icebreaker? More like muzzles once you two get going."

"Never mind. I want to talk to her first, so it's not on telling you about it, so just forget I mentioned it, okay? Tell me about Rebecca. Is she going to move in with you?"

"Ash...."

"I'm serious, Zach. I'm sorry, it's just personal, and I need to do this my way."

"Okay. Just, let me know if you, I don't know, need anything. I'd do whatever you asked, you know. No questions asked."

I smiled at him. He was such a protector, a fixer. No wonder I always put things on his shoulders; he'd been wide open to taking care of me since we were little. Rebecca was a lucky woman, and I was glad he'd found her.

ZACH DROPPED me at Gran's—I would stay the night with her and Zach would stay at Bernadette's. She and Frank only had the one guest room now they'd converted my former bedroom into a meditation zone. At Gran's, the spare room always had a couple of changes of my clothes.

Also, Gran's had the expansive fabric closet Pappa had built for her. It was a miracle of color and texture and organization, that closet, and we'd both spent hours there, over the years, letting a project take shape in our minds as we gathered the fabrics that would become quilt blocks and backers and binding. Right away, I found the brocade I wanted for *Patchy Men*. Soon I'd added some organza I might or might not want to appliqué, and began a pile of spearmint-hued calicos for a vague plan to do with images of women refracted through a garden tea-party setting. When I caught myself going over the pros and cons of taking a package of sewing machine needles, I knew I was avoiding talking to Gran about Pappa. So back to the kitchen I went, feeling grim.

And wimpy.

Instead of talking first, I presented her quilt. Gran loved it, no surprise—my goal had been to honor her with this manifestation of my love. Her response, the way she took in the fine details and overall impact, the way she kept moving her arthritic hands across the surface, showed she understood my work, both narratively and artistically, and her appreciation for *Chains of Love* was multi-leveled.

Mostly, she loved that I had made it for her—that she had been the inspiration for my work. I always acknowledged her teaching and her support as the base from which I had launched myself as an artist, but she rarely credited herself for the things about me that made her proud.

"It's not like I never mentioned how much I love you, you know," I laughed after her third or fourth round of 'I can't believe you did this for me, sweetheart.'

"Oh, sweetheart, I know you do, I've always known. Aren't I the one who can read your mind since birth?"

"Or the one who I've wanted to, anyway," I said with a kiss.

"And that being true," she pulled me towards the breakfast room and we sat at her small vinyl table—the yellow with gold and brown specks had greeted me most dinners of my youth. I traced the dots that always looked like the outline of a duck to me. "Who is he and what has he done to give you that secret little smile?" Gran asked. "If you can tell me without being crude."

"Gran!"

"I'm just asking, You're not the only one who reads romance novels here."

I laughed. "He's just another guy at the retreat, his name is Caleb and he actually was at Berkeley with Zach."

"As in, he still lives in California?"

"Get right to the heart of the matter, why don't you? Yeah, he does. But, I don't know, so far we haven't talked about it. I have this, I guess, premonition it'll be okay."

"Well, good girl, I'm glad for you. And I hope it works out to be everything you dream." Gran always talked about my life in terms of dreams. My name—she named me—was adapted from the

Gaelic for dream or vision, and she put a lot of store into the symbolism.

I served us some shortbread from the batch Gran had prepped for my arrival. Zach had obviously broken into it while I was lost in the fabrics, so I asked if he'd had a chance to chat with her.

"Yes, I got the news of his love life, too. I feel blessed both of you have found such happiness—you're reminding me of myself and Pappa, our early days in love with each other."

I bit into the shortbread and looked at the duck again.

"What is it, Ashlyn?"

"Just, well, not nothing. Something. Something I need to talk to you about."

"Goodness, girl-child, what is it? So serious all of the sudden."

"I know, I'm sorry. I need to have a serious kind of talk with you, but maybe we should wait until later, after dinner. It's not urgent."

"Well you've got me curious. Can we not talk now?"

I glanced at the kitchen clock—it was closing in on four, and the reservations were for seven. We'd have to leave by six-thirty at the latest to avoid Bernadette's sarcasm should we arrive after her, and I wanted to shower the patina of car trip off of me.

Mainly, though, I was avoiding it.

Gran was having none of my hedging, so I started in with the background of Lizzy's parents. Gran, being from the land of everyone knows everyone else, had a cousin who'd been at school with Agnes's mother and aunt. She didn't know Dub but wasn't surprised he knew of Pappa.

"And is this serious thing of yours about Dalkey seventy-odd years ago?"

I nodded. "Sounds silly, I know."

"Maybe not."

I glanced up at her. She was looking a tad wary. "Gran? Are you, um, aware of a secret from then?"

She sighed. "Just tell me what this Dub Murphy had to say, sweetheart. Just tell me."

She couldn't know already. Until her resigned sigh, I'd been convinced she couldn't. Gran wasn't known for her poker face, but I was getting nothing from her. So I talked.

"Okay, he told me Pappa didn't exactly come over here the way he said."

Gran didn't comment.

"He came the same route, I mean, through Liverpool, but not the same way with his family and all."

Gran put her hand over mine. Faltered over the words a little. "I—I suppose he knows the sister?"

Meeting her gaze, I said, "He knew the doctor, your father-in-law, that is, and he knew the doctor's, um, grandson. Matthew O'Connor." Her eyes went dull and moist like wet slate, but still not a word. Voicing this was a thousand pinpricks with not a thimble in sight.

I fumbled out the most straightforward words I could find to finish the story. "What he, Dub, says is that a boy—eighteen really, so a man—named Niall O'Connor, who was the son of Dr. Matthew O'Connor, went with his bride to England, and she came back saying he'd died on their wedding trip. She had a son, this other Matthew O'Connor, and the doctor and his family took them in and, well, that's about it. I guess."

I trailed off, and Gran was staring into the middle distance, and I paused before reopening my heart-crushing mouth. "The mom died already. So there's no…proof at all. It mayn't be true. You know the Irish and their blarney, and how many O'Connors might he be confusing Pappa with anyway."

Gran patted my hand lightly so I shut up but she wasn't talking. This wasn't good—Gran had never run out of things to say to me before. I mean, of course we had our companionable silences, but usually when we were occupied—quilting or cooking or whatnot. Otherwise, we were always talking; talking politics, talking history, gossiping about family and neighbors.

When I met her eyes again she was crying, which was enough to open the floodgates I'd been forcing closed for most of a week. So much for my theory the worst part delivering bad news was the anticipation.

"I'm sorry, Gran, I'm so sorry. I'm sorry if it's true and I'm sorry I mentioned it."

"No, no, sweetheart." And to my shame, she offered me the solace of her hug, and I took it. Of all the times to discover how like my mother I truly was.

No. I refused to be like Bernadette, sobbing across Pappa's side of the bed after his funeral. Gran had been forced to comfort the daughter whose lifelong message was that the men in her life were more important than her mother. First Pappa, then her brothers, or then Frank, and Zach. Or Zach, then Frank. No matter the order, it always went men first with Bernadette. Gran and I were tied for last.

Gran was forever first for me, and I'd done my best to be first for her since Pappa passed.

I disengaged and reached to the center of the table, plucking napkins from a basket I'd woven back in middle school. After we'd wiped our eyes, Gran told me what she knew.

"It nearly cost us the wedding." A minuscule smile graced her face. "A fortnight before the ceremony, and we were at a picnic, just the two of us. Talking about sex."

"Gran!"

"We were engaged. Are you and your Caleb engaged?"

Oops. "Well, you were still a teenager."

"An engaged teenager. And don't think I didn't know about you and Daryl."

Double oops. "Fine. You and Pappa were having teenage sex."

Her smile brightened enough to truly rearrange the lines on

her face. "Not until after we were legally bound, dream girl, and don't you forget it. We were only kissing on our picnic."

"Shocking behavior. I'm telling my uncles."

"They're to defend me against their own father now are they?"

"Well your brothers have all passed. I can't tell them."

Gran blessed herself. So did I. Although I've never been a church-goer—Frank and Bernadette opposed organized religion like the good new-new-age hippies they were—I'd picked up the habit of making the sign of the cross over my own chest when Gran's lost family members were mentioned. "Rest their souls," she said. "And my Niall's, too. He was a good man, Ashlyn."

"The best."

"I hope you find one as good yourself some day. I hope maybe you already have."

The stinging behind my eyes wasn't all due to missing Pappa. Just thinking about Caleb and the future sent bright pinwheels of hope and fear spinning within me. "Maybe," I said, but quietly. It wasn't time for those thoughts.

"And I got up the nerve to ask Niall about sex."

I laughed. Gran's timing couldn't be beat. "What'd he say?"

"Poor Niall. He looked like he wanted to sink beneath, well, if not the earth, at least our picnic blanket. Do you remember how his ears went all pink?"

I shook my head. Tons of memories of Pappa, but not one to do with his ears.

"Well, they did, when he was embarrassed. And his ears went pink, and I thought it was to do with us both being virgins. No more of your faces, young lady. As it happens, I was the unsullied one, so you can just wait until you get to heaven and scold your Pappa then about it."

I laughed. "Pretty sure he knew about Daryl, too."

"He's the one who caught you half-stripped behind the henhouse."

Now there was a memory of Pappa I'd never lose. Come to

think of it, his ears that afternoon had been rather bright. As bright as mine now felt.

"So no scolding in heaven. What Niall told me did break my heart that day. It truly did. But I was a teenager, and furious, and nervous about the rest of my life, and though I've never thought about it before—I've never talked about that day before now—I believe I was jealous." Gran traced patterns of her own in the tables gold dots. "Not of her. Alice. Well, not because she'd lain with Niall. What made me burn was how I was inexperienced, a child, and she a woman. I was facing moving from my home where my ma directed us all to this unknown where I had to manage everything. It was daunting, and on top of all that, I had to learn about intimacy. And here was Niall already knowing everything, and keeping it from me."

"What happened?"

"I accepted him, of course. How could I not?"

"But I mean, what happened with him and Alice?"

Gran huffed a short laugh. "Sex. Behind the henhouse, most likely."

"Not behind the henhouse," I said.

She squeezed my hand softly. "Well. Wherever it was. Alice was a neighbor, friendly with Niall's sister Kitty. They took walks together, all three, and sometimes just Niall and Alice. Kitty was sure they'd wed. And because neither of them had much else of a plan, they discussed it. They were curious. So they went behind the henhouse and no one's grandfather came along to stop them, and they ended up pregnant. He offered marriage. He said it was Alice's idea to go to England instead, for...to take care of it. Kitty helped them arrange it all. The always helpful Kitty."

Gran sarcasm about a sister-in-law she'd never met cracked a whip of blame in Kitty's direction.

"Once they were in Liverpool, Alice decided to see it through on her own. She said she never wanted to see him again, and I gather there were some words and some tears, but in the end, he gave her what money he had and promised to stay in Liverpool while she went back to Dalkey. He only corresponded with her via Kitty; ensured Alice made it home all right. Once he'd earned some money he wrote to offer his hand again, and promised if she didn't accept he would head to America on the next ship."

All the pinwheel pieces in my heart had crashed apart. "What did she say?"

"Nothing. The reply came from that bitch Kitty. He never heard from Alice, may she rest in peace." We crossed ourselves. "More than seventy years, and I've never forgotten Niall's face when he told me about it. He said Kitty's was the shortest letter he'd ever received. 'May the wind be at your back always, Niall.' Only that. She never answered the letters he sent from Texas, probably never passed his messages on to their parents."

"How horrible. Poor Pappa." Just reading the silly storybooks he wrote up for his children proved how dedicated he was to his family. Picturing him pushed out of his family of origin hurt.

"Poor Niall. And hearing all that, how could I deny him the chance to form a family with me?"

I sniffled. "You couldn't."

"Well, no, I could not. And in my heart I didn't want to. So," she tilted her head, sighing, "we married."

Poor Gran. Her teen bride self, grappling with such a change in who she thought her fiancé truly was. Poor Pappa, carrying the guilt of the abortion and the loss of his family, burdens he knew he had to put down to move forward with Gran. They couldn't know about the years of war and the miscarriages and the drought ahead of them; it would have seemed a glittering future only accessible via a rickety bridge of hope and faith.

And just as they were about to start across, a plank fell into the abyss.

It sent my tears overflowing, contemplating what would have happened if they hadn't trusted they could make the crossing together.

CHAPTER 15

*B*ut cross the bridge together they did, only as it turned out, it a more rickety crossing than Gran had realized. There I was sitting in her kitchen telling her the foundations of her life were shakier than she'd ever dreamed.

My gut curled further in on itself. "Oh, Gran. I don't—I mean, you don't think he ever knew? About the baby and the whole thing with his supposed death?"

She shook her head with the smallest of smiles. "I don't, sweetheart. No, not my Niall, he couldn't have. He wouldn't have stayed in England, or in Texas, knowing there was a child of his in Ireland. No. He never knew." Gran swallowed back a gasp. "He never knew."

I could feel my eyes jumping rapidly as they scanned her face. "I always thought he'd had a row with his family, or they'd died or something. He never mentioned much about them other than his childhood days, and I didn't think to ask."

"No, Niall was still devoted to them, as much as he could be. It broke him, I always thought, in so many little ways, being away. You don't remember when he found out his mam had died? You were, oh, nine or ten?" Pappa used to take a day every few weeks to go to the downtown library and read the papers from home. From Ireland, that is. "It was mid-winter, but he spent the next two months ripping down and rebuilding your precious henhouse. Hardly spoke a word to any of us."

She sat back, exhaling fully this time. Her movement seemed to break the closed system we'd made, beside each other at the table. I looked around. It was almost six. I hesitated. "I could make an excuse, say we can't make it."

"Pah! Your mother would have Frank here within minutes. I do love the girl but here she is turning sixty and behaving still like a pre-teen." We laughed, leaning our heads towards each other, a habit between us that reestablished our comfortable connection.

"Are you frightfully sad?"

"Oh, Sweetheart, I just can't say. If it had been when Niall was still here, I think I'd have raged at him, but now…. A child there, too. A man, now. He'd be older than your uncle Dermot." She stood. "Well, I'll need time to digest all this, and stomaching it with a plate of enchiladas is as good as anything else. Don't let me forget the gift, it's on the hall bookcase."

"I'll put it with mine right now." She patted my shoulder as she passed on the way to her bedroom, and I sighed. The telling of it was over, which was my hard part. Now the onus was on Gran, and she had stooped under its weight, though I watched her square her ever-more-sloping shoulders. Willing her pain to rest on me instead, my own heart sank a notch. I went to my shower.

It was a typical Frank and Bernadette evening—with the glorious addition of onlookers. I do know they love me. But she talks about me like I'm a kid being indulged in this silly little dream of quilting for a living, despite the fact I've managed to support myself through college and since, and Frank kicks in with his 'oh but she has some real talent, our little girl.' You'd think they'd never been hippies, hadn't been stuck in the 70s for decades. Meanwhile we all heard at length about Zach's wise career moves, his big success, his promising future. It amazed me they didn't tweet screen shots of his tax return.

Usually I have Gran to back me up, or at least appreciate my attempts at self-deprecating comic relief. Tonight, she wasn't taking in the celebration with her habitual three-sixty field of vision. I shuddered with an epiphany: I hadn't endured Frank and Bernadette without either Gran or Zach at my side for close to eight years. *Damn*, I thought, *am I afraid of my parents?* Well, probably not Frank. But maybe Bernadette.

Zach nudged me. "You look lost. Where'd you go, FireWind?"

I nudged back. "I wish. No. You wanna take a quick walk?"

"Think we're allowed?"

"We're adults, you know," I said, not without irony.

"Easy for you to say, you're bunking with Gran tonight." But he followed me out to the verandah anyway. "S'up?"

"Shitloads. Night of revelations." I sighed. "I'll tell you the Gran thing on the way back tomorrow. But answer this. Do you think I'm scared of Bernadette?"

He laughed.

"What?"

"Bernadette's scared of you, is what."

"You're full of it."

"I kid you not."

"She said that?"

"No, of course not. And maybe, yeah, it's less fear than...."

He was cut off by Frank bellowing out the door, "Kids! Candle time!"

"Goody, goody!" Zach jumped. "Last one in's a rotten egg!"

I got him with the old swerve and curve move, so he was the rotten egg and had to give me the bigger plate, so there.

Bernadette's friends had put together an aromatherapy massage spa day for her, which sent her into Zen mode, and not even Zach's first edition of *The Power of Non-Violence* could top that. When she opened *Mama Bear* she said, "Oh, Ashlyn, what a lovely blanket!" and passed it over to Frank for his perusal.

Ah, well. At least the presents signaled the end of the party.

But then of course was the return home with a silent Gran. She wanted to sleep on it all, so we headed off to our rooms without further re-hashing of the Pappa story. I fell into instant, dreamless sleep, that's how decidedly my brain wanted to avoid dealing with another thought by then.

All the FireWind breakfast duty had conditioned me to be up early. I made coffee and slipped back into Gran's sewing room, locating her stash of scraps and sorting through them for border pieces for *Patchy Men*. I would assemble blues and deep greens as if they were actual patches on an old army blanket, the one I'd snagged it from Uncle Dermot a few years before, knowing someday it'd come in handy. I was always doing that; going to thrift stores and estate sales to collect other people's junk I wanted to turn into art. My favorite form of recycling.

Again, I was avoiding.

I made her favorite tea and looked in on Gran.

I guess people don't tend to think their grandmothers are beautiful. Age and all. However, something about Gran made it easy to stare at her face, though it was just as wrinkled and spotty as those of the rest of her generation. Her cheekbones still high-lighted her eyes, and her lips, once almost over-full, had wrinkled down to a gentle cupid's bow that was still rosier than her browning skin.

At a recent check-up, her doctor had told her she had the spine of a fifty-year-old. Her posture was deceptive; I let her strong appearance and strong personality fool me into taking her resilience for granted. After last night, seeing her so still and mechanical after our talk, I knew with finality Gran was not as rock solid as she seemed. I closed my eyes and sank the welling moisture of my tears as I bent to kiss her forehead.

"Wake up sleepy-head. Zach's gonna be here in two hours and

I don't want him to catch you lolling around in your night clothes." Gran's apple-green dressing gown was like her second skin; Zach called her Granny Smith whenever he saw it, which was pretty much whenever he saw her.

Gran yawned and smiled. "I need you to move back home, sweetheart, so you can bring me my tea in bed every morning."

"Just give me a month," I promised. Gran had practically thrown me out after college—she'd re-subscribed to the Houston paper just for the 'For Rent' listings.

We sat over breakfast, not talking. Still, it wasn't like it was out of nowhere when Gran said, "Don't tell Zach." We both knew what was on our minds.

I swallowed. "You sure?"

"He'll only talk to Bernadette. Then she'll talk to Matthew and Dermot. And where would be the good in that?"

"But the kids, or grandkids, whatever they are? Are we?"

"Just going to leave them in Ireland? Yes, we are. What possible joy could it bring to their lives to know their grandfather deserted them before their da was even born? They wouldn't even have the chance to get to know Niall if they wanted to. He's gone."

"So, you're..."

"Going to leave it be." She held up her hand to quiet me. "No, sweetheart, I thought about it all night. It's a miserable thing, a thing that does no one any good." Then she squeezed my hand. "Except me."

"How?"

"Because I know that, receiving this burden, you trust and love me enough to share it with me. Even guessing how it would hurt, you did what I would have wanted you to do."

I was back to crying. Gran sighed. "There is one thing I thought I might do."

I used the heel of my hand to squeegee my face. "What?"

"I thought if you could find the number for that wicked Kitty O'Connor, I'd ring her up and give her a piece of my mind for letting Niall's baby grow up without knowing how pure and good his father was. And for letting Niall think his family had turned their backs on him, when really it was just her and her stupid schemes." Gran sighed again. "But I don't think I want you to. I think an evil minor part of my soul feels it's justified, but the rest of me knows it will serve no purpose."

Zach's car turned in the drive. "I'm gonna find her number anyway, Gran. You're too kind now, but if you wake up in the middle of the night sometime bent on vengeance, you'll have it and know it's morning time in Ireland."

At last, her face softened into a smile. It wasn't as rich as her usual, but it wasn't hollow, either.

Then Zach came in and teased us about being a couple of sour apples and we teased him about rushing us so he could get back to his Rebecca faster. I loaded up my bags of treasure and the alcohol requisitioned by the others at FireWind, and held Gran in an extra-long hug before kissing her goodbye.

ZACH WAS ANNOYED by my not telling him the Gran secret, but was distracted by our in-depth analysis of when, based on the birthday bash, would be a good time to spring Rebecca on Bernadette and Frank.

"And what the Freud were you talking about with this 'Bernadette is scared of me' crap, anyway?"

He snorted. "Like you didn't know."

"Oh, yeah, I knew. That's why I've never mentioned it and am currently looking at you like you're destined for the madhouse."

"You did too."

"Quit arguing with me, you big baby, and tell me what you're talking about."

"It's only the same thing as always your whole life. Bernadette knows you love Gran better, she knows you'd rather be with

Gran, and it scares the crap out of her she can't relate to her own daughter in a meaningful way."

"But I only spent so much time with Gran when we were little because Bernadette was too busy with work and with treating you like the king of the universe."

"But she only treated me like the king of the universe because I responded to it, and whenever she tried it with you, you acted like she was, as you so eloquently say, destined for the madhouse," he countered. "Plus there's the jealousy."

"Excuse me? The what?"

"You've heard the word before. You know, the little green-eyed boogie monsters all over the place because Bernadette's mommy treats Bernadette's baby like the child she's always dreamed of, excuse the obvious pun. Bernadette just can't measure up to the Dream Girl."

I didn't know how to begin to contradict him, but I threw out a, "You're so wrong," just to let him know I wasn't convinced.

"Seriously, Ash, you never thought about this? When for decades, you and Gran have been bonding over the story of how you only stopped crying as a baby when Gran held you?"

Okay, we did keep that one active in the family lore. I sighed. "But I thought Bernadette just didn't like me much."

"Now I know you're the crazy one. Ask Frank how many times she's wondered when you two were finally going to become real friends."

I shook my head. Bernadette had never displayed an iota of this frightened jealousy of me as far as I could remember. All the way past Columbus I moped over the idea Bernadette had secretly longed for me all these years.

You'd think she could have found some way to let me know, other than the obviously doomed strategy of building alters to my paragon of a brother. Which Zach now claimed was a misguided attempt to show me how rewarding it would be to be Bernadette's friend, so I would try harder to connect to her. *As if.* He was just attempting to hide his embarrassment at the preferential treatment he'd lapped up like an eager puppy for a good long while there, try as he might to deny it.

In this sulky manner, we reached FireWind. Fortunately, Caleb came over before we were done unloading the car, and Zach got to mutter, "Take her, but don't say you weren't warned about her loose grip on reality."

Caleb looked confused and I laughed, and then I was able to admit to Zach he might, in a very twisted and obscure way, have a point about Bernadette and me. Probably not, but there was a faint, faint hint of logic in his argument I was willing to examine.

"You do that, sis," he said, dropping a kiss on me before high-tailing it back to Austin, and Rebecca.

Caleb, showing an endearing level of perception, smothered me in a hug and ordered me inside for a back rub. Funny how walking back into the cabin with him felt like coming home.

"You look on the verge of collapse," he fussed as I sank into the sofa.

"Yeah, I'm not surprised." I closed my eyes. "It's good to be back with you, though."

I could feel his smile warming the room, though my lids were still shut. He said, "Who knew I'd miss you in one day?"

"I knew."

"Yeah?"

I moaned as his fingers dug at a knot in my muscles. "Course. Just look at how adorable I am. What did you expect?"

"What, indeed?" He began to kiss the arc of my skull, moving towards the nape of my neck. "So, missions accomplished?"

I didn't know if he meant my talk with Gran, my surviving the birthday party, or my run for supplies we wanted to procure without Margie's explicit knowledge. I nodded yes for all three of them. Over my massage, he agreed to keep what he knew about my grandfather a secret from Zach. "And your parents, of course," he added, leaning in to nuzzle my spine.

I opened an eye. "Were you planning on having many private conferences with Frank and Bernadette?"

"You never know."

I rolled over, pulling him down beside me. "True enough," I smiled. He tasted so good—mint and sun and a hint of sweet coffee. An overwhelming desire to seize him and absorb him just as he was took me and I think he was a little startled when I dashed into the studio for a length of silk and used it first to blindfold him while I took his shirt off—slowly, slowly—and then to bind his wrists to the headboard. But unless it was a moan of protest, he didn't mind.

I moved over him almost desperate to memorize his body, his reactions, his desires. I didn't want to think about anything other than Caleb Kendall and the energy between us. He was ticklish just under his ribs, but not unbearably so—that was reserved for the backs of his knees. When I tongued the hollow at his sternum he wriggled with voracious pleasure. His pelvic bones were sharp but his abdomen strong within them, and his pubic hair arced gently and beautifully upwards towards his belly. He was an innie.

As I took neat little bites of his shoulders and chest, he wrapped his thighs around my waist and trapped me, "Hey!" I protested, but he claimed turnabout was fair play, swearing he wouldn't let me up until I reached up to untie him. As I wriggled up to do so, he enveloped my nipple with his mouth and slid one leg in between my two for a meltdown of contact. Then when I was collapsing against him and his hands were free, he flipped us over and twisted my wrists into the silk.

Before I could tug them out, he had me bound to the corner of the bed and was grinning like he'd just won first prize in the county fair chili cook-off. "Well, what have we here?" he whispered deep into my ear. "A little lesson in equality for you, ma'am?"

I twisted a bit, just so he'd know I was objecting, but it only made the way his pelvis was pinning mine more liquid. "You may as well give in," he added, talking now to my clavicle, "it's no use struggling." His fingers brushed my thighs, his palms cupped my hips. He kissed lower, nibbling in a spiral that sent my breasts into a taut frenzy to be sucked. Caleb ignored my whimper, and laid his head on my stomach, breathing gently across my pubic mound as he told me it wasn't very nice of me to have trapped him earlier. I started to apologize but had to stop when he murmured, "Shushhh, shush," against my crotch.

Tears streamed down my cheeks and into my ears, and I thrashed my head to clear them. My hips were thrashing for another reason, and Caleb straddled my legs up over his shoulders and clamped my abdomen against the bed with his hands. He wasn't strong enough to still my bucking crotch, though, and his occasional bites to my inner thighs didn't do anything to convince me I should stay still. All I wanted in the world was for his mouth and tongue to follow the directions of my arching hips, but he kept whispering, "Now, now, who's in control here? Settle down," and pressing me back against the mattress. So I clamped my thighs against his head and held it in place, my will to move against him stronger than his to keep me still. After explosion four hundred and sixty-three, Caleb finally pulled himself away from me, and kneeled, straddling me as I panted.

"My, my, my," he grinned. "I missed you, too."

"Prove it," I managed to breathe, tugging at my ties. He moved forward to lean over my head and untie the knot on the headboard, which gave me a chance to ensure his erection was about as hard as it was possible for it to get. He froze in place, so I sat up enough to wrap my still-tied arms around his neck and lower us back to the sheets. He reached for a condom, moving quickly again as I teased him with kisses on his earlobes and gentle brushes of my soaking crotch against his. He moaned as he came into me and again I thought of how right it felt to be in a room with him.

I was drained by the time with my family, but Caleb was doing enough work for the two of us. Soon I found my legs and back responding independent of my brain. Our urgency grew and grew and grew and it wasn't long—not too short, but not long—before we imploded together.

Wow.

I lay there leaking silent tears, feeling a little like a shallow fool when the word 'love' kept flashing through my mind, as if incredible chemistry in bed was the main criterion. Caleb's eyes were glistening, too, as he looked at me, so I cheered up. He eased my hair behind my ears with some sweet soft touches and asked what I was thinking. I just smiled and sighed.

"No fair holding out, lady. I'm here for more than just the awesome sex, you know. I want to know what's on your mind."

"Just stuff about us. About chemistry and biology and history and psychology." I laughed. "Sounds like my senior year of high school, huh?"

"What, no cheerleading practice?"

"Naw, that was for the pretty, big haired girls. I was in the Latin Club, though, does that count?"

"Absolutely." How did he still taste like mint? I made a mental note to check what brand of toothpaste he used.

Footsteps on the path past my window to my door. We were just acing our timing. I shut the bedroom door as Lizzy let herself into my sitting room.

"Ash?"

"I'm in here," I answered. "Not alone, though."

The strides towards the bedroom stopped.

Caleb's sudden transfer of a pillow from under his head to over his crotch made me laugh. I called, "You want me to come by in half an hour?"

"Uh, sure, that okay?" Lizzy asked through the door.

"Yeah, I'm just going to shower and I'll head over. Oh, your beer is there in the box on the counter if you want to take it."

She rummaged. I wondered if I'd brought all of the condoms

and stuff into the bedroom. "Cheers, Ash, see you in a bit. Bye, Caleb!"

Through compressed lips, Caleb muttered, "Bye."

I peeked out the door—this not having direct access to the bathroom from the bedroom thing was getting to be a pain—checking the clarity of the coast. We dashed into the shower, giggling. Damn but I had a good time with this guy. Casting my mind back to the patchy men, I wondered if I would have said the same in the early phases with any of them. I didn't think I was lying to myself: none of them were like Caleb.

Even as I discovered the sticky note Lizzy had left with my great-aunt Kitty's Dublin phone number, his warmth and support grounded me. There was a lot of freedom with Caleb, a lot of feeling like it was the real me exploring life with the real him.

And I was learning that the real me felt even realer with him around, than without.

CHAPTER 16

beautiful rain was falling—the kind that goes straight down, no wind to make it gush and slant, and it hit the roof with loud round flops. We lay listening until I couldn't stand it and got up to watch out the studio windows. The trees barely moved and the clearing was developing little pits in the dirt where the drops dug into the earth. It was all just a precursor to the real weather, and simultaneously the temp dropped several degrees and the wind rushed in to drive the rain sloppily against the cabin. Within moments, rivulets streaked haphazardly down the panes and the dirt in the clearing became streams of mud. I sighed and turned back to my room to get a sweatshirt. The night would be cold again.

"You okay?"

"Yeah, I just don't feel like doing anything now."

"How long will this last?" I assumed he meant the storm, which was settling in for a loud party. But it looked to break for dinnertime, which was a blessing cause I was starving.

"Oh shit!"

Caleb sat up. "What?"

"We're on dinner duty. Did you order anything?" I knew the

answer—we'd been holed up in the cabin together for hours. He was, he claimed, thinking hard on what his next phase of the project would be, though thinking looked a hell of a lot like flopping across the love seat and drinking beer. He'd kept me supplied with glasses of ice water and kisses, and stayed quiet so I could concentrate on my two-dimensional men, so I wasn't complaining.

"There's bound to be something we can make," he ventured.

I sighed. "Exactly," and tossed his flannel shirt at him. "Let's go see if Lizzy will let us steal something from tomorrow."

Typically, it was warmer outside than in, if far wetter. The rain had slowed but the trees were shedding unpredictable drips and torrents. I laughed when Caleb jumped at the thunder. He was such a Californian; the Gulf Coast weather gave me plenty of storm experience.

After semi-successful scrounging, we goofed around the Main House, listening to the rain. Gran had written back to my email with Kitty's contact info:

"Sweetheart—first the good news. I opened the packet that just arrived for you from Bluebonnet Expo and you've been juried! Both *Hibiscus Nights* and *Comfort Food* (my favorite excepting *Chains*, you know) are going to be exhibited. I'm delighted for you, and won't stand for less than a grand prize from those people, if they know what's good for them.

"On to other matters. Naturally, I don't mind you passing on the information from the Murphys. I was still in two (probably more) minds about getting the information, but once I had it, I realized I was glad.

"I don't think I'll be doing anything about it. At least not at this juncture. Much as I would love to give that Kitty a piece of my mind, I can see nothing more than more hurt coming from that. I know you still honor it, but my request that you not tell your mother or anyone about it all still stands. Don't be annoyed with me for repeating it, just put it down to your doddery old Gran's quirky ways.

"Nothing else of note to report to you, except the opening of the magnolia buds. I imagine there aren't any up there in your woods, so think about mine and smile.

"Much love to you, my dream-girl.

"Gran."

IT LEFT me high and low. I was delighted about the show—it was great regional exposure and a likely forerunner for Houston's International Quilt Festival in the fall. Plus they'd rejected my submissions the last two years, so I felt vindicated.

But I ached that Gran was so torn about the Pappa news. If she'd been raging, I could have been strident in my support; if she'd been stricken with sadness, I could have been her shoulder to lean on; if she'd not minded, I could have been her sounding board about next steps. Instead, she was somewhat all of those things, and there was no definitive place for me to set up emotional camp. I worried I'd be too passionate in the wrong direction. Having only written communication about it, too, was hard. I'd reply to the tone of one message, and by the time she got it, she was in another place.

I did my best, knowing good enough was still no good. The next family email I received, the following morning, wasn't from Gran. It was the first time since my arrival at FireWind that Bernadette had written:

"Dear Ashlyn—It was lovely to see you at my party, and thank you again for the pretty blanket. It means a lot to me. I know your Gran was happy to see you, too. We get more used than we know to having you so close, then when you're gone we find ourselves surprised to miss you so. I want when you return for you to partic-ipate in a conversation with me and your uncles about Mom's living arrangements. I don't want to spring this on you suddenly, so I'm planting the seed now. It's not urgent, but I know you want the best situation for her and I wouldn't want to upset you by failing to include you. I've cause to worry about her mind-set and as you know, one cannot thrive in any environment without the mental peace to breathe deeply and sleep well. If we can do anything to help Mom attain that, I feel we owe it to her. I hope you agree. And again, I hope I've not unsettled you by bringing this up this way. It had been in my mind to touch on it, but now I feel I should open the dialogue in whatever way I can. Hence this message. I wish you many pleasant sleeps and all the energy to create that you seek up there. Frank and I send our love, Bernadette."

WELL. I sprang up to pace, scaring one of Margie's hummingbirds from the window feeder. The room wasn't big enough for the strides I needed, so I hit the still-muddy trail out towards the lake. I managed to scare Hester, too, in a real communing with nature moment. Damn these birds.

I mean, what the hell brought this on? Bernadette a) treating me like an adult b) bringing up this nursing home threat in a freakin email c) acknowledging my gift almost as if she meant it d) sounding like maybe Zach was right and she's scared of me and e) obviously reacting to some change in Gran that made her want to reach out to me sooner rather than when I got back to Houston.

Gran wouldn't have talked to her about Pappa two days after telling me not to, would she?

I mean, if anyone was going to talk to Bernadette about it, it should be Gran. I realized that. But she'd said she didn't want her kids to know. She'd been opposed to me mentioning it to a soul. So what was the deal? Was she so devastated and indrawn even Bernadette noted the change?

I had to reply.

I didn't want to. I didn't know what to say. Glancing at Rafa's cabin, which looked empty, I let rip with a primal scream the likes of which I hadn't loosed upon the world since the Inner Peace workshop Frank and Bernadette had enrolled me in senior year of high school.

After dinner, the gang showed up in my cabin. I tossed the printout of Bernadette's message to the coffee table, then yanked the cork out of a bottle of Chablis.

"I need to be there to figure out what's going on," I ranted. "She had to have said something. Otherwise this makes no sense, right? Either she said something or she is so bummed out she's letting it show to Bernadette, and that's just not her style." I poured. "Or it wasn't her style ever before. Maybe she is so depressed about this she's letting it show, in which case I am an idiotic and callous fool for telling her about it."

Wren took her glass. "Ash, you're overreacting. No, you are. I see why you're saying what you're saying, but it's not so bad."

"She's right," muttered Caleb into his wine, avoiding meeting my eye. I was beginning to think I was a too-severe person if the people I loved were afraid to stand up and contradict me.

And now I was thinking about loving Caleb as if it was for granted. Great, even more grist for my emotional mill, as if I weren't overflowing with grist. I sat heavily in the rolling desk chair.

"Well, I think I should talk to Zach about this," I said. "Maybe he can go to Houston and check the lay of the land."

Lizzy was shaking her head.

"What?"

"Your gran told you not to."

"Yeah, well, I'm not seven. I don't have to do everything she says."

"Fine, so don't act like you're seven," she retorted. "She asked you not to, and it's her relationships you're talking about here, so you honor that."

"It affects Zach and me, too."

"How, exactly?"

"How? Because it's our grandfather! It's our aunts or cousins or whatever out there, unknown to us."

"So?"

"So, we should have a voice in talking to Gran about what she'll do with the information."

"No, not really." Lizzy sat forward. "Look, it makes no difference in your life to know or not know these Irish people. You don't stand to gain anything from it, you're not likely to stage a family get-together, and you would just screw up their lives, too, if they knew about you."

Wren nodded. "Yeah, the only one this affects is your gran. She's the one who should decide how to disseminate the information, or even if she should. And she said don't talk to Zach about it."

"He wouldn't tell her I told him, if I said not to."

"And, what, you think she wouldn't be able to tell?" Caleb asked. "Zach couldn't hide that from her."

He wasn't exactly the most opaque person.

All my dramatic sighing was starting to irritate even me.

"Fine, I'll keep it to myself." I glared. "For now. When I get back home if she's not doing okay and I can't make her better I'll tell Zach, so he can help me."

"How's he going to help?"

"I don't know. He just will. He's a helpful guy."

"Don't fight with me, I was just asking." Caleb was getting defensive on me, and worse, Lizzy and Wren weren't sticking up for me. So fine. I dropped it and told them about the Bluebonnet Expo. Of course, being foreigners to my great state, they hadn't heard much about our state flower and thought it sounded all very bucolic, but I took the high road and ignored them.

CHAPTER 17

Wednesday morning Caleb slipped out of our warm bed pre-dawn and hadn't made it back in time for breakfast. He slammed into the dining room just as I was finishing my coffee and grinned widely at me.

"Oh, Ash, babe, I'm sorry I was so long. It was incredible—the trail up the stream was bursting with dragonflies and blue jays, and then I swung back by my cabin and Brandon had left some coffee cups on the porch and, oh my God, I couldn't believe my luck, there were I kid you not, three crows hopping around on the rims and all over. I even got some shots of one of them bowing over the tray like a supercilious waiter while the other two were gazing at each other like star-crossed lovers. Just wait till you see it." He finished this little outburst with a loud smooch on my cheek as he reached for his coffee cup.

"Great."

"Yeah, it was." He poured and I passed him the cream and he finally stood still. "Hey, I'm sorry I woke you this morning."

"It's okay, I know you need to catch the light, and I'm glad you got some great work done." I squeezed the strong muscle of his upper arm as he returned for the coffeepot. "Just don't call me babe. I hate that. You didn't give birth to me, and I'm not an infant."

"Oh."

"It's not a big deal. Just try to not do it, okay?"

He nodded, still jazzed from his morning. "'Kay."

But then Thursday and Friday mornings he did the same thing, and Friday night I suggested maybe he should sleep in his own cabin, since he was getting less and less subtle in his morning ablutions and we were staying up late enough for the lack of sleep to turn me crankier than I needed to be. He got all puppy-pouty and promised to be super-quiet if I'd let him stay.

I gave in.

Big surprise, he woke me when the door slammed behind him before six the next morning, and to make it worse he came back in to apologize and decided somehow it would help if he rubbed my shoulder to get me relaxed again. All it did was wake me up further. He was getting impatient to get out in the dawn, jiggling his foot against the bed's side rail so I had to practically shove him off the quilt to get him to leave. He said, "Sorry," three more times on his way out. I buried my head under the pillows but never managed to get back to sleep.

Then it got bad. We went to his studio after lunch. He wanted to show me the new prints, and we made the usual jokes about skanky artists inviting women up to see their etchings, and then we got there and, well, I just didn't like them.

I didn't like his composition of the crow and coffee shots, and the deer at the salt lick looked derivative of some hunting lodge oil painting, and the hatching chrysalis, which he was going to put into a maternity-ward setting, were so soft-focus they were hard to decipher. It's not like they were the finished product, I knew that. I knew my reaction to them raw might be vastly different to my reaction to them when composed, but I just couldn't grasp the frayed ends of his enthusiasm and turn it into excitement on my part.

So, I wasn't jumping up and down for him.

I wasn't rude. I'm not that big an idiot. I did what I could to praise the prints, to look for the good points and stoke his ego. Apparently, Caleb was getting damn perceptive when it came to reading my body language, or my mind, or my aura, or something.

"What's so terrible about them, then?" he asked, all mopey.

"Wrong? Who said anything was wrong?"

"No one. No one said they were right, either, did they?"

I knitted my brow at him. "I said they were good. How is my reaction so important anyway?"

"Don't play me for an idiot, Ash. You know damn well you're my sounding board here. If you don't like them you should just be honest with me."

So I told him he was wrong, told him he was imagining it and being defensive and even paranoid. In the end, he wasn't so happy with me, and I wasn't so happy with myself. The longer we went into it and into it, the more I realized I hadn't been nice about the prints. I still thought my reactions were valid—I wasn't crazy about the work itself. But I wasn't crazy about the way I'd expressed myself. Instead of treading carefully, I'd figured a slightly glib path was good enough to get me through.

Eventually I asked, "Do you want me to stay and talk about this some more, or go?"

"Go."

He didn't move a muscle, so I had to stretch pretty far across the space between us to brush his cheek with my lips. "Come by and get me for dinner?"

He exhaled. "I'll be working here for a while. Why don't I just see you there?"

I nodded, and couldn't think of much else to say. I left.

Dinner would be a pasta salad—no cooking time to speak of, but I expected him to show up about ten minutes earlier than he did. I wasn't waiting for him or anything—I was sitting in the common room sketching while I listened to the radio. Wimberley got several country stations and, after I played with the antenna a little, an alternative rock station out of Austin.

I wasn't going to be the first one in the kitchen again. Been there, done that, written the cookbook. So I didn't rise until after I'd heard him run the water and clank the pot on the stove and open the sticky door of the cabinet where the cutting boards lived.

He didn't say anything, so I didn't say anything. I just got my favorite knife and started dicing the tomatoes. He spooned the cornbread into the pan. I scooched aside so he could open the oven door. He closed it with a bit more of a bang than I considered strictly necessary.

The water was bubbling.

He was looking, presumably, for the penne, but since he hadn't bothered to put the mixing bowl in the sink he couldn't tell it was tucked behind it against the knife block. After his third trip to the pantry, I scraped the tomatoes into the serving bowl and slid the pasta bag out from its hiding place, handing it towards his chest.

"I know," he snapped, then opened it and dumped the contents into the pot, sending scalding bubbles up to land on his hand.

"Fuck."

He didn't elaborate, and when he unwrapped the dishtowel from his wounds, I took it to give me leverage in opening the jar of artichoke hearts.

"Operating with your usual thoughtful sympathy, I see," he muttered.

"Excuse me?"

"You heard me."

"I can't say I understood you, though. You apparently have some problem with my behavior, Mr. Paragon of Romance?"

He gave the pasta a quick stir. "Oh now I'm not romantic enough as well as being crap at my job?"

"I never said that. Either of that."

"What are you saying, then, Ash? You're doing your best to be as unclear as possible, if you don't mind my saying so."

"Gee, why would I mind?"

We locked eyes for a moment before I reached around him to get the mayo out of the fridge. My back was to him as I dumped it in with the olives and tomatoes and everything, and then reached for some dry mustard and tarragon. "I never said you were crap at your job, not even remotely. I liked your stuff, I like talking to you about it, and I think what you have is going to turn out great. Just because I can't see in it the same things you can doesn't mean your vision is bad, it just means I see it differently."

"Yeah, we seem to see a lot of things differently."

I didn't think that deserved a reply, and I suspect my look told him so. I tasted the penne. "That's ready, drain it and mix it in cold water."

He pulled out the colander. "Don't tell me what to do, I know how to cook fucking pasta."

My vegetable dressing tasted perfect. I added one more dash of pepper, then pushed the bowl towards him. "Fine then, you finish it. If I'm such an overbearing person you maybe want to talk to Margie about it, see if she'll assign you to Angelica. I'm sure she'd love to get a crack at rounding off her tour of men. You get sex, I don't have to cook with you; everyone's happy."

The timer for the oven went off as I left the room, so whatever Caleb may or may not have said was lost in the buzz and the slamming door.

Fine then. Being alone gave me a chance to throw myself into my art, which had been suffering some neglect. I worked with the quick assurance and precision I loved but only found in maybe thirty percent of my labors. I woke up in the middle of the night with a clear plan for the patch about Jason, how to put me in his temple as both individual and a generic Venus from his brain. Since I had just the right fabric scrap for the marble-look of my figure, I got up to dig through the box until I found it. As pitch dark as it was in the country at two a.m., the windows reflected back the colors and motion in my studio, fish-bowlish and yet safely encompassing in the silence. I sat at the machine, and stitched, and cut, and basted, and sang along to the old country tunes on the radio, and drank a lot of water, and worked.

I was becoming all too aware of the time during this reign of Margie's food schedules—I should have gone to a normal retreat where they didn't make you cook the communal meal. So I knew it was just past five when the dawn light intruded into my space. My spine screeched as I stood, and my eyes were gritty and dry. The radio was playing some post-*Gambler* Kenny Rogers, which I never much liked, so I switched it off.

I'd done good. The patch for Jason was as close to my mind's eye as I ever got, and technically, it shined. It only took a couple of moments for me to iron it flat and hot and press it against my hanging felt.

The birds were intent on their business. Caleb would probably be up among them, unless he'd been up late with the raccoons. Rolling my shoulders under the pulse of the shower sent me deeper and deeper towards comatose. I didn't even put my clothes on, just climbed under the sheets with a towel on my head and one around my chest. It was Sunday. No one was looking for me. I slept for hours, dressed, munched some cereal in the kitchen, walked up the river an easy ways with my coffee, then went back to ValeSong and slept through lunch.

The thing is, with that second nap, I'd cried myself to sleep. It was unexpected. It made me mad. Since when does Ashlyn May cry herself to sleep over a man? Then I cried some more and told my pillow I was really crying because I was mad he'd made me feel like crying, and then told my pillow (it was skeptical about the first reason) really I was crying because of the pent up worry about Gran, and not knowing what to tell Zach, and what had happened in my life to make my own mother scared to talk to me. (The pillow let me get away with that, though it pointed out my worries were hardly pent up, what with my sharing them with everyone I could get my hands on. I told it to shut up and balled it up into my chest and buried my head in it, and it relented softly.)

It was one of those groggy awakenings, confusing because of the afternoon light and the sheets crumpled under my neck and ribs. Someone was knocking at my door—a refreshing change from the usual walking right in. My pillow was still damp and my legs were cold, and I barely breathed until I heard the steps walking down my porch.

Presumably, it had been Caleb. There was a tray outside with a bowl of fruit salad and a cheese sandwich, but no note. It seemed to me he was making an awful lot of assumptions in bringing me a late lunch, but I was, after all, hungry, so I brought it inside. He was probably hiding behind the scrub oak taking pictures for his *Food in the Wood* series. I stuck my tongue out towards the trees, just in case.

At dinner I sat between Lizzy and Wren, and when Caleb passed me the salt before I'd tasted my tomatoes, I said, "No thank you," even though, when I bit into the salad, it needed the extra flavor boost.

On Monday, we sat next to each other at breakfast and dinner but when he bumped into me with his shoulders, I scooted my chair away, politely ensuring he had all the personal space he could ever need.

On Tuesday after lunch he caught up with me as I went back to finish the Wig patch.

"Ash, babe, aren't you ever going to talk to me?"

"Haven't I asked you not to call me that?"

He blushed. His skin was such a lovely deep color that blushing was a cranberry affair for him, gentler than my own cherry-red flames. "I'm sorry."

I shrugged. "Doesn't matter."

Silence. Then, "Can we go talk?"

"About what?"

Slightly more hostile silence. "About the fact you're avoiding me for no good reason, maybe?"

"That's not what I'm seeing. I just happen to be busy with my work."

Definitely not silence as Caleb ripped a dry branch off of the mesquite and hurled it towards the creek. "Damn, Ash! Whatever the hell I did, and to tell you the truth, I don't know what was so bad, is freezing me out like this really the way you're going to deal with it? How the fuck is that fair to me?"

He was staring nastily at me, but it was my turn to generate hostile silence. "Last I checked, screaming obscenities and throwing things wasn't in the 'How to achieve effective communication' relationship guide, Caleb. Please excuse me, I have some work to do." And I turned slowly and paced myself until I was, probably, out of his line of vision, then stomped back to my room to tell the pillow all about the latest agony in my life.

On Wednesday morning I was trying to sleep in again, having stayed up past two drinking coffee and pacing between the final assembly of the X patch. All in service of a less than inspired plan to make my stomach feel abused.

When Caleb came in and sat on the edge of the mattress, brushing the hair back from my cheek, my first half-asleep thought was of the wrenching sweetness that suffused me at his touch. Then as I woke enough to open my cracked eyes, I was flushed with irritation he'd invade my privacy. That's what I started to say as I sat up gruffly and moved my face away from his hand. My words died when I saw my brother standing in the doorway behind him.

Both men told the same story with their eyes, and I knew it was not something I wanted to read. Looking at Caleb ripped me in half before I knew, so I looked at Zach and said, "What?" softly, and did not move.

So Zach had to kneel at my bedside like I was an invalid, and lean his elbows on the sheet. He reached for my hand, saying, "We need to go see Gran, Ash. She had a stroke, and she's not responding to anyone."

I fell against him.

He said, "I know, I know," and for the first time I registered the red rims of his own frightened eyes.

I honestly do not know how I moved through the cold fog around me and ended up sitting between Caleb and Zach on the front bench seat of Zach's car, headed to Houston with a thermos of coffee on my lap. Even it didn't warm me.

Caleb was driving. Closing my eyes and reliving select parts of the previous forty minutes, I saw myself nodding to him as he wrapped a towel around me and said, "I'm coming with you, okay?"

Glancing at him, I touched my damp hair. His, too, was slick, though I had no memory of him showering with me; where had Zach been during all of this? Embarrassment that my brother may have seen me naked burned worse than the thought of Caleb cleaning me without my realizing it, so I accepted the latter version of events.

Turning to view the back seat—brushing shoulders with Caleb —I took in the backpack stuffed with Zach's clothes, Caleb's camera bag and his vest full of the actual camera gear draped across it, and my small duffel full enough to see the outline of my sandal. It was the left one.

Zach's voice turned me back around. He was lifting a bag from the foot space. "Are you hungry? That director woman packed you fruit and...oh, they're scones." He held one towards me.

I shook my head.

"Are you sure? They're warm still."

"You should eat." Caleb.

He didn't take his eyes off the road, didn't speak my name. His voice was quiet, distant.

Zach hesitated, or maybe I just imagined it, then passed a

scone to Caleb, and one to me. "You should both eat. Come on Caleb, I interrupted your breakfast."

Instant mental video of Zach's car puling up the Main House road; Caleb sitting in his usual chair at the foot of the table, about to take a bite of cereal; the two of them conferring on the porch, Caleb's hand on Zach's shoulder; their heads turning towards the cabin where I slept.

I opened the thermos and half-filled the wide, shallow plastic cup, then held it towards Caleb, taking the scone from his hand. "Here, drink this, I think it's the Indonesian bean you like."

He glanced at me then, and took it (the heat of the coffee and his magnet hand triggering a storm to finally wash away the fog), smiled his thanks.

Crying again, but quiet tears just looking for another place to be, I mustered the resolve to look at Zach with the questions he knew, sooner or later, I would ask. It was yet another blessing of my brother that I could be spared the actual voicing of those questions. Looking at him with my furrowed brow prompted him to nodded and take my hand, tell me about it.

Gran had talked to Bernadette after lunch the day before, and she mentioned Mr. Weimer was going to drive her in for their grocery shopping that afternoon. When she didn't show up at three-thirty on the dot, he knew something was odd. Not getting an answer from her phone, he called Bernadette at the store.

He was next door and she was in Spring, but she was barley five minutes behind him when they met at Gran's house. He'd let himself in using the key under the potted hibiscus and found her, unresponsive, in the dining room. The municipal fire department's EMS, with their oxygen tanks and their stretcher and their kindly rush of activity, was close behind Bernadette.

She was at the Medical Center in downtown Houston. Bernadette was with her. Frank had called Zach first thing this morning, claiming he'd wanted to wait until they'd had some news from the doctors, but we knew he and Bernadette were trying to manipulate us into one last peaceful night's sleep. Little did they know.

Uncle Matthew was already on a plane, but swore he didn't want a lift from the airport, so we were heading straight to the ICU.

"And she hasn't...?"

"Frank said they didn't think it was permanent brain damage, but she'll have to wake up for the scan to be definitive."

I nodded, sighed, stared as Caleb ran the wipers to try clearing the bug splats off the windshield. The coffee cup was resting on his thighs, and I replaced it with a scone. Zach poured himself the next cup while I sank into the seat.

It just didn't seem credible. Gran wasn't even on blood thinners like half her friends. She walked every day. She had plans, she always said, to live into her hundreds. She's said she refused to die before taking a great-grandchild trick-or-treating. Maybe it was foolhardy, given her age, but she'd been so rock-solid we had no trouble believing her.

Except last time I'd seen her, I'd taken a sledgehammer to her rock.

"Don't, it's not that," Caleb murmured to me, holding my hand in his warm palm. I hadn't realized I was so cold.

"You don't know that."

"Yes. I do."

The only way I could survive this trip was to believe him, so I clung to his assurance, and his hand, as if they held the deepest truth I'd ever know.

"Not what?" Zach wiped the cup out with a paper towel and screwed it onto the thermos.

"Not anything." Caleb was firm. I was going to cry again if I couldn't tell Zach about Pappa, but with a squeeze of my fingers, Caleb told me I had to honor Gran's request, even now.

With a swipe of rough paper towel to my raw eyes and nose, I sniffed and rested my head on Zach's shoulder. "Nothing. Thanks for coming for us."

"Sure," he said. We were coming into Brookshire. Caleb must have been speeding. "Hey, stop at the gas station, we'll wash up and stretch our legs. I'll drive into town."

"You sure?" Goddess love Caleb, he was as concerned for Zach as he was for me.

"Yeah, it's fine. It's easier than telling you directions."

Caleb nodded and signaled the exit. Suddenly I was desperate to pee, though I didn't remember drinking anything that day. Maybe I just hadn't yet been, between the men waking me and cleaning me and loading me into the car.

The restroom was clean but hot. I splashed cool water on my face and raked damp hands through my hair. My knees were rubber and the right calf was asleep. Goosebumps erupted on my forearms as I stepped back outside.

They'd cleared the trash from the car and refueled. Caleb had bought me a jar of peach iced tea and himself a bottle of water. Zach finished off a chocolate bar and asked if we were ready to go.

The trip to the hospital was barely more than an hour, most of which I dozed away curled up under Caleb's arm. We arrived at midday, which meant the parking garages were near capacity, and after circling the lower levels for a few minutes, Zach headed for the uncovered roof spaces. We shut our bags in the trunk, bagging the rest of the scones and a banana for Bernadette. She wouldn't have left Gran's side to eat.

The profusion of glass and stucco towers was overwhelming and intimidating, but we navigated through the signboards and cryptic posted maps until we reached the correct wing. Sixty-three percent sure we'd trespassed to get there and already confused about where the parking garage was, it was a near-Holy Grail experience to walk into the waiting area and actually find Frank sitting there. He looked as dazed as I felt, but he blinked it off and stood to hug the three of us.

"Frank, this is Caleb Kendall," I said, once he'd released me but still, oddly, had his arm wrapped around Caleb's shoulder. They rearranged themselves to shake hands. "You're the one who was at Berkeley with Zach, right?"

Caleb confirmed while I darted a glance at Zach, who half-shrugged at me. At any other time, I'd have censured him for sharing my secrets, but right then it just wasn't worth it.

"What's happening? Can we go in?"

Frank reached for my hand. "They're just checking her responses now, and the next visiting window is in twenty minutes. Your mom's still in there with her, but they needed a little room, so I came out here."

"Responses?" Zach was pale. Caleb eased us all into seats.

"Reflexes, audio and visual stimulation, that sort of thing." Frank rubbed his eyes. "Your Gran hasn't done much since they found her. They think it was at least four hours before Bernadette got there, and 911..."

"Four hours! But—"

Frank squeezed my hand again to quiet me. "It must have been right after Bernadette talked to her. It looked like she was making lunch." Behind my eyes, I saw the blue and white Corning-ware bowl she tossed her salads in sitting abandoned on her counter. Caleb moved me into his waiting arms, and I could feel, outside his warm envelope, the defeated slumps of Frank and Zach, who had both moved to hug me.

Then the nurse came by and told Frank we could see Gran again, but only two at a time. They all looked right at me. I stood without bothering to ask if I could be the one to join Bernadette in there. The nurse led me through the wide swinging doors, indicating the intercom for when I was trying to visit without her escort. I didn't like that: the presumption I'd be back and forth with some frequency while my Gran was in ICU.

I looked at Bernadette first. Well, first after a painful glance at Gran, who was an inversion of her former self. Bernadette stood; we held each other. Then I moved past her, and took a good look at Gran.

She was intensely small under the nubby blue hospital blanket. I looked past the plastic tubing with its slow drip of liquid, at her chalk-dry skin and wrinkled lips, at her hair that needed a wide brush and mist of hairspray, at her softly closed eyes.

My one and only Gran. I cried. Bernadette leaned in over me, an awkward arm across my shoulder, silent

I wanted Bernadette to go away, so I could take it in. So I could bend over Gran and hold her face between my hands and tell her I was sorry, and if she would just wake we could make it all better. So my grief and anger and love and fear could form a vortex of healing energy that would magically restore the Gran I'd seen the week before.

But even I recognized I couldn't send Bernadette away, when it was her mother lying there in the bed before us. So I suffered her pincer-grip as if it was the hug of strength she intended, and together we looked down at Gran.

After a while, she sighed and let me go. I almost staggered. I didn't know I'd been leaning against her. Lacking chairs, we perched on either side of Gran's cold feet, taking one each to gently rub and warm. Bernadette tried to explain what the doctors had said, which left me perplexed, but at least it was something to talk about. Otherwise, we were haltingly quiet.

An artery in Gran's brain had ruptured. Her blood-sugar levels were fine, so they provisionally blamed it on hypertension. Bernadette was clear on that much, still looking for someone to accept her protests about how Gran's blood pressure had always been very good. She couldn't name the profusion of plastic tubes —oxygen to her nose, and IV to carry glucose and meds, an arterial line invading her torso to monitor her blood. The awkward machines with their indecipherable codes were pure mystery voodoo to us both.

After a bit I told her Zach wanted to come in, and started to stand. She was first on her feet, though, claiming she needed to walk around anyway. I kept my hand on Gran's left foot, shifted to a slightly more comfortable pose.

While we were alone, I did talk to Gran, not that the monitors indicated she noticed. I couldn't bring up Pappa, in case she did hear me and reacted badly. I stuck to telling her I loved her and wanted her to get better and come back to me, as much as she could. I told her I'd always take care of her.

Zach, gently, came up beside me and took Gran's hand. He scanned her face, looked at me for an answer I didn't have, and knelt on the floor with closed eyes.

"Are you praying?" I didn't mean to blurt, but it surprised the heck out of me. We never prayed growing up.

After a moment, he looked at me. "It can't hurt."

"I know. I'm sorry, it's lovely. Thank you," I stammered. "I was...."

"I know. It's fine. Sometimes I go to church. I started at Berkeley, how's that for unexpected?" He stood and gave me a wry smile, apologetic about the decade of hiding it. "It makes me happy."

"Well. Good. I'm glad." It still seemed too odd to contemplate, but look at how strange everything in our family was right then. Bernadette, who'd just hugged me with no one to witness it, was off in the ICU waiting room with Frank and Caleb, and Zach and I were at our Gran's bedside, talking about church, while she was comatose.

Zach was teary, too. We hugged on each other and stared out the window at the top of a parking garage below, and I told him it was going to be okay, because, after all, what was the alternative?

Soon—it seemed soon—visiting time was over. We were

packed off back to the waiting area with the assurance of a doctor soon to follow.

Overall, his report wasn't encouraging. Gran's GP had been by, and would follow up with us after rounds, but hadn't given us much hope. If any. They were, I guessed, taking it easy on us. It didn't matter for Bernadette, who couldn't or wouldn't grasp a tenth of the medical information she'd been hearing. Maybe on some level the staff's gentle reports helped her, I don't know. Personally, I was angry at anything less than full disclosure. After the doctor headed away from our group, I pulled my arm from Caleb's hold and followed him to demand clarity.

He was sympathetic. What a crappy thing to have to learn to be, I thought, as I damned his glasses for reflecting the fluorescents and hindering my ability to read his expression.

"Ms. May, your grandmother is not in a good position. I don't know of any better way to put it. This, the cerebral bleed, is one of the worst types of stroke to recover from, particularly for someone elderly who was not presented for treatment right away."

"But she will—she could—recover?" I was speaking as levelly as I could. *Breathe in, Ashlyn, and then breathe out. Listen to what the man had to say.*

"Anything is possible at this point, of course. But I will tell you even if she does survive this stroke, she will most likely have mobility and functionality problems, some of them potentially severe. The stroke was inner-cerebral, and affected the part of her brain where many of her reflexes are controlled. You should prepare yourself, and your family, for that."

I stared some more at him, but he wasn't forthcoming.

I went back to the chairs where my family sat, now giving me the hopeful blank looks we must have all given Dr. Erie moments before. I could only shrug as I sat back down between Caleb and Bernadette. She took my hand, and I clung to it, and we all just sat.

"Matthew should be here in an hour," Frank said. He'd said the same thing twenty minutes earlier, but Zach had been the only one to reply, "Great," so this time I asked if I should go to the airport to get him. Between us, we'd had that conversation seven or eight times, but it kept resurfacing. Until Uncle Matthew—Gran's baby-love, the boy who never failed to light up her face, the one who'd taken her on an Alaskan cruise to help her over the hump of Pappa's death—until he arrived, we could go no further with discussing Gran's condition.

"I saw signs for a food court," Caleb volunteered. "I'll see what they have. Does anyone want coffee or a soda?"

"Let me go, too," I stood. It may have been the first time since we left FireWind I'd looked into his eyes. "Okay?"

He nodded, and pressing our palms together, we set off.

"CALEB," I started, but had to stop his walking beside me first. I spotted an alcove, and pulled us into it.

"Caleb," I began again, this time touching his beautiful face and locking his stormy eyes with mine. "Thank you. Thank you so much, it's...."

"Shhh, Ash, love, it's fine. It's nothing to thank me for. I wouldn't be anywhere else. Not now."

He pulled my body into his, holding me, a steel beam for my dripping limbs and drooping heart. He absorbed my tremors, quiet hmm-shusshing and gentle kisses in my hair, and I gasped because, in the midst of my meltdown, I was exalting that he'd called me 'love.'

Caleb eased us onto the floor and cradled me in his lap, my face buried in his neck, rocking us until I relaxed. The tears—that round of tears, anyway—subsided and I deep-breathed as I dried my face on the tail of my shirt.

"Thanks," I whispered, embarrassed.

One more kiss to my scalp. "Hey, no problem."

"Goddess help me, but you are a sweet man, Caleb."

He laughed silently. "Is that bad?"

I squeezed him to me. "No, not in the least."

When we stood, I was hit by the tight after-effects of the car ride, and my pent-up tension. There was a restroom a few steps away, so I excused myself in search of a wet paper towel and a place to straighten myself without looking like an idiot.

To my amazement, the signs for the cafeteria led us on a direct and easily-traceable route. I was relieved to see they had, in addition to cheese sandwiches, a decent-looking vegetarian pasta salad. Waiting for our to-go boxes and bag of drinks, I told Caleb I'd been acting far too snippy and judgmental at the retreat. He countered with self-accusatory self-centeredness and pettiness. We assured each other that we'd done nothing wrong, besides falling into a trap of not talking to each other, which we'd watch from now on. By then, we were back to our niche, and Caleb stepped into it, glancing back at me. I followed, blushing, and put the bag on the one wobbly table that furnished the area.

"You haven't replied yet, you know," he said, tracing my left eyebrow with his right forefinger. Delicate, delicate softness.

"About what?" I asked. Lying, of course. I just wanted him to say it again.

He shook his head. "I'm no sucker, Ashlyn May. You know perfectly well."

My hands moved from his neck to his shoulders, and on tiptoe I leaned in to whisper, "I love you, Caleb." The left ear, naturally— it's the one most sensitive to these things.

Turns out he was strong enough to twirl me around, a spin of happiness followed by a short, hard kiss on the lips.

I used to wonder who it was out there—in the world of movies and novels and the like—who would chose the moments of deep turmoil in their lives to delve into the grandiose emotional territory of love. But all of the sudden I had a new theory about it, one which made it utterly logical for Caleb and I to be sharing our first confessions of love while the grilled cheese was getting cold and Gran was still unresponsive sixty yards away. The rawness of my fear and guilt left no room for interference about trivial matters. The unfinished quilts and the reactions of Wren and Lizzy to Caleb leaving town with me and whether or not I'd left the alarm clock on had no place in my mind—or heart—while I was wandering the hospital corridors. It was inconsequential.

What was strong and obvious was our common emotion. Giving those words to him made going back with rubbery pasta spirals to the plastic sofas to wait for my uncle's galvanizing arrival an easier task.

Almost, if not quite, bearable.

CHAPTER 18

*L*ooking over my shoulder, Zach stood, grinning despite the circumstances, and went forward to take Uncle Matthew's bag. Uncle Matthew tousled his hair. No one else could do that, but it had been their gesture of affection back when Matthew was in his twenties, not minding but not admitting he liked that five-year-old Zach followed him everywhere. He hugged me in passing then kissed Bernadette's cheek with a, "Hi, sis, happy belated," which set her in tears again.

It killed off the rest of our initial euphoria at seeing him again, and we sank heavily into our chairs. Matthew shook Frank's hand and I introduced him to Caleb. We determined that his flight had been okay and that he'd had no trouble getting in from the airport, that he didn't want any lunch and that he'd stay at Frank and Bernadette's house, with 'the kids'—Caleb and Zach and I—at Gran's.

Then there was nothing else to talk about except Gran.

Frank, with a surprisingly good grip on the medical facts at hand, talked Uncle Matthew through the events as we knew them and the diagnosis, such as it was. He told Bernadette to stay in the waiting area with 'the kids' (it was becoming standard parlance) while he took Matthew into the ICU, which has just re-started afternoon visiting hours. After the wide doors swung shut behind them, I looked at Bernadette. "Will you come for a walk with me?"

She blinked, focused, thought for a moment. "I'd like that, yes."

We found a window looking out over actual green space and paused to take it in.

"He's so nice," Bernadette said.

"Matthew?"

"No, no. Your Caleb. A nice young man."

I smiled my thanks. And surprised myself by telling her I loved him.

"I can tell."

"You can?"

"I can. It's beautiful. Your Gran told me you were in love, and I was so, I don't know, sad you'd told her and not me."

Gran was the one who told them about Caleb? "But I didn't tell her I loved him," I said. "We only told each other today."

"I know, but it's the way you looked. She could tell, and I missed it when you came in for my party, but she knew. And when I saw you together, I could tell, too."

Fortunately, I had some of the thin cafeteria napkins in my pocket. We weren't generally the type to cry easily.

"How does she always know everything?"

"I don't know. She was always like that, even when your dad and I were living in Philadelphia, she knew everything I was feeling. She's good." Bernadette laughed, briefly. "She knew the day after I conceived you. She looked at me when she came to pick up Zach and told me, 'It's going to be a girl this time,' and I didn't even know myself yet."

"You never told me that."

"I didn't? I thought I had. It's true. I went running off to the doctor the next morning and had a blood test, and made him swear he wasn't lying about six times, because I was so astounded she was right."

Before we got back to the waiting room, not far, actually, from my magic alcove, Bernadette touched my arm.

"Ashlyn, I'm not leaving here tonight. You'll have to take them all back home. No." She shook her head as I tried to talk. "They'll never let us both stay here, there's too much maleness between them to allow it. Only one of us can manage it, and I know you want to, but please. Please, Ashlyn. Please let it be me, for tonight, okay?"

My heart, I think, stopped for a moment. Then I nodded slowly. "We'll stay until visiting hours are over," I said, "but you have to come have a good dinner with us, too. Something more than half a sandwich. You can't sleep all night on a plastic sofa on an empty stomach. And I'll be back for the first morning hours, and when I get here, Zach is going to run you home for a shower and a change and a rest, no matter what." Internally I winced at the last phrase, but tried not to let it show. She knew what I meant, though. She knew.

Bernadette kissed my cheek. Her lips were dry and scratchy, and I made a note to find my lip balm for her when we got back to the guys. Neither of us mentioned our plans. At six, I took Caleb into the room with me; I wanted him to finally meet Gran, after all our discussions about her.

"She's just like you, Ash," he said, quietly.

"Is she?" I'd never realized.

"Yes, she is. Your uncle's the same, the same face on all three of you. The same lips and cheeks. You didn't know?"

I knew I looked like Uncle Matthew. Zach looked more like Frank. Frank with Pappa's eyes. I was Matthew with Frank's hair. I'd never connected the dots from our faces to Gran's, though.

"Thanks," I whispered. We were both whispering, which was foolish, but it felt appropriate at the time. Caleb wanted to leave so Bernadette could come back in—they were still letting us in two at a time, since the bed next to Gran was empty—so he brushed his lips against my cheek and then, pausing, Gran's, and backed out.

I went back to holding Gran's hand and telling her I loved her. Then Frank came in with Bernadette, so I had to tell her good night.

"Don't let the bed bugs bite," I chanted with a smile as I kissed her forehead, an echo of the way she'd tucked us in as little ones.

"I asked at the desk; there's a pizza place we can walk to from here," Matthew was saying in the waiting area.

"What about your bag?" Zach glanced at me. "Matthew's staying."

"Bernadette's staying," I replied.

"She can't, she was here all yesterday and since six this morning," Matthew protested.

I shook my head. "Well, she says she's staying. She won't let me stay with her because she wants the rest of you to let her do it."

"Neither of you should stay. You'd be sleeping on a chair and can't be with her anyway," Zach said, weary. He's obviously been through this with Matthew.

"We should all go sleep and come back first thing in the morning," I said, not that I believed it. I believed the rest of them should all go sleep and come back first thing in the morning, and let me stay there. Just in case.

"I don't know if they'll even let you stay," Zach added.

"How can they stop us? We'll just be in this area, out of their way."

No one was saying the obvious. That the only reasons to be there were in case she woke up or in case she died, and every brief conference with Dr. Erie was making the first possibility seem increasingly remote. I sure as hell didn't want to say it, even to myself.

"Zach, if Bernadette's staying, I'd rather Matthew stayed with her. Frank will, too. I still think you should both go home, but I made Bernadette promise she'd let you or Frank take her home in the morning for a shower and a nap. There's plenty of time for a nap before the eleven a.m. visit, and we'll be here, and I think Matthew should promise the same thing."

"God, Ashlyn, when did you start telling your mom what to do?" Matthew asked. I cringed. "Oh, honey, I'm sorry. I didn't mean it like that. I'm so glad to see you talking to her."

"I know," I said, resigned. "I know what you meant. It's just too strange. I never could have had that talk with her a week ago, and now Gran's in ICU, and we're talking, and I don't even like it, because, I don't know why. I just don't like it that we're talking when Gran's in ICU, like…like this coma is such a bad and drastic thing it's forcing Bernadette and I to talk about stuff. I'd rather we just were still all normal with each other, even though normal with Bernadette wasn't the best place for us to be."

I don't think Matthew and Zach even heard much of that, since I mostly sniffled it into Caleb's chest, but Matthew took my hand and said, "I know, honey, I know," and Zach rubbed my back and said, "It's okay, Ash, it'll be okay."

It was dark as Zach merged onto 45 North. Caleb and I slumped in the back seat, holding hands loosely, and I studied the back of Frank's head in the streetlights. He'd gotten balder, and grayer. Mostly his hair was still thick and wavy brown. The same color as mine; the same texture as Zach's. I'd always wished it had been the other way around.

"This is killing her," Frank said, apropos of nothing.

Zach glanced at him. "Bernadette?"

He nodded. "Your mom. She keeps trying to figure out what she did, how, somehow, she caused Gran to have this aneurysm."

I started up, but Caleb tugged me back down. "No one caused it," he said, firmly.

"That's what I keep telling her. Dr. Erie says the same thing. It just happened."

"Why doesn't she believe it, then?" Zach asked.

Frank sighed. "Because she can't. She's so used to taking responsibility for your Gran that she wants to take this on board, too."

I couldn't speak past the vise on my throat. What responsibility did Bernadette ever take for Gran? I was the one who did that, who made sure her life was running smoothly, who helped her set up the computer to deal with her finances, who checked in with her every day when I was living in town, and emailed her while I was away. I was the one who she depended on, on the rare occasions she let herself depend on anyone. Bernadette just made her an occasional casserole and called her to talk about Bernadette, Bernadette, Bernadette. And Zach.

I looked out the window, clamping my lips together. I was the one who'd caused Gran's stroke. Bernadette had nothing to do with it, and acting like she did was just grandstanding in a crisis. Same as she had after Pappa's funeral, throwing her sobbing self across his side of the bed so Gran didn't have a hope of finding his scent on his pillow later.

I didn't have anything to say to anyone until we were sitting on the guest bed, door shut, lights off, and relatives gone quiet in the other rooms.

I closed my eyes and tipped my skull back against the headboard.

"Ash? You okay?"

I shook my head.

"I know. I mean, I know you're not okay. But, do you want to talk?"

I sank down, then, hugging one of the pillows, and looked at him. Caleb Kendall. There was something in his eyes, something sweet beyond just the love, something that took my spirit and gently wrapped it in cotton and held it warm against his own.

"Oh, love, I can't begin to say the mess of stuff on my mind."

"Do you want to try, or do you just want to go to sleep?"

I sighed again. "I want to, I don't know. I want to talk, but some of it's too painful, and some of it's so, I guess, so petty it makes me mad at myself, and I don't want you to see how ridiculous I am, and I'm sure you're sick of my crying all over you, too."

"No, I'm not."

"Well, you should be. I'm sick of my crying all over you."

"Well, I'm not, regardless. You can cry and scream and tell me whatever you want, and I'm not, no, I'm not, Ash, going to think worse of you for it. I love you. I like you. I know you're in knots, and I know you're blaming yourself for things not your fault. They're not. I've been listening to the doctors all day, and I'm telling you. It's nobody's fault, okay? Not yours or your mom's or your grandfather's or anyone. So stop thinking that, okay? Please?"

I shook. Not my head—all of me. I shook. "I can't."

"Well, do."

"No, Caleb, I can't. It was hypertension, they said it was hypertension. You heard them. That's stress. Stress, Caleb. And she's never had stress before, no high blood pressure, nothing. Her heart…her heart was in great shape."

He pulled tissues from the box on his side of the bed. "This wasn't her heart, Ash. It was her brain. It's a brain attack, you can have the best heart in the world and still have one, okay?"

"Not five days after your granddaughter tells you this horrible news and not have it be related."

"Yes, you can."

"No."

"Ash. Ashlyn, listen. You can, okay? She can. I listened to those doctors, okay? It's not good, where she's at now. It's not good, and I can't even tell you how sad that makes me for you, for you all, but I swear, you can't go blaming yourself."

I let him tell me that. I mean, he wasn't going to agree with me, no matter what I said, we both knew it. We settled under the covers and I let him rub my back until I fell asleep, but I only did it for him.

But at two o'clock, I was wide awake again, Caleb's warmth the only thing keeping me in bed beside him. I knew, then, what I'd have to do, and the knowledge, thinking about it, stung my dry desert eyes, until once again, I fell asleep.

WE WERE ALL UP, showered, somewhat fed, and waiting in the chairs for the staff to let the first two of us in by six the next morning. Gran had had an uneventful night. Although there was now another patient in the bed next to Gran, the shift nurse said, just for the six o'clock visits, we could still go in two at a time. Starting at eight, we'd have to follow the rules. Matthew and Bernadette, bleary and subdued, went first.

"How are you feeling?" Caleb whispered as we waited.

"Humph. Don't ask," I muttered back. Even without the tears and guilt, there were the nights on end of short, bad sleeps and the diet of coffee and sugary bread.

"Poor baby," he answered with a hug to my shoulders. He'd almost said 'babe', but caught himself in time.

It was my turn, Uncle Matthew indicated with a half-smile at me when he emerged from behind the swinging doors. Caleb pressed my hand as I stood, and the strength of his touch carried me through the now-routine procedure of getting in the ICU ward and navigating past the profusion of gurneys and equipment to Gran's semi-private room.

It's hard to describe, the differences between that morning and the night before. She wasn't exactly smaller, but she was flatter somehow. She did look more relaxed, which gave me pause. It was darker in the room—the only window faced west and the curtain was pulled. Bernadette said something about keeping the biorhythms going with natural day-night patterns of light, but I didn't know if that was from her or the medical team. She was gone for less than a minute before Zach came in to join me.

We held hands. It felt strange; comforting, but strange. We hadn't held hands for a dozen years or more. And Caleb's hand was broader than his; Zach's long fingers seemed cool and gangly in comparison.

"I think she's slipping, sis."

I shook my head.

"Sis."

"I know, Zach, I know, okay? I just don't want to talk about it in front of her."

I could see him trying to fight the emotional reaction with the logic of what we'd been told, but with a sigh he just said, "Okay. Sorry."

"Forget it. I'm sorry." Drawing a deep breath, I stepped from him and leaned over Gran. I smoothed back her hair, tried to fluff it on top a bit the way she liked, and adjusted the oxygen tube where it was pushing into her cheek. I kissed her forehead. "I'll see you in a bit, okay? Frank's going to come in for a little while, then after the doctor makes his rounds, I'll come back."

Gran didn't even exhale noticeably. I caught my tear before it landed on her, and turned to walk away.

FRANK TURNED INSISTENT ON US. Taking Matthew's bag and Bernadette's backpack, he handed Zach a twenty and sent us to the cafeteria while he drove them home.

"I know it's not looking good," I told Zach as we walked, "and I know she's not supposed to be able to hear us, but I don't care. I don't. I'm not going to stand there in front of her and talk about how bad she's doing like she's not a part of the conversation."

Zach, bless him, wasn't upset. He didn't take it as defensive, just as emotional.

"Okay, Ash. I can do that. I'm—I guess I'm worried about how you're taking this, cause I am just not getting a lot of good feeling off of you."

"I didn't expect you would."

"You know what I mean. You're tense and conflicted and vibrating with worry. If something happens to Gran, I don't want you to fall apart. I want to help you get ready."

We were staring at the line-up in the cafeteria. Caleb was looking at us, I realized, waiting for a break so he could steer us towards some food. I bit my lips and told him I guessed I'd eat some eggs. Zach said him, too. No coffee. Caleb nodded and sent us to a nearby empty table. The place was full of people in scrubs, some in suits, some as weary and faded looking as I felt.

Carefully, I answered Zach. "Thanks. I know you're trying to do your best for me, and I know you're torn up with worry, too, so it's not easy." I sighed. "And I know she's not okay. I know what the doctor is avoiding coming out and saying."

Caleb sat down between us and started parceling out plates and cups of tea. He offered me some orange juice, and I shook my head. "If she, if Gran dies, I'm going to be a mess, okay? I mean, I'm already a mess. But, that's okay, I think. I know it might happen, and I can't get ready for it somehow, I can't meditate and reach acceptance about it. I just can't. If it happens, I will figure out what to do next. And," I took both their hands—broad, thin, both gentle, "I know how lucky I am you two are here for me, I know how much you love me and want to protect me. Believe me, it's already helped more than I can tell you. So thanks."

"Oh, Ash," breathed Caleb, dropping his forehead to our linked fingers. "My sweet Ashlyn."

Zach was watching us, brow furrowed, not quite crying. "Thanks, too, sis."

I handed him a napkin, which he used to dab at his eyes. "Zach, what about you? I never ask you how you're doing."

He shrugged and stirred his tea. "About what you'd expect, I guess. I'm sad and worried and just want her to get better so we can all go home and be happy."

I smiled. "Yeah, me too."

Caleb sat back and breathed deeply. "You guys need to eat. That's good protein there, now, come on. And all the fruit, too, even the grapes, Ash. Eat."

We all relaxed a little. It was good, right then, to have someone tell us what to do, and it was good for Caleb to have us listen, to have us respond to his concern.

We still had an hour before we could see her again. Caleb wouldn't even let us go back up to check in with the nurses, leading us out to the park across the street instead. We walked several blocks of it, watching some ducks at one point and some golfers in the distance at another. The day was warming up quickly, a sign of the blazing summer moving in soon. Zach pointed out a brown-headed nuthatch, which was one of Gran's favorite birds. After that, we just turned and walked back to the waiting room in silence.

Dr. Erie had just finished his rounds, and nodded solemnly to us. I didn't feel like talking to him; I needed to concentrate on what I was going to say to Gran, instead. Caleb and Zach stood in the corridor, gravely listening to the morning report, and didn't mention a word of it to me when they sat down. The others returned, looking somewhat fresher but no less shell shocked.

It was eight o'clock.

Matthew went in first.

After a few pacing moments, Bernadette stood in front of the doors, waiting, and then they switched places.

Matthew stood at the window, crying, and I stared at him until Bernadette came out, sniffling herself, and Zach nudged me.

"You go next," I told him.

"Really?"

"Really."

So he went, and I looked at Frank, and he gazed into my face for a long moment, and told me, "I'm not going to go this time, sweetie. You take the last minutes."

Breathe in, Ashlyn. Breathe out. I didn't look at anyone else, just stood, holding my elbows in my hands, and watched people walking up and down the halls until Zach opened the doors and held it for me to enter. Our hands touched briefly as we passed, but we didn't say anything.

There I was, alone with my Gran. My breath was shuddery, and I forced it still, so I could talk to her. As I spoke, my eyes flickered to the monitors, anxious, desperate to know she did hear me, but desperate to know she didn't, as well.

"Hey, Granny bug." I held her hand, and knelt on the floor by her head. The same way Zach had when he'd come to tell me about her. Yesterday? Only yesterday. "Hey, there. I love you. You know that, I know you know that. We know each other, huh? That's what we always said, so why am I sitting here talking to you like, I don't know. Like you're a stranger or something? I'm sorry." I pressed her hand and then got up to pace. I opened the curtain fully. The sun was beginning to creep across the roof of the building below. It had a plastic owl shunting back and forth on a pole, looking far too large and chipped to fool any pigeons.

Again, I held Gran's hand, this time perched on the bed beside her. "Here's the thing, Gran. Here's what's what. Caleb keeps insisting that what I told you, it has nothing to do with how you ended up here. I can't accept that. I know you too well." Before I exhaled, I squeezed my eyes shut for a moment, imagining the darkness behind Gran's own eyelids. "I'd already told him about it before I told you; I hope that's okay. I needed to talk to someone before I could tell you. He won't tell Zach, he never would."

Her face was almost void of color. Parchment. "And that's what I want to tell you, too. I won't tell, either. No matter what, Gran.

I'll never tell my mom or Zach or anyone, I swear. I won't try to find them in Ireland. Even when everyone's gone, when I'm a grandmother myself. I won't tell, okay? It's my promise to you, Gran. It's," so hard to talk through the shuddery tears, "it's what I need you to know, now, to believe from me. I don't want you to lack peace about it. I don't want you to worry."

I was still holding her hand in my two, and as I turned my head to wipe my face on my sleeve, I saw the nurse standing near the door. I sat up. "Is it time?"

She nodded, and I nodded in return.

I stood, but still held onto Gran. Still held her. I bent close to her ear. I kissed her cheek, her pale, cool cheek. I whispered, "I love you, Gran, with all my heart. You have my word now."

And I kissed her one more time before I stood, placing her hand on her stomach. I smoothed out her arthritic fingers and said, "Bye, Gran."

The nurse held the door for me. She'd just started to close it when I heard the monitors beeping, and then she was no longer there, and then another nurse and a doctor brushed past me into the room. Slowly, I pushed the door back open, in time for the doctor to glance at her watch and say, "Eight twenty-one a.m." and turn off the high-pitched wail. She glanced at me and said, "I'm sorry," and then the first nurse was back at my side.

It had only been sixty seconds since we'd last stood in the doorway together.

In that time, my Gran had died.

CHAPTER 19

And then I was alone.

I crept back up to Gran, brushed back her hair, and laid my fingertips against the cool of her cheek, not wanting to touch her but not wanting any of my touches to be the last. The nurse came to put her arm across my shoulders and next thing I realized we were standing in front of my family in their chairs. She must have been well practiced in gently moving immobile people.

Matthew and Bernadette didn't get it at first. They thought it was my sadness at seeing Gran so ill. Frank knew. He read it in our posture, in the generically kind face of the nurse beside me. She transferred my body to him, and he held me and said to Bernadette, "Love, she's gone."

"She's?"

"She's gone, love." And then I was passed to Caleb and Frank was holding Bernadette and Zach and Matthew were staring at each other like they were drowning and the other was a distant life vest. The nurse still hovered, but closer to the doors. Caleb sank us into a chair and I couldn't hear anybody's words, although they were talking.

Everyone just kept talking. It seemed to go on for days, the talking. Through us heading back to Frank and Bernadette's house, through the phone calls and the meeting of Uncle Dermot at the airport and the awkwardly genial presence of Mr. and Mrs. Weimer, who made a tuna casserole only Dermot and Zach could eat.

Gran had made all of her own arrangements. It was a very Gran thing to do, said Frank's sister Elizabeth when she called to offer her condolences. She sent a rubber plant, too. Zach lobbied for us to bury her in the apple green dressing gown, but we decided instead on a navy dress with subtle green and white flowers across the bodice. It matched her favorite handbag, so we enclosed it, too, stuffed with photos of us all and her girlhood locket with the last picture of her sister Berneen.

Somewhere along the way I'd told Caleb we could get him a bus back to Wimberley, but he said no, he'd already emailed Margie we'd be a while longer. With Matthew, we moved over to Gran's house after Uncle Dermot arrived, Caleb borrowing some clothes off Zach, and disappearing for a couple of hours one morning only to return with a charcoal suit.

He shrugged. "I needed a new one anyway."

I sighed—I wasn't manage much speak in Gran's house without Gran there to speak back—and we held hands on the sofa for a while. The funeral was the next morning, and every time I started to actually hear all the words flowing around me, I thought of it and stopped being able to hear anything.

After lunch, Zach and Caleb ambushed me.

"Sis, on Monday we're driving back."

"Okay."

"You, too," added Caleb.

I shook my head. "I need to stay here."

"Why?"

I just stared at them. Wasn't it obvious? "Because."

"No, seriously, Ash. Why?"

"Just because, okay?"

"No, not okay."

"Ash," Caleb said. "Love, you need to get away for a bit. You'll be back in a few weeks."

"Bernadette can't take care of this house stuff on her own."

"Dermot and Matthew are going to stay all this week. Frank's got all kinds of people in to cover the store. She won't have to work for a month or more. You'll be back by then."

God, there really had been tornadoes of words around me. I had no idea. "You can't make me."

"Sis, no one's trying to make you do anything. But this is what makes sense, for everyone."

Every time I opened my mouth my lips clung together a moment too long. "So you're saying I'm just in the way?"

"No one's saying that, love." Caleb's hand on my arm. His gentle touch I'd barely been without since the hour of Gran's death. "They're saying you should get away from here for a bit. Staying here in your Gran's house is just going to rip you apart every day. It'd be better if you let them work on it first."

But what if they did it wrong? What if Gran had left behind some evidence of the Pappa thing, and they came to me for an explanation? What if they gave her favorite tea mug to the United Way? Looking at Caleb, beseeching him silently to understand what I couldn't talk about in front of Zach, I started to shake again.

He shushed me. "Ash, I promise, it's okay. This is the best thing. You need to get out of here. Just for a while."

I was still shaking my head, but the looks Caleb and Zach were trading proved they knew they'd gotten their way with me. Their ganging up angered me, but I didn't have a lot of energy just then to battle them. I half-hugged them both and went to be alone for my afternoon nap.

～

THE FUNERAL. Well, looking back, I can describe parts of it. The Sunday crowd in their somber Sunday best. The unnatural heat of the day, or the natural heat combined with the unnatural warmth of dark clothes and hosiery and too many people too close together. The crowd was larger than I'd expected. Between the neighbors and Gran's book club pals and friends from the store and the people who just knew her from her congregation and wanted to pay their respects, upwards of forty souls came together in the little chapel to say goodbye.

I spent the entire time sitting straight up ('train your spine to be straight, Sweetheart, it will always serve you well') between Caleb and Zach. I cried when they closed the casket, although I wasn't watching, and again when they lowered it graveside. Other than that, I didn't open my mouth the entire time. I know it was rude of me, with old acquaintances taking the trouble to offer me sympathy, but other than half-smiles and nods and clasped hands, I couldn't communicate with them.

Zach repeated, "Thank you for coming," over and over, and I was grateful. His girlfriend had come in late Saturday night, and was standing as quietly as I on his other side, frighteningly elegant in a simple black shift dress. Bernadette barely registered her, although Frank, I could see, was making an effort to treat her kindly and include her in conversation. I was glad about that, at least.

One other thing I recall vividly about the funeral. I was kneeling by Pappa's marker, brushing invisible dust off it just to feel cool marble against my sweating palm. A shadow over me proved to be Uncle Dermot. His eyes were moist.

"Your Pappa was a great man, you know," he said.

I nodded.

"He had his flaws. We all have our flaws. But not all of us are so aware of them, so intent on atoning for them."

I stood. *Atone?* What did Uncle Dermot know? But he wouldn't answer my puzzled look, and glancing at Gran's grave beside us, I couldn't ask him anything, no matter how veiled.

Uncle Dermot closed his eyes and then patted at my back. "A great man," he repeated, and then Bernadette was between us. We turned to take our seats under the green canvas canopy, ready to recite the Lord's Prayer and very much not ready to see Gran's remains descend into their final resting place.

Rebecca stayed the night with us, and after the rest of the guests had shuffled off in groups and twos, she and I sat on the sofa sandwiched together between Caleb and Zach on the ends. Frank and Bernadette and her brothers just kept moving. Not quickly, just consistently. Frank would carry a cup to the kitchen, then Matthew would wander past and pick up the napkin that had been under it. Even in my haze—I had succumbed to sudden-onset exhaustion—I realized I liked Rebecca a great deal. She was sensitive enough to sit holding Zach's hand and let us be as quiet as we wanted. After her initial offer to help clean up was refused, she recognized the way the prior generation was finding tasks was vital to them just then, and didn't try to interfere. She didn't shift around trying to get more comfortable as we squeezed against each other. I liked her calm and her acceptance of the prevailing mood. And Zach leant against her as if she was his stable doorway in the midst of an earthquake. I'm projecting that's how he felt, anyway, since I was doing the same thing with Caleb.

'THE KIDS' slept at Gran's house that night, and sooner than we'd have liked, Bernadette and Dermot came by with fresh berries and Bernadette's organic pancake mix. It gave me chills to use the rest of Gran's half-gallon of milk, and we all left her favorite mug in the cabinet when pouring our coffee, but no one discussed it.

Zach shared our plans; Bernadette seemed content with us leaving. Dermot was taking a week's bereavement leave, and he and Matthew would begin to go through Gran's house. Bernadette held my hand as she told me about it, giving me a look promising I would return and not feel violated.

"When you're home from the retreat, we all—Dermot and Matt and me—want to ask if you'll stay here. At Mom's. Just for a while, until we figure out what to do," Bernadette said, looking more at the pattern of the table than at me.

I knew they meant selling the house and dividing the proceeds, but I left my sealed lips as they were. Dermot was standing in the door to the den, leafing through the old Sears catalog and smiling briefly when he came across Pappa's war letters home.

"Look," he said, tilting the book towards her.

She nodded. "I know."

They smiled at each other, the smile of their father's children, transported from the days when the two of them were as tight with each other as Zach and I were now. Then I willed myself not to think, because my life sucked enough as it was without trying to figure out if Rebecca and Caleb would interrupt the always-there-for-you status quo of Zach and I.

Matthew came by in time to say goodbye. The cars were loaded—Rebecca would follow us out of town and veer towards Austin, and Zach would meet her there in time for an early dinner. We group-hugged, and I caught Zach's smile when Bernadette thanked Rebecca, who asked that Frank be told good-bye from her. Frank was at the store, unavoidably, and had told us to not worry about stopping by. In other words, he was too drained to say farewell to his kids, and Zach nodded without commenting. He refused Caleb's offer to drive.

I blinked, and we were on the road. I blinked again, and Caleb was driving after all, while Zach lay in the back seat with his eyes closed.

He wasn't sleeping, though. "I like her," I said.

He smiled slowly.

"Yeah, she's great," Caleb added.

"And Frank and Bernadette like her."

Then he opened his right eye, briefly. "They do, actually, don't they?"

I nodded. "They do."

"They like Caleb, too."

"Yeah."

"They do?" Caleb asked, with a quick grin.

"You know they do." I took hold of his forearm. "You've been great."

He shrugged. Each time our bodies moved against each other, I felt my spirit circling back down to rejoin my form, so I kept my hand on him. "Thanks."

Eventually, quietly, we reached Wimberley. The too-bright FireWind sign looked weather-beaten and friendly. Caleb brought us to my cabin, not even glancing at the turn to his own, popping the trunk before turning to my brother. "Are you okay to get back, man?"

Zach stretched. "Sure."

"Thanks again for all the rides."

"Anytime." He paused, shook his head vigorously. "Okay, I'm just going to go. Email me later on and let me know how you're doing."

We huddled in a hug, then Zach folded himself into the driver's seat and took off without a final wave through the windshield.

Caleb wrapped his arm around me. "He'll be fine."

"I know."

"So will you."

I looked up at him, at his strong cheekbones, his concerned brown eyes, his focus only on me. "I know," I repeated, and walked us inside.

We skipped lunch, falling instead into a peaceful long sleep on the top of my bed. The later afternoon was still bright, the sun through the bedroom window increasingly hot. Caleb was so gentle as he eased out of bed, but I woke up anyway.

"I'm not ready for real life to begin," I said, muffling a yawn.

"I know, sweetie."

"You should get your stuff done, though. Don't be sitting around babying me and neglecting yourself, you've done enough of that."

"I'm not neglected, and I've been doing nothing I haven't wanted to do."

Suppressing a groan, I sat up. "Would you like to walk up the creek with me?"

"As a matter of fact, I would."

"Shower first or later?"

"Later."

I nodded. "Let's go."

The woods were so much cooler than Houston, especially when compared with the forced barrenness of the Medical Center. I drew the oxygen-rich air into my lungs and sniff-sneezed at the pollen but my eyes actually felt good watering against the allergens. The itching was annoying, but having some reason for my eyes to self-lubricate after all the dry crying was a relief.

Caleb ended up going to dinner alone, bringing me back a plate as well as Lizzy and Wren. Before we'd finished with the condolences, Rafael stopped by with a large handful of maidenhair and black-eyed Susan, and a quiet, "I'm sorry for your loss." He refused my invitation to join us.

By Tuesday lunch, I'd climbed onto the swing of things. Theo, since his return from the hospital, was spending more time in the dining room with the four of us, though he hadn't sought any of us outside the Main House. He'd caught Caleb and me on the footpath the evening of his discharge to offer his quiet thanks, and otherwise never mentioned the emergency call. His increased presence at the Main House meant Brandon and Angelica tended to get out of there asap. Rafael continued to be late or not show for meals, but sometimes sat over coffee with the rest of us. He never said much, but Sargie's approving beam as she walked past and saw six artists sharing a plate of brownies did engender rolled eyes and sub-breath mutterings.

Most of the time, we were somehow past the point of talking about work. Once in a while, we'd get on the subject, in more than a general 'so how's it going?' kind of way. Wren pointed out, one night in my cabin, that Theo no longer talked divine inspiration. She was so perceptive it scared me. At least she was no longer pissed at Caleb and me. The time we'd been in Houston had probably helped—because she had some distance, or because she felt sorry for me, or because she saw a depth proving the relationship was more than a physical thing, I don't know. I didn't want to know; I just wanted to put it all behind us.

Caleb had moved into ValeSong, although he left most of his camera equipment at LakeFire, and fiddled around there a few hours a day. Developing, manipulating images, whatever. He and Lizzy and I had carted his small sofa over to ValeSong, so there was comfortable seating for five in my den. We had to shuffle to get to the coffee maker and fridge, but it worked. Theo found out about my stash of beer and started to drop by if the front porch light was on. Zach emailed a thumbs-up icon when I asked him and Rebecca to drive down over the weekend with more booze and to hang out.

Not when Caleb was around—he tended to see it coming and distract me, I think—but on those mornings when he slipped out of bed to shoot the dawn light, I'd wake up with wet eyes from sad Gran dreams. I kept wanting but not wanting to pack up her fabric scraps and use or not use them in *Patchy Men* or *Tea Time Mosaics*, which occupied me when I needed a break from my men.

Once or twice, Lizzy brought up the Irish O'Connors, but I didn't let her get into it, and she let it drop.

I felt like myself, but a sketch in pastel rather than an oil.

On Friday, without quite realizing how I'd gotten there, I finished *Nine Patchy Men*. I took a quick jog down to the road and back in along a side path to the creek, went straight to the shower, and came out with the towel still turbaned in my hair to take a look.

The first thing you noticed was the standard-issue masculinity of the army blanket against the incongruously bright patches. I had abandoned the more traditional nine-patch form in order to feature the blanket, and had concentrated on providing as much detail in as small a space as possible for the individual men. I wanted it to invite close inspection, for each patch to be it's own presentation of 'patchiness' rather than going for a cumulative effect. Wren had pointed out it would be more like a series of vignettes that way, rather than an overwhelming bash against the male gender. I couldn't even remember what she'd said; it was her usual intuitive way of drawing the ideas from my own vision rather than imposing her thoughts on my art.

So I headed to Wren's cabin to ask her to come and judge me. It started to drizzle as I walked, so I didn't see her clearly when she asked me in. Once I'd brushed the hair off my forehead and dried my eyes on the belly of my shirt, I noticed her own damp cheeks.

"Hon, what's up? Are you okay?"

She nodded, not in the least convincing, and sat down. I followed.

"So what's up then? You're not sick, are you?"

The breath she drew sucked half the air out of the room, but it didn't lighten her mood. "May as well be."

"Why?" Nothing. "Wren, why? What's wrong?" I sat back and looked at her. Beneath the rims, her eyes were smudged with black, and she was gnawing at a fingernail edged in orange ceramic glazes—which surely wasn't healthy snacking material. "Is it work?"

She rolled her eyes so dramatically I could hear the snide thoughts.

"Well, what about work, then?" I bit my snippy tongue. Impatience wouldn't help either of us.

She stood abruptly and said, "Come on," without looking to see if I was going to trail her into her studio. Though, naturally, I was.

With an upward jerk of her chin, she invited me to inspect the orange house. It was small, half of a one-bedroom duplex she'd left open at the adjoining wall, dollhouse-style. There wasn't much furniture: a brown-orange table and chair, a sunflower-gold bedspread over a futon on the floor, a tangerine carpet.

She had glazed it in preparation for firing, and then gone back to reshape the front door area and the sitting room. There were still raw clay edges and a distinct lack of detail around the front stoop.

"Well?"

I shrugged my left shoulder. "I like the open effect, that's cool. Like you're cutting yourself off from the world around you." The duplex was her current home, the place she was being forced to leave.

"And the door?"

"Well, I guess, I just don't know what you're doing there."

"Exactly," she snapped, bitter. "I know what I'm trying to do there, but I'm not doing it. I'm just creating a fucking huge mess."

"Wren."

"Don't patronize me, Ash! I know a fucking huge mess when I see one. And this is one."

"But, Mother God, you can fix it, right? I mean, maybe not this one, but you can use it as a template and do the next one the way you want," I paused to see if she was gonna listen. She slammed her left fist down on the house, crumbling it and splatter-staining us both in the process. "Wren—hey!"

Lauren's eyes glared under her furrowed brow. Her rant wasn't speaking to me so much as grousing at the air around me. "Supposed to be the happy one. Supposed to look like a beautiful sunset, a sunset and sunrise rolled into one, a new beginning and a place of rest. Supposed to be vibrant and fill you with a longing to come in, sit down, get to know this place. Supposed to put the others to shame but infuse them with power at the same time. Instead it's a big, fucking, damn mess!" And she flattened what was left of the roof with the heels of both hands.

"Wren, sweetie, come on. A lot of that was in there. It just, you just need to take another stab at it."

"Shut up, Ash. Just shut up, okay?"

"Fine. All right. Look, I'll just leave."

"What'd you even come here for, anyway?"

Well, that was a trap door to a whole snake pit of negativity if ever I saw one. I shook my head. "Just was taking a break, wanted to say hi."

"Sweet of you." She couldn't have meant it less.

"I was going to see if you wanted to take a walk," a half-truth. "But then it started to rain."

"So you probably guessed, my answer is no, I don't want to go on a fucking walk. Can you just leave now?"

"Yeah, I can." Shit, I should be more gracious. She was obviously beyond frustrated. "Wren, really, you'll get it. Come on by if you want to talk or get away from here. But you'll get it." I leaned toward her to hug her shoulder but she moved away, so I caught myself by turning towards the door. When I got home, I took down the *Men* so she wouldn't see it first thing, but she never even came by, anyway.

"I just don't get it, is all," I said to Caleb, later on. "It's not like I put her down or anything. I was trying to be supportive. Or I was until she got all snappy at me."

He was blasé. "That's how she is. I told you. It has nothing to do with you, but just wait—she'll treat you differently from now on."

"No she won't." I even sounded like I believed it.

"She will. She did me. She's not going to stop talking to you, not like before, but she'll stop trying to listen. She'll stop noticing if you're being nice or you're interested or whatever."

I looked in vain for his blush. "So, you were interested in her." I don't know how I said it—it just slipped out, unplanned. I kept letting my guard down with him. Alternatively, I was comfortable.

"Huh?"

"Don't stall. You told me that first night you weren't ever interested in her, and now you're admitting you were."

"No, I meant her work."

"No you didn't."

"Did too."

"Caleb, my love, you did not. Give me some credit. I don't mind, but you did lie."

He growled, softly. Kind of a variation on his pre-speaking hum. "Ash, I was never interested in Wren. Not really. Just like I told you, I knew she was interested and when I thought you weren't, I thought about it. For like a minute. But by then she was all weird with me, so I didn't pursue it."

"So if she'd responded, you'd have gone for it?"

"God, what are you, a lawyer? Stop putting words in my mouth!"

So to shut off his spigot of indignation, I put something else in his mouth. He pulled back a moment later and confessed he probably would have gone for it with Wren if she'd let him. I found the ticklish spot under his knees.

"But only because I was so dejected and frustrated about you not caring for me. I was feeling like such an idiot chasing after you all over the place." He found a sensitive spot of my own.

"You were not chasing after me." I tickled my way from knees to upper thighs. Higher.

"I was, too. You just ignored every one of my advances." His hands left my body to guide my fingers around his erection. He hummed before speaking again. "Anyway, I never could have fallen in love with Wren. You're the one for me, Ashlyn. You know it, too."

It restored significant piece of peace to my soul to be able to make love with Caleb again. We'd shared a bed but not our bodies while we were in Houston.

In the morning, even though he'd slipped out early, I didn't wake up crying. I felt rested for the first time in almost two weeks.

CHAPTER 20

The next afternoon, Zach and Rebecca took Caleb and I on a drive along the Devil's Backbone. It's a loop along the eroding Edwards Plateau, with long vistas of rolling hills and limestone outcroppings and cacti that takes about an hour and a half if you don't stop. We kept pulling into the scenic overlooks to wander off as couples and admire the views, and each other. Back in the car, we giggled ferociously at Rebecca's lampooning of all things Zach and at Caleb's and my stories of Sargie and the other charmers at FireWind. Rebecca turned out to be a huge Lisette Model fan, which pretty much bonded her and Caleb like epoxy.

Caleb got some great raw shots of grebes and green-backed herons on the Blanco River. Rebecca, who'd led tours at Meadows Center for Water and the Environment during her years at Texas State University, had us stop there so she could show Caleb the Wetlands Boardwalk.

They were exclaiming over his high-shutter-speed pics of the endangered San Marcos Salamander when I turned to Zach, brow raised. "Admit it. You only worried about introducing her to Frank and Bernadette because she's the exact human they'd want for you and they'd never let her escape."

He laughed. "Assuming they'd agree I'm allowed to love someone besides them."

"So you do love her." We grinned at each other. "Well, it's about time. Everyone else in the May family is way ahead of you. Including Caleb."

"He's in my family now, is he?" Zach's shoulder bump pushed me into the railing.

"You're the one who introduced us."

Zach laughed again. All the endangered salamanders were going to take cover if he kept it up. "Didn't mean to."

I searched his face. "You aren't saying there's a problem?"

"No, sis. No problem. I like the two of you together. I hope it works out."

We turned to look at our new loves, busy discussing rare fish and wild rice. My smile was small but tender. "Me, too."

LIFE back at FireWind was increasingly routine. With Angelica and Brandon keeping mainly to themselves, it was just the six of us who piled into Lizzy's studio to see *In Sickness and In Health*, which she'd completed more than a week ahead of schedule. It was the first time since the Margie-dictated studio visits we'd spent any extended time discussing our art. Mostly we expressed awe; she'd captured vulnerability and dependence and raw struggle when she'd put the two figures together. Caleb took some slide shots for her, Wren directing the angles and presentation.

With ten days left, I finally brought up Caleb's return to San Jose.

"I'm not going back."

"'Scuse me?"

He laughed and grabbed me for a twirl in the air. Good thing we were in the doe's clearing or I'da hit the underbrush. "Ash, you think I'm going to pack up and leave the love of my life sweltering in Texas without me?"

"How am I supposed to know?"

"Oh, don't pout."

"What? You make, apparently, all these plans and schemes and don't bother to mention them to me?"

He hugged me gently to him this time. His arms. His scent. His teasing soft voice. "Sweetie babe—sorry, just sweetie. I didn't know when you wanted to talk about it. I was going to say something a billion times, but you've still been so sad. I don't want to intrude with all my plans for our happily ever after."

I widened my eyes. "Happily ever after?"

"Well, why not? You never know. We may as well go into it planning for forever."

"Great, no pressure or anything." Though the thip-thump of my heart wasn't from a flight or flight instinct. I thrilled.

"No, no pressure. Seriously. But I'm not going through life regretting missed opportunities. If right now I feel like we could be happily ever after, I'm going to proceed like I may be right."

"That's just. I mean, I love you; you know I do. But, isn't it dangerous?"

"Dangerous how?"

He was daring me to meet his eyes, but I looked into the branches of the black willow instead. "I dunno. Just, dangerous. It makes the fall so much harder when you discover it won't work out."

"Ash. Come on." Then he physically created eye contact, his hand calm and steady on my jaw. "Ash, do you have the slightest of inklings it won't work out?"

Then he shook my head at the same time I, hesitantly, started to shake it myself.

"See? We're fine. There's no reason to plan a lot of half-steps and 'what if' clauses. Come on." We'd reached my porch, and I sat on the step beside him. "Let me tell you what I've been thinking about, and you tell me which of the things are good for you, and which ones scare you, and which seem terrible. And we'll go from there, okay?"

I nodded, slipped an arm behind his waist. The gentle press of his weight against my side felt made for me. Damn him his confidence, anyway. I still wasn't sure he was so right, and considered this just more of his dictatorial take-charge-and-make-gazpacho nature.

However, the plans were okay. Some of them. No way was I going to move back into my damn rental, which I was now sure had totally the wrong karmic balance for me, and which wasn't big enough for the two of us to work in at any rate. My sublease had already emailed about extending the lease, when I'd said I would be going straight to Gran's after FireWind.

I didn't want to go as far as Northern California. And Caleb had been adding distance between himself and his parents since he'd figured out their trick of turning him into their arbiter. As he ran down his ideas, we stuck on two plans. He could move into Gran's with me, or we could find someplace new entirely. He was partial to Arizona.

As if I could just up and change my entire life.

To be with him.

As if my entire life hadn't already changed.

Not just because of him.

I couldn't imagine leaving Gran's behind, but I couldn't fathom living there without her. I vibrated with Caleb's gentle suggestion that moving there—even with him—would just exacerbate my loneliness for Gran and make it harder for me to establish my own space to work and live. "Would you ever let her fabric closet get as messy as you keep your studio here?"

I shoved my shoulder into his side. Never mind that he was right.

That night, mid-darkness and peacefully quiet, I burst into giggles.

"Hmm?" he asked, mellow and deep laughter in his throat.

I shook my head a few times before I could answer. "The very thought."

"Come on, it can't be that funny."

"No, Caleb, really. Me moving to Prescott to hang out in the desert with you? Where it's all hot and dry and people don't know how to make decent iced tea?"

"How d'you know they can't make iced tea? You've never been."

"No one who don't live between the Rockies and the Appalachians knows how to make decent iced tea. It's documented."

"You're so full of it, babe."

I pinched his arm.

"Okay, then, you're so full of it, Ashlyn."

"Be that as it may be. It's still bizarre to be planning this."

"Why? You've got nothing holding you back."

He must have felt my flinch. "Oh, baby, I didn't mean it like that. You know I didn't. I just mean, in general, like Lizzy has a job waiting for her and Rafael has his kids."

"Rafael has kids?"

"Two of them. Didn't I tell you?"

"No! When did this come out?"

"I don't know. Last week sometime. Oh, I do know; I was down trying to get some pictures of Hester and he was walking around, started telling me how much his little girl loves peacocks. She's one of those pink fairy princess kind of kids."

"So, not to be rude, but where's the mom? And why is he sleeping with women the first night here?"

"Aren't you the nosy one?"

"Yes. So tell me."

"Make me."

"I will, if you're gonna be like that."

His three-second window of opportunity to speak ran up, so I pounced and tickled.

Later, he rolled over and said, "Okay, okay, I'll tell." He kissed the back of my hand and murmured into it. "His girlfriend got pregnant when they were in college and they got married and then when they graduated their daughter was born, and then she convinced him to get a vasectomy. And then divorced him the next year. He gets them all summer now they're older—that's why he wanted to go on retreat now, so he wouldn't be anxious to work when they're staying with him."

"Damn. You sure know how to withhold information."

"Come on, how's it relevant to anything?"

"Goddess, Caleb, how is anything relevant to anything we gossip about? It's gossip! You get some, you share it with me, I share it with Lizzy and Wren. It's the way the world goes round."

"Women."

"Sure, women. We're all horrid beasts. I notice your inherent blame of the ex-wife in Rafael's story. It could quite easily have been the way he sleeps around or the way he refuses to pitch in around the household. Or all of it together."

"Wow, a misandrist diatribe. At two in the morning, no less. If I promise I'll change all the diapers and read all the bedtime stories, will you save the ranting for daylight hours?"

"Okay, I've only just decided to move to the desert with you, and you're naming the children. Slow down."

He turned and propped himself on his elbow. "You're coming with me?"

I smiled, which maybe he couldn't see in the dark, but I could hear his, so maybe he knew. "Yeah, Caleb, I'm coming with you. I want to go, alone, to Gran's for two weeks first. I want to help Bernadette sort it all out."

She and Dermot and Matthew had gotten through a lot of the estate stuff and were dividing possessions without rancor, but both uncles would be gone by the end of the week and there were personal effects and paperwork piles to sort through. And I needed to get the rest of my stuff out of the rental and figure out what to take to Prescott. And I kinda needed to talk some more to Bernadette; it had all been so flustered and unfocused after Gran's death.

Caleb would just have to find us a place to live on his own.

Our future had been on my mind since before Bernadette's birthday party, but I never expected to go from tentative discussion to thousand-mile-moving plan in the space of a few hours. My breathing hitched with the return of my racing pulse.

"Ashlyn," Caleb traced whispery fingers along my hairline. "Thank you. Thanks for trusting me on this, I know it's not easy."

I exhaled. "No, it's not. But in some ways it's easier now than it would have been before." I stared at the moon-glow through the curtain. Not to get all anthropomorphic again, but it seemed to be winking at me. Gran used to wink when she wanted to quietly signal my doing something well.

I winked back at the moon and tucked myself in tighter against Caleb. We drifted off together.

I yawned through our penultimate breakfast prep, and Caleb wasn't much better. He just nodded when I suggested we order yogurt and toppings for a parfait buffet the next morning. And let Margie try to prevent me serving packaged muffins.

"Just think, next week we have to make dinner," he grumbled as he cleaned the waffle iron. Since we'd been away for the funeral, Sargie'd had the new Team Three (Wren and Lizzy) trade breakfast/lunch weeks with us, which meant they were now done with all of their FireWind cooking. Caleb and I felt the press of expectations. We were cooking the very last of the communal dinners. Week Eight was nigh.

After lunch, back in ValeSong, I gathered the sketches I'd done in that studio. All of the *Patchy Men* pages were a mess, and I culled them for a few showing my progression through it, as well as a couple with motifs I liked but hadn't used. I couldn't hardly look at the *Chains of Love* layouts, so I moved them directly to the recycling pile, except for the one from my first FireWind morning.

Once those were organized out of the way, I added notes to the plans for the mosaic series, and sorted through the scrap pile to find some Pima broadcloth I could test out my bleach-dyeing plans upon. There was a largish section of a pale pink as well as a damask that struck me as particularly tile-like, so I stretched it on a smaller hoop and carried them both to the sink.

Half of the broadcloth I brushed over in a crazed fashion, going for the look of cracked plaster, and on the other half I traced a grid of bleach, then carried it out to the clearing to set in the sun. I tried the grout lines effect on the damask but it didn't look like it would take well. I put it in the sun anyway.

Straightening, I saw Wren walking up the stream from her cabin. I waved, but she didn't notice. Or didn't care. I started to call out, but, for whatever reason, didn't. I was suddenly exhausted; drained. Things were not going well with her, and I just couldn't blame myself. Normally I blamed myself for all of the inter-personal problems around me, but this time, I just couldn't.

Still, there was the news about Rafael, so I checked the angle of the sun and went to Lizzy's to tell her. She was gratifyingly titillated, and after she'd shown me the rough cut of a small soapstone figure provisionally titled *Lonely Loner*, I brought up Wren's walking away.

"Ash, don't be putting me in the middle here. I don't let her talk to me about you two, and I won't let you talk to me about her."

"She tries to talk to you about me?"

"As you do her, so don't get stroppy. I'm your friend, I'm her friend, and if the two of yous want to work it out and be friends as well, it suits me beautifully. If not, I'll just be friends with you separately."

"Wow. I guess I didn't know we weren't still friends. I thought this was just a rough patch."

"And why shouldn't it be?"

I shrugged, guilty. "I dunno. It should be. She's not..." I stopped myself from complaining. "I'll see if we can't work it out."

"Good." Lizzy was better than most at declaring a subject closed with just her tone.

WREN WASN'T AT DINNER, and Caleb and I retired early, worn out. He tried to slip out without waking me Saturday morning, but the shower noises roused me, and together we plodded to the kitchen and silently set out all of the food. Part of it was being too groggy to talk much, but part of it was the syncopation of having worked together so often in that space. He handed me bowls when I was gathering the table setting, and I nudged myself closer into the pantry when he needed to get to the fridge. Our choreography was a security blanket whenever I startled myself by remembering we would leave FireWind to start an entirely new life together.

Anyway, maybe our silence was infectious, 'cause the breakfast people who showed up (Wren, Theo, Lizzy) were notably quiet. I planned to talk to Wren when we were done clearing up, but the only one left at the table was Theo.

"Hey," he said as Caleb and I emerged from the kitchen, water-wrinkled fingers interlaced.

"Hey," Caleb replied. These two were quite the conversationalists.

"Listen, can you guys come by my studio?"

Theo had been spending a lot of time in there working, from what Caleb had seen while walking past between our own rooms. But he'd never asked anyone to see his stuff since the *Angel by Starlight* showing. We didn't hesitate to join him.

In his den, he started pacing some, but kept us facing the

window so we wouldn't see over the low wall into his studio. "When I was gone, you know, in the hospital? Okay, so, that was a bad time for me, but it did give me a lot to think about. You know, artistically and all. And emotionally, but that's different stuff, that's not why you're here."

Caleb and I traded glances, still unsure exactly why we were there.

"So what I said before, remember? About the way the work just comes to me, I don't control it?" We nodded. "Yeah, I know, well, I know now, that was just a lot of bullshit. That was just my way of avoiding confrontation if I offended anyone. I mean, I offended people a lot. I still do, I don't think that's changed, I don't think I want it to change, right?" Again we nodded. His pacing—a cross between professorial and maniacal—combined with all the nodding was making me dizzy. "Because offended is a visceral reaction, and that's what I want, is something visceral.

"She," he spat the word towards the north, "doesn't understand about visceral, even though it's what she does, too. She doesn't think of it like that, which is why she won't ever really make a masterpiece. If she was looking for it, that'd be one thing, because she has the skill and imagination for it. But she's not, she thinks it's all beauty and light or something. But not me. I know about feeling it," he punched his small intestine, "feeling it here, getting offended and getting repulsed and getting angry, and having it come from something exterior, something presented to you, something so powerful you can't look away from it but you want to, you want to but you're drawn to it." He stopped. "Do you know what I mean? Am I explaining it well?"

Personally, I wanted people to be irresistibly drawn to my work for different reasons, but I knew well enough what he was getting at.

A deep breath from Theo. "Right, so now, after being there and all, after thinking about this, I can say yes, I do intend to procure the reactions I get, I do want to be in control of my art. Okay?"

More nods from us. "So that's what I've been working on since I got back, and I've got a canvas I want to show you two, if you'll look, and tell me, honestly, what it makes you feel, right? What's the effect, what's the deep down gut reaction, right?" He gauged us. My head was spinning but I must have looked on board. "So come in."

Caleb followed me following Theo into his studio. He walked all the way to the easel, but the two of us stopped short in the doorway. Gradually we moved apart a little and closer to it.

The canvas was mostly in reds and blacks, heavily overpainted and almost three-dimensional just from the paint layers. A pale gray skinny body, naked to the waist, lay on a stretcher between two red-suited paramedics. The tube emerging from his throat ended at the lip of a gleaming steel basin in the lower left quadrant of the painting. Emerging from the tube were the contents of Theo's torn-up soul: a profusion of aspirin tablets, torn canvases, shards of his heart, and primarily, a crucifix upon which was mounted a smaller but more intricate version of the gray Theo, the feet end of the crucifix itself emerging from the labia of a be-winged Angelica. She was fellating the dick-shaped lens of a camera.

I glanced at Caleb. He was still contemplating the painting. I glanced at Theo. He was contemplating Caleb. Then he smiled wryly at me, eyes gleaming. "It makes you uncomfortable, doesn't it?"

"It does."

"But you want to keep looking, right?"

No point in denying it. "I do."

He nodded. "Look, then."

I went a bit closer. The details were articulate and deft. As in *Starlight*, he used light and shadow to suggest emotion and highlight the storyline. The first thing you studied, despite it being among the smallest of elements, was the crucifix Theo. But you didn't see it until you had taken in the scene as a whole: the medics blurred by quick action, the tragedy on Theo's brow, the betrayal of the Angel. I moved away, to a chair.

"Well?"

Caleb had moved away as well, and was looking at Theo. "Man, it's great. It's repulsive, but great."

"I do feel like I've been kicked in the stomach," I agreed.

"Seriously, now? You're not just trying to prevent me o.d.ing again, right?"

Caleb barked a laugh. "Well, I wasn't until now. Damn."

"Naw, I'm not going to. I'm too into life now; I got things to do."

"I feel like I should approach it with caution, like if I don't, it's liable to attack," I said. "And skill-wise, it's excellent. The balance and the color and the light, all great. Still, the main thing is how dangerous but, I guess, fascinating it is. Like a panther."

"It's fuckin' scary, all right," Caleb affirmed.

Theo was doing a hyena imitation. "God I'm glad you're saying this. I didn't want to show the others, well, you know, not those assholes anyway but the girls, no, cause it still feels too raw to me myself. But you guys, you saved me, in more ways than one really cause if I hadn't gotten to that damn therapist they had there I never would have realized half this stuff about how I control my work, but mostly you saved me literally, and I never really said thanks about that. So, thanks and all, and thanks for coming to look at it, and I guess I'm holding you up from cooking lunch, which should probably be good because all they're planning on is cheese sandwiches and tomato soup for dinner, so you two get going and thanks and I'll check you later."

Oh-kaaay. (And how did he know what Angelica and Brandon were going to cook?) We actually backed out of the studio, whether because Theo was actively herding as he talked at us or because we were subliminally worried about the art attacking us, I don't know. Seconds later we were out the door and on the path to the Main House.

"Well, that was," Caleb started.

"Yes, indeed it was," I agreed. "Do you, um…."

"Want to grab some cheese sandwiches and fruit on our own and not go to dinner tonight? Why, yes, yes I do." Caleb ran his fingers under my shirt and up my spine, then kissed my neck three fast but sharp times. "Let's go have that picnic on the rise we've been threatening."

What a relief.

I didn't see Wren until the next day, and by then, somehow, the moment for talking out the tensions and moving back towards closeness had passed.

CHAPTER 21

Our last week at FireWind was a bit of a flurry. First off, it rained gully washers all day Tuesday and Wednesday. The all-knowing founders hadn't provided umbrellas or entry mats to wipe mud from our shoes, so for the most part we all stayed in our cabins. Caleb and I dutifully dashed down the path to get dinner going, but we took the easy road of doubling the portions of rice and beans. For a couple of nights anyone staggering in for hot food found my burrito-making instructions stuck to the fridge. Meanwhile, Rafa and Theo were supposed to be on breakfast/lunch duty but they'd arranged to each prep one meal a day, and they seemed to be in competition over who could make a more bare-bones meal.

On Thursday, Margie posted a note on the Main House door:

"As the earliest flight out of Austin on Saturday is at eleven a.m., the shuttle will be arriving at eight a.m. for loading and departing at exactly nine a.m. Anyone who fails to make it onto the shuttle will be responsible for their own transportation arrangements. Please remember the telephone in the common room is for local calls only. There will be no lunch served on

Saturday, although participants are welcome to pack themselves a 'to go' meal after the breakfast service is completed. All participants are expected to have departed, leaving their cabins and work areas in a clean and tidy condition—WITH ALL FURNITURE RETURNED TO ITS ORIGINAL LOCATION—by noon on Saturday. Please speak to me directly if these arrangements pose any difficulty, although you should note special accommodation is not available. Thank you."

I nudged Caleb. "I think she's been spying on your cabin."

"I know. Now I'm worried. What if she has cameras everywhere?"

I giggled.

"Stop laughing. What if she has cameras up in that tree on the rise?" We had been ever so slightly indiscreet after our picnic up in the knoll.

"I'd wager she does. But there's nothing we can do about it now."

"Unless we want to give her a repeat performance," he said, dipping me down swiftly despite my squeal of protest.

"Break it up, you two, this is a family retreat," Lizzy said, climbing up the porch.

"We were just..." I grinned.

"Yeah, yeah, I saw. What's that?"

"Dictate from the Sarge."

She read it. "Just when I was getting used to sleeping in."

"I know. So, will you help move back the sofa?"

"Sure, we'll get it after lunch. Have they actually cooked?"

"Nope. Theo came by and tossed a salad, though. I was impressed."

"Mmm, mmm, good. I wonder if I can steal his recipe and use it at the new job?"

"I highly recommend it," Caleb said. "The can of artichoke hearts was an inspired touch."

"Well," Lizzy said, "that's our Theo for you, divine inspiration and all."

We'd told her, of course, about the painting. But it was funnier to pretend he hadn't had a work-related revelation.

ZACH WAS COMING for me Saturday late morning. Caleb's flight was at noon, which nixed any hope of his hitching a ride to Austin with us, so I wouldn't get much of a private farewell. He was going to San Jose for a couple of days to sort out his stuff, and would drive to Arizona to settle in. After I was finished at Gran's house—or as finished as I was capable of being—I would drive to our new place myself. With plenty of loud music and scheduled stops to keep the old hypersomnia at bay.

Margie joined us for our final dinner, so for once the dining table was crowded. Seating arrangements were mutually careful— Brandon and Angelica were buffered from Theo by Margie on one side and Wren on the other. Lizzy blocked Wren from Caleb and I. It was sure proof of our creativity as a group.

I expected Sargie to make a speech, but she kept it brief. She did tell us all how unique our group had been, among the many previous FireWind participants. She patted at Theo's hand as she said, "I doubt I will forget this experience," and he recoiled away. We passed around a contact sheet and filled in our email addresses and phone numbers—I didn't see what Caleb put for address, but I listed Frank and Bernadette's house. It was the first time I'd used their address as a default contact since leaving high school. The rest of my junk mail went to Gran's house; I'd have to file a change of address for both places, as well as the damn rental.

Margie promised copies for us all in the morning. She didn't leave when dinner was over, or when the brownies and coffee were served. Brandon and Angelica kept glancing at the door, and Caleb eventually went to the kitchen to start the dishes. Trying to read Wren's and Lizzy's faces, I got nothing, so I gathered up some cups and followed him. When I went back to collect plates, Theo was gone, and Angelica's tears dripped down her immobile face. Lizzy moued at me but no one said anything. So I returned to Caleb.

He was goofing off, pretending he needed to use the sprayer to defend himself from me. I couldn't stop giggling. The last damn dishes we'd wash there! Domestic life in Prescott was going to be a comparative breeze—not least because Caleb had promised to never make me join him for breakfast. *Hello, late mornings.*

I pressed up against his back to stop the spray attack. "You done with packing, or what?"

"Just about. I'm going to bring it all to yours in a bit, okay?"

"Sure."

"What's happening out there?"

I leaned away from him enough to peek through the pass-thru. "Umm, Margie's still there. The girls are there, but Rafa's moved on. He said he'd come to ValeSong tonight to help finish off the booze, though. What does she want?"

He shrugged, shoulder blades shifting across me. "Maybe she just likes us."

"Weird ways of showing it."

"Yeah," he turned. "Let's let the rest air dry, eh?"

Ten minutes after chocolate and Brazilian roast, and he still tasted of peppermint. It was somehow inherent in him. Crap, I was gonna miss his peppermint tongue over the next couple of weeks.

"Hey, no crying, not yet. I can't cry yet, so you can't cry yet."

My internal compass said he didn't need to hear I might just be crying because of the fear-tinged excitement of self-reliance. I had been through hell and emerged in a spot from which it appeared I could miss Caleb not because I needed him beside me, but because I treasured the way I felt about myself when we were together.

I would be, I knew, still strong on my own.

Without Caleb. Without Zach.

Without Gran.

I found a dry dishtowel and scrubbed my face. "I have some more packing to do before people show up to drink me out of house and home."

He kissed my cheek. "See you in a bit."

"'Kay." I skirted past the people still silent at the table. What a tableaux. Not that I was much better a sight, I imagined.

IT WAS time to pack up my machine. I wasn't sure how much sewing, if any, I'd accomplish between FireWind and Arizona, so I brushed it carefully and blew compressed air through the bobbin case to chase out any lingering lint. I unclamped the needle and stored it with the others, checked my box of embroidery wheels to ensure they were all gathered and stored.

Then I oiled the machine parts, brushing lubricant as well on the gears within the base plate. I moved on to my spools and bobbins, locking them all down in their traveling case, and dug out the cardboard carton where I would nestle the jars of beads, notions, floss, tapes, and pins. Finally, I spread large sheets of tissue and set *Nine Patchy Men* and *Mint Tea Mosaic* upon them, folding each carefully away.

The studio was bereft. I would miss its space—the light and the peace of the woods, the feeling of having everything at my oft-pricked fingertips, yet being able to spread out like I needed.

Before I could sink into a true reverie, Caleb barged in loaded down with camera bags. Sweet man. He was wearing my favorite black jeans.

"Just about done here?"

I stood. "Yeah, I think I'll do the rest after you go. Zach won't be here at the crack of dawn or anything."

"Like brother, like sister."

"Learn to live with it."

"I will, thanks." He started in on my neck again. "How much time till the horde arrives?"

"Um, not much, I'm afraid. We'll just have to drink fast to get them out."

"It's a plan."

Indeed, the horde—a.k.a. Lizzy, Theo, Rafa, and later Wren—did descend. It was a heck of a lot more relaxing sitting around on the floor with them sipping beer and talking about the 'what nexts' of our lives than it had been at the dining table. In deference to Theo and Rafael, we didn't mention Angelica, though we did have a couple of good laughs at Brandon's expense. Wren arrived in the middle of Caleb detailing our Arizona plan, and left after half a glass of wine. I attributed her shining eyes to an alcohol buzz, more to salve my own conscious than from conviction. Lizzy gave everyone hugs and walked her out.

"I guess you two are ready for us to leave, then?" Theo asked, draining his longneck. Rafael didn't say anything, but gathered up the empties around him and stuck them back in the carton.

"It's cool," Caleb said, friendly enough but he stood and started tidying, too. I just leaned my head back against the wall, eyes closed, smiling.

And then we were two. I made a slow rondo through the cabin, turning off lights, shutting down the evening, and shutting out the woods, the suitcases, the people in other cabins and other cities. My dance ended at the bedroom doorway, where Caleb was leaning, watching me, silent and smiling from his eyes but serious from his lips. His ever-minty lips.

"We'll be fine."

"Who said we wouldn't be fine?"

"No one. But you were worrying."

I laced together our fingers. "No. Not worrying. We will be

fine. I may have a hell of a next two weeks, but I'm not worried about the moving across the country part."

Together we moved across the floor, sank down upon the bed. "I love you, Caleb. And," I smiled back into his eyes, before he could say it, "you love me, too. That's the beauty. The chaff is getting Frank to not freak about me crossing three states to be with you, and Bernadette to become convinced I can survive and do my art at the same time. If I get her to stop calling them 'your little quilts', so much the better. But even with all of that, even in Gran's house without Gran, I'm okay."

"You're better than okay. You're fantastic."

"No, you're fantastic."

"No, you are."

"Well, you are too, then," I moved into him. "And I'll prove it."

The other thing, I thought, hands again memorizing the seat of those black jeans, was when Caleb told me I was fantastic, my little internal note of protest was quiet. I was beginning to truly believe it. And if I cried a little bit more about that, on top of everything else, he never said a thing. Like the first night we slept tight in my bed, he just held my body to his, gently kissed my hair, and let me cry within his embrace.

Sargie Margie's careful notes notwithstanding, the morning was chaos. I sent a blessing to the sun gods for Zach's habitual sleeping in, so I could get past all the shuttle bus mania before having to deal with my own packages and bags. As it was, we were hauling *In Sickness and In Health* to Houston to ship it for Lizzy, because she didn't trust the amount of crating she could accomplish at FireWind. I assured her for the fourteenth time I didn't mind, and I'd make sure every one of her specifications was met. She trusted *A Loner Alone* to the airline, but I was custodian of her masterpiece.

Even without *Sickness* the shuttle was packed full of art, barely leaving room for the artists. At the last minute, Brandon's ride fell through, so he was going along to Austin in hopes of catching a bus to Tulsa from there. No mention of Angelica joining him or vice-versa spilled out of any conversation, and they were behaving as if they barely knew each other. Apparently, she was ready to move on.

Wren let me help with her suitcase, and clutched me in a good-bye grasp. Caleb stepped away to help Rafa carry up several large boxes. Unlike Theo, who'd generated drama at every turn regarding his traveling frames, the quality of the interleaf paper protecting his canvases, and the Tetris-level stacking of luggage he required before he would load his work into the bus, Rafa sauntered up and shoved the boxes into the cargo space. He boarded the bus without looking to see if Caleb had safely stowed the three boxes he carried.

Not a one of us had seen his painting. The boxes, which weighed little, were our only clue: probably he painted on flat canvas boards, and clearly his scale was small. I decided he was an enviable genius and let it go. Maybe one day we'd run across a show of his.

We. Yeah, we. Me and Caleb. Going together to a gallery, talking about the artists we knew, and the ones we didn't. Now that was a life I could picture without needing a telephoto lens.

Margie stood on the porch watching everyone board the bus. "Don't let her bite you after we're gone," whispered Lizzy, coming up behind me.

"Let's hope Zach gets here soon," I agreed.

"I'll call yous from Dublin."

"You have Gran's number?" I knew she did, but I couldn't phrase everything else I wanted to say: she'd been a true friend, she'd only ever done what she felt was right, she'd be deeply missed. I would carry Lizzy's voice in my head as one of my trusted advisors. I settled for a long hug and a squeeze of her hand.

She pushed those wire-rims back up her nose. "Okay, then, you be good."

I smiled. "And yourself as well. Safe home. And my best to your folks."

"My folks! What a Texan. Only call me when you're drunk, right? No point hearing your voice unless I get the drawl as well."

"I'll make sure of it."

She nodded. "Right, then." And boarded the bus.

The driver was definitely ready to go. Margie came down two of the porch steps, pointedly glancing between Caleb and the bus door.

He led me around the back of the bus, out of sight of both Margie and, hopefully, most of the inhabitants.

"So."

"Hmm?" he breathed, more a vibration from his voice box to my skull than an audible reply.

"Okay, let's not make it too long. You have a good flight, call me tonight sometime, and kiss me goodbye now."

The crinkly eyes. "Now who's getting all dictatorial?"

"I learn from the best, my love."

One more time, my hands on his shoulders. One more time, his palms on my back. A kiss, then another. Then another. Longer, longing.

Together we clung on, and together we broke apart.

"See you soon."

I nodded. "See you real soon."

"Why? Because I like you."

"You goof."

"You first."

"You more."

"One more."

"Yes, please." I kissed him. He agreed. And then the bus started up, baleful exhaust sending smoke signals our direction.

I sighed. "Subtle." Which got a laugh, the last laugh I'd see from him for a while, so I locked it in my heart and walked him to the door.

"Bye, Ash, I love you."

"I love you too. Tonight?"

He nodded. "Tonight." With that promise, and with one last kiss to brand my cheek, he was on board, and the bus was gone.

CHAPTER 22

Zach arrived; we left FireWind. The hills and streams had given way to foothills that were threatening to give way to the flat plains of I-10 before I roused myself for conversation.

"So, you okay? You all sad and stuff?"

I shrugged defensively. "It's only two weeks."

"Which seems like an eternity?"

"Ha ha. No, the only eternity is the future in the desert. He'd better test out the a/c real good before he signs a lease."

"You're really going, then?"

"Yeah, why not?"

"I dunno. I just have trouble picturing you living so far away."

"It's not as far as Berkeley."

"I know, but that wasn't far for me. It was barely far enough."

"The young runaway. They roped you back in the end though, didn't they?"

"Shuddup. I'm not here for them, it just worked out that way."

"Uh-huh."

"Shuddup." He tried to clean the windshield with the spray, but it just streaked bug innards across the field of vision. "Besides, who's running from who now?"

"I'm not running, we just picked a place that doesn't happen to be in Texas."

"Uh-huh, and have you told Frank and Bernadette about this plan?"

"What am I, twelve? I don't need their approval."

No answer.

"Shuddup. I don't."

"I didn't say anything."

"I think after a quarter-century I've come to accept their disapproval."

"God, Ash, not your self-pitying bullshit again."

"What?"

"The whole mom and dad don't love me thing, I mean, haven't we done it to death already?"

Where was all the anger coming from? "Well, excuse me, it's not like you know where I'm coming from here, is it?"

"Oh, right, I forget, they never criticize me. They wholeheartedly refute everything I do as an adult, but they don't criticize."

"I never said they criticize me, I said they don't approve of me."

"Well they don't send you articles about the ways the computerization of our world is destroying the environment, do they? They don't treat every girlfriend you've ever introduced them to like a no-good Martian, do they?"

"They like Rebecca."

"They treated her well at the funeral. And then they sent me another clipping with a note that said, 'give our best to Roxana.' I mean, Roxana? That's a stretch even for them."

From somewhere in the part of my psyche not overcome with offense at him and worry about my own life, it occurred to me I'd never heard him rant so much about Frank and Bernadette. I'd heard some snide comments, and we had plenty of anecdotes for the party crowd, but never this wholesale bitterness. "My goodness, Zachary May, you are truly in love!"

He glanced at me. "Come again?"

"You. You're in love, you're happy, you're secure and content. I knew you two were into each other, but I didn't pick up on how deep it went." I slid across the seat to kiss his cheek. "Way to go."

He shook his head. "Do I even ask where this came from all the sudden?"

"Nah."

"Right." Again, he tried the wipers. "Well, anyway, you're right about the love thing. But don't tell Frank and Bernadette. And don't tell them how Rebecca is their ideal daughter-in-law, either. We'd end up planning a big church wedding and roast beef reception just to keep them a reasonable distance from us."

I grinned, happier than I'd been all day, but it didn't take. "Yeah, I'll be too busy convincing Frank I can drive a thousand miles safely and Caleb won't axe me once I get there. And Bernadette that we won't starve to death with only our 'little quilts and snapshots' for an income."

"You know, if you need some cash to get you settled...."

"No, big spender, the point is, I don't. We don't. Save it for your giant carbon footprint honeymoon. We'll be fine, we'll be okay. Two starving artists are easier to keep alive than one starving artist." I backed off some. "But it's totally sweet of you to offer, thanks."

"Sure. And I mean it, so call anytime."

A half-laugh. "Well, I'm more likely to call you than Bernadette."

"She really does like your art, you know."

"Uh-huh. She raves about it."

"No, seriously, Ash, she told me *Chains of Love* one was your best yet. It brought tears to her eyes."

"Beg pardon?"

"God strike me down for a sinner."

"When?"

"I dunno. Like, two-three days after the party."

"You never told me."

He shrugged. "Other stuff happened. I forgot."

Other stuff. Stuff like, Gran dying. That kind of thing. And then it mattered not how many bugs were smeared on the windshield, 'cause I couldn't see a thing.

"Oh, man, Ash, I'm sorry."

I shook my head, sniffled, "It's not your fault. It's just," a couple of minutes to find a way to phrase it, "how, I mean, what am I going to do? Who do I talk to about stuff? Where do I go at Christmas? I need her. I need my Gran, Zach, and she's gone."

He was rubbing my shoulder with his free hand. "Come on, Ash, come on. You'll be okay." I found a tissue in his glove box. "You got me, ya know. And Caleb." I nodded with my face buried. "And Bernadette, and Frank, too. No, you do. You gotta grow up out of this self-pity thing, cause you gotta see you do have them, okay? I don't want to get harsh on you right now, but it's important. You need to know it, all right?"

I nodded, to shut him up, which worked. Most of the rest of the drive was quiet. I didn't want to retreat back into my cocoon, but just for a couple of hours, I needed it. Quiet. Bless him, Zach gave it to me. That Rebecca was a lucky woman.

THEY'D NEGLECTED HER BUSHES. In the late spring like this it got dry and if the azaleas were going to bloom they needed to be watered regularly. I switched on the sprinklers on the way in.

It was the first time Zach had been there since the funeral, too. It wasn't quite ransacked and wasn't quite tidied up. The dining room was almost empty, just the sideboard left to be taken out. The pictures were, by and large, off the walls. But the hall table was piled high with envelopes and stacks of paper, and the kitchen hadn't been touched. The beds were stripped and her clothes had been packed up. Only our quilts remained in the linen closet. I turned away from it and closed the door.

"You sure you're okay to stay here?"

I nodded.

"I'll stay tonight too if you want."

"Nah. I think it's better if I do it on my own. Besides, you have to get back."

"Not really."

"Well, if you stay, we're gonna have to have dinner with Frank and Bernadette, and I'm gonna tell them Rebecca moved in."

"You wouldn't."

"Try me."

"I'll tell them you're off to some strange city with a man you hardly know."

"I've known him longer than you have her, plus you can vouch for him. For all we know, this Roxanna of yours is a high-tech bank robber who runs her CPU all night regardless of the energy waste."

"You are such a brat."

"Just trying to make sure you won't miss me too much when I've gone."

"I won't miss hauling your stuff all over creation, that's for sure."

"Okay, special treat. This time I'll unload the trunk, and you make up my bed for me. Deal?"

"Somehow your deal still has me doing chores."

"And look how sympathetic I am. Hand over your keys."

I stacked most of my stuff in the dining room, not anticipating I'd use any of it until I was re-settled with Caleb. It was strange to think of not sewing for weeks. Even when my art hadn't been going well, I did a few basic stitches every day—piecing, or turning somebody's great-grandmother's antique quilt tops into finished products for extra spending dollars. Practically no one realized the tops their bygone ancestors hadn't bothered to quilt were the ones deemed unworthy. But value is a relative thing; few people today could piece a top half as well as the less adept quilters of a hundred and fifty years ago. Hell, even I didn't have the patience to hand quilt my non-art pieces, not the way Gran did.

Past tense did.

I put the suitcase and duffle in the utility room. Zach found me there, folding Gran's clothes from the dryer. Smoothing wrinkles from the apple green housecoat.

"Are you sure about this?" he asked.

"As sure as I am about anything. Will you be okay driving back?"

He shrugged. "I'm always okay to drive. Unlike some people. Hey, can I ask a favor?"

"You know it."

"Not now, but someday? Can you…make me something with that?"

I was still holding the half-folded robe. I tucked it into quarters and set it squarely on top of the pile. After a bit, I managed, "I can. Thanks for asking."

He got me in a bear hug. "You be strong, Ashlyn, and call me whenever you need, okay?"

"Okay."

"I mean it."

"Of course you do. You're an anchor."

I was almost overloaded on leave-takings for the day, but survived this one more. By the time he drove off, it was getting on towards dinner, but I couldn't be moved to go in search of food. I scrounged. There were rolls in the freezer and cans of soup in the pantry. It lacked panache, but it filled my stomach.

My heart was a different matter. Even curled up in bed talking to Caleb, my heart refused to fill. I gave him credit for enforcing a limit to my time at Gran's house; the morass was threatening to claim me permanently after only a few hours.

In the morning, after she'd had time to open the store and see to the early customers and paperwork, Bernadette came by. We took a slow tour of the house together.

The three siblings had divided the furniture according to their wants and some basic feeling of fairness. Matthew had taken some smaller mementos back to California. Dermot had arranged for his selections—the dining set, the large carpet from the living room, an armoire—to ship on a truck headed his way later in the month. Together they'd packed up the clothes and towels to donate to Gran's parish, and had taken most of the books to the library. The only real sorting jobs for Bernadette and me to finish up were the sewing things, which she left entirely to my discretion, and the paperwork. Her plan for the kitchen was for me to take whatever I needed or wanted, pack up the china for Zach, the crystal to save for me, and donate the rest.

We didn't get tons done before she had to get back to the store for the lunch crowd. I headed to my rental to clear all traces of myself from it. I had left most things packed away so the subleaser could use the space, but what was left took a couple of days of solid hauling. Very little of the furniture was mine, but I still didn't see how I would get everything to Prescott without a trailer. Caleb was looking for an unfurnished house, so we needed whatever I could bring. That meant my bed from Gran's house, the sideboard Uncle Dermot didn't have room for, and the dinette set.

On Wednesday, I got a trailer hitch installed on my little car. It would have to be a very lightweight trailer, but it should do the trick. After a determined campaign, Zach had convinced Caleb to ignore my protests about driving myself to Arizona. Zach shared every story from my entire life about my falling asleep in cars. And buses. And boats. And once on horseback. It didn't offend me so much as annoy me that Zach thought Caleb was the one to be persuaded.

Persuaded he was, though he claimed his impatience to hold

me again was more of an influence than my brother's heavy-handed scare tactics. So he was flying to Houston once he found us a house, and together we would haul whatever fit on the largest trailer my car could manage.

Wednesday night, Caleb called from Los Angeles, where he was crashing for the night at another of the Zeke's pads. "And how are you?"

"Not thinking about anything, and staying sane that way."

"Are you taking care of yourself? Are you eating?"

"Yes, sir."

"Don't tease me, I'm worrying about you. I'm not used to worrying about someone so much."

"Sweet man, you don't need to worry, okay? I'm fine. For now. I miss you, that's a given, but I'm fine."

"Only ten more days."

"Wow."

"Will you be ready? Is that okay?"

"I think so. I'm finally out of the rental. From now on, I'll be concentrating on this house."

"Is it going okay with your parents?"

"Yeah. I haven't seen much of them yet. As a matter of fact, I haven't seen Frank at all. I'm supposed to have dinner there tomorrow. I'll tell them about Arizona then."

"I'll call you late tomorrow then. I'll call you from bed."

Caleb kept my heart open just thinking about him. I smiled. "I'd like that."

"Not as much as I'm planning on liking it."

I laughed. "Dirty. Hey. Caleb."

"Hey, Ash?"

"I wanted a future with you, you know? Before Gran, I mean. Just so you know, this isn't escapism on my part."

"Ash." He cleared his throat. The deep emotion in his voice stung my eyes. "Me, too."

"Thanks. Thanks for running away with me."

"Running towards you."

"Towards you, too. Towards each other."

I could hear his smile. "Yeah. Good night, Ash, love."

"Sweet dreams, Caleb. I love you."

"Good night."

I HAD LEARNED to sew on Gran's Singer. By my eighth birthday, I could thread it blindfolded. I know, because Zach bet me I couldn't, and I won. He had to wear the blindfold the rest of the day.

The summer before I turned fourteen, Pappa took me on a 'secret mission' to the sewing machine shop, to help him pick out a new multi-purpose machine for his and Gran's anniversary. I couldn't imagine her giving up the Singer, but we settled on a beautiful Janome that stitched multiple layers with perfect ease. Then, even though it was months early, they gave it to me for my birthday.

"No, sweetheart, that was always our plan. I'm not giving up my trusty friend here," she'd said, patting it. "You can have it when I'm dead. Until then, you use this."

And I did. I loved my machine. But I was taking them both.

After Bernadette left on Thursday with an armload of official-looking documents to sort while at the store, I found Gran's case of lint and oil brushes and the tube of lubricant, and set to work. Gran hadn't cleaned it often once her arthritis got bad, but there wasn't a lot of build up. I just liked doing it; it was satisfying to know I was treating the equipment well. The way Gran had taught me.

I didn't start crying again until I opened the fabric closet. The boxes she'd labeled 'scraps' and 'quarters' and '1/2 yd or more' in red permanent marker did me in. She was always so organized. I was constantly fighting the urge to just toss my leftovers on the top of the pile when I finished a piece, but the Gran-voice in my head made me fold them neatly and jot the remaining yardage on the bias. The partial bolts in Gran's closet were all lined up straight, with darker fabrics to the left and lighter ones to the right. I screwed up the organization right away by sitting in the middle of the closet and digging through the quarters box to see if anything in particular caught my eye. The only way I could get through it was to dive in and be as ruthless as I could manage, and I had my black garbage bags at the ready. I wasn't even going to look in the box of scraps. Everything I didn't want was going to the church auxiliary's blankets for the homeless project.

After I'd bagged the desirable textiles, and created a 'maybe' pile to look at again in the morning, I moved on to the threads. Most of the spools weren't colors I needed, but I filled up my thread case and took the colors matching any unusual bobbins she'd made up.

I kept every one of Gran's button jars.

Before I could sew a stitch, I used to empty them over her floor to sort and play, delighting when I found a white in the pink/red jar or a fabric frog in with the wood buttons. Gran didn't often make clothes, but it took years for me to guess she was mis-sorting the buttons just for me.

Big old treasure trove of devastatingly happy memories in one small room. I wandered back into the kitchen and opened a beer. Anesthesia was definitely the way to go. I tuned in the eighties rock station—anything to avoid an oldie or one of Gran's mockingly loved country songs—and took a deep breath.

They're just things, Ash. Some cloth, some embroidery floss, a few pairs of scissors. Figure out what could be useful, figure out what's sentimental important, and pack up the rest.

I ended up with the buttons, three bags full of cloth, my favorite embroidery hoop, and a collection of beads stashed on a shelf too high for Gran to have reached in a long time. I also found the Singer's long-absent embroidery disk no. 19, for block stitches. Gran would have gotten a big kick out of seeing that gap in the disk box finally filled.

Ultimately the phone stopped me from packing more.

"Baby girl, dinner's on the table. Are you coming?"

"Oh, Frank, I'm sorry. I didn't realize the time." Glancing down at myself, I volunteered, "Why don't you two go ahead and eat, and I'll clean up and come by for a drink?"

"No, we'll wait for you. Nothing will spoil. You take your time."

"Are you sure?"

"We are. See you in an hour or so."

I rushed. Bernadette wouldn't appreciate my near miss of standing her up.

She was treading gently, though. Even told me I looked nice, which was unique. I had to smile when I saw they were serving gazpacho, Caleb's favorite. It made it easier to just come right out with Project: Arizona.

I glanced sidelong at Frank. He was the one who'd give me problems over this. He started with, "But, why there?"

"I can't stay here. This week," I spooned a bite and stalled, "this week's been hard enough. I just can't stay here right now."

"So far away, though?"

"It's the half-way point. Just as easy to get to his family as mine." Or as hard, I didn't say.

"What are you going to do there?" This from Bernadette.

"My art. Same as Caleb."

"But, for rent, for food?"

"We've got it under control. We've got our commercial sites, too." I attempted a smile. "Come on, you two taught me so much about living frugal and simple. I don't need much more than air conditioning and room for some tomato plants."

"How well do you think you know this Caleb, anyway?"

I patted his hand. "Don't worry, Frank, I'm getting bigger by the day. I'm not making a mistake, not this time." It came out steady, but inside I was stammering.

It was all going so damn predictably. He questions my emotional judgment, she questions my practical judgment, I defend and deflect while trying to sound reasoned. Finally I set down my spoon and said, "Look, Frank, would you like to read my cards? Would that help?"

As he dealt, his frame lightened. The past was predictable enough—three of swords for heartbreak. Better then than now. Frank squeezed my hand and moved to the present. "A new beginning for your heart," he said, almost triumphantly, laying the ace of cups.

Bernadette stopped clearing the bowls and leaned on him to watch, a soft smile spreading when Frank turned the king of cups. "True love," she read for him, though we all knew already. I'd known for weeks, but it warmed me to see the proof laid out on my parents' dining table. Considerably more accepting of my new life-course, they turned the conversation to more immediate concerns.

Over chai, we made plans for the rest of my stay. They would walk through with a realtor on Sunday. Frank would help me load the trailer on Wednesday before Caleb's flight came in, and he and I would leave early enough to eat dinner with Zach and Rebecca (Bernadette used her correct name) in Austin, aiming for New Mexico by Thursday night and our new home, wherever precisely home was, by Friday.

Logistically, there wasn't much left to do at Gran's. Bernadette and Dermot and Matthew had accomplished a lot.

"I could use your help going through all the papers," Bernadette told me.

I nodded. "Okay."

"The mail is piling up. Well, you know, you saw it. You could start to sort through all that. I've arranged to cover the store on

Saturday, so we can stay over there together and figure it all out. Okay?"

I nodded again.

The parental dinner wasn't quite as hard as I'd feared, I reported to Caleb later, in bed. He'd made it to Arizona.

"Oh, Ash, it's beautiful. Wait until you see. You'll be so happy."

"I'll be happy wherever we are," I smiled down the wire at him.

"Hey, me too! Hmm, I do miss you." His voice was dipping and growling.

"And I you."

He would look at properties from our shortlist in the morning, texting me pictures and opinions. I started my last Friday in Texas scrolling online property listings while waiting for any early reports from Caleb.

There was nothing from him, but there was an email from Lizzy. She'd been tracking her crate, and was anticipating it in another week. And based on the slides Caleb had shot of it, coupled with some advice from Wren, she'd been able to secure a top notch agent, who in turn had secured her a couple of exhibitions in the next month. Moira had begged again for her to come back to Carmel's, but not to her arms, which was fine. Lizzy would have rejected either option. She was getting on well at the brasserie and had met a tall blonde who was flirting mercilessly with her.

All in all, she was in grand form.

She had a postscript: "Wren has put aside her houses for the nonce. She barreled into a gallery there in Norwich trying to flog her stuff, and ended up talking her way into a job. She claims to be ecstatic about it all, but as this is Wren we're talking about, is sure to change her mind. Happy thoughts going out to her, though, and to you and Caleb. Lotsa love, Lizzy."

Right, I told myself. The mail pile wouldn't shrink just because I ignored it. Carrying the stack from the hall to the breakfast room, I couldn't help noticing on the way the house was colder and emptier than I'd ever imagined it could be.

Setting the recycling bin next to me, I got to work. A profusion of AARP-type bulk mails went out first. Following that, the credit card offers and local coupons. A bank statement and three bills stayed on the table, as well as four envelopes suspiciously sympathy-card-shaped, which I left for Bernadette. Over two week's worth of mail, and only eight things worth saving.

I didn't want to mess with the bank statement—and there I was, professing to be a grown up—so I opened the bills. Electricity, long distance, and, predictably, a statement from the hospital. At least the water bill was straightforward. I put the remittance slip and envelope with the ones for the long distance, and started to toss the rest. But the phone bill was close to fifty dollars. Gran never called long distance. Were they pulling something funny knowing it was the final bill?

So I read the itemization.

International calls: Ireland. The morning of her brain attack. Thirty-six minutes to a suspiciously familiar number.

Kitty O'Connor.

On the morning leading to her death, Gran had phoned her estranged sister-in-law and found her at home.

And that's where my mind stopped churning. It didn't go into the implications; it didn't try to recreate what their conversation was. It didn't think to stand up and throw away the billing and not be sitting there gripping it when Bernadette walked in with yogurt smoothies for our lunch.

Sure, I tried to snap out of it. When Bernadette glanced into the dining room as she entered and said, "Wow, Ashlyn, you've been working so hard here. Thank you," I looked up with an automatic smile. But I didn't manage to say anything, or to put aside the papers. Bernadette's round eyes narrowed at me before she sat down in the other chair.

"What is that?"

I stammered some. "It's just, it's a bill of Gran's." Handing over the payment voucher and the envelope, I added, "It's due next week."

Instead she took the detailed bill, scanning it to figure out the line items before saying, "She called her."

Who? "Who called who?"

"Mom called that traitorous aunt of mine. I can't believe she did it."

"She told you?" She didn't tell me she would tell Bernadette. She didn't tell me she would call Kitty. She didn't even email me afterwards, just started making a salad.

"No, she said she wasn't going to do it, and then look, she did."

"But. Gran told you about Kitty and…and Pappa?"

Bernadette's eyes went all round again. "Oh, Ashlyn. You didn't know she told me? I'm so sorry." When she took my hand, I let her. "I thought you just didn't want to talk about it."

Brushing my eyes with my shirtsleeve, I said, "No, she told me she didn't want me to talk to anyone about it. I, that's what, on her last day…."

"Ash. My poor girl."

I shook my head. Sniffled. "I promised her. I didn't think anyone else knew, and she said she didn't want me to contact them, and didn't want me to tell you guys. I promised her, there, there in the hospital, I wouldn't. And then, right after. That's when." I sank, fetal, defeated, to the floor. Whispered, "That's when she died."

"Oh, my Ash." Bernadette was holding me. "Okay, it's okay."

We rocked together, cried together.

"Shhh, it's okay. It's okay." She wouldn't let me shake my head 'no', holding it against her shoulder. "It is. It's okay. Just cry, then we'll talk, but just cry."

I did what she told me to do.

❧

LATER, we took a walk around what used to be the farm. Most of it was half-completed subdivision now. With some work, Bernadette convinced me what Gran had meant with her requests for my silence was that she wanted to be the one to talk to Bernadette and her brothers about it all.

"She told Dermot and Matthew?" I was genuinely surprised.

"No, she was going to. But she wanted to do it in person."

Bernadette believed Gran had felt my presence when she released herself from life, but also that she hadn't been hanging on because of lingering concern about Pappa's secret.

"But we both agree," I said, stopping her in front of a cul-de-sac of framed out houses that used to be the path to the creek, "her call to Kitty was critical. That her hemorrhaging just hours later was related."

"We do," confirmed Bernadette.

"Then there's no doubt if I had just kept all this to myself, Gran would never have known to call Kitty and then she'd still be alive. So it all comes back to me."

"Baby," Bernadette brushed my hair off my forehead but I shook her hand away. "There's a reason you're an artist and not a lawyer. The argument does not hold. You are not, could never be, the reason your Gran died. Directly or indirectly."

She'd never called me an artist before.

"Ashlyn, you were the light of her life. She loved you." Bernadette looked away. "Loved you more than the rest of us put together, I think. And even if this knowledge about Dad was the reason she passed on to him—"

I swallowed heavily.

Now she fixed her eyes on me, "Do you think it came to you by accident? You weren't seeking anything like this, you were off secluding yourself for your work, and the knowledge found its way to you. You were fated to be the messenger, because you were the one she was most receptive to hearing it from. You didn't kill your Gran, love."

Sentimental hippie foolishness. But the stranglehold on my solar plexus loosened, and I could once again take a deep cleansing breath.

"Come on." Bernadette took my arm in hers. "I'm showing you our secret fishing hole."

Like I didn't know where the secret fishing hole was. Just cause I hated fishing didn't mean I wouldn't accompany Pappa on his clandestine trips down there. I wouldn't gut the poor creatures, but for a few youthful years, I'd eat them once they were charred over Pappa's fire.

We went anyway. It was probably somebody's backyard, now, but who cared. It was still peaceful. I climbed into the crook of the live oak, while Bernadette found a long stick and poked around the water. "There are still some mud puppies down here, if nothing else."

"Jordie-cat used to always bring those back for Gran."

"I remember. His mama used to do the same thing."

We watched the water, listened to the wind in the trees. Communed.

"Bernadette?"

"Yes?"

"She told you the whole thing?"

She nodded. "On the Monday, I think. When we had lunch."

"How was she?"

"Oh, goodness. She was upset some, but she was okay. Calm."

Bernadette told me about their lunch, and about Gran's upset that Pappa had been severed from his family at the whim of his sister, and how secretly—she was laughing at herself about this, by then—she was glad of it. Because if Pappa had known his son was living in Ireland, he'd have returned, and Gran would not have had him herself. I nodded at this truth about Gran and Pappa.

We got back to the house, and found separate bathrooms to wash our splotchy faces. I'd missed a message: "Ash love, check your email, see what you think. I'll call you later."

Bernadette said, "You're sure about this moving with him thing, aren't you?"

"Yes. Absolutely."

"But so far away?"

"Now you sound like Frank." I looked from the screen to her. "You know, you've always wanted to see the Grand Canyon. And the hiking out there is supposed to be fantastic."

We smiled at each other and dabbed at our eyes as I clicked on the links and photos Caleb had sent me. The first three places were fine, nothing bad but nothing great. The next one though, made Bernadette gasp.

"Oh, Ash. Click over there," she pointed to the pics of the rooms. I enlarged them, and one by one, we scrolled through the big open living area, the three bedrooms with great light, and the garden with a pinion tree in the middle and a small fishpond in the corner.

I looked at my mom. At the shot of an eat-in kitchen with walls three shades lighter than Gran's kitchenette set. Back at my mom. "So? What do you think?"

"Ashlyn." She closed her hand over mine. "I think he's found your home."

EPILOGUE

"What are you up to?" Caleb asked, leaning over my shoulder as I typed.

I laughed, which turned into a squeal as he nipped at that ticklish spot where neck meets collarbone. Cupping my hand over his jaw, I slid the laptop across our kitchen table so he could see the Dublin news site. "I'm trying to tweet that article about Lizzy."

"You're adorable." Caleb liked to pull out his computing knowledge to act superior to me, but I'd figured out how to turn his smug attitude to my advantage within weeks of our moving in together. My redesigned website was getting more hits than ever, and I was able to be increasingly selective about the side jobs that helped pay our bills.

"Hush." My kiss ensured Caleb's silence. "Anyway, guess what?"

"What?"

"I heard from Bernadette this morning. Uncle Dermot's headed to some training in Germany next month, but he's going a couple of days early so he can stop in Ireland and meet the O'Connor clan." Of all Gran and Pappa's kids, rigid Dermot had bent most easily to accommodate the new shape of our family.

Uncle Matthew—my Uncle Matthew, not the half-brother—was in denial, and Bernadette feigned indifference. However, she was the one who'd phoned my great-aunt Kitty to share the news of Gran's death, and allowed the transatlantic door to creak further open in the months since.

"That'll be an adventure."

I nodded.

"Almost as big an adventure as our road trip."

I swiveled to face him. Caleb was biting back a grin. "What road trip?"

"Unless you'd rather fly?"

"Caleb...." I warned. "What are you talking about?" It was possible I knew. I hoped I knew. I'd been lurking by the computer all day, daring myself to check my email only once per hour. Notifications were supposed to be in mid-September, and it was officially mid-September, and Caleb was sneaky. Back when I'd been named a finalist, he'd offered to set up an alert so I would know when winners began posting online about their success. I'd declined, feeling virtuous and restrained, all the while knowing Caleb would set the alert for himself.

And it was mid-September. And Caleb was grinning.

He sat, shifting me onto his lap, and clicked into my professional email. He'd added it to his mobile accounts when he took over managing my online store. I tucked my head against his shoulder, unwilling to watch the messages populate the screen.

Instead, I glanced around the bright kitchen we shared. The walls were covered in Caleb's prints, a mix of Gran's and Caleb's dishes rested in the drying rack, and my fragrant black bean soup simmered on the stove. A box in on the counter was overflowing with fabric I'd been meaning to put away for several days. Caleb's photography vest hung from the door to the den.

The room centered me. I turned back to the computer and said, "If you're toying with me, I'm changing my password."

"I do love toying with you."

"Dirty."

"Love that, too." Caleb kissed my temple. "Love you, Ashlyn May, Judged Show Winner."

I near about leapt from his encircling arms. "I won?"

He laughed. "Of course you won."

"For real?"

"Look for yourself." Caleb highlighted the message. *Chains of Love* was going to be in the International Quilt Show at the end of October. We would go to Houston, and Frank and Bernadette and Zach and Rebecca and tens of thousands of other people would see it. Would see Gran as I'd seen her.

"Wow," I said, breath hitching. "Wow."

"Congratulations."

"But you don't understand. I've been entering for years."

"I know, love. You told me." He wiped a tear from my cheek.

"I've never won before. I can't believe *Chains* won."

"It's your best work."

"It's because of Gran."

Caleb kissed me. "It's you, Ash. She gave you the dream, but you made it real. You, and your talent, and your love, and your vision."

"And you."

He laughed. "I'm not sure I had a whole lot to do with anything. You could have taken the photographs yourself."

I buried my fingers in his dark hair, rested my forehead on his. "You believed in me, and you supported my ambition. You've helped me find my voice, and I need my voice, so I can go out and ask the world to give me what I want."

"The world would be crazy to deny you. You deserve it all."

I kissed the man I loved.

"And that's just what I have."

THANK YOU!

I hope Ashlyn and Caleb filled your heart with their creativity and love, as they did mine.

Ratings and reviews help me grow as an author, and I appreciate all of your feedback. Please take a moment to review me! Goodreads ~ Bookstore

Not done with me yet? Read on!

My 'also by' page has links to the rest of my books. My 'about the author' page has links to my newsletter, website, and social buttons. I'd love to connect with you!

Happy Reading,

Melanie

ACKNOWLEDGMENTS

Ashlyn and Caleb's story has been a part of my life for so many years, and it's such a joy to bring it to the world at last. Without my grandmothers, the one a Texan, the other an immigrant, Ashlyn's world would lack color and depth. I miss them both, but I know they would both be proud that I'm flying after my own dreams.

Jennifer and Jennifer, my sisters, know when to comfort and when to light a fire. Jen W in particular inspired me to never stop seeking the creative life I craved. Thank you for saying such nice things about this novel. My godmother Charlotte, my mom Karen, and my friend Karen all gave me background on their sculpture, sewing, and photography. Thank you for letting me pick your brains! Mom, you raised me without suspecting I would end up stealing your button jars; I can only repay you with my thanks.

R, D, K: nothing about my life as a writer would exist without my life as your wife and mom.

ABOUT THE AUTHOR

Melanie Greene is a native Houstonian. She shares her life with her hometown hunk of a husband and children so amazing they defy superlatives.

For more info:
Sign up for Melanie's Newsletter to access new releases and bonus content.

www.melaniegreene.com

ALSO BY MELANIE GREENE

Roll of the Dice Series

Rocket Man (*Serena & Dillon*)

Ready to Roll (*Janice & Miguel*)

Eye of the Tiger (*Natalie & Evan*)

Let the Good Times Roll (*Chloe & Gabriel*)

Roll of a Lifetime (*Rachel & Theo*)

Roll Play (*Kim-ly & Tómas*)

On a Roll (*Gillian & Vic*)

Other Contemporary Romances

Retreat to Love (*Ashlyn & Caleb*)

Feather in Her Cap (*Jeannie & Brendan*)

Twelve Scorching Days (*Sarita & Scorch*)

EXCERPT FROM ROCKET MAN

Book 1 of Melanie Greene's sizzling contemporary Roll of the Dice series:

Though order-loving Serena shies away from Dillon's messy complications, she can't escape her fantasies. When Dillon's determined pursuit leaves Serena breathless, it might just be 'all systems are go' for Rocket Man.

~

CHAPTER 1

IT WAS 8:12 ON A WEEKDAY MORNING, which meant that Serena Colby was negotiating with the finicky lock to her scummy-butt apartment's front door.

It also meant that she jumped a little at the unwelcome sound of Joey coming up behind her. And jumping a little meant Serena risked dropping either her keys or her mug of steaming Earl Grey. Drop the keys, and the drawing case dragging down her shoulder would follow, and she'd just finished the Mooney account mock-ups. Drop the mug, and she'd be reminded that no matter how much she loved its paprika-and-nutmeg swirl of color, that particular to-go cup had a loose lid, and Serena was wearing sandals.

She dropped the keys, trusting her case's integrity more than her mug's. Catching the strap before her work hit the floor, Serena turned, tight-lipped, to face Joey.

Other ex-boyfriends would have been polite enough to pick up her keys. Of course, other ex-boyfriends would also have been polite enough to remember that Serena left her apartment at 8:12 every morning, and would avoid their common hallway for the three minutes it took for her to get out to her car. Or at the very least, other ex-boyfriends would have been polite enough to wait until she was done locking her apartment door before approaching.

One thing that was sure about Joey: he wasn't like Serena's other ex-boyfriends. Not that she'd been stuck living two doors down from other ex-boyfriends before, so maybe she was giving the others too much credit. She counted to six before speaking, since that was the number of weeks she had left before her lease was up. When she'd regained some patience, she greeted him. "Joey."

He was barefoot. Khakis and his work polo, but barefoot on the sticky hallway linoleum, just in case Serena thought it was coincidence that he was leaving for his store at the same time that Serena was headed out to Lanigan Printing and Advertising.

"Hey, I was wondering if I could borrow some coffee."

"I don't drink coffee." Which should have been apparent after eight and a half months of dating.

"But you have that instant stuff in your freezer."

"I threw that out." On the first morning of January, actually, cursing herself for keeping it throughout December, just in case he came knocking. A long, fun, revelatory New Year's Eve with her former college housemates had been the push she'd needed to get up the next morning and throw out Joey's coffee, Joey's toothbrush, and Joey's Christmas present (she'd bought it the week before he broke up with her, which she did confess to the gals; she hadn't admitted to wrapping it, prettily, post-breakup). In the weeks since, Serena's early rising and Joey's later working hours had kept the hallway encounters to a minimum. But every time they did meet, Serena ended up with a longer list of prohibitions about the next guy. Not younger than her. Not a coffee addict. Not afraid of cockroaches. Not laid back about being on time. Not a food mooch. Not obsessed with his stupid gaming. Not living in a scummy-butt apartment within steps of her own scummy-butt apartment.

"Why'd you do that?"

"Throw it out? Because I don't drink coffee."

"You could have given it to me. The Brackenbridge kids were having some sort of tennis match all morning."

"It was a sword fight." The Brackenbridge family lived in the apartment between theirs. The walls were thin. Cammie Brackenbridge had pointed out, early in Joey and Serena's relationship, that the boys and Joey shared a bedroom wall. Serena had averted her eyes around the kids for a good long while. On the up side, Serena was petty and the boys hated waking up at seven for school. Each whining protest about missing shoes and bad-mood-induced loud game that floated on the air waves while she got ready for work delighted her, knowing that Joey was piling pillows on his head and grumbling into his mattress about it.

"It was loud. And I ran out of coffee last week."

"Well, you're up now. You should have time to go buy some before work." Serena retrieved her keys and finessed the lock before shouldering her drawing case again. "Gotta go."

"Where'd you get it, though?" Joey was walking alongside her.

"Get what?" She knew. But she liked irritating him. More proof of her pettiness.

"The coffee."

"I threw it out."

"I mean where'd you get it to start with?"

She'd told him, at least twice. Probably more. It was bad enough that she'd once spent a couple of hours online researching instant coffee brands, searching for something flavorful, fair trade, organic, and also available from a locally owned store somewhere in Houston. Never mind that it was at the same place where she got her olive oil and shampoo, and she might have just grabbed the coffee off their shelves without the research time. But she'd told him the whole story when he'd complimented the flavor. Joey had even gone to the co-op with her, back when they sometimes ran errands together.

"Oh, just the grocery store. I think it was HEB." The chain carried organic coffee; it wasn't impossible that Joey would find the same stuff there.

"Okay. Fine. I guess I have to go shopping."

"Bye, Joe." He hated being called Joe. Serena took the stairs instead of waiting for the elevator. Sure, her case banged repeatedly against her thigh and a few drops of tea spilled out onto her hand, but the thud of the fire door slamming shut between her and her ex-boyfriend was more than worth it.

Despite the Joey delay, Serena was at work early enough to grab a minute to herself. She spent it rearranging her poster frames. The first thing she'd done when she was hired by Lanigan was to install two rows of a deep crown molding along a couple of her office walls, which she used in place of an easel to display client mockups, past campaigns, and some of her own personal, more artistic work.

Right at nine, Serena's friend Janice came in and caught her repositioning the Mooney account frames.

"You know, Toots, I'll have those Mangoes and Moonshine posters for you tomorrow at two. You're just going to want to move everything around again." Janice was Lanigan's Operations Manager. She knew the schedules for a million things at once, and how to deal when any of those million processes threatened her deadlines. If Janice promised a poster at two, Serena would have a poster at two.

Serena laughed. "Yeah, I know. But Anica took my HouGreen mockups to give to Mr. Kenzi, and I can't leave these poor walls with a big gaping hole showing, can I?"

"Your walls aren't sentient, Toots."

"Shh! They'll hear you."

"They don't really have ears, you know. I'm beginning to think you're clinically disordered here. Or maybe it's clinically ordered? Ducks don't come in rows that straight. Some people let paper stack up in their in-boxes, or keep the 'to be filed' pile hidden behind the door." Janice made a show of looking, but of course only found a white board outlining the quarter's work flow. "Seriously. I dare you to just leave your walls the way they are until Monday."

As if she'd leave them a mess for four days. Janice was toying with her, but Serena could play right back. She knew Janice's obsessions as well as Janice knew hers. "I dare you to only go to the gym once this weekend."

Janice cocked her head, considering. "Does Friday count?"

"If it's after five, it counts."

"No deal. I'd miss my kickboxing class."

"You have a sickness."

"Which I think was my point to you." Janice sighed. "We need boyfriends."

"Speak for yourself," Serena said, and turned to nudge one of her collages to the left an inch. "You're addicted to exercise endorphins, so a nice physical outlet is just the ticket for you. As for me, there's nothing wrong with making my environment nice. And besides, even if I could find anyone worth dating, I'd still keep my filing done."

Janice snorted. "I want to know which one of your thirteen evil stepparents beat you black, blue, and purple unless you folded your laundry on time. You have a deeply scarred psyche, my friend."

"There were only seven stepparents, and I never even lived with Number Seven. I mean, Zane. I promised Mom I'd stop calling him Number Seven. What's your point?"

"Want to go for Cuban food and talk about it?"

"Is that a subtle way of making me go out dancing with you tonight?"

"Maybe."

"Will you glare at me for the poor dietary choices I will definitely make?"

"Not if you promise to shake your hips afterwards."

Serena grinned and tapped the last frame a tiny bit to fix the spacing. "You're on."

Before Janice had even cleared the room, Anica called Serena in for an unexpected meeting, and told her to bring everything she was working on. Not always a good thing, being summoned by the boss, but Serena's conscious was clear. And as it turned out, Anica had only slightly nerve-wracking news.

"I need you to sit in on these interviews today for Margaret's replacement."

Serena blinked. Margaret, one of the copy writers, was moving to Alabama rather suddenly, but Anica had always done the hiring on her own. "You want my help?"

Anica stopped flipping through the paperwork Serena had handed over and glanced up. "It looks like these spots can go to Eddie as-is, and I'll have Philip and Johnnie do some initial mock-ups of the gala brochure based on your notes. That should give you a few hours free to talk with the copy writers."

"Right," Serena tried not to sound as nonplussed as she felt. It didn't seem bad, exactly, but it was unexpected, and Anica was many things, but few of them were spontaneous.

Anica smiled at her. "Relax. I've decided to groom you for more responsibility, and I thought you'd benefit by sitting in. It's hardly a death sentence. Besides, you worked most closely with Margaret, so you'll know the essentials we're looking for in a replacement."

Well, then. Serena smiled back, hoping she looked at ease. She'd been eyeing the management tier; after almost four years at Lanigan she was eager to do more than strictly graphic design, but hadn't yet formulated her plan for approaching Anica about it. Seems that first step had been taken without her realizing it. Trying to expel her nervous energy, Serena picked up the applicant's folders. "Okay, then, thanks. Just these three? Can't HR rustle up anyone else?"

"Oh, Emily had several applicants. Of the ones she put through to me, these are my top choices. If this process goes well, next time we have to hire I'll show you how I go through the applicants to decide who to talk to. Listen," Anica took off her glasses and tossed them to the side, "I know everyone is used to Margaret, and the way she works, and maybe your team will resent the new guy a little...."

"Or gal," Serena added, reading the applicant names. "But if I'm one of the interviewers, I'll stand up for him or her and smooth things over, yes, I get that. It's not subtle."

"I never said it was."

Serena tried to get ahold of her mouth before it shot her in the foot. "No, no, of course not. It's a solid plan. I'll do what I can, but there is going to be some fallout. I'm not the only one who's going to miss Margaret, or her efficiency. For the group's sake, I can't be seen as rising up solely on the back of her departure. So, how else will you be giving me more oversight?"

Anica swept her hair back from her forehead and put her glasses back on. "You're not so subtle yourself, Serena. But this isn't a fast track, so don't get too rebellious on me. For now, you will sit in on sales meetings between Eddie and me, and take over some of the direct communication with clients. Select clients. Lanigan wants to build a stronger base in the hospitality industry, and we think you can help with that. For now, these interviews. The first one's in about thirty minutes—have a seat over there and look over the resumes and portfolios."

Moving to the small conference table Anica had indicated, Serena checked the time on her cell phone. There were two interviews before lunch. And while their talk with the first applicant took most of the hour between ten and eleven, the next guy was so monosyllabic and almost hostile that Serena and Anica both were happy to shut the door behind him a half-hour after he first walked in.

"What was that? Misogyny?"

Anica shook her head. "I do not know. What year is it again? Do they still make blatant chauvinists in this millennium? Let's hope that Dillon has a little easier time with the idea of female bosses."

"Cheri was fine with us, at least."

"My only question with her is her experience. She has talent, but her resume just isn't very deep."

"Okay. Dillon at one?"

Anica nodded. "See you then."

1:10 rolled around; Dillon Hamilton was late.

Anica shot Serena a wry look and made noises about the file of other applicants, but before they could open it, Hamilton was announced. He propelled himself into the office, jacket flying behind him, and seemed anchored to the earth only via the messenger bag he wore over one shoulder. He was all apologies, kinetic charm and a tumble of dark hair.

"What a disaster, I'm so sorry. Do you still have time for me? All my fault, inexcusable. But not typical." He turned to Serena.

"Sorry, I didn't know I'd meet you, too, just Ms. Sands. Dillon Hamilton, hi."

"Serena Colby." They shook, his long fingers wrapping around the back of her hand, enveloping it. His height when they were right up close was a little overwhelming, but he was lanky, only his broad shoulders filling up his otherwise flapping blazer. At her name, he grinned one of those lights-up-the-face grins. Charm. The guy had dangerous levels of charm.

"Right, hi, Serena, nice. I saw your picture on the Lanigan site. You did their new logo, right?"

Serena confirmed she had, and Dillon complimented her before turning his eyes (Serena hadn't decided if they were cobalt or Egyptian blue) and his attention back to Anica. "I feel bad I kept you waiting. My references will tell you, I'm really prompt. Oh, you have my samples there, good. Let me show you a couple of other things. This is recent, similar to what Lanigan did for McMahan Foods, I think. Similar tone. I've just done some food writing, and I'm not sure my application materials show you enough of that."

They discussed his work, Lanigan's history, Houston, and the industry.

"Why are you looking to move from freelance to a permanent position?" Serena asked. Over the course of the day she'd gotten more comfortable with questioning the applicants, but something was tying her tongue a little with this one. She didn't want to think that it was the fact that he was gorgeous, so she refused to think about it and kept her eyes on his resume and on Anica.

"It's what I always wanted. I moved to Houston to be near my sister, she's having a baby soon, and they're my only family. Anyway, I came here because she's here, and I'm staying because she's here. And I like it. I'm a huge Rockets fan. I've been searching for a permanent position since I got here, looking at different companies, and Lanigan is just perfect for me. The size and the team and the work you've all done. The location. It's exactly what I hoped for."

His enthusiasm was sweet. And she'd never fault a fan of her hometown basketball team, since she was rather rabid about them herself. Serena remembered her own interview at Lanigan; she'd probably been about Dillon's age, and was just as eager to be hired on. But she didn't think she'd come across as open about it. Not that it was a bad thing. He was just so...so there. So tall and happy and that dark hair and those cobalt eyes and Serena was not inclined to gladness that she was so aware of his thereness. But he interviewed well, and they'd liked his work best of the three candidates. As Dillon packed up, Serena and Anica shared a relieved smile behind his back.

"We should be making a decision in the next couple of days," Anica said, returning to her desk. "Serena will show you out. Nice to meet you, Dillon."

"And you. I'll look for your call."

They strolled to the lobby, chatting. Lanigan's halls were lined with completed campaigns—not updated as frequently as Serena's office walls, but still a strong recommendation for the work they did there. And it gave her a secret little smile that several of the pieces Dillon commented on had her graphics. At the front desk, he turned fully towards her. "Thanks, Serena. I can call you Serena? I know I said it, but I can start right away."

"That's great." Despite being fairly sure Dillon would be their hire, Serena didn't want to give anything away. Plus she'd caught sight of Philip, their other writer, headed into Margaret's office with a grim look on his face. Clearly the word of Margaret's potential replacements and, with it, Serena's semi-promotion, was spreading through the building. She was mentally running damage control, but Dillon still stood facing her, blue eyes unwavering.

"I can ask you a question?"

Serena nodded.

"I don't want to come on too hard. And I know it's maybe stupid of me to mention this. But," he ducked his head some, rubbing the back of his neck. "Can I call you?"

"Well, sure. Like Anica said, we're going to contact all the candidates by early next week, but if you want to just check in, that's fine."

"No. I appreciate that, but...I mean, you, specifically. No matter what happens with the job decision, can I call you? For coffee or something?"

"I don't drink coffee." What a stupid response. Serena sent a mental slap to her forehead, but this adorable puppy of a man was asking a maybe future boss on a date? What if Anica had been the one to walk him out, would he have asked her instead? Was this strategy, or just strange? And why did the idea of his offering Anica a coffee set Serena's mind at disgruntled alert? "I like tea."

"Well, for tea then."

"Sorry. I mean, sorry, it's not the coffee. I appreciate it, Dillon, but I don't...it's not...."

"You're with someone?" He shook his head. "Never mind. You said 'no' and I'll let it go. I just didn't want to wait until I started working with you and have to wonder how to fit my asking you out in with the job stuff. Or if I don't get it, for you to think I'm trying to get a second chance. I mean, when I say it like that, it's obvious the right answer is to not ask you out at all. Which is what you're trying to say. I was right to start with and it was stupid to ask. Forget it all, please. What an impression I make. Show up late and won't go away and incapable of biting back my words when I should."

"No. It's fine. Nice of you to ask." Unsettling, but nice. Serena was not looking to date. The post-Joey list of things to avoid was too long, and she had a promotion to chase, and Dillon was too young and too handsome and too likely to be her subordinate and too much a whirlwind and anyway, Serena was not looking.

He took her hand in hers, squeezed. Serena resisted pulling

away from the warmth of it. "I'll leave now. Thanks for your time today. And when you choose someone else for this job, I'd still like to hear from you. If you want. I won't pester you. Thanks, Serena. You're really nice. And pretty. But mainly nice. I'm going, I promise. Bye."

And like that, he slung his messenger bag around his neck and strode away, shoulders set, not looking back.